Luan Goldie is a primary school teacher, and formerly a business journalist. She has written several short stories and is the winner of the Costa Short Story Award 2017 for her short story 'Two Steak Bakes and Two Chelsea Buns'. She was also shortlisted for the London Short Story Prize in 2018 and the *Grazia*/Orange First Chapter competition in 2012, and was chosen to take part in the Almasi League, an Arts Council-funded mentorship programme for emerging writers of colour. In 2019 she was shortlisted for the h100 awards in the Publishing and Writing category. *Nightingale Point* is Luan's debut novel and was a BBC Radio 2 Book Club pick.

Nightingale Point

Luan Goldie

ONE PLACE. MANY STORIES

This novel is entirely a work of fiction. The names, characters and incidents portrayed in it are the work of the author's imagination. Any resemblance to actual persons, living or dead, events or localities is entirely coincidental.

HQ
An imprint of HarperCollins*Publishers* Ltd
1 London Bridge Street
London SE1 9GF

This edition 2020

3
First published in Great Britain by
HQ, an imprint of HarperCollins*Publishers* Ltd 2019

Luan Goldie asserts the moral right to be
identified as the author of this work.
A catalogue record for this book is
available from the British Library.

ISBN: 978-0-00-831461-3

MIX
Paper from
responsible sources
FSC™ C007454

This book is produced from independently certified FSC™ paper
to ensure responsible forest management.

For more information visit: www.harpercollins.co.uk/green

Printed and bound in Great Britain by
CPI Group (UK) Ltd, Croydon, CR0 4YY

For Patrick

SATURDAY, 4 MAY 1996

The evacuation began this morning. No sooner had the bins been collected than the hundreds of residents from the three blocks that make up Morpeth Estate began streaming away in their droves.

Bob the caretaker sat in his cubbyhole on the ground floor, telling anyone who would listen that 'it's only a heatwave if it goes on ten days'. But no one listened, instead they asked when the intercom was getting fixed, if he knew the lifts were out and what he was planning on doing about the woman on the third floor who kept sticking a chair out on the landing. Moan, moan, moan.

Bob stubs out his cigarette and looks up at the grey face of Nightingale Point, smiling at the way the sun illuminates each balcony, every single one a little personal gallery, showcasing lines of washing, surplus furniture, bikes, scooters, and pushchairs. Towards the top a balcony glints with CDs held by pieces of string; a few of the residents have started doing it and Bob doesn't have a clue why. He must ask someone.

Mary is amazed at how well it works. Who would believe that hanging a few CDs on the balcony stops pigeons from shitting on your washing? She had seen the tip on *GMTV* and immediately rushed to the flat next door to ask Tristan for any old discs. His music was no good anyway, all that gangbanging West Coast, East Coast stuff.

Mary wraps a towel around her hair. Her husband could show up any minute and the least she can do for him, after being apart for over a year, is not smell of fried fish. She switches on the TV, but the picture bounces and fuzzes. She doesn't even try to understand technology these days, but heads next door to get Malachi.

Malachi sits behind a pile of overdue library books and tries to think of a thesis statement for his *Design and the Environment* essay that is due next Friday, but instead he thinks about Pamela. If only he could talk to her, explain, apologise, grab her by the hand and run away. No, it's over. He has to stop this.

Distraction, he needs a distraction.

On cue, Tristan walks over with *The Sun* and opens it to Emma, 22, from Bournemouth.

'Your type?' he asks, grinning.

But Malachi's not in the mood to see Bournemouth Emma, or talk to Tristan, or write a thesis. He only wants Pamela.

Tristan sulks back out to the balcony to read his newspaper cover to cover, just as any fifteen-year-old, with a keen interest in current affairs, would. After this he will continue with his mission to help Malachi get over Pamela, and the only way to do it is to get under someone else. Tristan once heard some sixth-former girls describe his brother as 'dark and brooding', which apparently doesn't just mean that he's black and grumpy, women actually find him *attractive*. So it shouldn't be that hard to get him laid.

There's a smashing sound from the foot of the block and Tristan looks over the balcony.

The jar of chocolate spread has smashed everywhere and Lina doesn't have a clue how to clean up such a thing, so she walks off and hopes no one saw her.

Inside the cool, tiled ground floor of Nightingale Point, the caretaker shakes his head at the mess. 'Don't worry, dear, I'll get that cleaned up. Don't you worry a bit.'

'Thanks,' Lina says. A small blessing in the sea of shit that is her day so far. She hits the call button for the lift but nothing. 'Please tell me they're working?'

The caretaker cups his ear at her. 'What's that, dear?'

'The lifts,' she says.

He fills his travel kettle and shrugs. 'I've logged a call but it's bank holiday, innit.'

Lina pushes on the heavy door to the stairwell and sighs as she looks at the first of ten flights of stairs. 'By the way,' she calls back at the caretaker, 'I think there's kids on the roof again.'

Pamela loves being on the roof, for the solitude, for the freedom, and for the small possibility that she might spot, walking across the field below, Malachi. She has to see him today and they have to talk. Today's the day; it has to be.

At the foot of the block the caretaker tips a kettle of water over a dark splodge on the floor and gets his mop out. Just another mess to clean up at Nightingale Point.

CHAPTER ONE

Elvis

Elvis hates to leave his flat, as it is so full of perfect things. Like the sparkly grey lino in the bathroom, the television, and the laminated pictures tacked up everywhere reminding him how to lock the door securely and use the grill.

'Elvis?' Lina calls. 'You want curried chicken or steak and kidney?'

Elvis does not answer; he is too busy hiding behind the sliding door that separates the kitchen and living room, watching Lina unpack the Weetabix, bread and strawberry jam. She unscrews the jar and puts one of her fingers inside, which is a bad thing to do because of germs, but Elvis understands because strawberry jam can be so tasty.

This is the nineteenth day of Lina being Elvis's nurse. He knows this as he marked her first day on the calendar with a big smiley face. There are fourteen smiley faces on the calendar and five sad faces because this is when Lina was late.

She puts the jar of jam in the cupboard and returns to the shopping bags, taking out a net of oranges. Elvis hates oranges; they are sticky and smelly. He had asked for tomatoes but Lina said that tomatoes are an ingredient not a snack and that oranges are full of the kind of vitamins Elvis needed to make his brain work better and stop him from being a pest.

Lina's face disappears behind a cupboard door and Elvis watches as her pink coloured nails rap on the outside. He likes Lina's shiny pink nails, especially when her hair is pink too.

'Elllviiiis?' she sings.

He puts a big hand over his mouth to muffle the laughter, but then sees Lina has removed the red tin from the shopping bag – the curried chicken pie. He gasps as he realises he wants steak and kidney.

'Bloody hell!' She jumps and raises the tinned pie above her head, as if ready to throw it. 'What the hell you doing? You spying on me?'

'No, no, no.'

'Elvis, why are you wearing a sweatshirt? It's too hot for that.' She slams the tin down on the counter.

'Steak and kidney pie,' he tells her. 'I want steak and kidney pie. It's the blue tin.'

'Yeah, all right, all right.'

'Can I have two?' he tries, knowing his food has been limited. He is unsure why.

'No, Elvis, that's greedy. Now go. Get changed. You're sweating.'

'Get changed into what?' he asks.

'A T-shirt, Elvis. It's bloody baking out; go put on a T-shirt.'

Elvis goes through to his bedroom and removes his sweat-shirt. He stands for a moment and looks over his round belly in the mirror, moisture glistening among the curly ginger hairs that cover his whole front. When he takes off his glasses his reflection looks watery, like one of his dreams. He then pulls on his favourite new T-shirt, which is bright blue and has a picture of the King on it. It also has the words *The King* in gold swirly writing. He smiles at himself before going to the living room to sit on his new squashy sofa.

Elvis listens carefully to the steps Lina takes to make the pie: the flick of the ignition, the slam of a pot on the gas ring. Then, the sound he likes best, the click of her pearly plastic nails on the worktops. He loves all the flavours the tinned pies come in and he likes the curried chicken pie most days, but today he really does want steak and kidney.

'Right, master, your pie is on the boil,' Lina says as she walks into the living room. 'Nice,' she says, acknowledging his T-shirt.

'Are we going to the bank holiday fair?' He had seen posters for it Sellotaped up on bus shelters and in the windows of off-licences: *Wilson and Sons Fairground on the Heath, 3–6 May. Helter Skelter, Dodgems, Ghost Train!* He really wants to go.

'Yeah, maybe when it cools down a bit.' Lina flops on the sofa next to him and picks up the phone. 'Go.' She waves him away. 'Why you sitting so close to me? I *am* entitled to a break.'

But Elvis is comfy on the sofa and he has already sorted the stickers from his *Merlin's Premier League* sticker book and watered his tomato plants on the windowsills. He has already carefully used his razor to remove the wispy orange hairs from his face as George, his care worker, had taught him, and rubbed the coconut suntan lotion into his skin as he knows to do on hot days. This morning Elvis has already done everything he was meant to and now he wants to eat his steak and kidney pie and go to the fair.

Lina has his new special phone in her hand. Elvis loves his phone; it is his favourite thing in his new living room, after the television. The phone is so special that you can only make a call when you put money inside and you can only get the money out with a special key that George looks after. Beside the phone sits a laminated sheet with all the numbers Elvis will ever need: a little drawing of a policeman – 999; a photograph of Elvis's mum wearing the purple hat she reserves for church and having her photograph taken – 018 566 1641; and a photograph of George behind his desk – 018 522 7573. Elvis is trying to learn all the numbers by heart but sometimes when he tries, he gets distracted by the fantastic noise the laminated sheet makes if you wave it in the air fast. Next to the phone is a ceramic dish shaped like a boat that says *Margate* on it. The dish is kept filled with change for when Elvis needs to make a call.

He watches carefully as Lina feeds the phone with his change and starts to dial, her lovely pink nails hitting the dial pad: 018 557.

'Go and sit somewhere else,' she snaps.

But there is nowhere else to sit apart from the perfect squashy sofa, so Elvis goes into the kitchen where he can watch and listen to Lina from behind the door. In secret.

'Hi . . . I'm at work. Elvis is driving me nuts today,' she says into the phone. 'He keeps bloody staring at me . . . Yeah I know . . . Tell me about it . . . Ha ha. Yeah, true true . . . ' She slides off her plimsolls and pulls the coffee table closer, putting her little feet up on it. 'But you know what my mum's like, always busting my arse over something: look after your baby, wash the dishes, get more shifts. I thought the whole point of having a baby was that you didn't have to go work no more . . . Exactly . . . Especially on a day like this. Bloody roasting out.'

Even from behind the door Elvis can see that the nails on Lina's toes are the same colour as those on her fingers, but shorter. The colour looks like the insides of the seashells Elvis collected at Margate last summer. He likes Lina's toes; this is the first time he has ever seen Lina's toes. He likes them but knows he is not allowed to touch them.

'Can I have a biscuit?' Elvis asks as he comes out from behind the door, now peckish and unable to wait for the pie to boil.

'Hang on. What?' Lina rests the phone under her chin like one of the office girls at the Waterside Centre, the place where Elvis used to live before he was clever enough to live by himself in Nightingale Point.

'Can I have a biscuit?' he asks again.

'I'm on the phone, leave me in peace.' She tuts then returns to her call. 'But look, yeah, I'm coming to the fair later. Soon as I'm done with the dumb giant here I'll be down . . . I'll get it; pay me later.' Lina slides the rest of the money from the ceramic boat into her pocket.

Elvis pictures the laminated sheet of Golden Rules that hangs in his bedroom. Rule Number One: Do not let strangers into your flat. Rule Number Two: Do not let anybody touch your private swimming costume parts. Rule Number Three: Do not let anyone take your things. Lina is breaking one of the Golden Rules. Elvis must call George and report her immediately.

Lina picks up the laminated sheet of phone numbers and uses it to fan herself. It makes her pink fringe flap up and down, and Elvis wants to watch it but he also knows that he must report her rule break. George once told him that if he could not get to the house phone and it was an emergency, he could go outside to the phone box to make a call. The phone box, on the other side of the little field in front of the estate, is the second emergency phone. Elvis must now go there. He leaves the living room and slips on his sandals at the door. *Jesus sandals*, Lina calls them, but Elvis does not think Jesus would have worn such stylish footwear in the olden days. He opens the front door gently, quietly enough that Lina will not hear. Then, and only because he knows he is allowed to leave the flat to use the second phone for when he cannot use the first phone, Elvis steps out of flat thirty-seven and heads into the hallway of the tenth floor.

CHAPTER TWO

Mary

Ever since Mary woke up she has been feeling uneasy. And as the mother of two, grandmother of four, nurse of thirty-three years and wife to a fame-chasing husband, Mary knows what uneasy feels like. Her elbow has been twitching and she can't shake the feeling that something is wrong. Something is coming.

She opens the pink plastic banana clip and allows her long greying hair to fall about her shoulders. Everything is cooked and cooling but she now needs something else to occupy her mind, to stop herself from worrying.

She covers the last plate – vegetable spring rolls – and stands within the tiny space of bulging cupboards and greasy appliances as she looks for a place to lay them. The worktops are already loaded with plates of food; each one gives off a different fried smell from under sweating pieces of kitchen roll.

'Ah, too small, too small,' she mutters. But no one could accuse Mary of failing to make the best use of her space. In each corner of the lino two-litre bottles of Coke are stacked like bowling pins; on tops of cupboards tins upon tins are stashed, heading slowly towards their expiry date; and on a small shelf above the fridge sits no less than seven boxes of brightly branded breakfast cereals. She buys them for her grandbabies. Though after a long shift on the ward she loves nothing more than to peel off her tights and eat two bowls of Frosties while lying on the sofa listening to *The Hour of Inspiration* on Filipino radio. Mary shuffles around some things, swears to finally get rid of the dusty sandwich maker and to stop buying five-kilo bags of long grain rice.

Her elbow. Twitch twitch twitch.

'Stupid old woman,' she mumbles. She knows she is being ridiculous, worrying too much about everything and nothing. She makes a mental list of her worries and tries to remember what the doctor on *The Oprah Winfrey Show* said to do with them.

'You think of a worry, you cross the street,' she says as she pictures the studio audience of determined, applauding, crying American women.

Mary thinks of each worry: talk that teenagers are gathering in the swing park at night to watch dogs fight; the cockroaches that continuously plague her kitchen; the smell of gas that sometimes lingers on the ninth floor; the woman from the top floor who was robbed of her shopping money last week as she got in the lift. It's a long list.

'Cross the street, cross the street.' Mary waves her arms as she imagines each worry float off behind her. But then larger worries, those that are more likely to happen, these are things she can't dismiss as easily, namely the imminent arrival of her estranged husband, David. Fifteen months he had been gone and then a call from Manila Aquino Airport two days ago: 'My love, I am coming home, but I am on standby. You know what these airlines are like: locals back of the queue.' She has heard this from him before, claims of him booking a ticket, being at the airport, getting on the next flight. Even once a call to say he had been diverted to Birmingham and would arrive the next day. She had wrung her fingers with anxiety for almost a week until he finally landed on her doorstep – their doorstep – with an excuse she now struggles to remember. For David, there is always some excuse, some distraction, some offer of money he can't turn down. Whenever he is due to return home the world is full of people desperate for a poor Johnny Cash tribute act. Or maybe he is with one of his many floozies. Mary has never gotten over her own brother's accusation that David had 'a floozy waiting at the side of each stage'.

'Cross the street,' she says more weakly as she pictures David's travel-weary face, greasy rise of hair and fake Louis Vuitton suitcase. 'Cross the street.' She cringes as she imagines David pulling her in for an obligatory married couple kiss. 'Cross the street.'

'Talking to yourself again, Mary?' Malachi waves a hand as he enters the kitchen.

She felt bad for pulling him away from his studies, but also pleased for an excuse to check in on him and his younger brother Tristan. When had she turned into such a meddling old woman?

'I've fixed the TV,' Malachi says.

Mary takes the two small steps needed to cross the kitchen and throws her arms around his middle.

'It wasn't even broken.' He shakes free from her arms and wipes the small beads of sweat on his dark brown skin. 'Your aerial was unplugged. Tell the kids to stop playing behind the TV.'

Mary nods, knowing she will never tell her grandbabies any such thing – those perfect little girls would have to throw the TV out of the window before she dare aim a cross word at them. Each time they come to stay they leave her exhausted, and the small flat trashed, yet she can't wait till they come again.

'Why don't you open a window in here? It's twenty-four degrees already.' Malachi leans over the sink and pushes on the condensation-streaked glass. It screeches loudly as it gives way, allowing the heat from outside to do battle with the steam from Mary's cooking.

'I have the vent on, see.' She indicates the tiny, spinning, dust-covered fan. 'You look tired,' she says gently, keen not to nag the boy. 'Too much study, study, study.'

He looks up at the window and undoes the top button on his shirt. Mary does not like the way he has taken to wearing collarless shirts; she watches *MTV* sometimes, and knows this is not a fashion among young people. She notices too, as he goes under the sink, that his trousers – muted green cotton with a sharp crease down the middle – are for a much older man.

'What you looking for?' she asks as he rummages around her collection of multi-buy discount cleaning products, fifty pack of sponges and long abandoned, but not yet disposed of, cutlery holders and soap dishes.

'You need to oil your window.' He twists the nozzle on a rusty can of WD-40.

'Don't worry about my window.'

He stops and looks down at her. His almond-shaped eyes search for something.

'What?' She touches her face, wondering if a stray Rice Krispie is stuck on her cheek.

'You're saying *I* look tired. You all right? You look a bit . . . frazzled.'

'I worked forty-eight hours already this week – what do you expect me to look like? Imelda Marcos?'

Malachi blesses her with one of his rare smiles and then positions his knees into the two small free spots on the worktop. He seems more sullen than usual.

'Are *you* okay?' Mary asks as he squirts the window frame.

'Yep. I'm always okay. Just hot and this smog, it plays havoc with my asthma.' He jumps down and stares blankly across the kitchen.

Mary knows he's still hung up on the blonde girl from upstairs. 'Well, I'm glad you're not still sad about whatshername.'

'I have a hundred other things to think about,' he snaps.

She was the first girl of Malachi's Mary had ever met. He even brought her over for dinner once, one wet afternoon where they sat, with plates on their laps, eating chicken bistek.

'Some things are not meant to be. I could see it from the start,' Mary lies, for all she saw that afternoon was Malachi buzzing around the girl like she was the best thing since they started slicing bread. 'I always know when couples don't match. I even said it about Charles and Diana, but did anyone listen to me?'

'I really don't want to talk about this.'

Mary throws her arms up. 'Me neither. Goodbye, Blondie. Plenty more pussy in the cattery.'

He wipes his face to hide his embarrassment and she's pleased to see the tiniest of smiles emerge on his sad face.

'Why'd you make so much food?' he asks.

'I told you, I need to work every day next week so I'm stockpiling. Like a squirrel.' She wraps an old washed out ice-cream tub with cling film and hands it to him. 'This is for your tutor.' She had been sending food parcels to anyone related to Malachi's education since his first semester of university. Anything to boost the boy's chances. 'The rest is for your freezer.'

'Thanks. I appreciate it.'

'And I appreciate if you put on some weight. What is this?' She pinches the flesh of his side.

'Ow.'

'Heroin chic!' she announces. 'I saw it on *GMTV*. Teenagers with bodies like this.' Mary holds up her pinkie finger. 'No woman wants that, Malachi. You need to eat properly.'

She had looked in Malachi's and Tristan's fridge a few days ago and saw nothing but a loaf of value bread and jar of lemon curd. The freezer was even worse: a half empty box of fish fingers and two frosty bottles of Hooch, which Tristan explained were 'for the ladies'. If their nan knew they were eating so poorly under Mary's watch there would be murder.

'Freezer, you hear me? Tell your brother he can't eat, eat, eat all in one sitting. And why has he got zigzags shaved in his hair? Does he think he's a pop star or something?'

'You know what he's like. He's a little wild.'

'He can't afford to be *wild*.' Mary tries to put the word in

15

air quotes but uses eight fingers and makes a baby waving motion. 'Too many riffraffs around here going wild like this.' She makes a stabbing gesture and tries to look menacing, but her only reference point is *West Side Story* and she makes a dance of it.

Malachi puts a hand under a piece of kitchen roll and drags out a bamboo skewer of prawns. Mary slaps him.

'Did you hear me say help yourself? Does this look like the Pizza Hut buffet to you?'

'You just told me I need to eat.'

'Not prawn. Too early for prawn.' She turns her back to him as she rewraps the skewers. His eyes burn her; she must explain her snappy mood. 'I need to leave my spare keys with you in case David gets in early. He's on standby for a flight so could be here tonight, tomorrow or next week. Oh God.' The reality of him arriving hits her again. It sends her elbow into overdrive.

'David?'

'Yes, David, my husband. Remember him?' There's a hysterical edge to her voice. She puts a hand on her forehead to save herself as Oprah has taught her. 'I don't even want to talk about it.'

'I didn't know David was coming back.'

'No. But we didn't know Jesus was coming back either.'

Mary takes her nurse fob watch from her pocket – a present from David on one of his rare jaunts back home. An obscure-looking Virgin Mary with oversized arms ticks around the clock, hung on a thick, gold link chain. Well, it was gold once, now it's more silver, the shine, like everything else to do with David, rubbed away by the sweat and grime of real life. Quarter to twelve.

'Mary?' Malachi waves his arms to get her attention. 'Hand me these keys then. I need to get back home.'

Mary nods as she looks in the junk drawer, rifling through papers, wires and replacement batteries for the smoke alarm until she finds the spare keys. Tristan had once attached a plastic marijuana leaf to them thinking it was funny. Mary had given him a lecture about the dangers of drugs but never bothered to remove the key ring.

She fusses with the catch on the watch as she pins it to her uniform, swearing to get it fixed. 'You want some tea before you go?' she asks Malachi.

He spins the keys around a long finger. 'No, thanks. Too hot.'

'You call this hot? It's thirty-five degrees in Manila today.' She lifts the kettle and gives it a shake before she flicks the switch.

'Right,' Malachi says. 'I better get back to my books.'

He sulks off and she rolls her eyes at his constant grumpiness. But as she hears the front door close she stops cold. The twitch becomes a scratch. Something is wrong, for her feelings never are. Today, something horrible will happen.

CHAPTER THREE

Pamela

There is not a stitch of breeze on the roof of Nightingale Point. Today, up here is just as suffocating as being in the flat with Dad. Pamela places her new running shoes on the ground and holds onto the metal railing; her long rope of blonde hair falls forward and dangles over the edge. The sunrays hit the nape of her neck and she feels her skin, so dangerously pale and thin, begin to burn. She shifts her body into the shade of the vast grey water tanks and imagines the water as it rolls between them and into the maze of pipes around the block's fifty-six flats. Pamela loves the roof. Since she returned to London a few days ago it's become the only space Dad does not watch over her. Sometimes she wishes she was back in Portishead with her mum, just for the freedom from his eyes. But in a way being there was worse, because it meant Malachi was over a hundred miles away rather than two floors. At least here there is a chance she will see him, run into him in the lift, or bump into him in the stairwell.

Blood runs into her face as she leans further over the

railings. Her head feels heavy. She wonders, not for the first time, how it would feel to fall from this spot, to flail past all fourteen floors and land at the bottom among the cars and bins. It would probably feel like running the 200 metres. Air hitting your face and taking your hair, your lungs shocked into working harder than you ever knew they could. Pink and yellow splodges dance in front of her eyes as she lifts her head. It's coming up to noon, only halfway through another monotonous, never-ending day.

She assumes it's other teenagers that repeatedly bust the locks on the door that leads up to the roof. They leave their crushed cans of Special Brew and ketchup-smeared fish and chip papers across the floor as evidence that they are having a life. She often fantasizes about coming up here at night, catching them in the throes of their late-night parties, tasting beer and throwing fag butts among the pigeon shit with them. If only Dad would let her out of the flat past 6 p.m. No chance.

The sky appears endless. Unnaturally blue today, almost unworldly, not a blemish on it apart from the single white smear of a plane.

Does she need to run back? Has it already been twenty minutes? She doesn't care. What does time matter if you're all alone? What difference does any of it make if you're about to throw yourself from the top of a tower block? She takes three deep breaths but knows that she doesn't have the confidence to do it. But the thought alone makes her feel like she has some edge on Dad, something that she *can* do without his permission.

In front of the estate people are living their lives: a child runs, the drunks drink, some girls sunbathe in pink bras and denim shorts, and a lone large figure in billowing purple crosses the grass at speed. Pamela tries to picture who the bodies are, how they would feel if they witnessed a girl fall from the building, their faces upon discovering her body bashed at the bottom. They would be traumatised, she thinks, for a while at least, and then her death would become another estate anecdote. *The tale of the broken-hearted teenager with the strict dad.* It would become just another story to get passed around the swing park and across balconies, along with tales of who is screwing who and which flat plays host to the biggest number of squatters.

Pamela wishes she could go for a run. She needs to clear her head. Surely Dad will let her out.

'Please, one hour out,' she rehearses. It sounds so feeble out loud, so knowing of a negative answer.

Her running shoes swing by her sides as she pads across the greyness in her socks. She steps over the glossy ripped pages of a magazine; a girl in a peephole leather catsuit stares back at her. The door bounces against its splintered frame as Pamela enters the building. Her world starts to shrink. With each step down to the eleventh floor the brightness of the unending blue sky disappears and the stairwell begins to close in on her. The concrete walls suck the air away until there is only the suffocating stink of other people's lives.

'Do you think it will be okay if I went out today? Maybe. Perhaps.' Her voice echoes eerily; she feels even more alone. 'I'm thinking of going out today.' This time with more confidence. But what's the point? He will say no. He will never trust her again.

She opens the door onto the puke-coloured hallway and the shouts and music of her neighbours. Outside flat forty-one she stops and rests her head on the security gate, takes a few breaths and then pulls it open. She looks down at the letterbox and for a moment feels like she has a choice. She could still go back to the roof. But, as always, the choice is taken away from her as the lock clicks from within and the front door swings open.

Dad fills the doorway; a fag hangs from the corner of his mouth. 'You're pushing your luck, girl.' Patches of psoriasis flame red on his expressionless face. He's put back on the same sweat-stained yellow T-shirt and army combat trousers from yesterday.

'I was getting some air.' She pushes past him into the dim, smoky living room.

He follows her, sits on the sofa and pulls his black boots on. 'Air?' He methodically ties up each of the long mustard laces. The woven burgundy throw falls from the back of the sofa to reveal the holes and poverty beneath it. 'We got a balcony for that. I don't wanna start locking the gate, Pamela, but if you're gonna be running off every opportunity—'

'I didn't run off. It's a nice day. I was on the roof.'

'Well, I've heard that before. You can't blame me for not trusting you.'

She rearranges the throw and stands back. She only wants an hour outside, just enough time to clear her head. So much can change in that time; like the day she first met Malachi. Dad had given her an hour then too, explained how grateful she should be for it. 'More than enough time to go round the field and straight back home.' She grabbed that time, and even though he was watching her from the window, she felt free as she ran loops around the frosty field.

The drunks, immune to the freezing temperatures of the morning, watched from their bench as she ran past them several times that hour. 'You should be running this way, blondie,' one called, while shaping his hands in a V towards his crotch on her last lap. They all laughed and she ran faster. She could always go faster and with time ticking she needed to get home before Dad came out for her. She cut onto the grass, slipped and fell awkwardly. It hurt straight away. Her ponytail caught the side of her face as she turned to check if the drunks were still laughing at her, but they hadn't even noticed her fall. The dew began to seep through her leggings and she tried to stand, but buckled immediately with the pain.

'Hey,' someone called. 'You okay?' A tall man came running towards her and put out a gloved hand. 'You really went down hard there.'

'Yeah.'

'Here, let me help you.'

As he helped her to a bench she tried to concentrate on the hole in his glove to stop herself from blushing.

'You really do run out here in all weathers, don't you?' he asked.

'Sorry?'

'I live up in Nightingale Point. I always see you out here.'

He had seen her before. How had she never seen him? She tried not to stare, or lean into his arms too much.

Tristan Roberts came over too. He was from her school, one of those loud, obnoxious boys everyone seemed to know.

'Oh, shit, did you break your leg?'

'No, she ain't broken her leg. This is my brother.'

They looked nothing alike.

'Ain't you cold?' Tristan pulled the drawstrings on his hoodie tighter. 'Running round out here? That's long.'

She could see Dad coming across the field now, his face red from fatigue and panic.

'I'm fine, really. Thanks. I need to get home.' She tried to rise but the pain shot through and she winced. He grabbed her again; the pain was almost worth it.

'Get off her. Pam.' Dad was closer. 'Pam, Pam.' He pushed past Tristan and put his hands either side of her face. 'I knew I should have been watching you. What happened?'

'She's all right, man, she just tripped, innit,' Tristan said.

'Who are you? Why are you two even near my girl?'

'Dad, stop it. Tristan goes to my school.'

Tristan looked confused. He obviously didn't recognise her. It confirmed she had no presence at her new school; she was nobody.

'I'm Malachi. We live in the same block. We were making sure she was all right. That's all.'

'Well, she's fine 'cause I'm here now, ain't I?' Dad snapped. 'Come on. Let's get you home.' His grip on her arm was tighter than it needed to be. She could see Malachi noticed it too.

'This looks bad, Pam. Don't think you'll be running again for a while.' Dad looked relieved, happy because injuries meant she had no reason to go out.

Even now, with the injury long healed, he still won't let her out, but then he has other reasons for wanting to keep her inside the flat these days. She pulls the curtains open and the room brightens, but even the sun's glare is not enough to chase the perpetual gloom out.

Dad inspects his roll-up for life before roughly squeezing it onto a saucer. It's from her nan's set, cream with tiny brown corgis around the edge, once used for special occasions but now reduced to holding ash.

'I'm going to the bookies,' he says. 'Will be back for dinner. We'll heat up that corned beef.'

'They're fighting again,' she says.

'Who?'

'Next door. Can't you hear them?'

They stop for a moment to listen to the searing soap opera from flat forty-two that plays itself out so regularly. It sounds particularly theatrical today. What is the woman shrieking about this time? She always seems to be arguing with her teenage daughter over something. Pamela longs for that kind of relationship, one so freely volatile that you could scream and shout at a parent, rather than stand there and soak up their disappointment.

'They been at it all morning,' he huffs. 'Their voices go right through me.'

Pamela tries to block out the domestic so she can focus on Dad, her own situation. She tries to assess his mood by the way he clears his throat and collects his wallet. She wonders at her chances of success and waits to pick her moment.

He looks straight at her. 'Why you dragging those about?' He nods towards the pair of pink and lilac trainers in her hands.

The tip of her ponytail tastes chemically; he always buys the cheapest shampoo.

'I won't go anywhere other than around the field. I promise.'

'You've only been home a few days. You expect me to let you start running wild again?' He holds his anger in so well, but she can see it behind his eyes, ready to pop like glass. 'No chance. You're staying in.'

'You know it rained the whole month I was at Mum's. I haven't been out running in ages.'

He shakes his head again.

'I want to go round the field a few times. It's the middle of the day,' she tries. 'You can watch me from here.'

'Told you. I'm going out.' His keys jangle as he taps his pockets and walks away, her chances dissipating.

'What about swimming? Can I go to the pool?'

He laughs. 'Yeah, right, the pool. Why? You arranged to meet someone there, have you?'

'No. Dad, please.' She follows him into the hallway, not content to let it end there. She knows she's already in trouble anyway. 'So you expect me to stay in all day listening to that?'

The walls leak more cries from the quarrelling neighbours.

He checks the handle on his bedroom door: locked. 'You can use the phone. Call one of your mates for a chat.'

'I don't want to chat. I want to go out. I want to run.'

He stops by the front door and gently takes her plait in one of his hands. 'No.' So calm. So fixed. 'I don't trust you out the flat. In fact, I don't even know if I trust you to be alone *in the flat*.' He lets the long plait fall and kisses her on the head.

'What do you mean?'

'Well, how can I be sure that the minute I go out your little boyfriend won't come running up?'

'Because I don't have a boyfriend anymore. Remember?'

He holds her gaze but what can he say? He knows he ruined it for her; he ruined everything.

'Dad?'

He turns to face her, keys now in his hands as he opens the front door. 'Yeah? Come on, Pam, what you wanting now?'

I hate you. 'Nothing.'

The door closes and she listens for the Chubb lock, but hears no footsteps. He's still outside; maybe he will change his mind and give her permission to start living again. But then, seconds later, there is the distinct clank of the security gate and the crunch of it being locked: the confirmation that she will spend today locked inside her home. Trapped.

CHAPTER FOUR

Tristan

Tristan had already picked the clothes from the floor, stacked the videotapes and lined up his and Malachi's trainers by the front door. He now sits on the window ledge, his place of choice, observing the world nine floors below him. He is wearing white shorts today, white T-shirt, white socks, white trainers, and a large cubic zirconia stud in his left ear. It's a good look. He feels pristine. He wonders if he should hoover but decides against it, as nothing will make the carpet, so full of cigarette burns and bleach stains, look any better.

Malachi walks in and slumps himself back into the Malachi-shaped dent on the sofa.

'So what's wrong with Mary's TV?' Tristan asks his brother.

'Nothing. One of her grandkids must have unplugged the aerial.'

Tristan laughs, once again glad that Mary never asked him to fix stuff around her flat. It's one of the perks of having a brother like Malachi, who is not only the clever one, the tall one and the 'traditionally handsome' one, but also the one that can 'fix stuff'.

'Did she make you watch *Ricki Lake* with her?' Tristan laughs. '*Girlfriend, you need to get a new man, get a man with a job,*' he mimics in an American accent.

Malachi shakes his head and pulls a pile of books onto his lap.

'Mal, you all right?'

'I'm always all right.' He holds his book in front of his face.

'You're proper squinting. You need glasses, man, stop denying it. Specs will complete this whole student look you've gone for.'

Malachi puts the book down and pulls some keys from his pocket. 'Mary's spare keys,' he says as they slide across the table into a pile of papers. 'Tris, if you drop out that window I can't save you.'

'You don't always need to save me,' Tristan snaps. 'I'm almost sixteen – old enough to vote and go to war.'

'You need to be eighteen to vote.'

'Whatever. Don't need my big brother saving me.'

Malachi always thinks he needs to play the hero, but looking at his outfit today he's the one that needs saving. Where did he even buy a pair of green trousers? No wonder he can't keep a girl.

Malachi starts writing a shopping list, like Nan used to, except Nan wouldn't have subjected them to pasta five nights out of seven.

'What?' Malachi looks up from his list of cheap meals. 'Why'd you keep staring at me?'

'Nothing. Was thinking, we should go West End, man. Get some new clothes for summer and that.'

'New clothes? Cool, right after I figure out how to stretch my last money over our meals for the week.'

'You were a lot more generous with the old purse strings when you were getting some action.' Tristan is fed up of Malachi's sulking. It's been going on for ages now. All over some girl. She wasn't even that fit. Proper Plain Jane. No need to get so upset over her. Tristan would never let a girl mess up his head the way Pamela messed up Malachi's.

He starts tapping a beat on the window and runs through his latest lyrics. *'It's Saturday, I'm out to play. Girls get ready 'cause I'm gonna pay, pay your way, so you can stay, in my bed, but I ain't gonna stay.* Yes. You like that one, Mal? I was born to do this, man.'

But there's no applause from the one-man audience on the sofa, only another huff.

'Pay your way, so you can stay, in my bed, we do it hard all day. So what you saying, Mal?'

Malachi raises his eyebrow. 'Keep working on it.'

'Ha. You coming out later?' Tristan asks hopefully.

'No.'

'How comes?'

'Busy.'

'Ah, don't give me that, it's bank holiday weekend.' He picks up one of Malachi's plastic-wrapped library books. *'The History of the Urban Environment.* Hmm, looks like a riveting read. But I'm sure it can wait. Come on, come out with me.'

'No.'

'You seriously telling me you can't take one day off from studying? Your brain gonna get stretch marks if you carry on like this.' How long is Malachi planning on hiding out behind his books? It's getting ridiculous. 'You gotta get back to normal sometime. Whole estate's gonna be at this fair up at the Heath. Plenty girls, Mal, plenty girls. Gonna keep me busy. Don't expect me home early. Don't expect me home *at all*. You can have the place to yourself, bring someone over if you want. Get a little study relief.' He pumps his hips.

Malachi rubs his eyes and groans. 'Tris, stop going on.'

'Calm down, bruv. I'm talking about girls in general. I wasn't gonna bring up Blondie.'

'You just did,' he snaps. 'You and Mary are doing my head in with this.'

'What?'

'You're both telling me to move on, yet you're bringing her up every minute. Why can't you both drop it?'

''Cause everyone's fed up with you sulking about Pamela. Time to get over it. It's time for a next girl. It's time, bruv, I'm telling you. That's why you need to come fair. You need to watch me in action.' He stands up and performs his lyrics just as he would on stage. '*Me settle down? You're having a laugh. A pocket full of Durex, girl meet me in the car park.*'

Malachi throws his books on the table. 'Don't you have somewhere to go?'

'Nah, not yet. I'm tryna cheer your long face up. I even put up that hotness for you.' Tristan nods over to the wall. Earlier he had taped up an A3 poster of Lil' Kim lying spread-eagle across an animal fur rug. Now that's the kind of girl worth having a broken heart over, not some skinny little blonde from the flats.

Tristan pushes the window open further, in need of air

after working himself up with all his talent. Now relaxed, he takes his Rizla from his pocket and what's left of his weed.

'Quickest way to get over one girl is to move on to a next.'

'Outside with that.' Malachi jabs a thumb towards the front door.

'You serious? The window's wide open. You can't smell it if I sit here,' Tristan says, demonstrating how carefully he will blow smoke out of the window.

'I don't care. Take it out.'

'Just 'cause you ain't smoking no more. Why should I have to go out?'

'Out.' Malachi repeats as he begins flicking through his books.

'Whatever.' Tristan rubs his brother's head roughly as he passes the sofa on his way out of the flat. Surely one of the benefits of having a twenty-one year old as your guardian should be that you can openly smoke a bit of weed at home. But no such luck with Malachi and that stick up his arse. Still, Tristan doesn't mind getting out, jogging down to his much-loved spot, between the sixth and fifth floor, where he selects the middle step.

'I'm more than a thug, girl get to know me, king of the block, T.H.U.G.'

He likes the echo of his voice in the stairwell and imagines how it would sound on a real microphone. He pictures himself in a recording booth, one headphone on, one headphone off, like the rappers in the videos, all his boys drinking in the studio, some girls dancing about.

'Gimme a kiss, I'll light up a spliff, take you to Oxford Street, buy you nice shit. Nah, don't sound right.' He looks again at his stingy stash. 'Hard times, hard times,' he mumbles.

Then he hears something, someone coming down the stairs. It stops. He cranes his neck to look up and down. Nothing. But there's someone breathing. It feels like he's being watched, maybe by one of those crazy girls from the youth club. He had stopped going after he got involved with one too many of them. Some even know where he lives; they're probably stalking him. Though he wouldn't mind being stalked by the girl with the red weave – she looked like the kind of trouble he could enjoy.

Again, the shuffle of feet, heavy, though, not like a girl. Footsteps. He looks up and down but can't see anyone. He's being paranoid, but it pays to be paranoid living around here. Last week some woman got her handbag nicked as she was getting out of the lift.

'I'll give that ghetto ghetto love, weed and sex, and some crazy drugs.'

'No smoking in the stairwell.'

Tristan is startled. His papers flutter to the floor.

'What the fuck?' he shouts.

A man stands at the top of the stairs. He looks down at Tristan. He is tall and chubby, and has crazy bright ginger hair.

'No smoking in the stairwell,' he commands.

'You what? You spying on me?'

'No smoking in the stairwell,' the man repeats, and his face breaks out into high red blotches. 'It's a rule. You cannot break the rules of Nightingale Point.'

'Fuck off. Go. Go past.'

But the man stands there, straight-faced. 'No smoking in the stairwell.'

There is definitely something off about him; he's wearing a T-shirt with a picture of Elvis Presley on it, for a start.

'Rule breaker. Rule breaker,' the man chants.

Tristan pounces up the stairs and grabs the idiot by the sleeve of his T-shirt. The man is bigger than Tristan but unsteady on his feet and he topples down easily with a tug. He lets out a small cry as he falls, then grabs the bannister and pulls himself back to his feet.

'Stop looking at me!' Tristan shouts. 'Move. Go before I chuck you down the next five flights.'

The man bends over to pick up his glasses. His grey shorts are too big for him and he gives Tristan an eyeful of his white fleshly arse cheeks before he runs off down the stairs.

'Fucking retard.' Tristan picks up his papers and returns to making the spliff. He empties his tobacco in and sprinkles the little weed he has left on the top. But he's pissed off now. He has nowhere peaceful to call his own, except for this place in the stairwell, and now some dumb fucker wants to talk to him about rules and try to kill his vibe.

Tristan lights up and waits a few moments to enjoy his first puff. It takes him a while to chill out again but finally he relaxes into his familiar routine, lounging back on the step and listening to the muffled sounds of the block.

'Oh, look who it's not.' Mary's voice echoes from above.

'Fuck,' he mutters and rubs the spliff against the steps. 'Didn't hear you, Mary. Boy, you're so silent. Like a ninja.'

'What you doing, sunshine?' Her little plimsolled feet patter down the steps till she reaches him. 'I was looking for you yesterday. Malachi tells me you're not going kiddie club anymore.'

'What?' He laughs and fans the air between them. 'Youth club? Nah, nah. I'm too old for that, man.'

'Don't *man* me. What is this?' She pulls the spliff from behind his ear and he awaits the lecture. Mary's got a lecture for everything these days. It's almost like when Nan left last summer she handed Mary some kind of oracle of lectures, one for every minor deviance.

'It's Saturday. I'm allowed a little relief from life.'

'Why not go and relieve yourself with a book?' Mary rolls her head around like the African American women she's always watching on TV. She leans towards him and sniffs his T-shirt till he moves away self-consciously.

'What you doing? I'm clean. You know me, fresh like daisies.'

'You stink like drugs.'

He laughs. 'Oh my days. Leave me alone. It's bank holiday weekend.'

'You don't work. Every day is bank holiday weekend for you. This is no good, Tristan.' She holds the spliff in her hands. 'If you smoke too much wacky backy you'll get voices in your head.'

'Is that a fact? Is that what the NHS is training you nurses to tell people nowadays?'

It's obvious how hard she's trying to hold a look of disappointment in her creased face, so he hits her with his biggest smile. 'Come on, Mary, marijuana is a natural product. It's grows alongside roses and shit.'

'Don't *shit* me.'

Her lips soften into a smile as Tristan laughs. She reaches up and puts the white roll-up back behind his ear. Such a pushover.

'You come with me,' she demands.

'What?'

'Walk me to the bus stop.'

He groans, knowing this will be Mary's time to grill him on school, smoking, girls and anything else that needs to be filled in for her regular report back to Nan.

'I can't walk you, Mary. I'm busy. Meeting friends and going fair later, innit.'

'You don't have a choice. Come.'

She takes him by the arm and they walk down the stairs in silence. The ground floor is filled with the smell of the caretaker's lunch – egg salad – and the sound of football on his radio.

'Why you wearing so much white?' Mary asks as they emerge into the heat and light of day.

''Cause it makes me look like an angel.'

'Angel, ha. That earring makes you look like George Michael.'

'Boy, you're giving me a hard time.'

She snorts then let's go of his arm as something hard and metallic falls to the ground in front of them. It's her nurse's fob watch.

Tristan picks it up and hands it back. 'It's broke. Why you still dragging this about? It looks so old.'

'Because it *is* old.'

'Get a new one. Get a digital.'

'I don't need new anything,' she snaps while trying to re-pin it. 'David gave it to me.'

A woman in hot pants and a bright red halter top, covering very little, walks past. She's too old for both Tristan and her choice of outfit. Just his type.

'It's hot out here,' he calls in an attempt to get her attention.

Mary grabs his arm again and pulls him away from the woman. 'This temperature would be like winter in Manila. It is thirty-five degrees there. Where you going today?'

'Told you. There's a funfair over on the Heath.'

She stops and grabs her elbows in that nervous way she often does. 'I hate funfairs. There's always trouble at funfairs. Always someone getting robbed or getting their head broken on a ride.'

'Yeah, that's why I don't get involved with rides. Those gypsies don't do health and safety checks. I'm going to check a few gal and that.'

Mary reaches up and takes hold of one of his cheeks. 'Eh, sunshine, put a sock on it. Don't want any babies running around here.'

'Oh my days, you're tryna embarrass me. As if I would have a baby with any of these mad estate girls.'

They both turn to face the car park where a few boys cycle about in circles, shouting at each other. Tristan hadn't even noticed them coming round. Behind them, on the wall, sit three older boys: Ben Munday, who has been able to grow a full beard since he was thirteen, and two others, who wear red bandanas around their heads like rap superstars. Tristan still owes Ben Munday twenty quid. Shit.

'You know them ragamuffins?' Mary asks.

He shrugs. 'Nope. Not really.'

'But they're looking at you.' She scratches at her left elbow and inspects it, as if she has been bitten by something.

Tristan really doesn't have twenty quid right now, his

own cash depleted weeks ago, and Malachi is being tighter than usual with the student grants and carer benefits that keep them both ticking over. He considers asking Mary but something about the way she frowns and fidgets tells him she's not in the most giving of moods.

'Tristan Roberts,' Ben Munday calls.

Mary widens her eyes. 'You don't know them? Liar. They look like crack dealers, like Bloods and Crisps.'

He laughs so hard he needs to use her little shoulder to support himself, 'It's Bloods and *Crips*. Where you getting this stuff from?'

'Don't make fun of me.' She shakes him off. 'I see it on *Oprah*. I know all about gangbanging.'

'Please, never say gangbanging again. And stop being so judgey. They're kids from my school.' Though they both know the wall boys are long past school age.

'Eh, Tristan?' Ben Munday calls again.

This time Tristan knows there's no escape. 'I better go check them out, all right?' He nods at her as he walks off slowly, already thinking of how to downplay knowing a 'gang' when his nan next asks him about it. 'And Mary, get rid of that nasty old watch.'

CHAPTER FIVE

Mary

She watches Tristan walk over to the ragamuffins that line the wall. He touches fists with each of them, and Mary catches a glimpse of the big Cheshire cat smile that makes him so endearing. She doesn't want to think anything bad of Tristan, who deserves a million chances to get it right, but he's smoking too much marijuana and surrounding himself with too many bad influences.

When Mary promised the boys' nan she would keep a close eye on them, she thought it would be an easy job. She had known them since they were babies and, despite their chaotic upbringing, they were mostly good boys. But Tristan worries her at the moment. It's no longer as easy as telling him to stay off the streets and he stays off the streets. She can't fool herself: she has no real control over him. It's like what you see on *Oprah*. Boy listens to rap music telling him to go shoot a policeman. Next day boy goes and shoots a policeman. She worries about him. All the time she worries about him.

Again it comes: twitch, twitch, twitch. She pushes her short blunt nails into her bony elbow in an effort to stop the tic.

Right now, there is a worry bigger and more urgent than Tristan. Mary's husband, David, will descend on her any day and she is sure her guilt will shine through like a firefly in a jar. She will slip up somehow, maybe smell differently or perhaps refer to something only a woman in love would know. He will watch her and he will realise: his wife is an adulteress. When he came last, just over a year ago, she had started seeing Harris Jones outside of their nurse and patient relationship. Nothing more than long walks around the Jewish graveyard behind his house. A place safe from the prying eyes of others, somewhere they could be together to look at the bluebells and put the world to rights. An innocent friendship. But now, now things were so different.

'Hot enough for you?' the big ginger man who lives in her block asks as he stands outside the phone box, his glasses sitting lopsided across his babyish face. He is new to the area, one of those care-in-the-community patients. He runs his hands down the front of his T-shirt; it has a print of a young Elvis Presley on it, all hair and curled lip. When Mary first met David he was working as an Elvis impersonator at The Manila Peninsula Hotel. Mary hates Elvis. She smiles politely at the man as she spots the number 53 pulling into the bus stop.

She flashes her bus pass and rubs her arms discreetly against her polyester white uniform. The door closes behind her and traps in the heat and smells of the passengers. Mary thinks of how she is breaking the vows she took all those years ago in the local church with the baskets of sun-bleached plastic flowers and the priest with the lisp. She falls into that awkward middle seat at the back of the bus and feels the woman to her right tighten her grip on a battered library book so their arms don't touch. Mary can just about make out the title: *Broken Homes Make Broken Children*. An omen? It's like the world is conspiring to tell her something about her own wrongness, her dishonesty. But broken children? Her twins were hardly children anymore, thirty-five this year, and with careers and families of their own. Mary can't imagine John's or Julia's life being affected by her having an affair or finally divorcing David. *Divorce*. As the word enters her mind the scratch becomes a searing itch and she tries to distract herself. She pulls a tissue from her bag and dabs her clammy face; the sun catches her wedding ring and it glints sadly, as if to mock her failure as a wife.

The bus picks up speed and a welcome breeze flows through the narrow windows. The woman with the cursed book gives Mary a sideways glance, their eyes meet and she adjusts herself to face out of the window. No one wants to deal with a crying nurse on public transport. As the bus nears Vanbrugh Close, Mary stands and presses the bell. She squeezes herself past the other sweaty passengers, towards the exit, ready to get off and face her second life. The doors hiss open and she steps into the full force of the sun. Immediately, her state of guilt gives way to something like joy, for although her affair is sordid and secret it is also satisfying, and her heart thumps with schoolgirl excitement at the prospect of seeing him again.

The walk towards the close of bungalows fills her with a feeling she remembers first having when she was nineteen and on the cusp of marrying David. A feeling she enjoys but knows she should not have in relation to a man other than her husband. Pop music plays from a stereo; a father and teenage daughter wash down a car together. They both glance up and smile at her. They look like a television advert: perfect and happy. On the other side of the road an elderly lady in a straw hat and pink gardening gloves picks at a blooming brood of hydrangeas. Vanbrugh Close is a world away from Nightingale Point and its smelly stairwell, blinking strip lights and cockroaches. And as Mary turns into the small neat drive of Harris's home, she realises the life she has created with this man is a world away from herself, from the woman she has grown to be: the mother of two, grandmother of four, nurse of thirty-three years and wife to a fame-chasing husband.

CHAPTER SIX

Pamela

She lies on the sofa listening to the neighbours' argument as it sinks through the wall. The mother–daughter screaming matches have become an almost weekly occurrence, both of them going back and forth at each other in their matching catty voices. Pamela closes her eyes and imagines what it would feel like to scream and shout at Dad the way the girl next door does with her mum. Pamela could never; she would be too scared to say all the things she really thinks about him. She jumps at the sound of a door slamming in the neighbours' flat, the sound that usually signals the end of the row. And now there's nothing to distract her. She stretches each leg out above her head. She misses running so much. How long will this go on for?

On the train back from Portishead Dad had told her not to expect to return to London and fall back into her normal routines, but she never expected this, for him to actually lock her in the flat, to put a complete ban on her going out. There was only ever a slim chance of him letting her take up running again, but it was him that pushed her to start swimming after her injury, so why rule that out as well? There's no way he could have found out how little she actually swam.

'I've circled the ladies-only sessions for you,' he had said as he handed her the pool timetable. He even went out and bought her a costume.

She knew she wasn't going to like swimming as soon as she got into the cold changing rooms. Most of the locks on the cubicles were broken and women of all shapes and sizes roamed about naked. Pamela looked the other way as old ladies stood with their swimming costumes half hanging down, applying deodorant and chatting to friends. There were used cotton buds left on the wooden slat bench, the floor dusty with talc. Quickly, she changed into the overly modest costume and made her way out to the pool, her eyes already stinging from the chlorine.

As she waded through the water her fingers caught long strands of black hair. She couldn't get a rhythm going, the pool was too small and crowded, and she found herself gripping the scaly tiles at the far end, waiting for someone to complete a lap so she could have a turn. There was no freedom, no clearing of the mind and no possibility of losing herself in the monotony of the movement. It was the opposite of everything she loved about running.

She flipped her collar up while she stood under the awning outside, watching the bus home pull away. If she ran she could be home in fifteen minutes, but there was no rush to get back there, to sit in the dreary living room alone.

Two people came towards her with their hoods up. One went through the sliding doors but the other one stopped.

'Hey.' It was Malachi. He removed his hood and wiped the rain from his face.

'Hi.' She wanted to smile back but instead looked around cautiously in case Dad appeared from somewhere.

'How's your leg?'

'Fine. Well, no, it's sprained, so I'm giving it a bit of a break from running.'

The sliding doors kept opening and closing until Tristan stepped out from them. 'Mal, we're not allowed in.'

'What?'

'Oh, it's a women-only swim session,' Pamela said.

Tristan stood between the two of them. 'What kind of sexist nonsense is that? I bet they don't run men-only sessions, do they?'

Malachi rolled his eyes.

'Let's go gym instead?' Tristan said.

'I told you, you're too young for it.'

'Come on, swimming never gave anybody a six-pack. Ain't that right, Blondie?' He nudged her side.

'Maybe you should take up running?' she suggested, still looking at Malachi.

'I'd like that.' Malachi smiled and held her gaze.

Tristan laughed. 'Yeah, running is a great choice of sport for a chronic asthmatic.'

'Tristan, I'm going to meet you back home, all right?'

'For real?' Tristan looked at Pamela like he wanted to laugh. But of course, it didn't make sense that someone like Malachi, who was tall and perfect, would want to spend time with a girl like Pamela, who was plain and invisible.

Malachi dug in a pocket and pulled out a crumpled fiver. 'Here, go cinema or something. I'll see you later.'

Tristan kissed his teeth as he took the note. 'All right, see you back home. Laters, Blondie.' He threw up his hood and sulked off into the rain.

They stood and faced the road, the rain coming down heavier now.

She wanted to wait for him to speak first, but couldn't hold it in. 'You know it's too wet to run, right?'

He looked at her. He had amazing eyes. 'I know. And you've been swimming already. You hungry?'

She shook her head. She didn't have money to eat out anywhere.

'What about a drink then? There's a greasy spoon over there, it does good milkshakes. I'll race you.'

It was awkward as they ran to the café together, as if they both knew straight away there was something more happening. The smell of burnt onions hit her as they stepped inside. They sat opposite each other in metal chairs and he picked up the laminated menu and held it closely to his face, studying it for way too long. Frowning, his forehead wrinkling, he looked so serious, so utterly different from every other boy she came across at school.

'How old are you?' She felt embarrassed straight after asking it.

'Twenty-one.' He put the menu down and folded his arms. 'Twenty-one going on sixty.'

She smiled at him. 'I know the feeling.'

He looked at her for a beat too long.

'I'm almost seventeen. I'm the oldest in my year group at school,' she said, trying to justify their age gap. 'Seventeen in September. If I was born one day earlier I would already be in college.' She paused. 'You and Tristan don't look very much alike.'

'No. We're not alike in lots of ways.'

'Do you have the same dad?' she asked.

'What kind of question is that?'

The milkshakes came and she felt she had blown it, asked a stupid question and revealed herself to be a stupid schoolgirl after all.

'I'm sorry, I didn't mean to be nosy.'

'He's my brother. That's all there is to it.'

She nodded and mixed the milkshake with the end of the straw.

'Tristan said he's never seen you at school before.'

'No one sees me at school. No one sees me anywhere.'

'I see you.' Malachi smiled.

As they came out of the café, back into the real world, Pamela felt cautious again. 'Do you mind if we walk back separately?' she asked.

'But we're going to the same place.'

'You met my dad – he's quite strict about who I hang out with. He doesn't really let me see boys.'

The word 'see' almost implied that she thought they had started a relationship.

'I understand.'

How could this work? Could she really see him again? She wanted to. But there were lots of things she wanted to do but wasn't allowed.

'I don't really have time to, you know . . . do stuff outside of school and sport. My timetable is quite packed.'

He straightened up and rubbed his face.

School and sport, that's all her life was. Surely she could take the risk of having something else going on?

'My dad wants me to go swimming every Tuesday and Thursday between six and eight. But I hate swimming.'

'So what are you saying?'

'That I'm free every Tuesday and Thursday between six and eight.'

He nodded. 'Got it.'

They separated as they reached the field in front of the estate. He sat on a bench and she walked off, trying her best not to keep looking back at him. She pulled her hair in front of her face, smelling its mix of chlorine and fried food, and knew she would never set foot in the pool again.

*

Pamela paces the flat like the caged animal she is, stopping each time to look at the front door. She misses Malachi so much. She doesn't want to chase him, but he needs to know the truth. That she didn't want things to end the way they did and hopes they can work out a way to still be together. But first, there's something else she needs to tell him.

What can she do? She doesn't want to talk over the phone; he's always awkward on the phone. Half the time his phone is cut off anyway. But what choice does she have?

She picks up the phone and dials.

Thank God, it rings.

CHAPTER SEVEN

Malachi

Malachi pulls his books back onto his lap and tries again. He's behind on his reading and hasn't even made a start on the essay. There's no way they will let him have an extension on the deadline again. The tutor won't understand that he's behind because he has a broken heart. It's pathetic.

His eyes hurt and so does his head. Maybe Tristan's right about the eyesight thing. He can't concentrate. He sifts through the morning's post. Junk mail and another bill. Where does all the money go anyway? He's only just managed to clear the rent arrears and get the phone put back on. The electric bill looks steeper than usual this time, probably because of Tristan's habit of running the hoover every day and putting on a wash for one or two T-shirts. Their mum never taught them anything about keeping home. They were learning as they went; they didn't have a choice.

Malachi allows his head to fall back onto the beaten sofa, the plush long gone from previous owners, and puts his hands over his face. There's got to be an easier way to get by than this.

'Get it together,' he says to himself. He wonders if there's anything he can do to get some cash in. Well, there are things: someone had talked about selling knock-off TVs, and he'd also heard rumblings about single men with British passports being paid for taking part in bogus marriages. But both these things seem to come with a lot of risk. And Malachi has a lot to lose if things go wrong.

There's no other option; it's time to call Nan. The last thing he wants to do is stress her, or make her feel like she's made a bad decision leaving him in charge here, but what choice does he have? He needs to watch the money more closely this month. He wishes he never bought that pair of pink and lilac running shoes for Pamela – they were so expensive. But her old ones were almost worn through and she seemed serious about taking up running again once she recovered from her injury. He wonders if she's allowed out to run in Portishead. She's probably not allowed to do anything there. Anyway, after what happened between them Pamela probably threw the trainers off the roof. She must hate him after what he did, how he denied her. It hurts to imagine her feeling this way; it's so far from how she was at the start, back when she was completely into him. He misses those early days with her, when her dad worked long hours and she had freedom. Back when being in this flat, in his bedroom, felt like they were a million miles off the estate and away from all their problems. They would lie in bed and allow themselves to believe it would all work out, that her dad would relax and let go of whatever his prejudice against Malachi was.

He wishes he could stop thinking about her, stop using his memories of them together as a place to escape to. But how can he? When everything here and now is so challenging, so dull and so lifeless without her? He wants her back, back here in the flat with him, talking to him and making him laugh. He can't stop thinking about those wintery afternoons; he can't stop imagining he is there again.

'It's so cold. What time does your heating come on?' Pamela had asked as she came back into the bedroom.

'It doesn't.' He didn't want to weigh her down with money problems, to soil their time together by talking about a situation he felt was drowning him.

She jumped back in the bed next to him and shivered. 'Your brother's home. He didn't seem too pleased to see me here. Asked if I had permission from my dad to have a sleepover.'

Idiot. Malachi laughed. 'He's a wind-up. Ignore him.'

'He doesn't like me.'

Malachi was never quite able to work out what his brother's problem with Pamela was. Especially as Tristan was always going on about Malachi having a girl and now he had one.

'I try with Tristan. I really do. But he openly yawns every time I speak to him,' she said. 'He does it on purpose.'

Malachi stifled a laugh. It did sound like the kind of thing Tristan would do. 'He's not used to someone other than himself getting attention, that's all.' Malachi put his arm around her and twisted a lock of her hair around his finger.

'You're not scared of my dad, are you?' she asked suddenly.

'It depends. What did he do to your last boyfriend?'

'I told you, I've not had boyfriends.' She moved away from him then, as far as the single bed would allow, and he braced himself to hear bad news. 'But when I first moved to London one of the youth coaches from running club called my house to ask me out.'

'And?'

'Well, Dad answered. He went nuts because the coach was twenty-one.'

'So you *do* like older guys then?'

She picked up the pillow and hit his shoulder with it. She was constantly trying to play down their age gap, it embarrassed her, but to him it wasn't an issue, she felt so much older, more mature than most of the girls he met at university.

'Dad accused the guy of being a predator, almost got him fired. He said if I saw him again he would send me back to Portishead. That's always the threat, sending me back.'

'The coach thing is a bit dodgy, though. It's like that teacher and student barrier. It's not meant to be crossed. Let's wait till you're out of school, then you can tell your dad.'

Malachi pictured it often, the first time he would meet her dad, Jay, properly. How it would be awkward at the start but eventually Jay would be won over by the fact that his daughter was with someone about to gain a university degree, someone with goals and ambitions, someone who would look after Pamela and make sure she was always happy.

She shook her head. 'He never needs to know. It's not worth the aggro.'

This issue, it was the only thing that ever annoyed him about her, this feeling that he needed to be kept hidden. It didn't make any sense, especially when they talked about long-term plans, the trips they would take, the cities they would work in and the home he would design for them in some perfect location far from the city. But none of that stuff could happen if their relationship was to remain a secret.

Malachi hated to give a voice to the thing in his head, but it was there and wouldn't go away. 'So apart from my age, there isn't anything else your dad would have a problem with about me, is there?'

'What do you mean?'

'You know what I mean, Pam. Don't make me ask you outright.'

She pulled her hair up into a ponytail and looked away. 'Mal, I've told you already, he's not like that. He doesn't like me seeing anyone. Black, white, purple, green.'

'You say that, but have you ever heard *him* say that?'

'He hates everyone and everything. He wants me sitting in the living room, right under his nose, where he can see me. I'm all he's got.'

Malachi nodded. It wasn't a conversation worth ruining their afternoon for. 'So, you wouldn't want to live with your mum again?'

'She doesn't want me. She's got her new life now, new husband, new job. Why would she want her teenage daughter messing it all up? She always made Dad out to be the bad one, but he's the one who looks after me. He's a little over-protective sometimes, that's all.'

Malachi pictured her dad waiting at the front door for her to return home each evening, ready with his interrogation about where she had been and who she had been with.

'A *little* over-protective?' he says.

'Dad's sister got pregnant at fifteen and it ruined her life. He doesn't want me going the same way.'

'That would never happen with us.'

She rolled back into the bed next to him. 'Boys are troublesome.'

'Except me. I'm the least troublesome boy you could have found.'

'Really? We'll see.'

*

Why did he allow himself to mess up so badly with her? How could he let her dad get the better of him?

He needs some air, some perspective. He scribbles a note for Tristan: *Gone out for a walk. Need to clear head* and goes out. As he walks down the stairs he hears humming on the third floor. *Shit*, Beryl must be tending to her plastic garden again. He could do without being caught up listening to her go on today.

'Hello, Mr Long Legs,' she calls.

'Hi Beryl, can't stop.' He catches her disappointment as he runs past and immediately feels guilty; swears to pop by later. Beryl, like most women in the block of a certain age, seems to have a certain fondness for him. Tristan says it's sometimes like Nan has them all on payroll for interfering.

He takes the steps two at a time till he reaches the ground floor.

'Your lifts are out again?' he shouts towards the open door of the caretaker's cubbyhole.

A grey head pops out, mop in hand. 'What did you say, son?'

'The lifts are out.'

'Yep. Both on the blink.' The caretaker smiles, as if having announced some welcome news. 'And you're not the first person today to point that out to me either.'

The sun is searing, it's full summer already and Malachi's clothes feel too heavy and warm for the day. He hadn't even registered the seasons change.

There's a crack of laughter from by the car park. He spots Tristan, glowing in his white shorts and T-shirt, with the local hoods. Malachi doesn't want to be called over to touch fists with them like he is part of their group, like he won't, later on today, have a go at Tristan for associating with them. He jogs off quickly across Sandford Road and out onto the green. He looks back at Nightingale Point and counts up the floors to Pamela's flat, half expecting to see her on the balcony, chewing her ponytail and observing the world below. But of course she's not there, she's gone. He didn't expect to still feel this way, a month on. He thought being without her would have gotten easier, that he would have stopped missing her. But every day it seems to get worse.

There are more people than usual on the grass. Some look prepared for the weather, with supermarket food, blankets and sunglasses. Though most, like him, are caught off guard and look uncomfortable in their dark colours and too-warm clothes. Malachi used to love summer; him and Tristan would sit out on the balcony and suck on the coloured chunks of ice they would make themselves by pouring diluted juice into ice cube trays. Mum loved the summer too; it made her want to get out of the house. He can't remember her depression ever taking hold during the summer months. But then he tries not to remember too much about her.

It wasn't planned but when he looks up he realises he's walked all the way to the swimming pool, the place he and Pamela first started talking, and across from it the café where they spent so much time together. He walks in alone and sits at the usual table, hidden near the back. With Pamela it was always a milkshake each and a plate of chips to share – his one extravagance.

The waitress comes and buries a hand in her thick curly hair. 'Hey, honey,' she says overly familiar, 'ain't seen you in ages.'

Pamela used to tease Malachi about the waitress having a crush on him.

'Where's your girlfriend today?'

'Oh.' His head falls to the side and he feels an overwhelming desire to confess all to her, just for someone to talk to, but it's not in him to do that. 'She's around. You know.' He pulls his gaze away from her face to the blue evil eye at her neck.

The woman smiles and wipes the table. 'Trouble in paradise?' She asks so gently he feels he might break.

'Ah, actually . . . Well, we broke up.'

'I'm sorry to hear that.' The crumbs fly from the table onto his lap as she pushes about a blue cloth. 'Well, it won't take you long to find someone else. I'm sure they're lining up.'

But he doesn't want anyone else, he wants to sit here with Pamela and share a plate of chips and laugh about last week's episode of *Father Ted*. It hurts being here, reliving all those times they sat in this very booth, getting to know each other and making plans.

He puts his head in his hands.

The waitress comes back over and puts a milkshake on the table. 'On the house,' she says, tapping his shoulder. The kindness of it, of her and the way she looks at him, reminds him of all those teachers and social workers who would give him extra attention when they knew his mum was having a turn for the worse. It's not empathy, it's pity, and it still breaks his heart.

He can't bear to see the pink glob of powder at the bottom of the glass so he drinks it to the halfway point. He misses Pamela so much. He's not going to be able to concentrate on studying this afternoon. He can't imagine being able to concentrate on anything ever again. Not without her.

'Get it together,' he mumbles. 'Get it together.'

He knows he can't speak to Pamela now; she surely wouldn't want to hear anything he's got to say. But maybe, just maybe, he can speak to her dad.

CHAPTER EIGHT

Elvis

Elvis runs across the field to the other side. On his way he passes some girls who are sunbathing with not a lot of clothes on, some friendly drunk men, and an old man who walks a giant, scary dog, which he does not stop to pet. He pulls open the door of the phone box and shields his eyes from the photo cards of women with their breasts exposed.

He cannot remember George's phone number and Elvis wishes he had spent more time trying to learn it and less time flapping the laminated sheet in the air. He takes his notepad from the pocket of his grey shorts and flicks through the pages to see if the number is written down in there. It isn't. Instead, the notepad is filled with other important information, such as what takeaway dish is best from Express Burger (quarter pounder with chilli sauce and salad) and what time the postman arrives on his floor (8.57 a.m.).

It is too hot inside the phone box and it smells of wee, so he steps back outside. Elvis wonders if Archie, his friend from the Waterside Centre, was telling him the truth when he said that teenage black boys were dangerous. Archie had warned, 'You can't live on a council estate. It's full of bad black boys that will try to stab you.' Archie is Elvis's best friend. Elvis misses Archie. He also misses the Waterside Centre. He misses the small bathroom attached to his bedroom, the paintings of lily ponds in the hallways and Tuesday night bingo with Bill.

As he stands outside the second emergency phone and looks across the green he sees the Filipina nurse he knows coming towards him. This makes him smile again. She lives in his block. Elvis likes her as once, when they were in the lift together, she told him a long but nice story about storms in the Philippines. The Filipina nurse is so small and Elvis always has an urge to pick her up, but he knows you cannot do that to strangers as it will scare them and some short people do not like to be reminded that they are short.

'Hot enough for you?' he asks as she walks quickly towards the bus stop. But she is in a rush today and has no time to stop and chat about storms. She needs to catch the number 53 bus because that goes to the Queen Elizabeth Hospital where she works. Elvis hates the Queen Elizabeth Hospital as it is where he went when his arm was broken by the car that time and it hurt so badly and he screamed and cried. Then, worst of all, he bit a nurse, which made him scream and cry all over again because he had done something so terrible.

Elvis's leg hurts now from where he bashed it on the stairs. He looks down at the purple bruise on his glowing white skin and wishes the Filipina nurse had time to look at it for him, but the 53 now pulls away with her on it.

If Elvis tells George, his care worker, all the things that have happened today, maybe he will make him go back into assisted living. Elvis does not want to go back into assisted living. He has only been living alone six weeks, which he knows for sure because he puts a red dot on his calendar each morning.

His glasses will not balance on his face correctly because the left arm is all bent, so he puts them in his pocket along with the packet of Euro '96 stickers he bought yesterday, then he slowly walks back across the green. He likes the way Nightingale Point gets bigger and bigger the closer you get. He looks up a few times to feel the sun hit his face. It feels lovely. But because he is a ginger he should not get too much of it. One summer Elvis had fallen asleep in the sunshine without his coconut suntan lotion on and his skin had burnt red raw, even his eyelids.

He crosses Sandford Road carefully, after looking both ways and listening for traffic, then heads into the estate. A group of teenage boys sit on the wall that lines the car park; one has a very impressive beard and Elvis wonders if he has a special little brown comb for it like his Sikh friend Mandeep. Some other boys cycle about and laugh loudly, and one sings a song Elvis does not know but would like to. In the middle of the group he notices the bad black boy from the stairs again, the one with the zigzags in his hair who pushed Elvis earlier and made his glasses all bent.

The boy has a bright blue ice pole hanging from his mouth, the kind Lina bought Elvis last week when she was in a happy mood. Elvis has an idea. He stops and gets out his notepad. This is his chance. He will make a description of the boy so that he can report him to George and then maybe even to the police. He sketches the boy's white trainers, white shorts, white T-shirt, and shiny diamond earring. The trainers are very difficult to draw correctly. He scribbles them out and tries again. He looks up to check what the laces look like and it is then he sees that all the boys are staring at him.

Rumbled.

He tries to place his notepad back in his pocket inconspicuously and pretends to be very busy kicking the stones from the path into a neat pile. Which is a very valid job.

'What were you drawing there, fatty?' a voice from the wall calls.

Elvis says nothing, just concentrates on making the path straight. Of course he knows it is rude to ignore someone, but then it is also very rude to call someone 'fatty'.

'Oi, I'm chatting to you,' the voice calls again.

Elvis feels a little bit scared now and no longer wants to kick the stones back into place. He wants to go home. Two of the boys cycle over. One of the bikes has colourful spokes that go *click clack click*.

'What you drawing?'

Elvis tries to remember what is best: to ignore or to lie. He chooses to ignore and tries to squeeze himself between the two bikes and off towards home, but he is not as small as he thinks and his T-shirt gets stuck on one of the handlebars. Maybe he is a fatty. He wriggles free and starts to walk away fast.

'Why you walking off? I'm talking to you, brer.'

He feels someone grab him and pull at his shorts. His notepad is pulled from the pocket. The biker, who Elvis really does not like and is very scared of, now holds the notepad and flicks through all the pages of Elvis's important information about what takeaway dish is best and what time the postman comes. Then he stops and begins to laugh. He shows his friend, who laughs as well and shouts, 'Oi, Tris, is this man your bum chum? Didn't know you were into gingers.'

The notepad is cycled back to the wall, where each of the boys has a look and a laugh.

'Please,' Elvis says, 'can I have it back?'

The boy with the impressive beard lets out a laugh, which sounds like the little girl who lives next door. He then stuffs his free hand down the front of his jogging bottoms, which is not socially acceptable no matter how much your penis needs to be adjusted.

'Please, can I have it back?' Elvis repeats, this time slightly louder than the last. He really does want it back.

But the bearded boy ignores him and hands it to the bad black boy from the stairs, who looks at it, then shouts, 'Is this meant to be me?'

Elvis does not want to look at the boy's very angry face, so instead focuses on the shiny diamond earring and the bright blue stain across the – otherwise – very white T-shirt.

'What's your problem, man? First you're spying on me in the stairs and now you're drawing pictures of me.'

The other boys gasp; some laugh quietly.

'Eh, Tris, this is proper creepy. This brer been stalking you?' one of them says. 'That's some gay bunny boiler shit.'

Elvis plans to grab the notepad very quickly, then run into Nightingale Point and up all the stairs and back into his perfect flat with all his perfect things, but as he reaches out the bad black boy grabs his fingers and twists them. It hurts. Elvis screams. He breaks free and tries to run away but two of the boys on bikes block his path. The bad black boy comes forward and starts to rip each page from the notepad and scrunch them up. Finally, he flicks the notepad over into the car park. The boys all laugh and the bad black boy hoots with them.

'Sicko,' he shouts.

'Don't let him get away with it, Tris,' says the bearded one.

Elvis is very frightened of being hurt again. He wraps his arms around his head and squeezes his shoulders up to his ears. The bad black boy takes a step closer but instead of pain Elvis feels a glob of wet spit cover his lips and chin.

The boys all laugh and the bad black boy shouts, 'Stay away from me, you fucking retard.'

CHAPTER NINE

Tristan

The boys hover around the wall in order of importance, headed by Ben Munday, who sits in the shade offered by Nightingale Point, pride of place. He's got on the latest Air Jordans, the type of footwear Tristan can only dream of owning.

'What's up, Tris? You look nuff prang,' asks one of the younger boys from his bike.

'Aw, it's this heat.' Tristan wipes his brow with a flourish but is embarrassed when he discovers the back of his hand glistening. 'What you lot saying then?'

'Chilling,' answers the boy.

'Yeah, yeah. Chilling.' Tristan relaxes a little, allows his shoulders to drop. What's twenty quid anyway? Ben Munday probably has so much money he doesn't even remember lending it. Now that's the kind of flex Tristan needs to be on. This relying on your big brother for handouts thing is getting long. Really tedious.

'Here.' One of the older boys hands Tristan a blue ice pole from a striped off-licence bag.

Ben Munday stands up and fusses with his hands down the front of his joggers, then pulls out a small washing powder net filled with £10 bags of cannabis. Tristan swears he can smell the weed, heated up by this boy's groin. The thought is kind of repulsive.

'Eh,' one of the cycling boys says, 'you seen Mustafa from Barton Point about? I'm gonna get him today, y'know.' He punches one fist into the other.

'For real?' Tristan feigns interest, distracted by the tightness of the wrapper on the ice pole. He puts it between his teeth and tries to rip it.

'He tried to chat up my sister. Man needs to be taught a lesson. You know me, how I protect my family and that.'

'Yeah, yeah, get him good,' Tristan says as he battles with the plastic seal. It bursts open and a blue juice sprays across his T-shirt. 'Shit.'

The boys laugh.

'You look like a sanitary towel advert.'

'For fuck's sake, man.' Tristan is furious. 'This is clean on.'

'You were asking for it wearing that much white,' Ben Munday says.

The toxic-looking blue colours the pavement as Tristan throws it to the floor. He leans down to wipe the bright drips off the trainers he takes so much pride in keeping spotless.

'Eh, Tris, you know him?'

'Who?' He licks a finger and scrubs it along the stain. As he looks up he spots the man in the Elvis T-shirt from earlier in the stairwell. But this time he's got a book out, a notepad or something, and is scribbling away. The boys cycle over and take it from him. Then they burst out laughing. Tristan tries to work out what's going on.

'Oi, Tris,' one of the boys shouts back, 'is this man your bum chum? Didn't know you were into gingers.'

'What's he on about?'

The notepad flaps by their sides as they cycle back and then pass it along the group. Each face breaks into laughter as they see whatever is written and Tristan waits for his turn to get in on the joke.

Elvis T-shirt follows. 'Please,' he says, 'can I have it back?'

Ben Munday shoves a hand back down his pants before letting out his one uncool trait: his high-pitched laugh.

'Please, can I have it back?' Elvis T-shirt reaches out for the notepad but it's finally passed to Tristan. The pencilled figure has lines shaved across its hair, a star in its ear and two skinny legs sticking out of a pair of big shorts. Tristan isn't sure what he's most annoyed about: that he's been spied on again or the unflattering portrayal of his physique, especially as he's been putting in up to sixty push-ups a night.

'Is this meant to be me?' It's humiliating, especially in front of Ben Munday. The heat creeps up behind his ears like a siren signalling the imminent loss of his temper.

The boys cackle and their energy builds behind him.

'What's your problem, man? First you're spying on me in the stairs and now you're drawing pictures of me.'

He hears a gasp.

'Eh, Tris, this is proper creepy,' says one of the boys on the bike, the spokes on his wheels click-clacking as he rocks back and forth. 'This brer been stalking you?'

Stalking. That's exactly what this is. Elvis T-shirt tries to grab the notepad but Tristan gets hold of his fingers and twists them tightly. He doesn't really want to break the guy's fingers, but this needs to hurt. He hopes he will know when to stop. Thankfully, the fingers are slippery with some kind of grease and slip from his grip. Elvis T-shirt looks proper scared now, huffing and almost in tears. He tries to run but the bikes block him, as if holding him for Tristan. For what? Not like Tristan is gonna fight this big idiot here in front of everyone. Ben Munday nods towards the notepad, as if giving the go-ahead. Tristan begins to rip out the pages, tearing at the little illustrations of postmen and bowls of food that appear alongside the scruffy handwriting. Then he flicks the notepad over into the car park. He laughs with the boys and shouts: 'Sicko'.

But Ben Munday isn't smiling; he's shaking his head like he's witnessed something substandard rather than business being taken care of. 'Don't let him get away with it, Tris,' he says.

Elvis T-shirt now has his arms wrapped around his head. Despite being scrunched up, he still has a few inches on Tristan. He takes a step closer and isn't sure what to do, how to make the biggest impact. Then it comes to him. He closes his eyes as he launches the spit. The boys gasp, someone snickers, there's even the slap of palms. He's done the right thing.

'Stay away from me, you fucking retard,' he shouts, and Elvis T-shirt wipes his face, then takes off in the direction of Nightingale Point.

'That's how to do it,' Ben Munday says, smiling. 'You gotta watch yourself with them care-in-the-community people.'

'Yeah, yeah,' Tristan agrees. He looks up at the flats and hopes no one saw what happened. Malachi would kill him. 'Well, man, I need to go get changed – can't be walking about like some tramp. Not my style.' He knocks fists with each of the boys. Ben Munday grabs Tristan by the shoulder and shakes him playfully; a proud smile breaks through his thick, curly beard.

*

Nightingale Point feels hotter than when Tristan left it, so as well as a blue ice pole stain, he feels the sweat seep into the cotton at his armpits. Nastiness.

'You again? Up, down, up, down,' the old biddie on the third floor says. She sits on a dining table chair out on the landing, surrounded by a mess of plastic plants and flowers. The sight of her dentures makes Tristan queasy as she smiles at him. 'No wonder you're so skinny.' She tuts. 'Get yourself outside. Too hot to stay in. Bet your lot are used to it, though, ain't ya?'

He pauses and retraces his steps back down. 'What?'

'The heat. You know.'

Is she serious? Old people have no filter whatsoever.

'I tell you, young man, once it got so hot here I could have fried an egg on the floor.' She points down to the narrow strip of grey concrete in front of her and sways. 'Szzzz.' She laughs. 'I sat out here with your nan that day. If she was here now, she'd be sitting out here with me. A lickle tipple of rum.' The woman mimics what he thinks is meant to be a Jamaican accent and laughs like a schoolgirl.

He rolls his eyes, trying to remember a time when his church-going, twin-set wearing nan would ever have sat out with his woman. There's no chance. Between working at the library five days a week, running around after Tristan and Malachi, and ferrying their mum back and forth to her hospital appointments, Nan had no time for anything other than standing in Mary's kitchen and complaining about life. That's Tristan's overriding image of her: tired, shoes off, tights in all weathers, holding a mug of tea and giving Mary a rundown of her ailments.

'When's your nan coming back?' the woman asks.

'Nan ain't coming back for a while.' Nan stuck out life in London for over forty years; she damn near swam back to the island the day she felt Malachi was old enough to look after things. Nan always said life in the city was 'nothing but bad luck and bad weather'. Guess she had more than her fair share of both.

'Well, tell her I've got the rum in the cupboard for when she does, hee hee.' The woman giggles again.

He waves off her comments, then carries on up the stairs, taking them two at a time.

Once home, the flat is stifling, the windows all closed. He pulls off his T-shirt and starts to fill the sink, adding a bit of bleach, before spotting a note on Malachi's abandoned pile of books. If it's the shopping list, Tristan's definitely going to add a few meal ideas of his own. Instead he feels inspired to write and rap.

'Baby come and get this champagne and lobster, you're dining with the mobster, some curry goat to finish, and I know you're gonna want more. Hmm, don't quite rhyme.'

He crosses it out. '*I need to handle business, get this money, you see, before Mal turns me into fucking fusilli.*' He sighs. 'I'm getting worse. Off my game today.' On the back of the paper there's a note from Mal.

Gone out for a walk. Need to clear head.

When did he leave the flat? Tristan hopes Mal didn't see him with the wall boys. Or with Elvis T-shirt. Tristan will properly be in the shit if that's the case.

'Who goes for walks round here anyway?'

He goes to the mirror and takes in his profile. Yeah, he looks good, but that pigeon-legged depiction was kind of hurtful. Working out at home isn't enough to get the kind of Tupac body he's aiming for. Only a gym membership will do the trick.

'*Check out my abs, built to last, come rub my chest, let me feel your arse.*'

Tristan drops to the ground and starts doing push-ups. He's hitting his flow when the door knocks. He jumps up, then tiptoes over, half expecting the police to be standing on the other side. Surely spitting at someone isn't a crime? He's not too sure. But on the other side of the spyhole is Mary's husband, David Tuazon.

'Smooth motherfucker,' Tristan says as he unlocks the door. 'Hello.'

'Hey, man.' Tristan can't remember David ever shaking his hand before. Up until he was about twelve he can't remember David even acknowledging him directly. Only ever through Mary, and this often took the form of a questioning murmur about what *those kids* were doing in his home again.

Tristan gives a proper firm handshake, to which David pulls away and laughs. 'My, how you have grown.'

'Yeah.' Tristan puffs out his chest and taps it. 'I've had my Weetabix, innit.'

'Either you're hot or I am interrupting something?'

Tristan, so used to his own nakedness, shrugs his shoulders. 'Hot,' he explains. 'I ain't seen you in over a year, man.' There's a fake-looking Louis Vuitton suitcase in the hall.

'I'm looking for my wife. She's not home.'

'She gone work, innit. Saturday late shift.'

'Ah. So.' He runs his hand over one side of his hair; he has so much of it. 'I've had a long journey. I am keen to get home and get some rest. I can never sleep on planes. You know how it is, so uncomfortable.'

Tristan nods like he understands, despite never having been on a plane. His own passport, ordered for a school day trip to France that he couldn't afford, still sits expectantly in his chest of drawers, each page pristine and unstamped.

'I need the spare keys. I assume *you* have them?'

The keys, yes, he remembers vaguely, but can't remember anyone saying David would be back. He fears he's losing his memory at fifteen and vows to give up smoking weed after the bank holiday weekend.

'Oh yeah. Course. I mustn't have been listening 'cause I really didn't catch Mary say you were here.'

'That's because she doesn't know. Well, she knows I'm on my way but I didn't say when. I wanted to surprise her.'

Tristan leaves the front door wide as he looks around for the keys on the coffee table; the cool green leaf key ring he added makes them visible among the dullness of Malachi's architecture books.

David inspects the key ring. 'Thanks. See you later. Say hello to your brother.'

Tristan pulls a tight smile as he shuts the door.

'Dickhead.'

He takes the windows off the safety latches and pushes them all wide open. The phone rings, startling him. Month to month it gets cut off so he's always shocked when the thing actually works.

'Hallo?'

'Tristan?'

'Yup.'

'It's Pamela.'

'What is this? All the old ghosts are popping up today.' He untwists the phone cord and walks back over to the mirror. 'What you want?'

'I need to speak to Mal.' She has a desperate edge to her voice. It reminds Tristan of all the times he walked in on her and Malachi holding hands, knee-deep in a conversation about how much they loved each other. They were so intense.

'He ain't here. He's gone out.'

'Don't lie to me. He never goes out.'

'Well, you been gone a month; people change.'

She sighs into the phone. 'I really, really need to talk to him.'

'For what? Can't you find some mug in Portsmouth to buy you trainers?'

'It wasn't like that. And I'm from *Portishead*. But I'm not there anymore. I'm upstairs. Got back a few days ago. Is he really not there?'

Tristan huffs.

'Okay, listen. I need you to give him a letter from me. Will you come up in about fifteen minutes?'

'Do I look like Royal Mail to you? Post it!' Tristan doesn't want to go back to being the third wheel in their relationship. He's only just got his brother back.

'Please. You don't understand what these last few weeks have been like.'

She rabbits on, blah blah blah. He rubs his lower abs and wonders how much it would cost to get a tattoo across them. Maybe some scripture or something. Some Chinese writing.

Pamela is now crying down the other end. He has better things to do with his bank holiday.

'Look,' he cuts her off mid-sentence, 'why you giving me this breakdown of your relationship? I ain't Martin Bashir. What do you want from me?'

'My dad's locked me in,' she says. 'So, please, come up and take the letter.'

He flops down on the sofa, wondering if he should help. Pamela did make Malachi happy while it lasted. It was good for him to get his lanky leg over something, even if it was her. But the drama of them was exhausting, all the crying and the constant threat of her crazy dad hanging over everything. Tristan used to get proper paranoid whenever she was in the flat and the door would knock; he was almost waiting for her dad to bust in and kick Mal's arse. Or worse. So when Pamela up and left for Plymouth it was sort of a relief.

'Tris? Will you help me?'

'I'm busy,' he says, and it's true. Who has the time to go running about, trying to fix up other people's love lives? Tristan's not sure if the whole thing was even worth it. He knows plenty of hotter girls that would give it up for less than Pamela. A lot less. We're talking a bag of chips here.

'Tristan, please, come on. It's not going to kill you to leave your flat for five minutes.'

He purses his lips and remembers how Mal pestered him to find out who Pamela was after seeing her run around the field like a hamster in a wheel. It was unusual that he took an interest in any girl, but then he'd been so busy since Nan left, trying to juggle studying and 'playing dad'. Tristan was glad when Mal gave that up. Finally they started up their Donkey Kong tournament again in the evenings. Except for the times when he would be sneaking about with Pam, probably kissing around the back of the bins or something, or sharing a milkshake in that nasty little café near the swimming pool.

'Why won't you help me?' she pleads.

So pathetic. But they did kind of like each other and it was rare of Malachi to do anything other than frown most days.

'Tris, I'm begging you.'

'Okay,' Tristan finally says. 'I'll think about it.'

CHAPTER TEN

Mary

'Mary, I didn't know we were seeing each other today.'

Mary gives Harris a weak smile as she steps over the threshold and kicks her plimsolls onto either side of the stripy woven mat.

'I've just got in.' He closes the front door from the prying eyes of neighbours before kissing her. 'I had a union meeting about next year's exams. Can you believe it? On a Saturday? Went on and on.' He walks quickly into the large room that makes up the living space of the bungalow and over to the hob, where he fiddles with the knobs and stops the hiss of gas.

'I was trying out a new recipe – cannellini bean mash – but it doesn't quite look edible.' He laughs and wipes his hands on the tea towel that hangs over his shoulder. 'Sorry, I'm rambling. Are you okay, Mary? I really wasn't expecting you.'

'Harris, I need to talk with you.' She takes a deep breath but already feels her resolve waver. Something about the smell of lemons, Harris's frequent failed attempts to cook, and his thin, perpetually tanned arms make her want to change her mind, to not end the affair, to divorce David, to marry Harris and to be with him always.

'I can't sleep,' she says. 'I keep thinking about what we are doing. How wrong it is.'

'Oh, not this again.' He turns away.

'Yes, Harris. We need to stop. I am having nightmares. All week, these horrible dreams waking me up.' She does not want to say anymore, for speaking her visions out loud somehow makes them more real.

'You are stressed. Overworked again. I told you, stop taking on so many double shifts.' Harris sits down next to her; the smell of tobacco on his skin ignites a craving for a cigarette. She takes the fob watch from her pocket and passes it from hand to hand.

'Oh, your watch broke?'

'I've had it twelve years.' David had set the time eight hours ahead when he gave it to her. 'Now you always know what time it is where I am,' he said, but she immediately reset it to show *her* time.

'Here, let me see if I can fix it.' Harris takes the watch into his speckled hands.

'No.' She snatches it back. 'David's coming home.'

'When?'

Mary shrugs. 'He's on standby for a flight. I'm not sure if he's coming here directly or stopping by somewhere else. His brother is in Amsterdam – maybe he will go there first. What? Why are you laughing?'

'Typical. So he's going to show up anytime in the next few weeks and you will accommodate him?'

'He's my husband.'

'Yes, but he doesn't have to be,' Harris says with a raised voice.

As he turns away the heaviness of what is *not* being said fills the room: the weight of the question she's refused to answer, the unworn engagement ring studded with rubies as pink as the hibiscuses back home.

'We need a break, Harris. Please.' But she doesn't act on it. Instead, she sits on the sofa and pulls one of the Indian elephant cushions onto her lap for comfort. 'There is too much going on. I am stressed. My daughter is going back to work and I said I would help out with the kids.'

He groans. 'She's taking advantage. She only works two days a week.'

'Yes, but she needs my help. I'm her mother.'

'I know, but what's this got to do with us? With what I asked you last week? Why can't we talk about it, Mary?'

She taps the face of the fob watch with her short nails. 'I need to call my work. I'm going to be late.'

It rings for a long time before being finally answered. 'Hedley Ward, Nurses' Station.'

'Hello, it's Mary Tuazon. I'm running late for shift.'

'Okay, I'll let the sister know.'

Mary recognizes the voice as one of the latest in a long line of lazy ward interns.

'Tuazon? Hang on.' Papers rustle, machines purr and a metal spoon clinks against something ceramic. 'There's a message here for you. Your husband called.'

'My husband?'

Harris straightens his back, like a cat ready to pounce.

'That's what it says.' The girl's disinterest seeps through

the line. 'Says: *In Hong Kong. Got direct flight to Heathrow.*'
She pauses. 'That's all.'

'You are sure? When did he leave this?'

'Dunno.'

'Well, is there a time on the message?' Mary asks.

'Look, I didn't write this down, all right?' She tuts. 'It's busy here.'

'Okay, thank you.' Mary puts down the phone and smiles at Harris. 'Stupid girl got the message wrong. There's no way he got a flight so fast.'

Harris appears to puff up his chest; his body, still frail, seems flooded with energy. 'So he's on his way? I feel as if this is it, Mary. You need to tell him. We can do it together.' Harris uses a tone of voice Mary imagines he rolls out for his students with low self-esteem.

'I'm not ready.'

'You will never be ready. But you need to move on with your life.'

'I took vows.'

The tea towel slaps against the coffee table as Harris walks off through the net curtains onto the patio.

Mary waits. How long it will take David to notice the spring in her step, the smell on her skin? She lies back on the sofa and tries to imagine the two alternate versions of her life: one where she goes back on her vows and becomes a shameful divorcée, and another where she continues to be David's unhappy, waiting wife.

How can she make that decision?

Harris sits at the white wrought-iron table under the cherry blossom tree, which hangs over from the neighbour's garden, his bare feet surrounded by a smattering of rotten pink petals. Mary stoops to rub a fleshy pink flower between her fingers and he scrapes the chair towards the edge of the wooden decking to bask fully in the sun he worships so much, while lighting his cigarette.

'For olden time sake?' she asks.

He hands her one and furiously flicks at the lighter as she takes the other seat. They both face out onto the messy garden, much of it claimed by the growth of wild flowers and overflowing planters. Mary watches two bees as they make double loops around the struggling zebra plants and moss roses he planted for her after she told him about her childhood garden. How could she even consider saying goodbye to Harris? To this secret life she has been building with him for the last year? She would miss him too much. They had spent the winter smoking on the patio among the dead plants, watching as the foxes brazenly entered to hunt around the composting bins Harris keeps at the bottom of the garden. She blushes as she thinks of all the times she has cheated on her husband with Harris. How self-conscious she was the first time, her body covered with fake tanning lotion, which stained her loose flesh a sickly yellow, making it look like the skin of the outdoor-reared chickens on the street markets back home. But after that first time, she never again felt the need to hide herself from him. Just last week as she lay in his bed, the windows open, the curtains billowing, she felt as she had all those years ago when she first met David. She was confident then too, but over the years she began to worry she was ageing faster than him, and that, as she took off her clothes, he was comparing her naked body to those of the girls he was picking up while on tour. Those floozies at the side of the stage.

Mary smokes slowly and waits for the threat of tears to pass before she speaks again.

'He will not stay for long. He never does. A month, maybe. I will phone you when he leaves.'

'So you have made your decision then? Another decision that does not include me?' Petulantly, Harris uncrosses his legs and slides away from her, before crossing them again in the opposite direction.

She looks down at her uniform, at the fat white stitching in the wide hem below her knees.

'You don't have to choose him,' he says.

'I already did. He does not come home often; I owe him my time.'

'You've already given him so many years, years in which you've waited and waited. And now you want to pretend that I don't exist for a month.' He shrugs. 'So go ahead, imagine that I'm dead so you can get on with playing husband and wife.'

Why can't he understand? It's only a month. She pushes the nets aside as she storms through to the bathroom, where she rolls a large ball of tissue in her hand to help her get through the bus journey.

Harris waits by the front door.

'Let me at least drive you to work.' His eyes appear watery, but he does not look emotional, only annoyed, probably from having to go up against a man much lesser than himself, of competing against vows made in another time and anxieties that manifest themselves in the form of twitching elbows and bad dreams.

'Okay.'

He slides his feet into his brown sandals and picks up the keys from the slim wooden side table. As they set off towards the hospital, Mary tries to distract herself from the silence between them. His car is messier than usual: mud-caked walking boots and some shrivelled orange peelings on the floor, a pile of his students' workbooks on the backseat. He fusses with the tape player as the car slows at the traffic lights, pushing in the Simply Red album she bought him at Christmas. The first song is their song: 'You Make Me Believe'. They look at each other and smile.

They could never go a month without each other.

Then a sound from above, a sound so deep it makes the windows of the car shake within their frames. Then a blast. It vibrates through the car.

Harris turns the tape off.

Moments pass, odd, thick moments, before a softer tremor is felt. They turn to each other, this time for an explanation. The doors of the bus in front open and people start to scatter out, all of them turning to face the same way.

Mary steps from the car and looks as well, into the distance, to a huge fire in the sky.

'It hit the flats,' the bus driver shouts.

Harris leans across the hood of the car, his eyes wide and dazed by the scene.

It is clear but Mary can't yet accept it.

Then a voice, in shock and rambling to all who will listen, confirms, 'That block of flats exploded.'

Mary's block of flats.

CHAPTER ELEVEN

Elvis

Elvis peeps around the corner of the block. The bad black boy went inside Nightingale Point a few minutes ago. There are two boys left by the wall; they cycle in little circles and do tricks on their bikes.

Elvis needs to get back to his perfect flat with his perfect things. Now is a safe time to do it. Quickly, he comes out of hiding and walks into the block behind a man pulling a brown suitcase on tiny wheels. The man has shiny black hair slicked back neatly like the men in the photographs of barber shop windows. Elvis has never seen him before, but hopes he is here to sell encyclopaedias, the kind with the gold spines where you can look up words like Serengeti and Kathmandu. The man grunts as he presses the lift button. People were not only dangerous on council estates but they were also unfriendly. Archie had warned Elvis of this as they ate their last full English breakfast together. As Archie scooped beans onto his toast he informed Elvis that brown people especially would not give you the time of day. It was 'a cultural thing'.

'Do you have the time, please?' Elvis asks the man.

He checks his watch. 'Eight-forty. No, sorry.' The man counts some numbers under his breath. 'I have come from the Philippines and have not yet reset my watch. One-forty.'

Elvis has had a bad morning but it makes him happy to know that Archie could still be wrong about some things and that not all brown people were too 'cultural'. The man hits the call button for the lift again.

'They are both broken,' Elvis says.

Earlier Elvis had flicked through his notepad of information and found the lift engineer number. He called it to report its breakage but there was only a voicemail message saying: 'Bolton Lift Services are closed over the bank holiday weekend. Please do not leave a message on this number.'

The Filipino man gives Elvis a half nod and starts up the stairs. The back of his red T-shirt is darkened with sweat, like a knot in a tree. Elvis waits till he can no longer hear the shuffle of the man's shiny shoes on the steps before he slowly starts up the stairs himself. On the third floor he sees the plant lady, Beryl. She is the one who makes the third floor look so pretty with all the colourful plastic flowers. She sits on a dark wooden chair, which looks like it should not be outside in a stairwell landing but inside and around a table. She gives him a wide grin and he is happy to see someone friendly.

'Elvis, love, how you keeping?' she calls. 'You all right? You look a bit peaky.' She leans forward in her chair and squints at him. 'You gingers do get red in the sun, though, don't you? Need to slap on some sun lotion.' Beryl dips down and feels the fake soil of her pots. 'Good grief.' She makes a tutting noise like you do when there is a nice cat that you want to stroke. 'These are needing another watering,' she says to him. 'They're sucking it up today. Roses, you know what they're like. I went to the Chelsea Flower Show once, did I tell you? Even met Her Majesty. I've got some photos. Hang on, love, let me get them.' She waves a hand and gets up slowly off the chair and walks over to her front door.

Elvis waits patiently for her to return with a shoebox filled with photographs. He has seen the photos before, yesterday and the day before that. He likes them but wishes they had more flowers in them and less of the plant lady's blurred thumb and edges of people's raincoats.

His tummy rumbles as Beryl points out Her Majesty. His pie, his lovely steak and kidney pie. He had forgotten all about it. It will be cold now and Lina will be mad. She will flick her nails at him and call him an idiot. He hates it when she does that.

'I need to go home,' he says suddenly to the plant lady.

'Okay then, Elvis. See you later.' She sits back on her chair and smiles at her photos.

He slows as he reaches the spot between the fifth and sixth floor, but it is quiet, the bad black boy is not there, only the faint smell of his rule-breaking funny cigarette. On the tenth floor he stops and turns to the skinny window that lets you look down onto the green. The windowpane is thick with grey, dried mould spores, but beyond it the sky is so blue and the sun so bright. He loves days like this. Maybe living in Nightingale Point will not be so bad after all and the bad black boy will come and say sorry and never smoke in the stairwell again. Maybe Elvis will go to the Chelsea Flower Show with the plant lady and have his photo taken next to a giant Helianthus Annus, which is the posh name for sunflower.

He watches as a plane flies across in the sky. It curves around the three towers of the estate and disappears behind him. Then seconds later it comes back, but this time, it looks closer. It turns slightly. One wing goes straight up in the air and the other points straight down to the floor. Then its big, round nose points straight at Elvis. He can feel himself getting excited and scared at the same time. A small trail of black smoke curls out behind the plane, showing where it has been, but there is nothing to show him where it is going. It looks like it does not know. It gets larger and larger, like when you are walking closer and closer to Nightingale Point. Then, there is a huge noise that makes Elvis put his hands over his ears and push his palms in. But the sound goes right through them. He squeezes tighter and tighter. Tight enough to collapse his soft ears and squeeze his head like a piece of clay on the creative table at the Waterside Centre. But no matter how hard he squeezes he can still hear the horrible loud blaring noise and then his own voice as it escapes his body. He screams, loud. As loud as he can. He is frightened. He does not know what is happening. It feels like the skin is being blown off his face. Tears stream from the corners of his eyes and run off his face horizontally. His bottom lip is pulled down, his teeth bared to the wind, and they become cold. His mouth opens and he tries to scream but it does not come out, or maybe it does. He is not sure. He cannot hear it. But he can feel it in his chest, which goes raw from the effort; he feels his stomach empty of air, the muscles cramp down as they expel every ounce he has, until he has nothing.

CHAPTER TWELVE

Pamela

Pamela puts the phone down and bites her lip. She can't believe she has to rely on Tristan. He was always tolerant of her, as polite as he could manage, but then there was a slight edge, a kind of jealousy that radiated off him each time she was in the flat. It was to be expected, Malachi said. It had been just the two of them for the last year. Maybe it wasn't even jealously. She often wondered if perhaps Tristan simply didn't like her. She didn't like him that much either. So loud, flash and vain, he always needed to be the centre of everyone's attention. While Malachi . . . Well, Malachi was kind, quiet, measured and caring. The kind of man that saved up all his money to replace her running shoes after the seams split and Dad refused to buy a new pair. The kind of man who, even when in a rush, stops on the third floor to listen as some lonely old lady talks about her plastic flowers. The kind of man who stepped into Pamela's life and became everything she needed.

How long will Tristan *think* about helping? Maybe he

won't even do that. He could have put down the phone and laughed. Maybe Malachi is sitting there too, glad that he no longer has to put up with her. No, he's not like that. She must stop doubting him; this is exactly what Dad wants.

She starts writing him a letter, everything she feels and thinks. He needs to know that she understands why he turned her away, why he needed time. It hurt when he denied her, but she gets it now. Malachi was looking at the bigger picture. But most importantly, and this part is so hard to put into words, there's something else they both need to work out before they can get back together.

The pages slot into a white envelope and she sits by the front door, clutching the letter to her chest as fifteen minutes pass, then thirty, then almost forty. He's not coming. Why would he? Tristan's got his brother back; he's Malachi's number one priority again. Of course he's not going to help her.

If only she could get out of her flat and into his, it would be so much better to talk face to face. She always feels so comfortable in his flat, so at home. It was weird at first, being somewhere that was exactly the same as her home, but also opposite in every way. The rooms reversed, the plug sockets and light switches all in slightly different places. But the main difference is the light. Her own flat is always so dingy and dark, but Mal's is open and filled with brightness. She loved being there with him so much; she loved every minute of it.

Pamela pulls the letter from its envelope and rereads it. It's filled with the words she should have been brave enough to say a month ago, rather than allowing her dad to pack her off to her mum's house.

She presses it against her lips, glad that he will soon know the truth. Then he can make up his own mind. But how will she get it to him? She slides down the inside of her front door and wipes the tears from her cheeks.

The sound of life pours into the corridor behind her. Tristan? She opens the door and through the bars of the security gate sees the woman who lives in the opposite flat, all dressed up, in a white and green swirled head wrap and dress, green fabric heels to match the green handbag on her arm.

'Tunde, come,' the woman shouts into her flat.

'Hello,' Pamela tries. But the woman does not even turn her way.

Dad made a fast enemy out of her when, during their first week living in Nightingale Point, he stood between the flats and declared her 'food stinks out the whole bloody floor', in response to what smelt like fried fish.

'Hello, running girl,' Tunde shouts from behind his mum's legs, his smile, as always, set to full beam. He makes a jogging on the spot motion. He's dressed up too, in a white suit and embroidered hat, like a little prince. Pamela is used to seeing him on the green in his school uniform, dropping his game of football in an attempt to run alongside her and pester her with questions about the Olympics.

'Contenders ready? Gladiators ready?' he shouts.

'Come.' The woman pinches him by the sleeve. 'You are making me late.'

'Bye, running girl,' Tunde calls as he runs ahead to the lift. 'Broken again,' he sings as he pushes open the door and disappears into the stairwell, his mum trailing behind as she attempts to outrun their lateness.

Pamela rests her head on the bars. She does not know what she would have said or done if the woman had spoken to her anyway.

Then a voice Pamela used to dread, but today welcomes, says, 'Here comes the cavalry.'

Tristan's bare-chested, for some reason, and a fake diamond glints in his right ear. She's never been so pleased to see him, but quickly tries to set her face back to neutral.

'Really? It's not *that* hot.'

'Whatever.' He pulls at the bars. 'So it's true then. Can't believe your dad is locking you in. That's some crazy Fred West shit. And why you standing out here crying? You still upset about Take That splitting up?'

'This is serious. This is my life.'

He holds out his hand and clicks his fingers. 'Hand me this letter of yours.'

She passes it through the bars of the gate and he fans his face with it.

'So you'll give it to him?' she asks.

He shrugs. 'I'm here, aren't I? Your own personal Postman Pat.'

'Please don't read it. It's private.'

'I can't think of anything I'm less interested in.' He stuffs the letter roughly in the pocket of his white shorts and begins to walk off.

'Tristan,' she calls. 'Thanks. I owe you.'

'Yeah, yeah. Buy me a burger when you break free.' He waves an arm and disappears into the stairwell.

She leans against the locked security gate and looks into the gloom of the flat. Finally, a weight has been lifted. Her face lightens into a smile, but then freezes as she tries to locate the noise: a fizzing, a drill, hollow and sharp, closer and closer until it escalates into a rumble. Then a bang, loud and long, and with it a force that lifts Pamela off the gate. Her face cracks against something scratchy and flat. For a few seconds there is nothing but pain. Nothing makes sense. She realises her face is pushed against the carpet and she rolls her head away from it. Opens her eyes. Sees white. Everywhere white. Her eye sockets feel raw. She has broken her nose. Her mouth is full of tooth. She spits it out. Her tongue fills the wet, fleshy space behind her teeth. Then another force, smaller than the last, but it shakes her. She uses her arms to push herself up onto her knees and attempts to grab at something for support, but falls back down. Her hands feel around the floor and come to stop on the ash-filled saucer and cigarette butts. She is in the living room. Has she been knocked out by something? Lost time? The room is in semi-darkness. Has night fallen? She feels around more. Finally, she touches the sofa. She uses it to pull herself up and rests her face on the soft cushion of it. How did she get to the living room? She looks around. The white has begun to clear and now grey smoke billows past the balcony door, rich and silky. She crawls over and pushes on the door. It feels warm to the touch and outside there is no longer a view, but a thick curl of hypnotic smoke, which she coughs to clear from her throat. There has been an explosion and now there is a fire somewhere, somewhere close. From which flat? Her own?

She needs to get out. Her legs, the most reliable part of her body, let her down. They turn to loosely set jelly and she is forced to crawl. Back into the hallway, now littered with things, sharp and foreign. There's a light. Not the blinding white kind of after the explosion, but of daylight beyond the fire. She moves faster, ignoring the pain in her face and chest. Then, as she reaches the front door and gate, she remembers. She's trapped.

CHAPTER THIRTEEN

Tristan

Pamela didn't even lick the seal on the envelope. It's almost like she wants him to open it and read it. And why did she have to mention that it's *private*? Of course it is. She's trying to get him interested. But he's not interested. He's already way too involved in this soap opera. Why didn't Mal take his advice in the first place to hook up with a local hood rat? Minimal effort, maximum satisfaction.

He fans himself with the envelope. *Private*. There was nothing private about how loud they used to have sex while Tristan was playing Donkey Kong alone in the next room.

And why is her dad locking her in anyway? Not right, really. Tristan can think of plenty girls who would genuinely benefit from being put behind a locked gate, but Blondie isn't really one of them. If anything it's her dad who needs to be locked up, stomping about in big old army boots, regardless of the weather, always scowling and muttering under his breath.

Tristan never did tell Mal about the run-in he had with the

dad a few months back. He'd skipped his last lesson of the day because it was the most pointless subject of all: History. Craving a lie-down, he slipped out the school gates and started to head home for a nap when he saw him, hanging by the bus stop, like some pervert on the hunt for underage girls.

He spotted Tristan straight away and came marching over. 'Is it you?' he asked, getting all up in Tristan's face.

'What? Is what me?' Tristan had no issue giving adults a bit of backchat but was aware none of his boys were around if he needed reinforcement.

'I saw her with you this morning.'

Shit. Tristan knew walking with Pamela would come back to haunt him. But he was thinking more about how it would damage his reputation to be seen with some unknown.

'With Pam? Yeah, well, we live in the same place and go to the same school. So, surprise surprise, we do sometimes end up walking together in the morning.'

But her dad was having none of it. 'Keep your black hands off my daughter.'

Boom, there it was. The confirmation that Mal was never getting approval. It was so obvious, Tristan could tell from a mile off that this was the case with Blondie, but Mal kept denying it.

'I put my black hands wherever I like.'

The dad grabbed Tristan by the blazer and pushed him against the wall. Up close his face was red and flaky, and Tristan worried it was something contagious.

'You think my Pam would want you? If she's given you a minute of her time it's only 'cause she wants to piss me off. She's not really going to drop her standards for someone like you. Some estate scum. I know what you lot are like. I see you all sitting on the wall smoking weed every day.'

'Mate, you're spending too much time watching me.'

'Yeah, watching you doing nothing, going nowhere. Stay away from my daughter.'

Pamela appeared out of nowhere. 'Dad? What are you doing? He's a friend from school.'

But his grip remained tight. 'A friend? You don't need friends like this, Pam. Keep yourself to yourself.' He turned back to Tristan. There was spit gathered at the sides of his mouth like some rabid animal. 'And you, stay away from her.'

'As if I'd want *her*.' He just was being provocative, he couldn't help it. 'As if I go back to the same place twice.'

The dad pulled back his fist but Pamela grabbed him, so when the punch hit it didn't have as much power as intended. Thank God because it still hurt like a bitch.

'Are you crazy?' Pamela screamed. 'He's fifteen. They'll put you in prison.'

Tristan shook his head. He couldn't believe the guy actually hit him. He'd been in plenty of fights but never been hit full in the face before. He didn't know what to do; he couldn't exactly run back to school or the police. All he wanted was to get away. He waited till he rounded the corner before he stopped and wiped the blood from his split bottom lip.

That evening when Tristan got home, Mal took one look at the busted lip and his face ran through shock, anger and amusement before getting to concern. 'What have you done now?' he asked.

Tristan already had a lie prepared. 'I fell in the stairwell.

Was proper lean.' He sank down on the sofa and picked up the controller.

Malachi grabbed his face and inspected the cut. 'You fell? When?'

'This afternoon. A little post-school smoke.'

'I don't get it – you fell because you were high?'

'Yeah, stop making a big deal out of it.'

What would be the point in telling him? Besides, Tristan took the hit for *him*. Surely that would take the scent off Mal. For once, Tristan got to be the hero.

'Mal, you wanna play Kong? You ain't beat me in months man. You need to get some practice in.'

He looked at Tristan closely, as if trying to figure out whether to pry more or not. 'I'd like to but Pam's dad is on a night shift, so she can get out. We're going to the cinema.'

Tristan wanted to say something then, to warn Mal that Pamela's dad was an aggressive racist and that Pamela was probably only using Malachi to rebel. But Mal looked so happy, so damn eager to go out and get laid, that Tristan didn't have the heart to say anything other than, 'Great. Enjoy yourself.'

*

As if Tristan would ever get lean enough to fall down some steps. Mal is smart but he's also gullible as fuck and Pamela knows that. Tristan pulls the letter from his pocket. Yeah, it definitely makes sense to check out what this girl is up to before he passes it on. *If* he passes it on. He unfolds the letter and starts to read, skipping past the pages with details about

94

'their love' and quotes from Aaliyah songs. He flicks to the third page and stalls halfway down.

What is she playing at? She's trying to throw Mal's whole life off-track, his degree, his internship, the career he's planned, everything he's worked for. This girl saw Mal's virgin arse coming and now sees him as a ticket off the estate. No way. Not going to happen.

Tristan roughly shoves the paper into the envelope and puts it back in the pocket of his shorts.

'Dumb bitch,' he mumbles as a noise approaches. *Zzz*, like last summer when a random mosquito flew straight into his ear. *Zzz*. It escalates quickly and then there is a huge burst of air, which smacks his body. The floor disappears from beneath his feet. He feels weightless and insubstantial as he's thrown, then heavy as a ton as his body smacks the glass window on the exit door that leads to the stairwell. It feels as if his bones are loose within his skin; they rattle around, joints bounce out of place and crash back into each other wrongly, awkwardly. The door to the corridor falls open slightly and he lays half in and half out. He pushes his body through. Then another vibration, where he feels something hit his face and explode in his left eye. Then it all goes quiet.

CHAPTER FOURTEEN

Malachi

He takes a long zigzagging route back to the estate, across the field, thinking over what to say to Pamela's dad. The words aren't coming easily. There's so much he has to get across to Jay in order to get Pamela back.

On the edge of the grass near the block lies a group of sunbathing teenage girls with their stomachs out. One smiles at him as she turns up a stereo set to dance music.

'*Let me be your fantasy. Let me be your fantasy, yeah.*' She sings along and Malachi looks away quickly. No other girl even comes close to Pamela.

He remembers how he described himself to her that first time they sat in the café: 'twenty-one going on sixty'. It was true and it was tragic. But when he was with her he was no longer this struggling, moping, sad person. He was happy.

His thoughts are interrupted by a din creeping up, the unmistakable sound of an aircraft, flying low, flying close. Must be a flyover. He used to love them as a kid, the way they would leave streams of red, white and blue coloured smoke across the city on commemorative days. But there's no formation of jets, just one large plane, the disappointing normality of a commercial airliner going somewhere he will never go. It makes a loop and turns on its side. That doesn't look right. Every hair on his body stands as the plane vanishes into Nightingale Point and is replaced by a giant ball of fire. The explosion rolls up the building and coats everything in flames. The force and fright knock him to the ground, and the sting of something hot and acidic in the air makes him cover his face. He shuffles backwards till the firm rubber of a car tyre blocks his movements. The skin on his palms has been scratched off by the pavement. Shakily, he stands and dares to look again. The top half of Nightingale Point is lit up like a flare. A huge white sheet of metal lands a few feet from where he stands. A small line of flames flicker along one side of it.

The boys on the wall shout and holler, but their sounds seem muffled and distorted against the roar of the fire above and the smash of glass. One of them pulls a bike from the ground with a shaky hand, throws a leg over and peddles away, his survival instincts more finely tuned than everyone else who remains motionless. Wreckage and dust falls from the building. As the boy passes, his eyes catch Malachi's and for a second they share a look that can't be explained, a mixture of confusion and terror. The boy's escape seems to kick-start something and every one of those previously frozen in shock now run like a tableau brought to life.

People stream from the main front door of Nightingale Point, pushing their way through the exit that usually suffices, but today seems tiny and mean in its proportions. Everyone yells, swears. A collective racket Malachi can't quite make sense of. Then a second bang, which sounds hollow, followed by a heavier scattering of debris. Malachi puts his arms above his head and squeezes his eyes shut. A shower of fragments scratches the back of his neck and arms. Then, as he stands in the centre of the carnage, he looks to the wall again. Where's Tristan?

As he runs through the main entrance of Nightingale Point, the heat intensifies like an oven with its door left open. It dries his lips and causes his eyes to stream. The caretaker stands by the bottom of the stairs with a cordless phone in one hand, while the other pushes onto people's backs as if they are unwanted guests.

He calls on Malachi, 'Young man, young man, you mustn't.' But his voice disappears into the sounds of the building, the roars and clanks, a song Malachi can't quite place but feels his body squirm to escape from.

People push their way out, a few scream, but most are silent, focused only on their exit. They hold onto each other, onto children, onto things, photo albums and teddy bears. On the first floor Malachi collides with a shirtless elderly man, a brown book under his arm, his chest skin loose and freckled. He shakes his head – an apology – out of habit and then throws a worried look behind himself like a thief caught in the act. Water pours down the stairs and masses of feet, bare and soled, splash past as Malachi pushes against the tide. He scans each face for Tristan as he takes the steps two at a time. His right hand tightly clutches the bannister as he pulls himself up, while everyone else floods down. On the second floor a man with a knot of dreadlocks on top of his head puts two hands on Malachi's chest and tries to push him into the flow of evacuees.

'Get out!' he shouts. 'There's been a gas explosion.'

Malachi has seen him before, leaving early in the morning in paint-splattered clothes. They've even exchanged nods while waiting for those first sleepy morning buses, populated by cleaners and builders. Malachi has to grip the bannisters with both hands to stop himself from sliding back down all the steps he has fought to climb. They both startle as an alarm sounds, old and tinny like a school fire bell, and Malachi writhes free of the man's grip. The sound ignites further panic, causing people to flee faster, push harder. Malachi has lived on the estate his whole life and this is only the second time he has ever heard it. The first was years ago, when the fire brigade came to check the alarm system and for one afternoon the block was alive with ringing and chat as neighbours gathered outside the caretaker's office to collect the free smoke alarms they promised to buy batteries for.

He climbs another set of stairs and registers faces everywhere, as familiar as the stairwell itself. His throat hurts as the smoke enters it. But worse than that, there's a vibration in his chest, the familiar shortness of breath that has plagued him since childhood. The crowds become thin enough for him to push through with less opposition as he reaches the third floor. But he trips over a plastic plant pot and smacks his shins across the top step. A panic of footsteps builds and people step over him.

The smoke becomes thicker, denser, harder to tolerate. He can't deny the wheeze he feels. Then a voice comes, high and loud, above the storm. It's Beryl. Her words fall out in an endless tumble, punctuated with screams before they die back down below the soundtrack of the block. The door that separates the stairwell and corridor to the third floor is propped by a wooden dining room chair, knocked over in someone's haste to escape.

'Beryl?'

She stands outside her front door, a shoebox in her hands. It falls to the ground as something crashes close by, photographs scattering everywhere.

'What are you doing? Get out.' Malachi kicks the chair out of the way as he heads towards her. He now understands the fury the dreadlocked man felt when faced with someone who seemed to be opting out of survival. Beryl continues to talk, she stops and tuts, her eyes darting about unfocused as if she does not even register his presence. There is another sharp crack and Malachi offers his hand, but she ducks down to collect the photos instead. He grabs her by the arm, his aggression fuelled by anger and the feeling that time is running out. She shrieks, as if on a rollercoaster, like someone who enjoys their fear too much. With each breath Malachi can hear the clock as it ticks in his head. Where is Tristan?

'Come,' he orders her.

'My photos,' she cries as he pulls her into the stairwell.

The ninth floor seems so far away, an impossible journey. Maybe Tristan is not in Nightingale Point at all. He was last seen outside, with the wall boys. Where was he going?

Beryl grips Malachi's arm tightly as they move down the stairs, her ringed fingers digging into his flesh and the few photos she managed to save becoming scrunched in her clutched hands.

His chest tightens; his heart begins to wind like an old clock. He glances up into the blackness and realises, to his horror, that no one else is likely to emerge from above them. Of course Tristan's not in here; no one is.

As they pass down onto the first floor the twist in his chest threatens to keel him over. He slows his breath, as his doctor taught him, picturing his lungs as a pair of brown paper bags, slowly expanding. Out of habit, he pats his trouser pocket, one puff, just one puff. But of course it's not there. He wasn't expecting to be out of the flat for so long.

The ground floor is deserted, and they both stumble out to the car park, where people run in different directions. Malachi feels himself being grabbed by a group of hands and pulled away from the source of heat against his back.

He allows them to take him, his head flopping back, and he stares up in awe at the fire.

Something pops from within the building and the crowd gasp, as if at a fireworks display. They are pushed again and again until Malachi finds himself on Sandford Road, barely on his own two feet, each breath a struggle. Beryl's still by his side and the two of them rest their weight against an abandoned car, its blue roof smashed in by something machine-like.

A voice, loud and authoritative, bellows, 'Move. Everyone get back.'

There's more crashing, more popping and banging, a hiss, a roar. Malachi's head spins with the noises. Then the voices, so many of them, all calling out.

' . . . another explosion . . . '

'. . . army use them. Jets . . . '

' . . . they'd do anything. IRA . . .'

Beryl pulls him along, into the throng, as they are swept further onto the field. A lone ambulance draws his eye. Two people begin to chase it and knock desperately on the back doors. With the road blocked it is forced to ride onto the field, where it bumps along the uneven grass.

The air feels too fresh and after each deep inhale Malachi coughs. His legs buckle and he hits the gravelly border of green. The grass is cool against his face. He opens his mouth and has an urge to taste it. There are more voices now, talk of smoke inhalation, shock, treatment, standing back. Hands and bodies he does not know pull him to sitting, strangers stare, their faces etched with concern. A bottle of water appears. He doesn't want it. He tries to shake off Beryl's hand, which still grips his own tightly. She refuses to let go. How can he find Tristan with all these people crowding him? The water comes again and he allows someone to tip it into his mouth. It hurts as it gushes down his throat and he coughs some up.

There are shouts. Cries. Then sirens. Lots of them.

From the corner of his eye he makes out two paramedics in high-visibility jumpsuits. Then they are close. One kneels in front of him and says, 'Calm down, mate. Take it easy.'

'He was trapped in the building; he's asphyxiating,' some-one says above him.

Malachi hears his own breath, shallow and slow, but can't manage to get his words out.

The paramedics talk between themselves. One pulls him fully upright and he squints at the sunlight, suddenly over-whelmingly bright.

'You escaped.' She smiles. 'You're safe.'

An elastic band stretches around his head and a ring of rubber is pulled tightly against the lower part of his face. He makes the gesture of an asthma pump.

'You use an inhaler?' she confirms, and the white diamond glued to her front tooth glints in the sun.

There's a familiar humiliation in his nod, the confession of being a grown man still weak enough to be brought down by a childhood ailment. Beryl pushes her fingers through the holes in her tights and inspects her bloodied knees. She pats his arm before turning back to the block, as if they are a couple sitting on the beach, her looking out at the sea while he lies in the sun.

'We're waiting on our vehicles getting through,' the paramedic explains. 'We'll get you in, you'll be fine.'

A shirtless man covered in abrasions staggers over. He holds his arm across his chest and looks around, bewildered. The paramedic jumps to his aid and Beryl screams and pulls herself in tighter towards Malachi.

The mask comes off easily. 'I need to go.' His voice is hoarse.

The paramedic clocks him and calls, 'No, wait.' But the shirtless man shivers and blood streams faster from several points on his body. Beryl cries and tries to grab hold of Malachi, but he shoves her away and runs.

The density of the crowd inspires faith in him, and he calls for Tristan between slow, careful breaths. Someone else yells another name louder than him and at one point they come face to face like mirror images of each other. They hold eye contact for a few seconds to share their distress before they move on to continue with their mission.

Malachi walks and walks, looking everywhere, at every face. His shoes are soaked through and he feels his feet begin to blister, but he carries on. Some people try to stop him and talk, but he can't, he needs to find his brother. His breath grows shallow again, the air slowly thickens and he stops for a moment to sit on the grass with his head between his knees. Occasionally he looks up at the blaze, which denies going out despite the continuous streams of water. He's glad Pamela isn't here to see this; she left weeks ago. He had watched from his window, her sitting with her dad at the bus stop, a bag at her feet. The threat of being sent back to the coastal town she hated finally realised.

Tristan had joined him at the window. 'So that's that then. It's done?'

'Yeah.' Malachi shrugged. That was it, his relationship with Pamela was over.

What a shitty ending, though he swears there was something about the way she looked up from the bus stop, directing her face to his window, which told him she was still thinking about him too. He had dropped his elbows to the window ledge and pushed the balls of his hands against his closed eyes.

Tristan put a hand on his back. 'You all right, man?'

'I'm always all right.'

It was the worst day, the very worst day he could have imagined, until now.

'Mate,' a police officer says. 'Sorry, but you're going to have to move.' He waves a roll of yellow tape as explanation. Malachi feels himself begin to unravel and falls to the ground. The officer crouches down to his level. 'You all right?' The radio crackles on his belt.

'I'm always all right,' Malachi tries, but his breathing grows ragged.

'I'm going to get you some help. Hang on in there. Where's your family, mate?'

Malachi lifts his head and takes a breath. 'I've lost them.'

CHAPTER FIFTEEN

Elvis

Elvis is hurt. His whole body hurts, from the neat line of hair Alan at the Waterside Centre shaved so straight for him last Thursday, down to the soles of his soft pale feet. The skin on his face is hot and he touches every part of it to try and find out why. He feels a big gash on his forehead, running downwards above his right eye like the crack in the wall of his old bedroom, a space so large you could slot 2p coins in.

There's the smell of smoke too, strong like the time he left the rice boiling on the hob while he was watching an Arsenal versus Chelsea match. It went into overtime and he did not want to miss the penalties, so sat there with the fingers on one hand crossed for Arsenal to win and the fingers on the other hand crossed that the rice would wait for him. It did not and there was a fire that time, small and smelly, and George, his care worker, was cross. So cross.

There is a fire somewhere in Nightingale Point now, and it is far bigger than the rice fire and much smellier. But Elvis cannot remember how it started or if it is his fault.

'No, no, no.' He pushes his hands against his ears tightly. He does not want to hear that horrible whooshing noise again or the boys on the wall laughing at him or Lina calling him a dumb giant.

'No, no, no, no, no.'

Elvis wants to stand up and run away. He can run fast – not as fast as the pretty blonde girl from the eleventh floor, who runs across the green in the sun and rain, her red sweatshirt a swishing blur – but fast.

Kaboom.

Something hard and flat hurts his head. The shock of the impact makes his eyes pop open. A group of tiny pale yellow flames skate across a shiny pool of liquid. The flames look so pretty but he knows that fire is extremely dangerous and resists the urge to touch. Someone or something brushes against his back and he shuffles into a ball, scared and confused. If only George was here, or even Lina. They would know what to do. Elvis does not know what to do. He never does.

'No, no, no.' He coughs out a mouthful of smoke, then remembers. 999. The easiest phone number in the world. If he can get to a phone, he can call the fire brigade. They will definitely know what to do.

Some people run. They look bloody and scary and Elvis does not want to be near them, so he skirts his bottom closer towards the exit that leads to the tenth floor corridor. If he can get back into his flat he can use his new special phone to telephone 999. He pushes hard on the door but it does not open. The little yellow flames begin to grow into big orange ones and pale grey smoke swirls around everywhere like a thunder cloud. Something watery trickles into his eyes and he uses his fingers to wipe it away.

The wide gash on his head feels horrible, like the slices of orange Lina is always forcing him to eat, even though they make his fingers sticky and smelly.

'No, no, no.'

Lina will be furious. The pie will be cold. He does not think he would mind eating a cold pie but Lina never lets him. Instead she will show it to him, tell him he is wasteful and that he should think of all the starving kids in Africa. Then she will let the food slide off the plate and into the rubbish bin to sit alongside banana peels and toast crusts. Waste makes Lina angry.

Three men run past, their clothes raggedy and bloody. One stops and tries to pick Elvis up. He screams. At least he thinks he does, he cannot hear it, as it feels like his ears have been switched off. It is dark now and very scary. His hands are covered in blood. What a mess. He takes a deep breath, like he has been taught to do in Monday drama class at the Waterside Centre. *Relax and breathe: one, two, three.* Then a burst of his favourite colour, macaroni cheese yellow, runs past. It's a lady's headscarf, and over her shoulder is the face of a crying child. Elvis does not like it when children are crying as it makes him feel like crying too. He pushes on the door that leads to where the flats are, where a phone will be, but it feels heavy and stuck. He pushes again. He wants to reach the phone and save the day. The door slides open a little wider. There's a hand behind it. An arm. A whole person. The person grabs Elvis and starts to pull too, like tug of war but not as fun. Elvis rises to his knees to make his pull stronger, then finally manages to drag the person onto his side of the stairwell. The person looks like a zombie and Elvis is frightened at first, but it is a boy, one who has been hurt very badly. Elvis sits against the wall and pulls the boy's head onto his lap, like he does with the nice Labrador dog George sometimes brings to the Waterside Centre. Elvis knows if he was hurt very badly he would like someone to put his head onto their lap and stroke his hair too. The hurt person does not have a top on, only a pair of white shorts and one white sock and one white trainer. The other sock is only on a little bit as the foot is all red and broken apart; a flap of brown flesh hangs off the ankle and Elvis has to look away because it looks so horrible.

The boy's face is covered in blood, one eye purple and swollen, like when you leave plums in the fruit bowl for too long because you do not like them, and only want to eat kiwis that week. The lights in the stairwell begin to flash and Elvis sees that the boy's head has thick lines of zigzags shaved into the hair, not like a Labrador dog at all.

Elvis looks closer. It is the bad black boy who spat on him and called him the horrible R word.

CHAPTER SIXTEEN

Mary

She took down the crystal angel that hung in front of her living room window. She was conscious of unplugging the deep fat fryer each night. She reported, to the hopeless caretaker, that the old woman on the third floor was blocking the building's only stairwell again with her plastic plants and flower pots. But still, the dreams continued. Night after night. Dreams of sofas going up in flames, glass popping onto balconies and water pouring down the concrete stairwell. Dreams from which Mary would wake in a bed empty of sheets, alone in her flat on the ninth floor. Something was going to happen. The dreams were trying to warn her. But what could she do? They were just dreams.

Mary steadies herself against the hot roof of the car and looks up at the tower of flames in the distance. Her fingers crush against the metal of her fob watch as she slides her hands into the closely stitched pockets of her dress. She fights the urge to pull out the watch and check the time. Maybe out of habit, or maybe so she will be able to, when asked, relay information about this event. People were always doing that on the news, discussing factually where they were, at what time the war started, the train came off the rails, the plane crashed into the building.

'Harris?' She can only see the back of his head, that comforting patch of fuzzy grey hair.

The sun's glare bounces off the car and makes his eyes water, and then, instinctively, they both get back in. The doors slam and Mary feels herself shake as they fight their way through traffic and edge towards Nightingale Point. The street that runs in front of the estate is blocked with people in varying states of undress, exhibiting different levels of suffering. They run, gather, hug and direct their stunned faces to the sky. The dense crowd spills across the usually empty green opposite the estate. How will she find them in this? Her boys, she needs to find them.

An image from a dream crystallises slowly in her mind, of Tristan aged six or seven, asleep in bed, wearing worn-out Spiderman pyjamas. His nose is crusty from the cold he never seemed to shake. His little feet stick out, his toenails unclipped and dirty. She wants to take care of him, she wants to give him a bath and put him in something clean. But she can't reach him.

There's a familiar flash of red bandana in the crowd.

'Stop the car.'

Harris makes to pull in but she can't wait and throws the door open. She slows only to push at those who stagger distractedly into her path. The boy in the red bandana stands astride his bike, alone under one of the beech trees. He looks like he wants more than anything to flee but has forgotten how to cycle.

'Where is Tristan?'

He breaks from his trance and looks at her like a child caught and about to be scolded for some misdemeanour he has forgotten. As he shakes his head Mary sees, for the first time, how young he is and she feels stupid for all the times she gripped her handbag as she walked past him.

'Where is Tristan? Please.' His arms tremble as she holds him.

'Tristan?' He looks vacant as he tries to place the name.

'Yes. He was with you earlier, and the other boys. Is he with them now? Did he go to the fair?'

'They ran. But Tristan, I dunno.' The boy pulls his arms away and puts them behind his head. His face softens, his voice barely audible. 'My auntie lives there.'

She follows his eyeline to the tower of flame-filled windows. Half of its fourteen storeys are lost. Small flares escape from various balconies high and low, as if the fire whirs around inside in search of an escape route. Then she runs. The nearer she gets to the block, the more agitated and less stagnant the crowd. There is energy, a buzz, like her early days on the accident and emergency wards, those draining twelve-hour shifts where one lost life would roll into another.

A figure on a low balcony of Nightingale Point waves down sombrely. A pushchair is knocked on its side and a tea-filled bottle rolls out. The three small trees closest to the building, planted a few years ago as part of some mismanaged attempt to spruce up the estate, are burnt naked of their leaves. Her thirty-two years of experience on hospital wards allows her to easily block out the screams of pain and the cries of shock, but she knows some of these sights will haunt her forever.

There are flashes of high-visibility jumpsuits as paramedics run to attend to the many injured, while the police, who never miss a chance to descend on the estate and execute a round of stop and searches, are everywhere. Mary runs past two of them doing CPR, one sweaty and red-faced pumps at a dark-haired chest, while the other counts aloud as he rolls up his own shirt sleeves.

The fire brigade move swiftly despite their heavy uniforms. They unfurl hoses and Mary jumps across the thick, grey crisscross of them to get closer to the heart of the chaos. She passes the wall, the place where she had, just two hours before, waved Tristan off, her elbow twitching in warning that something was worth worrying about.

'Nurse, can you help me?' It's Christopher Palmer from the ground floor. His arms are bloody, his face redder than usual under the snowy beard. When Mary's twins were very small they convinced themselves he was Father Christmas and for a whole year they obsessed over catching him doing mundane tasks: humming in the lift, eating a banana on his balcony, swimming lengths at the local pool, his big belly flopped over a pair of red shorts.

'Some glass fell on me.' He starts to cry.

Mary is glad the twins are not here to see this figure from their childhoods, scared and in pain. She wants to help him, but can't. He doesn't need it enough. He's alive. He grabs her and she shrugs away from the wet bloodiness of his touch.

But as she escapes him, guilt fills her. She is betraying the uniform she wears each day, one which makes her public property, someone always trusted for advice, care and helping old ladies cross the street.

A large group of women with sunburnt shoulders huddle. Inside their circle sits an old man on the ground. His hacking cough triggers a chorus of cries. One of the women seizes Mary's arm for assistance. Her immediate reaction is to help them but she knows she can't stop. She pushes the woman's hand off and glances down at the old man, whose head hangs forward as a stream of bile, thin and black, falls from his mouth.

Everyone is swept up in the swarm, people running from what is left of Nightingale Point and the two neighbouring towers. The road is pockmarked with pieces of debris, some of it aflame, some of it already burnt out.

A group of people, wet and distraught, run past. Where are they are going? Two bloodied figures stagger behind; one of them falls limply to the grass. He has blackened nostrils and the cotton and skin from one shoulder is torn away. He bounces up with his arms stretched out in front, like a monster in a comedy horror, and unleashes a scream of pain and panic.

Within the cloud of smoke a child holds a blow-up ball above her badly scuffed knees. She wipes her face tiredly and looks around at a world of adults too overwhelmed to notice, to scoop her up and take her to safety. Mary looks straight into the little girl's eyes. Her pain is all Mary's fault. She knew something was going to happen today, she felt it, it rattled her all morning, and she ignored it.

The child is snatched up by a police officer who, in his focused bravery, does not notice Mary as she ducks under the white and blue plastic cordon. She heads past the small swing park, where no children, other than the most uncared for, play. It is covered with chunks of debris. A flat white sheet of metal lies partly over the long ago condemned roundabout. Something has fallen into the eye of the bouncing pink elephant and begun to melt its face away.

She stops in front of the block, and not since she first laid eyes on it in the late 1960s has she ever been so overwhelmed by its size. She tries to count the floors up but anything above the fifth floor is covered in flames, and again, there's a clear vision of her boys inside: Malachi on the old busted sofa, his books covered in soot; Tristan on the floor, under something fallen. Then she does not hear anything anymore, not the screams or cries, not the plaster as it blisters or steel as it curls, only the blood in her ears as she runs towards the door. But she can't reach it. Someone pulls her back.

'Get off me, Harris.'

His hands snake around her stomach from behind. He has a strength that surprises her, one that denies he has ever been a sick man. Her legs flail out in front, the white of her shoes so out of place against the darkness that floods from the building. She kicks and screams before he manages to pull her down to the grass.

'You stupid woman,' he spits, before exhaustion takes his breath.

Mary looks up at the sky, the pure blue clearness of it obscured by smoke.

'I didn't warn them.' The tears pool in the hollow between her eyes and nose before they roll down her face and off onto the concrete. Harris's chest rises and falls aggressively as he chases his breath.

Then the twitch, the worry, the overwhelming feeling of dread that began this morning stops.

CHAPTER SEVENTEEN

Tristan

Tristan is unsure of anything other than the throb in his left eye. He has been attacked. But why? Surely not over owing Ben Munday twenty quid? He keeps his eyes shut tightly and tries to concentrate on not screaming. If his attacker is still stood above him, then shrieking like a girl would only make things worse. He can't hear anything, just a loud whistle in his ears. He has been hit hard.

I'm gonna die young in the wars, the hoes gonna cry on my corpse.

There is a strange smell, one he can't place, doesn't want to. His eyes feel sticky. Blinks don't seem to clear them. The left eyelid isn't moving at all, it feels stuck together. His perspective is off and when he looks around, the corridor seems to disappear into a circle of flames like a circus hoop. It's so hot. An unbelievable heat. Is he on fire? Does he need to shed burning clothes?

There are no flames on his body. His coughs make no sound, but he can feel it in his chest. His left leg glistens below the knee with something he can't quite make out in the darkness. It doesn't hurt so he presses it, along with the rest of his body, against the door to the stairwell in an attempt to get further away from the fire. The door moves from the other side. His body slides easily across the floor. A hand reaches around the frame and he grabs it. Help is here. The door continues to open and Tristan allows the person to pull him through to the other side where the heat is less intense.

Someone takes his cheeks in their hands. Soft hands, like Mum. The way she used to hold his face when looking for clues if he was telling the truth or not. But he was always telling the truth, she just never believed him.

'It wasn't my fault, Mum. I swear. This time I didn't do anything.'

As his head is lowered onto her lap he can smell the coconut oil she used to rub in her hair. The best smell in the world.

'I got attacked,' he tells her. 'It wasn't my fault. I didn't do anything.'

The flames fall away and her face is lit by a string of fairy lights. Red, green and white. Malachi is here too, the three of them on the mattress on the living room floor. Mum pulls at the sleeves of Malachi's jacket in an attempt to close the gap between the cuffs and his magic stretchy gloves.

'Mum. My foot hurts. My chest is sore.'

She doesn't hear him, bending down and twisting at one of the fairy lights until it twinkles. Red, green and white. Her eyes hazel like the tiger eye stone she used to keep on the windowsill next to the poetry books they weren't allowed to touch.

'I think I need help.'

Malachi falls asleep at the other end of the mattress. His sleeves have ridden up and his ashy wrists stick out.

Why is no one answering?

Mum's face breaks into a smile. She strokes his head and sings.

All the angels sang for him. The bells of Heaven rang for him.

'Mum, please help me.'

For a boy was born, king of all the world.

The colours fade as Tristan rolls his head in her lap. The twinkling lights bleach away until she is a blur of white.

'Mum? No.'

His eyes are drawn to another pair above him, those of a large figure, which shakes its head side to side.

'Mum?' But as the word leaves his lips he sees freckled white skin, red hair and a familiar face. The mouth is round and moves fast as it repeats something over and over.

'No, no, no.'

Shit. It's the guy in the Elvis T-shirt. This is his revenge. Ben did say it: 'You gotta watch yourself with them care-in-the-community people.' Tristan was warned but like always he didn't listen and now he's alone in the stairwell with his bust-up head in this nutcase's lap. The man lifts one of his big hands and Tristan flinches, cowering himself into a ball on the floor.

'I'm sorry. I'm sorry.' The words slur as they leave his mouth.

Elvis T-shirt stands, ready to run, to kick a man when he's down, but he doesn't. He pulls Tristan up and pushes him so he's leaning against the wall.

'I'm sorry. It was a joke,' Tristan tries.

Elvis T-shirt brings his face close and his green eyes look small and uncontrolled. The pupils dart about quickly, like the midge larvae that collected in the plastic bucket on Mary's balcony last spring.

'You did this?' But even as Tristan says it he knows the answer, that whatever happened here is bigger than revenge, bigger than this man in the comedy T-shirt.

Tristan sways side to side and his left leg buckles. Elvis T-shirt catches him and helps to lower him onto the first step, where he pushes him gently, encouraging him to slide down. Tristan looks away from the bloody tangle of flesh and bone where his foot should be and begins to slide down the steps on his arse, like a kid.

In between billows of smoke he can make out the white signage with the blue plastic lettering, the floor indicators he used to spend so long scratching off with his house keys. Ninth Floor. Eighth Floor. Seventh Floor. Where is everyone else? Sixth Floor. The stairs run with water and are scattered with dark objects: a blackened wooden disc, a small green jelly shoe, a plug with a wire sticking out of it but no appliance attached.

Fifth Floor. He slides down another step but his foot folds awkwardly and he lets out a scream, so loud that he can't even hear it. The cry takes all his energy and he blacks out.

He comes to with an urge to throw up; his stomach churns as it does after every session of drinking too much with the boys. He doubles over and vomits. But afterwards he doesn't feel better, just shivery and dizzy.

Bury me like a thug, give me all your love, bag of weed in my coffin, I swear you'll miss me often.

Another step. Fourth Floor. The tiredness is overwhelming. But Elvis T-shirt pushes again, encouraging him to keep going.

'I can't, man. I can't.' His tongue feels fat in his mouth, his head swollen and weighty. 'I can't. I can't do it. Go without me. Go.'

Elvis T-shirt shakes his head and takes Tristan by the hand, holding it tightly and pulling him down onto the next step. But Tristan has nothing left, he's exhausted, done. Even the effort it takes to shake his head makes him cry. This is it: he's going to die here in the stairwell.

Then Elvis T-shirt picks him up like a sack of potatoes.

'What the fuck, man? Leave me.'

He catches glances of the stairs at awkward angles. Smoke, flames, sky, the sign that announces Second Floor. Just a bit more rest. That's all he needs. He closes his eye. Opens it again. First Floor. So close. Tristan can see the white light of day, of freedom, of salvation. The air comes so easily all of a sudden, it chokes him. Elvis T-shirt shakes violently as he coughs and Tristan comes off his shoulder and tumbles down the wet steps onto the final landing. The windows are blown out and huge puffs of smoke escape from the confines of the stairwell.

Elvis T-shirt slowly sits, still coughing, his nose and mouth streaming. Apart from a gash on his head he looks uninjured.

'Go!' Tristan shouts at him. 'Run.'

But Elvis T-shirt shakes his head and tries to pull at Tristan again.

'No. Leave me.'

He blacks out.

This time when he wakes up she's there again.

'Mum? You came back.'

She's singing. Her scarf blows across her face, pink and purple, too thick for the weather. She tucks it into her jacket collar. She's so perfect and beautiful. So unlike what she became.

For a boy was born, king of all the world.

He misses her singing more than anything else. In a way it's worth going through this, whatever *this* is, in order to hear it again. The corners of her mouth go up slightly, her smile like Malachi's, modest and rare. She looks away, off to the side, to one of the many things that distracted her from their life.

'Wait,' Tristan tries to call but his voice catches in his throat. There's no more breath. There's no more strength.

CHAPTER EIGHTEEN

Elvis

Bloody spit hits Elvis's face as the boy tries to speak, but Elvis cannot hear him. He cannot hear anything as his ears are definitely broken. They are on the ground floor landing now. The way out seems very far away and he is too tired to get up and pull himself and the boy out. Help will come if they wait here sensibly. People are always coming in and out of the front door; it is the best place, after the bus stop, to meet people on the estate.

Elvis does not want to see it again but he cannot help himself from looking down at the brown skin of the boy's foot to where it gives way to a mess of flesh and bone. Like the meat that hangs on the hooks in the windows of the butchers on the high street.

The urge to cough becomes stronger and stronger as his lungs fill up with the horrible thick black smoke. An ache crawls up his back and arms from carrying the boy. His limbs are hot and tired like they were six weeks ago when he first moved into Nightingale Point. Back and forth from

George's car to the lift, carrying the blue suitcase of clothes and boxes of books.

The black boy's eyes open and roll backwards. He looks scary, like something from a horror film. Elvis looks away as he does not like horror and does not want to scare himself. There is a white light at the door and Elvis wants to walk through it, to leave now. But he is also tired and wants to go to sleep, in his old bedroom with the blue and white striped sheet and the red pillow.

The boy has stopped blowing the bloody spit bubbles. Elvis lowers his face and watches for movement, the way he has learnt to do when playing musical statues at parties. But it's hard to stare closely and cough at the same time as you are not allowed to cough on people, especially not in their faces.

Maybe the bad black boy is dead. He has never seen a dead person before. The last dead thing he saw was a frog in the park, which was horrible because it had gone all hard and black and had cut grass stuck to its legs. That made him very sad.

Elvis lays his head on the ground and watches the water run off each step and onto the next like a little concrete waterfall. It feels like it is time to have a catnap. He loves catnaps as they are the best kind of naps because you do not have to wear pyjamas for them or even go to bed. You can catnap anywhere. But you would have to be super sleepy to be able to fall asleep on the ground floor landing of Nightingale Point. He is not sure he is *that* tired. Also, he is very thirsty and wants a drink more than he wants a catnap. A big glass of juice. Though he no longer wants his pie as there is sick on his shorts from the where the bad black boy vomited and it has put Elvis off eating.

'I will come back,' Elvis says as he begins to crawl away towards the light of the door. Off he goes, out into the smoky sunshine, where there are sure to be people who can help the boy.

CHAPTER NINETEEN

Pamela

Pamela pulls herself up using the bars of the locked security gate. The front doors on the other side of the corridor are in varying states of destruction, Tunde's one blown off completely to reveal the sky outside and flashes of flames. She can't see down to the end of the corridor but catches glimpses of her neighbours as they run through the smoke, the fast blurs of blue shorts, brown legs and babes in arms. She puts her hands through the gate and, because she doesn't know what else to do, cries out, 'Someone, help. Please!' Her mouth is clumsy; blood splutters.

Nobody stops. Maybe they can't hear her. She can't hear herself.

A woman in a yellow headscarf comes into view. There's a child on her hip and as she nears the gate Pamela notices her face is covered with black patches, as if rubbed with charcoal. The child screams between coughs and the woman grabs Pamela's wrist with her free hand.

'Open?' Her mouth moves but the sound is lost to the buzz

in Pamela's ears. The woman looks up and down the gate, her eyes questioning why Pamela's response is not urgency, only tears. She pulls at the gate while the child puts its hand into the gap between her scarf and dress and pulls tightly at her neck.

'Open?' the woman demands again over her child's screams. She shouts something else but Pamela can't quite make it out.

'It's locked. I can't open it. Help me. I don't have the keys.' Her nose streams and as she sniffs, she chokes on the blood that runs into the back of her throat.

The woman shoves the child further up her hip. 'Unlock?' she says, her eyes wide, strands of black hair in her face. The way she pulls at the gate, it's as if she expects to find the strength to pry the metal apart with her hands. Others run past and disappear into the stairwell.

The floor is almost empty now. They both notice. Tears leave two clear paths through the soot under the woman's eyes as she squeezes Pamela's fingers tightly and says something, her face stern but calm.

Pamela knows she can't hold the woman here, that she can't help.

She tries to order her thoughts, to think of a way out. The sprinklers open and fill the corridor with uneven spurts of water, causing her to look away, back into her own flat, which is filled with pale, thin smoke. A phrase comes to her head from a safety video she had once seen in school: *stay low*. She shuts the front door and slides down the inside of it until she is on her knees, watching as a determined slink of smoke pours across the mat. She crawls into the living room where the sun and sky are gone, the whole world outside of the room is gone, and only darkness and fear are there to greet her. The room is disordered; the phone lies on the carpet by the television. She dials 999 but there is no answer, no sound.

'Can you hear me?' But she can't even hear herself. The phone falls to the ground.

How can she escape this? Which way can she run? A flash of brightness catches her attention as one of the sand-coloured curtains catches light, flames quickly sucking up the fabric and curling into itself before melting away into nothing. She pulls the throw from the sofa and scuttles through to the kitchen, where she whacks the taps on and pushes the blanket under the water. She doubles over the sink, hacking, attempting to clear her mouth of the blood and grit.

What were the points from the fire safety video? You wet a towel? You put it over your face? Around your head? You keep the towel dry and use it to stop smoke coming under the doors?

She can't remember, and now her breath feels thick and scratchy as she runs through her darkened home to the bathroom. The light blinks as she sits on the toilet seat. Under the smoke she can still smell the grey emulsion and gloss from the skirting boards. One of Dad's attempts to smarten up the flat. The water from the damp blanket dribbles down her face, mixing with the blood from her nose and mouth. Has she come in here to wait to be saved? Or to die?

She takes a deep breath, the fullest she can manage, and feels the paint fumes, smoke and vapours of something else chemical fill her body and graze her lungs, like freezing fog on a February morning. That cold hour each day she was allowed to run the field, back when she was free.

She struggles for another breath and pulls the wet material from her face to gulp at the air, but finds none. Her head rolls back. There's a bare light bulb, hazy within the smoke, like the moon on a cloudy night. She's running again now, outside in the air, in the space and sparseness of the field in front of the flats. It's cold and crisp, like that first day she spoke to Malachi. The first time he ever put his hands on her. The start of it all when things could have gone so right. The iciness tears at her chest, uncomfortable yet freeing. Where is he now? Tristan said he was out somewhere. Where? For how long? He's always at home. Or maybe he's in the library, squinting into a book. Yes, that's where he is. He's safe.

She squeezes her eyes shut, feeling Malachi kiss her good-bye outside his flat. The last time they were okay and happy, the last time they were together. That kiss was the last one and they didn't even know it then.

She had kept her head down as she leapt up the stairs two at a time, back to her flat on the eleventh floor. It was impossible to stop smiling, thinking of all the things she had done with Malachi that afternoon. But as she reached the flat her heart sank to see the gate lying open, unlocked. Dad was home early.

Inside, the lights were on and the cream saucer was piled with fresh ash. He stood in the doorway and it was clear from his expression there was no point going through the charade of hanging the wet swimming costume up above the bath.

'I've been trying to work out who you've been spending all this time with,' he said. 'For a while I thought that paedophile coach was back on the scene.'

'Dad, please—'

He held up a hand. 'Don't bother. Who is it?' He looked helpless, not angry as she expected him to be. 'Tell me, Pam, 'cause I need to know. Who's been with you? If someone's been taking advantage . . . '

Her skin crawled at the suggestion that she was some child being exploited.

'Who is it?' he demanded. 'Is it that black guy from downstairs?'

She dug her nails into her palms and hoped her face wouldn't betray her.

'Even after I smacked him one.'

'Tristan? No.' She almost laughed with relief. 'Of course not.'

'So who is it?' he shouted.

'He's a nice guy.' It came out so weakly, her voice tiny and scared. 'He's smart, he's kind and he's good. He's at university and—'

'University? How old is he?'

Was it too late to lie? Would it even help matters?

'Tell me how old he is.'

'He's twenty-one.'

'No, Pam. Not again.' He grabbed his head. 'Why? It's like they see you coming.' His face clouded. 'It's over. From now on you go to school. You come home from school. No running. No swimming. Just focus on your GCSEs.'

'Dad, please listen to me—'

'No!' he shouted.

'If you'd meet him, if you'd give Malachi a chance, you would—'

'He's Irish?'

'No, he's black.' She wanted to take it back straight away. The way her dad's face fell at her words. She knew in that moment that Malachi had been right. 'You're not even going to give him a chance, are you?'

'I don't need to.' His reply was calm, but Pamela felt herself stepping away, backing into her room in case he lashed out. 'Just 'cause this one's at university doesn't make him any better than the rest. You want to end up like all these other dumb white girls left with black babies? Is that what you want for yourself?'

'You're wrong. And I won't stop seeing him. I love him.'

'You're just a girl.' His voice softened. 'You really think he loves you? That he's taking you, a schoolgirl, seriously? He's using you.'

'I know he's not. He's not like that.'

'Pam, if you keep seeing him, if you break my trust, then that's it, I'll send you back to stay with your mum.'

'No. You won't.' She knew then the right thing to say, the thing that made perfect sense. 'Because I'm moving in with Malachi.'

Dad's face reddened as the anger returned, his shoulders shifting back.

'Well, then maybe you should go now.'

*

The light flickers in the bathroom. On. Off. On. Then goes out completely. Only a strip of light from under the door illuminates the grey as it creeps in. Something hot and wet falls on her face and she drops into a tight space on the warm, grimy lino floor.

Dad? In her mind she calls him.

'Dad? Dad?' She screams for him to come and save her. But nothing.

'Dad? I'm sorry. I'm sorry, you were right.'

The smell becomes pungent, different from the bin fires she became used to the first winter she lived on the estate. It's a smell like no other. A wet blob of something heavy and searing falls on her shoulder and she flinches away from it. She blocks out the smell and taste of the smoke, looking up to see if the moon is still there. Instead, there is only the ceiling, an orange glow around its edges, like a frame around something beautiful. The frame gets larger and larger, and she knows it is the last thing she will ever see.

CHAPTER TWENTY

Elvis

He pulls himself to standing and staggers over to the cubbyhole, but there is no one to help. Outside there is noise and people, and Elvis runs towards it, grateful that finally someone can take over and sort out this very bad mess that he hopes was not his fault.

A group of firefighters come close; they look scary in their masks and are rushing.

'Please can you help—' But they do not stop to hear what he has to say.

More firefighters come and one of them pushes Elvis out of the way and shouts something at him. There is so much noise and still a strange buzzing in his ears so he does not hear the exact words.

Outside someone grabs Elvis and tries to sit him down to help him, but he is not the one who needs help. He tries to explain this to the person but they are not paying attention. No one is. Who is going to help the boy? He is hurt, hurt very badly. His eye is smashed like an old plum and a bone is sticking out of his foot. Maybe he is dead now. Dead like the frog Elvis found in the park once, blackened and hard.

There are police on the field, Elvis can see their blue flashing lights and wants to find them. He runs through the car park, trying not to look at the smashed cars and broken glass and injured people all around. It is too horrible. He runs across the road and onto the field where there are people, so many of them, hundreds and thousands and millions. But none look like they know what to do.

'Can someone help? Someone is hurt on the ground floor,' he calls into the crowd.

Some of the people look hurt too, but not as badly as the boy, who cannot even walk because his foot is so broken.

'Who can help?' he asks again.

They are staring at him, and he does not like to be stared at, especially not now because he is crying and dirty and smelly. There is blood on his clothes, vomit all over his shorts.

A police officer walks past and Elvis stops him.

'Someone is stuck in there,' he shouts at the officer.

'Yes, we are working to get everyone out.'

'He's hurt.'

The officer pushes Elvis away a little and shouts to another, 'Can someone assist this man?'

'He's on the ground floor. He's lying there.'

'Yes. Okay. Okay. Someone help this man?' he shouts again before running off.

But no one comes. No one is listening. Not even the police, who are usually so kind to Elvis. This is all taking too long. Time is running out and time is important when there is an emergency, just like Michael Buerk says on 999 Lifesavers.

Elvis cannot stop coughing and feels very sick. Maybe he does need help. Maybe he is hurt. He stumbles over to a bench, but there are too many people there so he sits next to it on the ground. His home is gone, his perfect home, destroyed in the fire. He hopes it was not his fault. He does not think so as he was not cooking rice or watching football when the fire began. He was not even in his flat. He was in the stairwell watching a plane; it was quite exciting. Planes are fun to watch but this plane got too close and went too fast and then *boom*.

His ears buzz, *bzzzzz*. His eyes sting too, like they do in cooking class at the Waterside Centre, where they teach you how to chop onions very carefully rather than very quickly like the chefs on television.

Someone passes him a bottle of water, then a lady with nice curly hair and a necklace with a blue eye on it says, 'I'm Ann-Marie. I'm going to stay with you till the ambulance comes, all right?'

But Elvis does not need an ambulance.

'What's your name, sweetheart? Do you live in the block?'

Elvis likes meeting new people, but not now, not today. Also, Ann-Marie is asking too many questions and he's finding it very hard to get the answers out as quickly as she wants them.

'The boy,' he manages between coughs. 'Has someone helped him?'

'They are trying to get everyone out. They are really trying.'

'But he is hurt. Very badly. And there is a fire inside.'

Ann-Marie shakes her head and says, 'Wait here, I'll be back.'

A man with too many tattoos and no top on falls on the ground next to Elvis. He pours a bottle of water over his face and laughs. 'I got out.' His face is covered with black smudges and black snot runs from his nose. He sniffs and laughs again. 'I got out of there. I can't believe it. I can't believe I was fast enough. Everyone from the eighth floor up is dead. Look at it, they've got to be.'

But Elvis does not want to look at Nightingale Point. He has just come from there and it was horrible.

There is a tattoo of a mermaid on the man's arm, which goes upside down as he wipes the blood from his head.

'They got us this time, didn't they? IRA. We didn't stand a chance. Even if they called, sent a warning. No chance. Not a chance. They got us.'

Elvis is scared of the IRA. Whenever he sees them on the television it is because they have done something bad, like kill some horses or hidden a bomb in a shopping centre.

Elvis does not like the noise on the field, or the way people are running about, or the upside-down mermaid on the man's arm. He wants to get away. He has to get away. He stands and runs. Runs and runs as fast as he can, like Linford Christie, but even faster. He keeps going right till he gets to the high street with the takeaways and betting shops. There he stops to catch his breath because he is feeling sick now, so sick.

A group of people dressed as basketball players stand outside a closed post office. Their shorts are so long they look like trousers. They are smoking funny-smelling cigarettes and talking very loudly. So loudly that Elvis, even with his slightly broken ears, can hear them.

'I knew it was gonna happen,' one of them shouts. 'I

watched it go like this and I knew it was gonna be some *Die Hard*-style terrorism. Woo,' he shouts, then claps his hands together.

Elvis does not hear the clapping noise but sees the boy bring his hands together with such a force it makes Elvis jump. One of the basketball players looks across the street at Elvis and then they all point and stare.

Elvis cries. He's scared but too tired to run anymore. He leans his head against the big window of a takeaway called Jade Garden. The TV is on inside, showing his perfect home burning. A golden gloved cat waves at him. Usually this would make him laugh, but he does not want to laugh today because he is sad and lost and dirty and scared. His ears hurt, his chest hurts, his feet are wet and hurt too from all the running, and he wants to go home.

A little boy stands on the other side of the glass. He is small, too small to have a job, but he looks up through the window at Elvis, then runs back behind the counter.

Elvis touches his forehead. It stings and now feels like when you do not finish your bowl of Weetabix quick enough and it goes all mushy with some crusty bits on the top.

'Hey, hey,' someone shouts. Elvis feels an arm slip around his chest as he starts to fall down.

There is lots of talking.

'Someone call an ambulance.'

'What happened to you?'

'Jesus, he smells.'

But Elvis does not want to talk anymore today. He wants to go home. He wants to go home and eat his steak and kidney pie.

CHAPTER TWENTY-ONE

Mary

Mary finds it hard to estimate how many people are in the sports hall of the Arches Leisure Centre. She looks across the wooden sprung floor, busily marked with different coloured lines and shapes, and thinks it could be anything from fifty to hundred. The vastness of the hall seems to swallow everyone up. There are so many faces here, faces that are not Malachi or Tristan. They dribble in and disperse themselves into the rows of plastic chairs at the far edge of the hall. She twists the hem of her dress, picks at a small scab on her finger and tries to bend the metal catch on her fob watch back into place.

There's a cry from a group of skinny teenage girls gathered around a stack of brightly coloured soft play equipment. They hold hands and wipe the remains of smudged eye make-up off each other's faces.

'What is happening?' she asks Harris. 'Why are we sitting here?'

He shrugs and they both turn to where three desks are being lined up at the other side of the hall. Chairs, papers, a computer monitor and modem are brought in by some of the police officers, all led by a sweaty woman in a grey trouser suit and tightly tied white trainers. There's a roll of Sellotape around her wrist and more of the photocopied sheets that are stuck up around the outside of the building, their large type declaring: CENTRE CLOSED FOR EMERGENCY SERVICES OCCUPATION.

Mary feels she should have gone to the hospital to help. It will be overwhelmed with patients: burns, shocks, lacerations. She should be doing her duty, but instead she is paralysed with guilt as she sits here like a patient in an overcrowded surgery, waiting, just waiting.

'Mary?' Harris turns to her. 'Someone is coming over.'

The glow from the strip lighting hits the silver badge on the lapel of one of the volunteers as he makes his way towards the rows of chairs.

'Great news,' he says like a proud host, keen to sell the merits of his party. 'We've got extra phone lines set up now. Follow me.'

Mary's son and daughter come to her mind for the first time since she arrived at the centre. She must let them know she is okay. She pictures the twins watching the news, hearing of this catastrophe and panicking. They were always such anxious children and have both grown to be – for reasons neither Mary nor David have ever been able to credit – apprehensive adults.

A stream of people follows the Salvation Army volunteer out of the hall and into an office. Who should she call first? Julia or John? John will ask too many questions, then drop everything to come and save her, while Julia will be capable of nothing more than crumbling into tears.

'This way, miss, there's a free phone here.' The keen volunteer directs her to a desk, strewn with mugs and coffee-ringed paper. She feels silly as she sits there in her nurse uniform. But everyone at each of the desks looks as out of place as her: one with sunglasses on his head, another with mascara running down her cheeks and a toddler on her lap, who bemusedly grabs at staplers and pens.

Mary's little feet kick at the black court shoes left under the desk by whomever ordinarily works there and Mary hopes she will know what to say by the time the phone is picked up.

'Julia?'

'Mum. Thank God. Thank God. I've been going crazy worrying about you. Are you okay?'

'I am fine. They have sent us all to this place . . . ' Mary looks around the office. A busy whiteboard occupies her eyeline: *Options for membership up-sales! Peak swim access – £4 a month. 1-1 gym training – £5 per session.*

'Where? Are you safe?'

Mary hears tears on the other end of the line and pictures the heavy make-up, which she has not seen her daughter without in years, run down her face.

'Yes, I am fine. But I need to wait here till I find Tristan and Malachi.'

The toddler begins to wail and Mary presses her index finger into the other ear and misses what is said. 'Huh?'

'I asked where they are. The boys?' Julia says.

'I don't know.'

'Well, where were they when it happened?'

The question irritates Mary because, of course, she does

not know the answer to it. 'I need to get off the phone. There are a lot of people waiting.'

'No, Mum. Where are you? I need to come and get you.'

'No. It's fine. I need to go.' Julia protests but Mary puts the phone down.

The toddler's cries quell as the mother replaces its dummy. A fax machine crackles and whines. And at the desk across from Mary a woman talks casually into the phone, as if having a chat with a friend.

'Yeah, new sofas,' she says. 'New bunk beds too, can you believe it? I can't believe it. No way. It didn't happen. No way. How come planes still crash? With all that technology?'

'Excuse me, miss.' There's a gentle hand on her shoulder from one of the volunteers. 'Sorry, but could I ask you to move on so the next person can use the phone?'

As she returns, the number of those in the hall suddenly seems so large, so vast. She tries to calculate how many flats made up Nightingale Point, how many families were likely to have been affected, but she can't even remember how many floors it has, what it looks like, where it is.

The crowd is a good thing – it means more lives saved. She stands on her tiptoes to look over their heads, across sunhats, burnt bald patches and hair dank from sweat or sprinklers. Malachi towers above most people and Tristan can usually be heard over a crowd. They must be in here somewhere.

'Mary?' Harris takes her hand. 'Come, they are beginning to register everyone.'

He pulls her to the other side of the hall, where lines have begun to form. Above each desk is a handwritten sign with the name of each block. The lines for Seacole Point and

Barton Point are long and winding, at least sixty people in each, but the line in front of Nightingale Point is shorter. She scans each one quickly. A dreadlocked man shouts to anyone who will listen about what he saw, a woman in a blue bathrobe shakes her head and a tearful pensioner clacks rosary beads.

On the desk someone has folded a sheet of card in half lengthways to make it stand up. REGISTER HERE, it says, as if it were a conference or staff training day that people would try and skip out of.

Mary presses her hands on the desk. 'I need to register Malachi Roberts and Tristan Roberts. Both from flat thirty-three. It's on the ninth floor.'

A woman in a bright orange top writes down the information while an overly animated young police officer types on the computer.

'Any more information, please? Ages? Appearance? Ethnicity?' The woman does not stop her pen to look up.

'Why?'

The officer chips in, 'Any information we can collect here will help with identifying.' He pauses, as if he realises for the first time the horror people on the other side are faced with. 'Fact is, if the authorities need to identify lost people, people who are confused, maybe knocked unconscious, descriptions help.' He looks at Mary's uniform. 'I'm sure you understand.'

'Malachi is twenty-one. Tall. Over six feet. He is . . . he is . . . ' How can she describe him? There are so many words. Beautiful. Clever. Sullen. Miserable. Missing.

'And your nationality?' The woman finally looks up from her papers, squints at Mary but decides against a guess.

'No. These are not my children. They are black.'

'Oh, right,' she says.

'Do you share a property in Nightingale Point with these men?' the officer asks.

'No.'

'I'm sorry, miss,' the woman glances behind Mary, 'but we have over six hundred people to account for and right now we're only registering the missing members of people's families and shared properties.'

'They are my family.'

The woman bites her bottom lip.

'Write it down,' Mary shouts. She grabs the pen and slams it in front of the woman. 'Tristan Roberts and Malachi Roberts. Flat thirty-three. Write it down.'

'Please, miss. Calm down or I can't help you.'

Harris takes Mary's arm and guides her from the line. 'You need to stop. You can see it's chaos. It will take ages for the police to fully evacuate the area and have everyone come through here. But they will. That door, Mary.' He looks over to the entrance of the hall, at the slow stream of people who are not Malachi or Tristan. 'People keep coming through it, every minute. The boys will come too.'

'How can she tell me they are not my family? Who is she to tell me?' Mary feels helpless, regretful and furious. How could someone suggest that she had no right to look for them? The boys were family in a way that no one else could understand. She had loved them and watched over them their whole lives and now some stranger dared tell her she could not even search for them, their relationship belittled, as if she were asking after a neighbour or distant friend.

'They are my boys, Harris. They have no one else. No one.'

'I know.'

'Where are they?' She doesn't want to shout, to be that woman crying and screaming, but at this moment she can't control it. 'Where could they be? They can't be hurt, Harris. It's not fair if they are hurt.'

'You must stay positive.' He puts his hands on her shoulders. 'You said Tristan was on his way out. Malachi probably joined him.'

Harris had never met Tristan and Malachi, but he had a habit of speaking like he knew them, as if their personalities were shared with every other young person he had ever taught.

Mary nods. She wants to believe that they were both out at the time of the accident, that Harris is right. But then Harris does not know how Tristan can lose whole weekends indoors to a computer game and that hot days are the worst for Malachi, as the city smog clogs his airwaves and has him constantly reaching for his inhaler. Like this morning, when she last saw him. He said he was staying in, yes, that's definitely what he told her.

'I can't take this,' she says. 'This waiting and not knowing.'

'We have no choice, Mary. This is where they will come.'

The air is stagnant and close, and Mary pulls her uniform from her chest to fan herself. It releases the stench of smoke.

'I need some air.' She walks towards the double doors that lead into the main part of the centre. The smell of chlorine reminds her of the endless humid hours she spent all those years ago teaching her children to swim. She tried to teach Tristan too, when he was eight. He was keen but unfocused, and would waste time thrashing about, laughing till the water streamed from his nose and his eyes went red. He had never been in a pool before. But then the boys' lives were like that, huge chunks of childhood unchecked because of their mum's depression. They were only just finding their feet. It can't all be taken away now. It wouldn't be fair.

The flicker of a television catches her eye from a window-less room; a sign on the outside door reads: *Staff Only*. She shuts it behind herself and climbs over boxes with their contents spilt across the stained carpet tiles: deflated footballs, bundles of paper timetables, plastic-wrapped tennis rackets. There is a large table in the middle of the room, bare apart from a few squashed pieces of chocolate cake on a silver tray, a note underneath: *It's my 21st. Enjoy. Bean x*

Mary sits on one of the burst fabric seats closest to the television. The screen is filled with an image of Nightingale Point. Over the picture, a calm and formal newsreader recites the details, a bunch of numbers that mean nothing and yet everything. Fifty-six flats, up to 600 feared missing, death count on the ground currently three. She thinks of the last Major Incident Training she had at the hospital, how they were told to expect up to three times as many injured as dead. The boys could be hurt.

An old woman comes on the screen, her skin ashen. 'I just popped out.' She looks behind her to where the flaming building is cut from shot and drops her head. There's an awkward silence as the camera waits for more. Then footage of the green, of crowds and ambulances. Mary holds a hand to her mouth at the sight of the flames and sound of sirens.

The same information is repeated again and again. Homes

destroyed. Many missing. Three confirmed dead. A distorted phone call from an airline official with a heavy Greek accent. An accident, a terrible accident. Five on-board. Cargo flight. Five crew assumed dead. No passengers. Eyewitnesses describe something that fell from the plane, heavy and dark, onto the field in front of the estate. The faces in the background are many and unfamiliar. Nine confirmed dead.

From outside the staffroom Mary hears a raised voice. Someone shouts for their daughter. She grabs the remote control and turns it up; she can cope with the trauma on the screen but does not want to play audience to someone else's tragedy in real life.

The shouts from beyond the wall are joined by an authoritative voice as it calls for calm. There's a thump, the sound of a struggle. Then a voice she knows.

CHAPTER TWENTY-TWO

Malachi

He pictures flat thirty-three on the ninth floor. The place him and Tristan, aged fourteen and nine, redecorated with their nan a few days after their mum's funeral. Each room was coated in white paint in an effort to erase the devil Nan saw in every corner. Malachi was so proud that he was tall enough to paint over the blackened patch of ceiling above the toaster, the result of him attempting to make himself and Tristan dinner. It was satisfying to erase the past by simply covering it up and bringing new things in. The old bed sheets were ripped down from the windows and replaced with bright white nets from the market, the black mould removed from around the bath with bleach, and the cupboards and fridge were filled.

They dragged bag after bag into the lift and out to the rubbish stores, until everything from the old days was gone. Everything except for Mum's pink and purple scarf, which was kept tied around a once leaky pipe under the sink. Neither Malachi nor Tristan ever acknowledged the scarf, yellow with age and London limescale, but they knew it was there, like a heartbeat. Maybe it offered comfort that she was still with them in some way. Its image kept appearing as Malachi followed the crowd off the field and towards the local leisure centre hall, as directed by the police.

He wonders now how long he can put off calling Nan. He doesn't know what to say to her anyway.

The tightness in his chest has not yet subsided; this kind of attack usually means he will be confined to bed for the next few days. Malachi always suspected Tristan enjoyed those days. He would park himself up on the end of the bed and subject his captive audience to endless trivia about warring rap stars and local girls.

The air is muggy as he stands in the line for Nightingale Point, but there is a small flow of air from the fire exit doors, propped open with a chair on each side. Huddles of people stand out there, in the sunshine of the staff car park; they smoke cigarettes and look up at the thin haze that fills the sky.

Everywhere people are talking, behind him, in front of him. Someone shouts from the front of the line, an official voice, one that does not wobble or question.

'This is the line for residents of Nightingale Point only. Please help us help you.'

Everyone talks over the voice. Why can't they stop? Just be quiet. Malachi's head hurts with all the noise. But he is almost at the front. Then the line stalls as a woman in a yellow headscarf faints. People rush over to help, to hold her child and fan her face with leaflets for the Salvation Army. The child screams by her side and calls at her to wake up till she comes to.

The woman behind the desk aggressively takes the lid off her bottle of water and tips it to her lips to find it empty. She mouths 'fuck' under her breath, her empathy for the situation exhausted.

The paper on the desk is glaringly white, scrawled with names. Some of the writing has been scored out. Why? Are these the people who have been listed as missing but then found? Found alive? Have they walked into the local hospital? He jumps as the fire exit doors slam shut.

'Open them back up,' a voice from the line calls.

'They can't,' says a volunteer behind Malachi. 'The smell is drifting in.'

The strip lighting is too bright in the hall. The long, thin windows above the basketball hoops allow in too much natural light. The space feels too tight, too airless. Malachi tries to breathe slower but it doesn't help. How can he stand this? He needs to get out, to get away. He leaves the line and runs from the hall, stopping by a bank of vending machines, where he slides down to the floor, facing away from the lit-up bottles of Lucozade and bars of chocolate. He wills the hum of the glowing box to drown out the searing sounds around him, the footsteps and cries and talk of so many.

'Only six phones calling out.'

'That poor girl, poor girl.'

'They're saying it was an accident but they never tell us the truth.'

He breathes slowly.

'The terrorists are getting more and more ruthless.'

'Call your dad. Call him now.'

Who would Malachi call? Mary will be busy, on shift at

the hospital. He had asked her earlier this week why she was working so much and taking on the busy afternoon shifts she usually complains about. She said she was not sleeping well, up with nightmares and worries, then struggling to wake early enough to get in.

As more time passes Malachi knows he will have to phone his nan, but he can't face telling her he's lost Tristan, that the last time he spoke to his little brother he was hanging with some hoods, probably buying or smoking weed.

Again he sees the image of his mum's scarf, but he pushes it from his mind and concentrates only on the rise and fall of his own chest. He is startled by a shout from the hall, loud and aggressive, a male's voice whose words can't be made out. The doors fly open and a man in a yellow T-shirt is bundled out, a police officer on each side.

'My daughter,' he says loudly. 'I need to find my girl.' His big black boots trip by Malachi's feet.

'You need to slow down, sir.' The police officer puts his palms up in an attempt to pacify the man. 'If you slow down, we can try to help you find her.'

'My daughter, my little girl, my little girl. I need you to find her. Flat forty-one. The eleventh floor.'

His back is to Malachi. But it's him, it's Jay, Pamela's dad. His eyes jump about fearfully at the faces that surround him, as if about to be set upon. The colour is drained from his skin, far from the angry red of the last time Malachi saw him on that excruciating morning outside of the flat.

Malachi had opened his front door, expecting to see Pamela; it was part of their routine, the ten minutes they would steal each weekday before she went to school. He loved the way she would smile at him when he opened the door, the knowledge that even though the minutes were short, they would be spent together. But that morning she didn't smile, her eyes were puffy and she twisted her fingers nervously.

'I'm sorry, Mal.'

Jay came up behind her, chucking two black bin liners by her feet. 'There it is,' he said.

'What's going on?' Malachi asked. He knew it was bad.

'What's wrong with you?' Jay was close enough that Malachi could smell the cigarettes on his breath. 'Why couldn't you find a girl your own age?'

'Dad, please.'

'You're a grown man and she's still in school. Don't you see a problem with that?'

Malachi felt it then, looking at Pamela standing there, crying in her school uniform, her hair tied in a neat ponytail. He felt like he was some kind of pervert.

'But obviously you're serious about her. Pam tells me you want her to move in?'

Malachi's heart raced.

'Dad, stop it, please.'

'Well, here she is.' He kicked at the bin liner and turned to his daughter. 'He doesn't look that keen now, does he?'

'Why are you doing this?' she cried.

'Because it's what you said you wanted.'

Malachi tried for her attention. 'Pam, we haven't even spoken about this.'

'So you're saying you *don't* want her then?' Jay laughed. 'Ain't that a surprise.'

Malachi rubbed his face. What was he meant to do now? The timing was wrong. He wasn't ready.

'Pam, can you come in and talk?'

'Talk? Is that what you've been doing with my sixteen-year-old all these months?'

'Dad, please stop it.' She grabbed his hand to pull him away but he threw her off.

'You wanted her, so have her. You support her, pay for the roof over her head, her food, her sports. You do it. Bet you don't even have a job, do you?'

Pamela stood opposite, like some unwanted pet. 'He's going to send me back to Portishead. I hate it there, you know I do.'

It was too much pressure, he couldn't think straight, not with her in front of him crying and Jay looking on, waiting to be proven right.

'Let's see if he really is different from the rest of them,' Jay said, then went back into the stairwell, leaving them alone.

'I'd love for you to move in.' Malachi sighed. He knew this would be the end of things. 'But I told you how crazy this year is going to be for me with studying and I need to find some work to top up my money, Pam, and I haven't—' He broke off as she started to cry again. He wanted to take her hand but didn't. 'I need to speak to Tristan about—'

'It's fine, Mal, it's fine.' She sniffed and grabbed at one of the bags. 'I get it. Seriously.'

'I need some time. I need to think about how I could do it properly, how I could support you.'

'Support? Is that how you see me? As another thing on your to-do list?'

'No, I didn't mean that. Stop.' He took her arm, but she pulled away, then ducked to collect her other bag of stuff.

'I can't believe my dad was right about you.'

And that was it, she moved off to Portishead the very next day.

That's where she should still be.

*

'My girl, my girl,' Jay shouts. 'My little girl.' His voice breaks and his words are no longer audible as he paces about the hallway.

Malachi rises to his feet. 'She came back?' he asks.

The man turns to face Malachi and suddenly lunges, slamming him against a vending machine, the contents rattling inside.

'Hey, hey, hey.' One of the officers rushes over. 'Lads, take it easy.'

At full height Malachi has a few inches on Pamela's dad, as he does with most people, but finds the closeness intimidating.

'You. You. You!' he screams, his white knuckles bunching handfuls of Malachi's shirt.

'Someone stop them,' a voice from the crowd shouts. 'We're all fired up here but this won't help.'

'It's because of you,' he says. 'I was protecting her from you. She needed me to protect her.' His eyes drop down and his body crumples as he falls into Malachi's chest and sobs. 'She's gone. She's gone.'

Pamela's not even meant to be here. Malachi saw her leave, her bags by her feet as she waited for the bus. Right now she's surely feeling the sun burn her pale nose, or having an awkward lunch with her mum and stepdad, or riding the bus to Bristol to see a friend whose shoulder she would cry on about her broken heart. Pamela's not here. She left.

Malachi's shirt becomes wet with her dad's tears. 'I didn't want you to have her. I wanted her to be safe.'

Why is he saying this? Pamela is running along the seafront right now, in her new pink and lilac trainers, her ponytail swinging, her thoughts only on how much she's missed the freedom of running. Malachi needs to believe this image so badly, but her dad's face, the way his body appears broken and shattered, says something else.

'My girl,' he says again.

'Come, let's step outside for a bit.' The officer, his tone now gentle, lays a hand on the man's curled shoulder. He walks him outside, his sobs still audible until the doors slide shut.

She was home. She was in the flat. Alone. He could have got her. Saved her.

Malachi screams, slamming against the vending machine repeatedly till the palms of his hands sting with heat.

'Stop,' someone shouts. 'Malachi, no, stop.'

Blurry faces surround him; a woman pulls her elderly mother closer to her side; a tattooed man puffs his chest up, as if ready to get involved; then a familiar face pushes through the wall of disapproval and fear.

'Malachi, please stop,' Mary says.

CHAPTER TWENTY-THREE

Mary

She's never heard Malachi scream this way, but as soon as she hears it she knows it's him. Quickly, Mary elbows her way through to get close and when she sees his face the twitch in her elbow returns. Something is very wrong.

'Eh? Look at me.' She puts her hand on his cheek and turns him to face her. But his body slowly falls to the floor, hands around his shaved head. She drops with him, distracted by the unwanted presence of the crowd, bystanders to his torment. 'Go away,' she calls. 'Go.'

Malachi looks up. 'Mary?'

'Yes, yes. I am here.' She strokes his face. She feels so many things right now: confusion, relief, but also anxiety. Even as a child Malachi rarely cried. When he was first born Mary didn't even know there was a baby in the flat. So to see him weep in front of so many breaks her heart.

'It's Pamela,' he says. 'She was home.'

Mary shushes him, tries to calm him. 'No, Malachi. She left, remember? You said her dad took her back to her town.'

'No, she came back. I don't know when. I don't know. But she was home, he told me. Why did no one help her? Maybe they couldn't get to her. I couldn't get up the stairs either, I tried, but it was just flames and bricks and rubble and people.'

It's difficult to see Malachi without his composure. There's a ragged edge to his breathing and she fears he will have an asthma attack, the kind he used to have as a child, when his mum would panic and call Mary into the flat.

'Slow down, slow down,' she tells him.

He stops and looks up at the ceiling, pulling his shirt to his face to wipe the tears. He takes a breath and Mary can see he's trying to compose himself.

A police officer comes over and indicates down to Malachi, but Mary gives a little shake of her head, thinking she is probably best placed to bring him back.

'She's dead, Mary.'

Pamela, she was just a girl. She was still at school. She can't be gone. Mary cries, 'I'm so sorry. So, so sorry.'

Malachi's face hardens and he doesn't look at her.

How could this happen to him? Hasn't he already been through enough?

A few hours ago she had encouraged Malachi to forget about the girl, to move onto another, and now that will never happen. She strokes the side of his face again. His skin is hot and he shakes like he has flu. She wants to comfort him, to get down into the deep hole of grief with him for the girl, but there is still too much she doesn't understand about today. She needs to know why Malachi is alone, why Tristan is not hovering close as always.

'Malachi, please.' She takes his hand. 'Where is he?'

Malachi shakes his head.

'No?' She mirrors his actions.

'I can't find him.'

There are flecks of white dust in his eyelashes and she rests a hand on his shoulder to comfort him, but also to steady herself as she balances on her haunches.

'He was on the wall with the others, but then I saw them and not him. I looked for him, I looked and looked. All over the field. I went to the hospital, but he's not there. It's hell there, Mary, so many people are hurt,' he looks up at her, 'dying. No one knew anything. They sent me here.'

The back of his neck is damp with sweat. He smells like Nightingale Point, of smoke and death, but underneath that he smells like Tristan and the overly floral washing powder he uses. She never noticed that the boys smelt the same before, as Malachi, so unlike his tactile brother, rarely let her get close enough.

His weight now bears down on her, it shakes her with each cry. 'I don't know where he is.'

Then, despite her dreams and the twitch in her elbow, she says, 'They will find him.'

*

The two of them sit within a row of plastic chairs in the hall. Both blank-faced and focused only on the doors. But the flow of people seems to be going out rather than in. Many of those, who have now endured hours in the hall, begin to gather in the centre. They give their names and details to an overweight woman with a clipboard. She had introduced herself to Malachi and Mary earlier as 'Tina from the council', in charge of arranging everyone's emergency accommodation for the night. She smiled at them as if this was what they wanted to hear, that a night on a camp bed in a church hall or some bedbug-infested local hostel was the missing component they needed for a good night's sleep.

Mary watches as Tina does a headcount. Some of those in the group beam as they realise their hours stuck in the stale hall have finally come to an end. They make their way eagerly to the exit, some stopping to collect their remaining possessions: a pair of sunglasses folded neatly on a chair, two transparent green swim bags, and a few plastic carriers of spoilt groceries, which leave a wet smear on the ground like a footprint.

A baby, naked apart from a nappy, lets out a strained cry from a few seats down. The father attempts to shush it. 'Sorry,' he says.

'It's okay.' Mary manages to raise a smile as the thin legs kick in the air.

'He's twenty-two weeks. Needs to be fed soon. Can't find my wife.' He states each line as if giving directions, his voice rising along with the baby's wails. 'We went for a walk to the high street. Needed to buy a fan. It was so hot this morning, wasn't it? I don't understand why the plane was flying so low,' he snaps. The baby's fussing increases. 'Shush, shush.' He stands and sways back and forth till the cries die down to a murmur.

'I'm sure she'll be okay,' Mary says.

Harris walks over and puts a cup of tea in Malachi's hand. Mary had watched Malachi earlier as he nervously broke three polystyrene cups into tiny pieces while they tried calling around the hospitals again.

'I can't take this,' she stands up, 'waiting here in this place.'

'Mary,' Harris says, 'this is where he will come.'

'No. We should be out looking for him.'

Malachi remains silent.

'And look where? We have been told a hundred times: everyone needs to come through here at some point. He will have to. He has nowhere else to go. Sit down, please.'

She drops back into the seat, folds and unfolds the leaflet the Salvation Army volunteer gave her: *Call if you need us*. She will never call. She watches as the caretaker from Nightingale Point, still bumbling in his incapability, taps an old lady on her hunched shoulder.

'Camp beds at St Marks,' he says loudly. 'You'll love it. It'll be like the war.'

The old lady gives him a vague nod, before she takes the arm of a volunteer and follows the crowd out of the Arches Leisure Centre.

'Good they found somewhere,' the caretaker announces to no one in particular. He sighs deeply, then surveys those left in the hall, like some captain of a sinking ship he has refused to leave until everyone else has gone. There are now no more than twenty people left, drawn, drained, disturbed.

Mary still can't believe that Tristan has been reduced to a few scribbled notes on a Missing Persons list. No body, no belongings, no home. Tristan Roberts is now just a name, age and description. She closes her eyes and pictures him walking into the hall, cocksure and full of bravado about how he escaped unscathed, how he spent his time saving others from the burning building while she and Malachi sat idly drinking tea.

Malachi still has the cup in his hands, untouched and going cold. Does he feel Tristan is gone? Surely he would know. He would feel it.

Harris, who has kept up dialogue with the woman in the trouser suit organizing the relief effort, walks over to the desk for Nightingale Point where she sits slumped, blazer discarded. He hands her a cup of tea.

'He's from your hospital?' Malachi nods towards Harris.

Mary is relieved to hear to his voice again. 'Yes,' she answers quickly. 'He's my friend.' But of course he's not. Malachi will see through this lie straight away. Stupid old woman.

'These lights are giving me a headache.' He rubs at his eyes. 'How long have we been here?'

Mary takes the watch from her pocket. 'Long. You are getting tired. You need to rest.'

'I'm fine.'

'You are not fine. You need the hospital.'

'I'm fine.'

'What help are you offering sitting here? Go.'

'Where to, Mary? There is nowhere to go,' he says, raising his voice at her. 'Sorry.'

She wants to hold him again, to rub his back, but he seems so closed off.

They turn away from each other and watch as Harris makes a slow return across the hall.

'Right, this is it. They're going to close this centre down for the night.' He puts out a hand for Mary to grab, to help her rise from her seat. 'Malachi, no one else from the estate is being sent here. Come to mine, it's close by, and in the morning I will drive you around the hospitals. By then things will be clearer.'

Malachi looks up at Harris and nods.

As they walk out of the hall Mary notices a stereo pushed up against a wall. The disc blinks on pause and she wonders what was taking place in the room before all this tragedy entered it.

The woman in the suit is being held by one of the last remaining volunteers. The others help to clear the desks of paper and put everything into cardboard boxes, while some stand with their handbags over arms, desperate to escape.

The caretaker pats Mary on the shoulder as she walks by. 'You're all right, love, you're all right.' There are liver spots on his hand, a tremble in his wrist. Mary never noticed him get old. But, of course, he has been on the Morpeth Estate since the first day she arrived. She had collected her keys from his cubbyhole on the ground floor. It was him that talked her through how to use the bin chute and central heating. She wonders if she will ever see him again.

'Mind how you go,' he calls after her.

AFTER

CHAPTER TWENTY-FOUR

Elvis

Elvis has never been in his care worker George's house before. He has been in his car, which he really enjoys because it smells like Aztec, George's Labrador dog, but he has never ever been in the house where George actually lives. He is excited about this and also very glad to be out of the Queen Elizabeth Hospital as he does not like it there, not one little bit. It was busy and noisy. But it was where the kind people from Jade Garden took him after he fell over and fell asleep on the street.

He follows George into a big hallway. On the wall is a huge framed map of the world and a wooden clock from the olden times, which does not have English numbers on it only Roman numbers. Elvis thinks this could be confusing if you are learning to tell the time.

'This way,' George says. He sounds very tired and the skin under his eyes is dark, like a panda, but Elvis does not tell him this because it would sound mean and Elvis is not a mean person. Instead he follows George through to the living room, where there is a familiar voice coming from a television. It is *Breakfast with Susan Hill*. Elvis loves Susan Hill's colourful jackets and the way she says: 'back to the studio'. It is his favourite breakfast time television show. But as soon as they arrive in the living room a woman stands up from a squashy-looking sofa and points the remote control at Susan Hill to switch her off.

'Elvis, this is my wife, Jenny,' George says.

George's wife Jenny is pretty but her eyes are all red and when she sniffs it sounds like she needs to give her nose a good blow. She has soft-looking blonde hair and green eyes, which are sparkly with her tears. This makes Elvis swoon a little as blonde women are his favourite kind of women. He feels his cheeks grow red so he looks away, out of the window to the willow tree in the garden.

'Morning, Elvis,' she says.

Elvis keeps his eyes on the tree. He does not want to look at Jenny the crying wife because he might stare and he knows you should not stare at blonde women just because they are your favourites. You should especially not stare at blonde women who are already married.

'You must both be hungry?' she asks. 'George?'

'No, thanks,' he says.

But Elvis is actually a little hungry and he also really wants to watch *Breakfast with Susan Hill*. He especially wants to watch the weather report, because yesterday it was so hot and he got his outfit wrong at first, wearing a big sweatshirt, until Lina told him to go and put a T-shirt on. Also, on the drive over from the hospital, the clouds looked dark. This worries him because he still has on his sandals, which, although stylish, are not appropriate footwear for rainy days.

'We had a sandwich at the hospital,' George says. 'Think it's best if we both get some sleep. Okay, Elvis?'

Elvis is not okay and he does not understand what George and Jenny the crying wife have decided. He says nothing and watches a blue tit as it lands in the willow tree and begins to sing a song. Elvis knows the names of a lot of different little birds but he will never say blue tit out loud because it makes him laugh and people will think he is a pervert.

'Is the room made up?' George asks.

'Yes.'

Suddenly, Jenny the crying wife puts her arms around Elvis and her head on his shoulder. A wisp of her blonde hair touches his nose. It smells good and feels lovely, but he knows he must not stroke it. Or can he? He is not sure. He is not used to people he has just met hugging him.

'Jenny, please,' George says.

But Jenny the crying wife holds on and it makes Elvis feel nice, nicer than he has felt all morning and all last night and all the day before, which was a horrible and confusing day. Finally, she lets go. Elvis feels like he may fall down again, like he did outside the takeaway.

'I'm sorry, it's just so horrific,' she says. She takes a big sniff and gives her head a little shake, the same way Lina does when Elvis makes a mess in the kitchen or forgets to put on his trousers before he answers the front door.

'Come on,' George says. 'I'll show you where you can sleep.'

Elvis follows him up the stairs, which has photographs of

little children along the wall. Elvis needs to look very closely as he does not have his glasses on as they were lost in the bad explosion yesterday. He has seen these children before, in a photo on George's desk, where they are all wearing blue blazers, white shirts and smiles that look like the kind of smile you make when you have been asked to smile for too long. But these photos are more fun: they are of Christmas time around a table of delicious-looking food and of summertime on a beach in swimsuits and sunhats. Elvis would like to spend some time looking at the photos properly but George is walking super fast and is already at the top of the stairs.

'I'll be down the hall. If you need anything or have any questions knock on my door.' George points out which door is his to knock on and then takes Elvis into a nice lemon-coloured room. It has a double bed in it, big enough for two people, but Elvis is only one person so decides he will sleep diagonally on it so no space is wasted.

'Bathroom is through here. Jenny has left some towels, so have a shower and leave your clothes outside the room. We'll get them washed for you.' George keeps his fingers held over his mouth. 'You've been very quiet. Is there anything you want to ask me?'

Elvis does have a lot of questions, like why can't he watch *Breakfast with Susan Hill*? What is he meant to wear while he waits for his dirty clothes to be cleaned? Why can't he go to his old bedroom at the Waterside Centre? Has someone told Lina where he is? Can he have a chicken sandwich? But instead, he says nothing.

'Okay,' George says, 'remember to try and keep your stitches dry.' He closes the door gently behind himself and

Elvis wants to ask for tips on how to have a shower while keeping the stitches across his forehead dry, but it is too late.

He takes off his sandals and then his shorts, T-shirt and pants. They are very dirty. He opens the bedroom door and throws them, one piece at a time, down the hall. The vomit-covered shorts go far but not as far as the T-shirt, which has nasty brown blood all over the front, and not as far as his pants, which he manages to get all the way to the top of the stairs. He quickly closes the door before anyone can see his naked body. In the shower he watches the water turn from dark grey, to light grey, to bubbly white as he washes himself down with all the lovely products from the little shelf. Grapefruit and Bergamot, Tea Tree and Papaya, Strawberry and Mandarin. It is a very nice shower. The water comes out much faster than his shower at the Waterside Centre and even faster than the water at his perfect flat in Nightingale Point. At first he finds it difficult to shower and keep his head dry at the same time but when he gets out and wipes a clear circle in the steamy mirror he sees that his body is squeaky clean and his forehead, which has a track of tiny string stitches, like Johnny Depp in *Edward Scissorhands*, is still dry.

As he sits naked on the bed he begins to feel very tired. He slept for a little bit last night in the hospital. He had tried to sleep for longer but there was too much noise; a woman kept crying loudly, and even though Elvis asked her what was wrong she didn't talk to him or stop crying. Also, his back hurt, he kept having bad dreams and a lady woke him up several times to tell him off for snoring, even though Elvis never snores.

He is still not sure what happened yesterday. There was an

explosion, a fire. The boy was hurt and Elvis helped him. He wants to ask George what caused the explosion, if he did the right thing by leaving the boy, and what made him fall asleep outside Jade Garden. George would tell him if he asked, but Elvis is a little bit embarrassed as he does not want George to think he was not concentrating.

He remembers going to the hospital in the ambulance. The lights were on but it did not move fast or go through red lights like they do on *Casualty*, the best hospital drama on television after *ER*. This was disappointing.

Elvis wanted to look for the boy last night at the hospital but instead he was made to sit and breathe into a funny machine that made a loud beeping noise. Then he had to have his head stitched up by a doctor, who was grey-haired and handsome like Dr Ross from *ER*, but better than Dr Ross because he was a real doctor, not an actor. Then Elvis had been very busy eating two Mars bars from the vending machine in the corridor. Then George came and Elvis cried. He felt silly after that and worried that he would be sent to Sonia, at the Waterside Centre, to talk about his feelings. Elvis does not like Sonia as she always carries around a big suitcase, which you think will be filled with something good but it is actually filled with ugly puppets she uses to tell stories about emotions.

Elvis knows he has a strong emotion now and it is sadness, like Sonia's blue puppet with the stitched on tears and yellow mouth that looks like an upside-down banana. Elvis feels sad that his perfect home has gone and that he has a big cut on his forehead that stings and that his chest hurts and that the ambulance did not drive fast and that he does not know where Lina is, because even though she is sometimes unkind to him, she is still his friend. He also feels sad that the boy got so badly hurt.

Elvis lies diagonally, as planned, on the double bed. It feels lovely and soft. He is hot but pulls the bed sheet, which has prints of tiny tulips on it, over himself in case someone comes through the door into the lemon-coloured bedroom and sees his penis. He wishes he had pyjamas. He wishes he knew if the boy was okay. Has his foot stopped bleeding so horribly? Does his eye still look like an old, squashed plum?

Elvis yawns and rolls onto his side. There's a lovely fruity smell coming from his body, but it is mixed with the horrible smell of smoke coming from his hair. When he wakes up he will go and knock on George's door down the hall and ask him all the questions he has. But before that he closes his eyes and falls asleep.

CHAPTER TWENTY-FIVE

Mary

The radio is playing a Fleetwood Mac song. David begins to sing along. He grabs Mary's hands, a tea towel in one, the cotton pad she puts in her bra to stop the milk leaking in the other.

'Dance with me.'

The pot is boiling over and Mary knows she has just half an hour left before one of the babies wakes up and steals her time.

'You used to love dancing.' David lets go of one of her hands to turn the radio up. 'Come on, dance with me.'

The washing machine beeps. The load needs to be emptied and pegged on the rope that goes across the small balcony.

'You never dance with me anymore.' He looks wounded, hurt. His first time home in weeks and his own wife has no time for him, no energy.

She catches her reflection in the kitchen window: the outline of her young face, hair pulled back, small body still swollen and saggy from carrying the babies.

'Why do I bother asking you?' he sulks. 'I'm going to the snooker club. I'll leave you to it.'

Relief. The front door closes gently, but as if the babies know their dad has gone again, they both wake up crying.

*

5.26 a.m.

Mary sits up in bed. The sheets are damp and the room filled with a harmony of birdsong, which feels baleful this morning. The curtain was not pulled all the way last night and the visible strip of overcast sky is at odds with the sticky, heavy heat she feels.

David. Where is David? She counts back to when she thinks he left the message yesterday, trying to calculate the hours of the flight between Hong Kong and London. Eight hours? Nine? Twelve, maybe? The last time she made the journey home to the Philippines was over two decades ago and then, with the twins sulking teenagers on either side of her, the flight had felt endless.

David. He never arrived yesterday. It was common for him to do this, though, to leave Manila one day, arrive in London ten days later. It was typical of him to go missing in transit. No one else knew he was coming. She had not told the children. In the back of her mind she still had that thing of not wanting to get their hopes up about their dad arriving home, especially Julia. Though for John, recently, the relationship with his father had changed. The last time David was home, John passed by as if ticking a box. Refusing to remove his jacket or eat, he stood against the kitchen counter, watching the clock on the oven before rushing off to do an errand.

Mary wipes the sweat off her body with the sheet and shuffles her legs to the side of the bed. She feels exhausted. Her sleep had been patchy and she remembers waking frequently through the night, seeing each hour pass until it was no longer the day the plane came, but the morning after. Harris always slept like his life had expired and no amount of her shuffling and twitching seemed to rouse him, for which she was grateful.

Her feet touch the rug and she tries to indulge herself in the thought that maybe it was not real. Perhaps it was just one of her dreams, another night time ordeal. But she can't ignore the change in atmosphere, the unpleasant lingering smell of smoke and syrupy aftertaste of the madeleine cake Harris made her eat at the relief centre. Her uniform is crumpled; she strokes the creases from it before the stench makes her drop it to the floor.

Harris stirs and she has an urge to get away from him, to be alone with her thoughts and figure out what to do next. From the wardrobe she pulls out one of his work shirts and the pair of navy jogging bottoms he bought her in the winter.

She creeps into the living room, embraces one of the Indian elephant cushions for comfort and pulls the telephone onto her lap. It does not even complete a full ring before being picked up.

'Julia?'

'Mum!' she screams. 'Do you have any idea what you've put us through?'

The phone sounds as if it has been dropped on the other end and Mary's son shouts in the background. He comes on the line. 'Are you okay? We've been going crazy with worry.'

She is suddenly too confused to speak. Why are the twins awake and together at this hour?

'Why didn't you call us back?' he shouts at her. 'One call, Mum. One. Then nothing.'

'I'm sorry. You don't under—'

'Where the hell are you? We've had no way of getting hold of you. I called that relief centre and nothing. No one has a clue what's going on. You just disappeared.' He shouts at her again, her own son, frantic and hysterical.

Julia is in the background now, shrieking the phrases: 'complete panic' and 'up all night'. They are within their rights to be angry. She feels guilty for putting them through it, the worry they must have felt, but she wasn't thinking. She wasn't able to think.

'I went round all the bloody church halls and community centres last night looking for you,' John continues. 'Julia called everyone. Where are you?'

'I'm with a friend.'

Mary can hear one of her grandbabies, the pitiful, stressed cry of a child woken before it's ready. Should she mention David? How can she bring him up? She would not even know what to say.

'It's all over the news. The footage,' John exhales loudly, 'it looks terrifying.' He sniffs into the phone and for a moment it sounds as if he's walked away. 'Where are you? I'm coming to get you.'

Mary does not want that, for her son to run over and save

her, to see her secret life. There are so many things she needs to get straight in her own head first.

'I am close by. I will get the bus.'

'Bus? No.' He sounds paranoid, as if everything is now a threat. 'No way. Give me the address.'

'It's fine, John. I will come now.'

'The address, Mum. Please.'

Harris stands in the doorway, his flamboyant gold and green dressing gown pulled around his reedy body.

Mary closes her eyes as she tells her son the address of the bungalow.

'I'm leaving now,' John says.

They hang up and Mary searches for how she will explain to her children what she is doing here, with a man neither of them knows about.

Harris walks towards the sofa, his face creased from sleep. 'Was that the hospital?'

She shakes her head.

He sits down next to her and pulls the phone from her lap. 'We should call that emergency line again. It's been several hours. They may have some news.' He uses that bright tone of his, the tenor of a man used to telling everyone everything will be okay.

Mary pictures how David could effortlessly sleep on flights. Seat reclined, mouth open to reveal the extensive NHS dental treatment he took advantage of every time he returned to the UK. Is he flying now? Or is he still waiting in a terminal somewhere? He used to treat layovers like mini holidays, binging on American fast food and flicking through *Sports Illustrated* in the newsagents, poring over young girls in bikinis. How can she not know where he is? Her own husband.

In all those dreams that plague her, those terrible, sweat-drenched nightmares, David never features. In them it's always something terrible happening to her neighbours, to strangers, to her own children, and to Malachi and Tristan. Never David. So why does she feel the weight of dread now sink in her stomach? Like a rock. She thinks of all the double shifts she accepted the last time David was in London. How she would rather work till her feet swelled and eyes stung with tiredness than spend a night lying next to him.

'I forgot about David,' she says to Harris.

His face clouds. 'He's in Hong Kong.'

'Yes.' The rock sinks further, deeper into the pit of her stomach. 'Of course he is.'

There have been so many times over the years David has left her messages to say he was getting on the next flight to London. How rarely he showed up when he said he would. But this time he *was* in Hong Kong. Where did he go from there? Maybe there was a woman he needed to spend a night with. *A floozy at the side of each stage.*

'Mary?' Harris takes her hand.

But she can't let him hold it. 'I need to go. My son is coming. I will wait outside.'

'Mary, did David have the keys to the flat?'

'I gave them to Malachi.' What does this mean? She can't think clearly for she is too overwhelmed by worries that can't be dealt with by simply following the advice of a chat show host like she used to. 'The only person who would know if he collected them is Tristan,' her voice wavers, 'and we can't find him.'

She raises her head and looks into the room where so many secret hours have been spent. It looks cold and lifeless today, washed in a milky grey light as the sun struggles to rise.

'I can't stay here.' Her legs wobble as she stands.

'Everything is very uncertain at the moment. Let's just stop and wait.'

At the front door she pulls on her plimsolls, spoilt with splashes of brown tea, a spray of rust-coloured blood. Her eyes settle on the curled photograph leant against the rubber plant, the image of them both outside St Augustine's Abbey during their first weekend away in Canterbury. How could she do it? Be that woman who smiled at the camera while allowing a man who was not her husband to put his arm around her? How could she look so happy and carefree, as if she was not betraying everyone in her family?

She opens the front door but Harris pushes it closed.

'Let me go.'

'You can't walk out like this. What about Malachi?'

It breaks her heart to hear his name, to know she is leaving him, but for once she needs to do the right thing. 'Please, look after him for me. I don't want him to be alone. But I can't be there for him, not now.' She wipes the tears from her face as the front door opens. A dark plume of smoke in the sky catches her attention as she begins to walk to the mouth of Vanbrugh Close, where she sits and waits for her son to take her away.

CHAPTER TWENTY-SIX

Malachi

He lies awake in the darkness. His eyes are drawn to the weak line of light that seeps in around the blind. Daylight? He can't face it. Not yet. An ache spreads across his body as he rolls onto his side. From under the door there's the gentle chat of voices, a radio, perhaps, or television. It flows in with the light and urges him to get up. Malachi can't think of the last morning he woke up on his own rather than from Tristan as he rapped to himself in front of a mirror or slammed doors in the flat as he walked about in search of his school uniform.

He pulls himself up and tugs the cord on the slat blinds. On the wall are two photos of the Kremlin in the snow, washed in blue light. Above the bed is a shelf crowded with thin books and ring binders labelled with phrases vaguely familiar from school: *Battle of the Somme, Britain 1905–1951, People & Poverty.*

His socks are crusted into the shape where they lay over his wet shoes. His mouth is dry, his teeth furry. But he's glad he managed to sleep, and is thankful that Mary's friend, Harris, had driven him to a twenty-four hour chemist to get a packet of sleeping pills. Malachi had been using them since he was tall enough, to pass for old enough, to buy them. Last night he needed them more than ever.

The hallway is plant-filled, crowded with old brown furniture, knick-knacks and wide bowls of potpourri – the kind of clutter Tristan would itch to sift through. It leads to a main room where Harris sits at a small wooden table, one hand curled around a mug. His face points towards the ceiling, as if listening attentively to some beautiful piece of music rather than a radio news report. Phrases jump out at Malachi: 'major incident declared', 'PM said', 'damaged wing fuel tank', 'complex rescue operation'. He tries to block it out. He wants to get Harris's attention but can think of no morning greeting that suits the situation. Finally, Harris must feel his presence and looks over, startled, as if he forgot Malachi was still in the house. He clears his throat. 'Mary has left. She needed to go and see her children.'

Malachi nods, glad Tristan is not here to feel the sting of being reminded that Mary, despite her relentless doting on them, does have children of her own.

'When is she coming back?' he asks, surprised that she left without speaking to him.

'I'm not sure. Her children are quite distressed.' Harris is not an old man but his long, thin arms and tired eyes give him a frail look, almost sickly. 'I have called the emergency line several times this morning, but it's a mess. They didn't even have Tristan on their lists, though your name seems to appear three times with three different spellings.' He shakes his head. 'I'm sorry, Malachi. There is no news.'

Malachi gasps as he catches sight of the clock. 'It's after seven. I can't believe I slept so late. I need to go.'

'The hospitals are advising against people showing up. They will send you to one of their so-called victim relief centres. It's sounds more chaotic this morning than yesterday afternoon.' Harris furrows his brow. 'Stay here, please. We've given this number – this is where they'll call when there's news.'

News. Malachi's not sure what kind of news he's waiting on. 'I can't just sit here.'

That's what he did yesterday, while Pamela's dad was locking her in the flat, he was sitting in the café, their café, thinking about all the things he should have said to her, to her dad, all the things that could have possibly saved her.

'Malachi? You don't look well,' Harris says. 'Please stay.'

'I need to find my brother.'

'I understand.' Harris scribbles something on an envelope. 'Here, this is my address and phone number. I will stay in *all day*. If you can get to a phone box, check in with me every few hours. Come back when you're ready.'

Malachi roughly folds the paper and has to try three times to get it into the pocket of his crushed and filthy trousers.

Harris's home is smaller from the outside than he noticed last night. It sits within a close, each bungalow lined with rose bushes. Malachi doesn't really know where he is. But beyond the immediate buildings he sees the two towers of the estate, fully formed and ugly, and next to them a thick trail of dark grey smoke oscillating to the left in the skyline. A shiver passes up his back as he realises he must walk towards it. The smoke pulls him like a magnet through a series of unfamiliar roads and streets, until he recognises one of the long residential roads that lead to the thin end of the green in front of the estate. A cool drizzle begins, mist-like. Pamela would have said it's the kind of rain you don't notice until you find yourself soaked. Even so, the warmth of yesterday hangs in the air and Malachi sweats in his unwashed clothes as he steps onto the green. He passes the pond, bits of paper floating on its top next to rubbish and several large foil blankets. They look like the tinfoil boats he used to make as a kid.

The grass is patchy and flattened, as if it hosted a large crowd for something celebratory, like a concert or funfair, not an evacuation. As he gets closer to the estate there is a sound typical of Sunday mornings: church songs. A large group of women in head wraps gather around a bench, some stand with their palms to the sky, others with closed eyes in tear-soaked faces, their song far from joyful.

Malachi steps over a plastic line of police tape, ripped and discarded. Officers stand on the edge of the green and talk among themselves. Occasionally one breaks away from the conversation to remind the line of media to move back.

'Away from the scene, please,' one of them calls, as if herding excitable girls from a celebrity.

There are so many people, traumatised, tired and shocked. But there are also heavily made-up women with blow-dried hair and men in boxy blazers and ties, here to pick at the bones of whatever is left of the burnt-out and destroyed building. They stand with their backs to the estate and talk into cameras in English, in French, in German, in a raft of different languages and accents. Last night at the relief centre people had complained about the flash of cameras at the exit doors, the persistent whir of news helicopters above and the worry that photos of their lost loved ones would appear on the news. Should he be worried about Tristan? That a photo of him will appear on a television screen somewhere?

An angry shout cuts through the crowd and Malachi pushes his way forward to see the dreadlocked man who yesterday tried to save him in the stairwell. He has on the same paint-splattered clothes, but there is a white bandage at his elbow.

'Kill them all,' he shouts as he prowls up and down and spits on the grass. 'You don't see this happening in Westminster. In Hampstead.' He stops and looks at Malachi without recognition. 'Crash the plane onto the poor. Say it's an accident. A technical failure. It's okay, no one will miss them.'

The inferno is no more, but huge, clear rainbows of water remain directed at the building. Firefighters, weary and oblivious to the crowds that watch them work, battle to put out the unseen blaze that must still live within the shell of Nightingale Point. Two firefighters return to their engine, faces drawn and blackened.

A man fusses with a video camera, while a journalist in a green dress reads to him from a pad of paper. Her eyes light up as Malachi passes. He drops his head low as he realises how worn he must look, how obvious a victim in his grass-stained trousers, torn at the knees and crushed from being slept in. Her energy almost pulls him in, her enthusiasm to be able to report on something other than the muggings and community centre closures that usually emanate from this area.

The last time the news crews came to the estate, after a series of robberies on the green, Tristan had been so pleased with himself that he managed to get in the background of all their footage. Smiling and throwing up some gang signs he saw in a Snoop Dogg video.

The woman in the yellow headscarf is here, the one who fainted at the relief centre. She looks distraught and Malachi gives her a wide berth, not wanting to invade her grief. A man he vaguely identifies from awkward encounters in the lift stands by her. Who have they lost?

A teenage girl becomes frustrated as she struggles to peel the price label off a bunch of hurriedly bought supermarket flowers. A well-dressed photographer circles the singing women and clicks away, keen to capture their grief. The journalist in the green dress approaches the crying woman and her husband, moving with caution and confidence.

Malachi needs to get away, he needs to find Tristan. Quickly he ducks under the cordon and walks onto Sandford Road, which is covered with smouldering craters and littered with pieces of twisted, unrecognisable metal. There are also items that once had a life in a home, with a family: a red plastic toy box slightly charred on one side; a roasting tin, blackened by a lifetime of Sunday lunches and the fire; the door of a fridge, splattered with sauces and inexplicably still holding a large fizzy drink bottle; a teddy bear; a toaster; and a highchair half melted. Everywhere the remnants of people's lives are ripped open and thrown around. How could this stuff, this household crap that no one will miss, survive to see another day? Yet so many people haven't?

He finds himself looking for something of hers, something

he can take, to prove that she was once real. It's stupid; he knows he's being stupid.

At the relief centre last night there had been so much talk from those who had just left their flat or missed their usual bus home. Countless tales from people who cheated death because they needed a pint of milk or a package picked up from the local post office. They had all been saved by something and were happy to brag about it, to shout their tales of good fortune while others waited for news of their dead.

'Hey.' A police officer waves over to him. 'Get back.'

Malachi scatters back under the line quickly, unwilling to draw attention to himself. He knew Tristan would not be here, so he is unsure why he came or what he is looking for. Maybe he just needed to see it for himself.

The group of trees the council planted last spring have been scorched and stripped naked of their summer leaves. Last week he scolded Tristan for using the white bark of them to stub his spliff out on. They look grey; a film of powdery grey dust coats the wood. Surely dead now. He turns away from them and walks back onto the field, towards the benches. Looking, looking, looking. What else can he do? Go back to that stranger's bungalow and sleep? That only happened last night because Malachi had no energy for anything else; he knew Pamela was gone and also he truly believed Tristan would turn up there. Knocking on the door in the middle of the night, accompanied by a police officer he would have built up camaraderie with on the drive over. Why didn't he turn up there? Where is he?

Malachi has to find him. Looking after his little brother is all he knows. His memories don't stretch back further than being five and visiting Tristan, who was born six weeks early, in the hospital. Malachi was used to seeing babies, but none as small as the one his mum cried over that day. In those first few years Malachi was always on the side lines, watching and waiting for Mum to ask for his help so he could step in and do things properly. Like check the temperature of the bottle, so Tristan's tongue wouldn't be scalded, or wash his school shirts, because he's always been fussy about the whiteness of his clothes. Mum was never calm, always frantic with anxiety over something. If she was alive now she wouldn't be able to cope with this situation, with not knowing. That's why eventually it made sense for Malachi to take charge of things, to shop for and make the food, to book the doctor's appointments and get himself and Tristan to and from school every day. Mum couldn't deal with it. Even when Nan moved in to help them, she worked so much that the duties still fell to Malachi, or maybe he just claimed them. He never thought about his role that much. He just got on with it.

'Tris, you need to learn to do this stuff yourself,' Malachi told him once. 'I'm not going to be here to tie up your laces all the time.' He was off to secondary school that September and it was playing on his mind that Tristan would be left alone in primary without him.

They sat in the school reception and waited for Mum to pick them up. She was late again. The school used to let him take Tristan home by himself, but had started keeping them in so they could check up on Mum. He hated waiting there, the way the secretary would continuously check the time, the knowledge of being the last kids in school, the smell of coffee and photocopier ink. Tristan kept getting up to look around, until Miss Hunt gave him a pot of pencils to sharpen, saying, 'The devil makes work for idle hands.'

Finally Mum arrived, oblivious to the time. 'Got you both something.' She pulled two packs of Quavers crisps from the big pocket of her duffle coat and handed one to Malachi, then knelt down in front of Tristan and asked, 'Did you stay out of trouble today?'

He nodded and grabbed at the bag, from which the air had been squeezed, leaving it flat.

'The Head would like to see you,' Miss Hunt said then. 'Leave the boys here, I'll watch them.'

Mum disappeared into the office to have another one of her 'supportive meetings'. When she finally came out, storming back through reception, her face was puffy and she was too angry to acknowledge them. They followed her home in silence, Tristan jogging to keep up.

'Those bloody teachers always think they can tell me what to do. How to raise my kids,' she shouted as they approached the tower of darkened flats. Nightingale Point looked its most unfriendly at dusk.

Tristan ran ahead to call the lift.

'If you'd stay out of trouble they wouldn't be on me so much,' she shouted at him. 'Why can't you be a bit more like your brother? Bet those teachers don't even have kids themselves. What do they know about how hard it is to do this alone?'

It was cold in the flat so they kept their coats on and Malachi made tea, watching Mum the whole time in case she lashed out. But she was too tired for that so sat on her mattress, fiddling with the string of Christmas lights that had stopped working.

'Why are they broken now?' Tristan sulked.

Mum threw the lights to the ground and laid her head on the pillow.

Malachi put a tea in front of her. 'They're just lights.'

She stared past him and said, not for the first time, 'I can't do this. It's too hard.'

'You're doing fine, Mum.'

'No.' The blank look was always the worst; he could reach her when she was in a rage or crying fit, but not when she checked out like that. She was unreachable.

'The teachers are right. I can't look after you two.'

It was true, but also it didn't matter because he could. It was always his role. He didn't know how to be anything else.

*

The rain picks up and the crowd of onlookers begin to disperse, apart from the most distraught of family members and macabre of voyeurs. The news crews retreat to their cars and vans. The sliding door of one remains open and inside a heavily made-up woman sits shoeless and laughs with a cameraman over polystyrene boxes of chips.

The woman in the yellow headscarf and her husband pass the bench. The man nods at Malachi, his shirt darkened and slick from the rain.

Malachi sits on the bench and waits for an answer.

His name is called by a voice he doesn't recognise and for a split second he imagines it's Pamela's dad, come to tell him that he's made a mistake, that she wasn't really in the flat and had gone back to Portishead after all.

'Malachi?'

Coming towards him is Harris, the man he never knew existed until yesterday. His hair has been pushed off his large sun-kissed forehead and Malachi catches a flash, in that way you sometimes do, of what someone looked like when they were young.

'So glad I found you.' He leans forward and puts his hands on Malachi's knees before he says, 'They found him. They found Tristan.'

TEN DAYS LATER

CHAPTER TWENTY-SEVEN

Tristan

Saying you hate hospital is kind of like saying Glenn Hoddle is a poor choice for England manager or Tupac is the greatest rapper alive. It's just a given. So Tristan knows it's weird that he actually *likes* hospitals, that they make him feel comforted and even calm. The Queen Elizabeth Hospital in particular makes him feel warm inside. It's where his mum went to get happy and medicated, and where Malachi spent a week after the asthma attack brought on by his Year Ten sports day. That was probably the closest they ever got to a holiday. Nurses snuck them bowls of rhubarb crumble and they had access to all the leftover chocolate on people's bedside tables. Tristan still can't believe there are people out there who don't eat coffee creams. They even got away with streaming down the corridors in a wheelchair before a porter caught them and called them both 'little fuckers'. That was hilarious.

He's in hospital now. It dawned on him a while back, as he lay on his back, tuning into the regular beeps, some near, some far, and the soft sound of wheels on lino. That smell, too – distinctive and clean.

What Tristan isn't sure of is how long he's been here. Hours? Days? Weeks? He knows he was attacked. Jumped in the stairwell. Though he doesn't remember much of it. He was thrown from behind and knocked out before he could fight. He would've fought, too, if only he had the chance. Gone out Tony Montana style, throwing punches left, right and centre. But now he's stuck, unable to move or talk. Man, this is some Christopher Reeve shit.

Where the hell was Malachi when Tristan was getting his arse kicked in the stairwell? Not that Malachi can fight, but still. Thank God that retard from the tenth floor was there. Tristan's sure of it. The big ginger guy with the Elvis Presley T-shirt. He scared off the attackers and helped Tristan get away.

But there was a fire too, for some reason, he's sure of it. It doesn't make sense. It's so confusing.

'Olisa, if you change the dressing then I'll do this, okay.'

'Yes. Looking good today.'

And all these people talking around him all the time, *blah blah blah*. Definitely nurses. He's never been able to work out why but they do love to go on. Like Mary. Guess they've got a captive audience. Though he can't hear it all. It's his left side that's the issue. There's some kind of warm thickness over his head, which is muffling the sound.

'Is he from the plane crash?' a voice above him whispers. London accent, bit common.

'Yes. Pass that to me.' This is the Nigerian nurse, her name's Olisa; she wears too much perfume and is always humming something irritating like a Celine Dion or Phil Collins song.

'Freaks me out. A plane just crashing like that. I don't get it. You expect that kind of stuff to happen somewhere like Iran or Africa. Not in the UK,' says the common nurse. 'Poor kid.'

'Why are you feeling sorry for him? He survived a plane crash.' Nigerian nurse breaks into the chorus of 'Because You Loved Me', which, to his shame, Tristan knows some of the words to.

But what are they going on about? Plane crash?

He keeps thinking of the crystal angel Mary used to hang from her curtains; it would catch the light and turn it into beams of purple, orange and green that would shoot off across the room. He's not sure if she still has it, he hasn't been in her flat in months now. She's always working or running errands or hanging out with her new friends from the hospital, whoever they are. Maybe she's got a bit on the side, that would explain why she's not spending so much time with him anymore, and why she's started wearing her hair down. He's not sure if she's come to visit him yet, he hasn't heard her voice. Maybe he was asleep when she came; he sleeps a lot at the moment. She'll be well pissed that he got himself attacked. Probably now stressing about gang warfare on the estate and talking about how she dreamt this was going to happen in one of her weird, creepy dreams, which are never about anything good.

Each time Tristan wakes up and smells the antiseptic it makes him think she's here. That it's one of those summer holiday afternoons and he's just arrived at the hospital to pester her to take an early lunch with him. To sit in the patients' garden and feed him whatever food she packed into her blue-lidded plastic tubs. He loved those days. Even though she would lecture him on finding something else to do with his weeks off and suggest ridiculous things, such as going to a 'Teenagers Read-A-Thon' at the local library or the summer camp at church. But really, he could tell she enjoyed their lunches together. What with David still peddling his crappy Abba act around the Philippines and her own children grown up and gone, Mary was sometimes a bit lonely. Tristan felt the same way too, especially when Malachi had to do all-nighters at the library or was shacked up with Blondie. So Tristan didn't mind getting the bus over to the hospital for lunch and sometimes waiting for Mary to come off shift, sitting in the hallway watching as the same woman in labour walked around and around for hours.

Oh shit. Tristan hopes he's not wearing one of those nasty hospital gowns, with his arse hanging out. That would be proper embarrassing. Especially when his visitors come by. They don't need to see him dressed like that. Despite Mary being a no-show, there have been loads of visitors. Like his boys from Barton Point. ('It's like he's dead, man. This is nuff weird.') His form tutor from school. ('Don't think this will get you out of doing your Maths GCSE next summer. I'm still expecting that A from you.') And the girl with the red weave from youth club. ('He's still fit, though.') He hopes he didn't get a semi when she visited. Now that would be shameful.

There have been a few weird visits too. From some brer who speaks like a kid but with a man's voice. He comes often and talks about the same boring stuff over and over again, like which tinned pie is the nicest, why Margate is the best seaside in the world and how to care for a tomato plant. Tristan zones out.

'Morning.' It's Malachi. The voice Tristan hears the most.

This time Tristan will ask him, find out what happened for real. He's ready to hear all the gory details of his attack. A chair is pulled up beside the bed. Tristan can feel Mal sit close but the smell is unfamiliar, like Indian food. Is that what Mal is doing with his time? Hanging out in curry houses? Probably back with Blondie.

A trolley rolls by and stops at the end of the bed. Water is poured. Papers rustled.

Tristan opens his eyes. Well, eye. The left one is still strapped down. Everything looks a bit blurry at first and he hopes his sight isn't messed up because glasses are not a look he will be able to pull off. It's all a bit hazy, but slowly the ceiling come into focus: white, grey piping, strip light. He manages to roll his head to one side. But shit. Mal's face. Huge dark bags under his eyes, his hair grown out of the carefully shaved lines Tristan put in for him the day before the attack. He looks like a proper hobo. This is exactly why he struggles to hook up with hotter girls, despite being all-right-looking. The hair on his face has grown too, more than Tristan has ever known it to. For a moment Tristan freaks out that he's waking from some sort of long coma and Mal is now an old man.

Mal squints at a clipboard, then returns it to the edge of the bed. He wipes his face in that stressed way he always does, sniffs, and then looks at something in the distance. He's got on a bright blue T-shirt, which looks terrible, because for some reason Mal just can't pull off wearing colours. He looks uncomfortable in it too, like when middle-aged women wear short skirts because they feel young inside and still have good legs but it looks wrong.

Tristan hears the words he wants to say in his head, but when he speaks his voice is someone else's. Husky. Dry. Quiet. But at least it doesn't sound that mashed up, not like Rocky or anything.

He tries again. Mal doesn't even respond.

Then, 'You still heartbroken, Romeo?'

Mal turns and looks at Tristan like he's seen a ghost. His head drops to the bed and he begins to cry onto the sheets.

Another set of feet walk close by and stop, but Tristan can't see who it is. Please keep walking. He doesn't want them to see his brother's tears. Crying is private. It's between the two of them, in their own rooms at night before falling asleep. Or for those Sunday afternoons when the distraction of TV or football or computer games isn't enough and their mum's absence feels like a weight that can only be acknowledged with tears. Crying is private. But what Mal is doing now is full-on, no-shame, snot-bubble crying in front of everyone. What's his problem? Nan had asked Tristan recently if Mal ever cried, her curiosity about her oldest grandchild's mental state pressed in between questions about if they were eating a diet more varied than fish fingers and baked beans, and if they were getting their correct benefits.

Tristan wants to put his hand on Mal's big tuft of hair and tell him it will be okay, but he can't because Mal's got his bony, but surprisingly heavy, arm on the bed and it's too weighty to move.

A woman in a bright purple dress comes over. She starts to speak but Tristan's too confused to understand what she's saying. Then he realises it's the doctor. Like a real doctor dressed as a Parma Violet. Since when do they not wear white coats?

'Malachi, please,' she says, and he gets out the way for her. He stands by the curtain, eyes and nose running freely, no shame, no attempt to sort himself out. What the hell is wrong with him?

Then two nurses come over. Tristan recognises the perfume of the Nigerian nurse, Olisa, as she leans over him. She's way younger than he imagined and definitely flirting with him.

'Did they get them, Mal?' he asks.

Malachi smiles, then shakes his head questioningly. 'Tris? You're all right. Don't talk, take it easy.'

'But did they get them? The police? Did they catch who attacked me?'

He shakes his head again and says, 'Just get some rest.'

*

Tristan's been awake for days now and no matter how many times he hears it, he still can't remember the doctor's name. He keeps wanting to say Dr Gonorrhoea, but there's no way that's right.

'It's common. How you're feeling.' She leans over the bed and flicks some switches behind his head.

'So you keep telling me.' He studies her closely but she doesn't even wear an ID badge on her red and yellow blouse. She starts rattling on about allowing things to come back to him slowly and he wishes she would go and put on a white coat so he could take her seriously. It's like going to McDonalds and someone in a tracksuit makes your quarter pounder – it just don't look right.

'There's no rush to try and remember everything at once,' she says.

He nods. 'I know, I know.'

'Take your time, you're doing great. It's a process, Tristan.'

She keeps giving him the same lecture as Malachi. *Allow your memory to come back in its own time. Don't push yourself. Blah blah blah.* But Tristan knows himself. He knows that once he wraps his head around what happened, he will be able to get himself back on track. It's not amnesia or anything; he's just a bit blurry on the details. Ten days is a lot of time to lose. And the reason he can't remember the doctor's name is because it has like fifteen letters.

'You have my stuff?' he asks her.

She picks up a carrier bag from the floor. 'Your clothes were damaged in A&E. This was all we had left.'

The bag is small – definitely no Nikes in there. So it *was* a robbery then. Someone fucked him up this much for a pair of trainers. He sighs heavily.

'Those trainers, man, fresh on last month and now gone. You think I'm shallow, don't you?'

'No, not at all. You'd be surprised by how fiercely patients demand their things back.' She leans closer and stage whispers, 'Especially the bikers.' She thrusts the bag forward. 'I know you think seeing your things will help you piece together the *incident*, but know there's a chance it may not.'

'Thank you.'

'No problem, Tristan. I will be right over there if you need me. Take your time.'

He opens it up and, surprisingly, there's one of his trainers, but in a real state. There's a smaller bag with his cubic zirconia stud earring and a long white piece of paper, crusted and hard, like it's been through a washing machine. It says *Malachi* on the front in faded blue pen, the i dotted with a loop. Typical girl's handwriting. Pamela's handwriting.

Then, clear as anything, he sees blue ice pole on a white T-shirt, smells toilet bleach in a sink and hears the phone in his flat ringing. He leans back on the bed. His ribs hurt. He swallows the thin saliva that has gathered in his mouth. He feels dizzy as the memories start coming back, a bunch of jumbled up images, sounds and smells, all hitting him, one after another. The letter falls onto his lap as pins and needles run down his arms and into his fingertips.

He had spoken to Pamela on the phone about something, then saw David and gave him the keys to the flat. But then he remembers being in the stairwell. Why? It was something to do with Pamela. He'd gone up to the eleventh floor to see her, for some reason. The flat was dark. The carpets were kind of brown and tattered. He didn't go inside. She had no keys or was in trouble or something.

He looks at his trainer again, spotted with dirt and blood. It's for the right foot. Tristan looks down his hospital bed at his left leg raised high and rolled in bandages. He wasn't attacked. There was an explosion. There was an explosion near Pamela's flat. Or in Pamela's flat. Did she escape? Did the guy in the Elvis T-shirt help her too? He was so strong. Tristan remembers being picked up and thrown over the guy's shoulder. But why would he have done that? Tristan was a dick to him earlier. It doesn't make sense at all. But there definitely was some kind of explosion. It must have burst his eardrum and something fucked up his eye too.

Tristan lifts the letter to his face; it smells of smoke and damp washing. He promised he would never read it. He didn't read it. Or did he? It doesn't look sealed. But it's in such a state, yellow and all dried up, it's hard to tell if it was ever opened. But if he didn't read it then how come he knows what it says? And where is Pamela now? Something happened in the flats, something really bad.

CHAPTER TWENTY-EIGHT

Mary

A tense group line the wooden benches in the hallway of the town hall. They are the mums and dads, brothers and sisters, friends and neighbours, the bereaved and waiting. There are several doors along the hallway, each one labelled with a handwritten sign: *Housing, Counselling, Financial Advice.* Each one hopes to offer a solution to a different problem brought on by the accident. But the door Mary and her children wait outside is simply identified with a number two.

John stands flat against the wall, as if he feels the need to anchor himself to something solid, while Julia taps her heavy foot continuously against the floor.

Mary wonders who would have come here to hear if Tristan had died in the building? Who was there, other than Malachi, to witness the news? Their nan must be in pieces about everything, but Mary can't bear to call her, just like she can't bear to see Tristan wired up to machines in a hospital bed.

Malachi had called Julia's house the other night but Mary

was too distraught to talk to him. Her guilt won't allow it. She knew something was going to happen that day, she had felt it ever since she woke up, yet she didn't stop them from getting hurt.

'It's almost three,' John whispers. The strip light casts dark shadows under his eyes. He went to work this morning, put on his suit and too much aftershave, and drove in for a half day at the office. Said he needed a distraction.

Julia leans forward to confirm the time against the slow ticking clock at the end of the hall, before she huffs and stretches out her gangly arms. Mary has never truly understood what made her children, who were both born frighteningly underweight, so much larger than the rest of the family. David blamed it on all the white bread Mary fed them. Bread with chocolate spread, with jam, with peanut butter, and after long shifts on the ward, bread topped with a fried egg and ketchup for dinner. 'The kids back home don't look like this,' David told her once when he returned home to find that thirteen-year-old John was taller than him. But David wasn't there; he didn't have to put up with the children turning their noses up at the foods from back home, while begging Mary to buy potato waffles and turkey drummers.

'I can hear movement inside,' Julia says. Her face is covered in a heavy layer of make-up, but underneath it she looks tired. 'They're coming out.' Tiny lines crack the powder around her mouth.

The door opens and a lady with a long fringe and big glasses steps out. She looks down the hallway and nods at Mary. 'Mrs Tuazon? Would you please come through?'

Mary places her small hands either side of her thighs to

grip the bench. She's floating, it's like she's not really here at all. It's time to enter room number two and get the news she came to hear.

John puts a hand on her back. 'We're going in together.'

If only she could go in alone, and hear the cold and official declaration of David's death without her children listening in. She doesn't want them to hear it like this, she wants to tell them herself, to package up the news and present it back softly to them. *Your father has passed away. Your father didn't make it. Your father is in a better place.*

'This way,' the woman says. Her eyes are amplified by her glasses and Mary feels they can see straight through her, that she has no right to mourn this man she was betraying right up until the moment of his death. 'Please take a seat.'

The people around the table introduce themselves. There is a police officer; a nodding wrinkled woman, from family support; someone from the council, an officiator of some sort. So many faces. Mary does not understand why they all need to be here, why this exchange has to be made so social.

'Mrs Tuazon,' the big-eyed woman begins, 'you know why we are here.'

But it's not true. Mary still can't understand why her husband, who spends so much time on the other side of the world, has been killed on her doorstep. Even after family back in Manila confirmed driving him to the airport and Air China confirmed that David Tuazon was one of their passengers to London that morning, it was still difficult to believe.

Mary tries to take herself away, to somewhere else, somewhere silent where the woman's words can't reach her. She places herself back home, in the yard of her childhood, and listens for the laugh of the cicadas and snap of branches as her neighbours make fires. But the smell of coffee and her son's sharp aftershave pull her back into the room. The others around the table begin to talk, and phrases manage to sink through Mary's resolve. 'What they have found is a certain match for your husband.' 'Now you can start the process.' 'We are here to support you in all areas.' The woman with the glasses leads the chorus; she talks with her hands and moves a white mug of coffee about as part of her gestures. The coffee looks cold; she must have been sitting in this room for hours, giving out the same news. Death after death.

'In cases like this, even the smallest amount of remains can be enough to get a positive identification. Your husband had dental records here, blood samples.'

It has been thirteen days since the plane crash. Thirteen days of fluctuating death counts and now the final toll as detectives cross-checked the list of those registered as missing with DNA, dental records and family accounts of the last known whereabouts of everyone that afternoon. Most of the bodies were brought out fast, plunging their relatives into grief as parts of bone and flesh were discovered among the metal of the plane and debris of the building. Each time remains were found the whole clearing operation would stop. The press and crowds, in which Mary stood herself one day, could only look on in fascination as the identification experts clambered on to do their work.

Each day the death count got further and further away from the original figure of 250, which was thrown around by the media.

Julia sniffs loudly and dives into her bag to rummage about. From somewhere unseen the family support woman produces a white flash of tissue, like a magic trick she had not wanted to reveal earlier.

'Thank you,' Julia says. 'So how can we do a funeral if we have no body to bury?'

'There are remains,' the big-eyed woman says. 'But as your father was at the point of impact—'

The point of impact. Why do people keep using this phrase? Mary purposely stops listening. She does not want to hear that David's body no longer exists. That he is gone. That he simply vanished.

'Mum?' Julia asks. Mary has missed the conversation. 'We're going to have the funeral here, right?'

Funeral? There has to be a funeral? How can they keep up with this? How do they know what to do next? How can their heads not spin, confused and bewildered by these events?

Everyone stands. It's over already and Mary did not get to ask her questions. She was sure she had some. John takes an envelope of papers from the big-eyed woman, who nods vigorously at him.

They walk back out into the marbled hallway. The bench where they sat moments before has been refilled with another family, red-eyed and anxious. Mary feels their faces tune into hers, as if for a glimpse of how they will feel once they have received a confirmation of death.

John and Julia argue as they walk to the car, they snap lines back and forth at each other.

'We need to say goodbye to him in his own country,' John says. 'It's what he would have wanted.'

The idea fills Mary with a fresh dread. She has not returned back in so long. She hates the gossipy old-fashioned village she and David grew up in just outside the city. Mary will be obliged to stay at David's family home, with the mother-in-law who detests her. There she will have to endure countless visits from extended family members she knows little of and can't relate to, the aunties and uncles who will cry for her loss and ask if this means she is finally coming 'home'.

'You're being ridiculous,' Julia says. 'Dad was a British citizen; he'd want to be buried here. Plus I'm not dragging my kids all the way to the Philippines.' She wipes the creamy lines of make-up from her face.

The smell of the bubblegum-scented magic tree, which Mary had bought to amuse her grandbabies, nauseates her as they step into the car. 'My passport,' she says suddenly. 'My passport is in the bedside cabinet.'

The twins turn to face each other for a few seconds, as if formulating their response, before they turn back to Mary.

'It is . . . ' Mary stalls, conscious of the tense. 'It was in the folder with your birth certificates, our marriage certificate.'

'We can sort it out. Get copies,' John says.

'No we won't,' Julia says, 'because we're not going to the Philippines.'

It has always been the three of them. Mary and her children. So why does it feel as if there is a giant hole, a substantial space that previously had some kind of warmth in it?

John looks over at his sister in the passenger seat. 'Julia, we'll get through this, okay? We'll get through it.' He starts the car and the radio comes on automatically, a newsreader's voice announcing: 'Authorities today have released the final death count for the tragedy in which—'

Julia hits the off button.

Mary never wanted this life of drama, she never wanted the estranged husband who had floozies all over the world, and she never wanted to fall in love again or have an affair. And she certainly never wanted to be a widow. These were all things that happened to others, the kinds of women who sat across from Oprah and told their stories of survival against all odds and rising up again. Mary did not want to be a survivor; she did not want to have to rise up. What would her life have been like had she married one of the earnest local boys that used to court her? The kind of boy who would come knocking in his shorts and rubber shoes, promising to build her a modest sturdy house and life. David had offered no such thing. She should have steered clear of him, she should have predicted that marrying a man like him would only bring her drama and heartache.

They had first met at nursing college in Manila, where David lasted three months before quitting to peddle his Elvis Presley act around a small cluster of hotels in a nearby beach town. Before he left he put the idea of going to London in Mary's head, presenting her with a newspaper article headed: *Want to Nurse in the United Kingdom?* She applied, got the job and eighteen months later found herself with that most coveted of documents – a visa.

The car stops and they sit in silence.

John checks the time. 'It'll already be late there. I'll call Granny Lola in the morning.'

Mary looks forward to her ascent to the spare room, to

take a sleeping pill and drift off while listening to the sounds of her grandbabies as they play and the washing machine as it whirs. She finds she can't wait for the silence that comes with sleep. To be away from the sounds of John and Julia as they swing between arguing, crying and discussing what Mary was doing sitting on the wet pavement outside a bungalow in Vanbrugh Close the day after the crash.

CHAPTER TWENTY-NINE

Malachi

Post-traumatic stress disorder. A normal reaction to an abnormal event. Malachi folds the leaflet in half and puts it in the pocket of the unfamiliar trousers he was given at the relief centre. There had been a drive to gather items for those who lost their homes. Posters went up on the hoardings that surrounded Nightingale Point, shouting: 'EMERGENCY APPEAL', with a list of everything that was needed. Things you wouldn't even think of: pillows, salt and pepper, irons, nappies.

When Malachi first asked for clothes, they pressed upon him two cardboard boxes, more than he had owned originally. Most of the clothes looked new too, and he began to believe they were. But small things would give away that they had a past life with another wearer: a button missing from a shirt, a one-day bus pass washed hard in the pocket of jeans.

He goes to Nightingale Point each morning. He's not sure why but as soon as his eyes open he needs to see it, to confirm that it happened. It changes with each visit. Every day another area swept clear of debris, a different set of vehicles and machinery on-site. Last week a yellow crane arrived and he watched as it unrolled itself and began collecting huge pieces of the plane. The authorities said that now all human remains had been identified, the plane itself was being moved to a hangar on the outskirts of the city to be investigated. He never wondered where the Boeing 747-200 had gone, even after he read in the papers about its 195-foot wing span and 230-foot length. It was startling when the crane began to extract parts of the plane, as if sifting gold.

Today all the damaged cars have been removed; each of them leaves behind an oblong patch of ground a different colour from the rest. It reminds Malachi of the time their mum sold off all the furniture and the carpet underneath was a shade lighter than the rest of the room.

He walks close by and looks up at the same balconies he always does on the seventh floor. One is completely wrecked, its wire foundations sticking out wildly, a wall broken down. But then next door, a balcony intact, a line of dust-coated washing still pegged across it.

In front of the hoardings are pools of dried coloured wax, teddies and cards. The usual suspects are here. 'Ambulance chasers', Harris calls them – those who purposely gawp at the scene and throw around their conspiracy theories. For some reason they have jumped on the tragedy and day after day come to press their homemade leaflets – claiming: *Flight GR-387 Contained Classified Cargo* – into the palms of anyone who will listen. Malachi watches as one of them approaches a young-looking reporter from the depleting line of media. Three weeks on, the twice-daily press conferences have stopped. The public have grown tired of the tragedy of Nightingale Point, of tales of squatters being among the unaccounted for and accusations that the remains of the dead were improperly handled.

Many of the flats' interiors are obscenely revealed. Wallpaper and bedrooms made public. It's discomforting to see the homes of so many, ripped open and thrown about for all to gaze at. A toilet cistern dangles off one of the walls six floors up and Malachi tries to identify the layout of the visible rooms. Toilet, bathroom, living room to the left, two bedrooms to the right. Pamela had once said that Malachi's flat on the ninth floor was a perfect reflection of her own – the location of the rooms, position of switches and plug sockets all opposite – but also that his flat was constantly flooded with light, while hers stayed in dingy darkness all day.

Pamela.

He can't stop thinking about her. Of how she must have died in that flat, unable to save herself. Why didn't she tell him she was back? They could have talked. He could have explained everything to her and told her how much he regretted doing what he did. She should have called him. How many days had she been back? Upstairs in that horrible dark flat with her nutty dad. Maybe she wanted to see him, call him or pass a message but was struggling to do anything with him watching her.

It took four days for Pamela's name and photo to appear in the papers, four days of Malachi thinking: maybe, just maybe, her dad was wrong and she would be found alive. But then he saw the photo of her printed among the others from that day: Mary's husband, David Tuazon; the elderly couple from Pamela's floor; and a young mum who didn't even live in the block but was visiting a friend.

Tristan and Mary are the only people who knew that Malachi was seeing Pamela. Their relationship was an easy secret to keep, she had so few friends at school and he spent all his time alone studying at home or in the library. It made sense at the time, how insular their relationship was, as they didn't need anyone else.

The only other person in the world hurting for Pamela as much as Malachi is her dad, Jay Harrogate. His photo had also appeared in the paper, along with the headline: *I LOST MY GIRL IN CRASH*. Malachi couldn't bring himself to take in the words of this man. If only he let her have a normal life, she would have been outside that day, running around the field or even sitting with Malachi in the café, safe, scooping up the pink milkshake powder at the bottom of her glass and declaring it the best part.

Malachi's eyes feel dry, his lips cracked again. He's had enough for today. He drags behind some teenagers who emerge from Barton Point, the only completely undamaged block on the estate. The residents beginning to move back in. Though there's a rumour that if you claim post-traumatic stress, the council will rehouse you elsewhere.

The bus comes and Malachi crams on with the loud school kids who talk about a loose girl in year eleven and the burdens of homework. Their noise distracts him for the entire journey; it allows him to forget about Pamela and the thirty-eight others.

As he gets off the bus, the drizzle turns into something more solid and he pulls up his hood and breaks into a jog towards the rose-lined bungalows of Vanbrugh Close.

The odour of toasted cumin seeds hits him as he opens the front door. At the kitchenette he takes down his hood and pulls the leaflet from his pocket.

'Smells good,' he calls over Harris's radio.

'Soup? It's winter food, I know, but I felt like it. Something warm and comforting.'

The cutlery drawer rattles and Malachi takes the spoons, grabs the pepper and they both slide their legs under the small table at the same time. They have fallen into such a quick rhythm with each other. The council offered Malachi a hostel room but it was two buses away from the hospital and Harris refused to let him go. Malachi suspects Harris is doing it out of some sort of obligation to Mary, to look after him while she's dealing with losing her husband.

A few days after the accident Harris took Malachi to C&A and filled a plastic basket with five packs of underpants and socks. He felt like one of those pampered students going off to live in halls for the first time. It seemed unnecessary, but then, at that point, he still hadn't realised how much he'd lost.

It was difficult at first, to return to the bare room at Harris's bungalow, the room with the slatted blinds that didn't quite sit correctly and the smell of potpourri that turned his stomach. The room where Malachi had woken up the morning after the crash. But within days the little house with the lifeless bedroom became exactly what he needed to return to after hours at the hospital, sitting outside the operating theatre.

The thunder claps and Malachi's spoon clatters onto the floor.

'Sorry.' He jumps up and reaches for the cloth that hangs over the kitchen tap.

'Leave it,' Harris says.

'No, I'll clean it up.

'It's just a little soup. Not the end of the world.'

Malachi wipes the mess and returns to the sink to rinse the cloth. The skin between his fingers is dry and ashy, his appetite gone.

'Quite a storm coming.' Harris joins Malachi by the window, taking his cigarette box from a pocket. A cool gust of air comes in as the window is opened. 'My goodness, I have neglected my garden, haven't I?'

It's wildly overgrown, the flowers bright and large. They look mockingly cheerful in such a dark time.

'Of course most of it is wild vetch – weeds, really, but still beautiful. Sometimes those things are. Mary hates it, is always chucking her cigarette butts in them.'

'I can't believe I never knew,' Malachi says.

'Yes, well, she told me how proud both of you were when she quit smoking. But it was only a sneaky one here and there. A nurse and patient rebelling.' He laughs. 'We were terribly unsupportive of each other.'

'No. I mean I can't believe I didn't know about you.'

Malachi finds it difficult to work out what their relationship is. 'Friends from the hospital' – that's what Mary said, but for Harris to take Malachi in, it's obvious their relationship was more than that. And then, the morning the newspaper came out with David's photo, Harris went to his bedroom and stayed there for the whole day.

He takes a long pull on his cigarette. There's a pleasure in his eyes and Malachi wishes he was a smoker, if not for the enjoyment then for something to occupy his shaking hands.

He thinks of all the times him and Tristan spent in Mary's company, eating dinner while standing in her cluttered kitchen and listening to her complain about her lazy colleagues and ungrateful children. How could they have believed that this was all there was to her?

'It's like she had a second life. A secret life.'

'Don't say that. I had no secret Mary. It was the same Mary with me as with you, with your brother, with David, even.'

The name hangs in the air awkwardly. Harris should never say it.

Malachi pushes a stray piece of brown onion skin about. 'You miss Mary, don't you?'

Harris nods, then quickly shuts the conversation down. 'Would you like me to make you something else? I can try and make some rice?' He adds vaguely.

But the cumin soup is one of five in Harris's rolling repertoire of recipes, each meal capable of filling his evenings with chopping, boiling and cleaning the small kitchen enough to keep the pests away, although Malachi swears he can hear the mice gnaw at the cupboards as he waits for the sleeping pills to take effect each night.

'There's no shame if you want to talk to someone professional.' Harris indicates behind them, to the leaflet between the two abandoned bowls of soup.

Malachi is feeling worse today than yesterday. Maybe it was reading the leaflet that did it, seeing the description of PTSD symptoms: *nightmares, flashbacks, feelings of isolation, guilt, difficulty sleeping.*

'I'm talking to you right now, aren't I?'

Harris nods. 'Yes, I guess you are.'

Malachi suddenly feels exhausted. He sighs and rubs his face.

'How did the call with your nan go this morning?'

It's still the most difficult part of his day, the brief calls Nan demands. After she was deemed too unwell to fly, Malachi promised he would keep her updated on everything, but he hates having to speak to her on the phone; between her hearing issues and the poor connection, it often feels like talking to someone down the bottom of a well.

'It was the same as every other call. She cried. Prayed. Thinks it's time I told Tris the whole truth about the plane crash.'

'Maybe she's right.'

As Malachi sits back at the table, the smell of soup reminds him of his hunger – he's not eaten anything since last night.

'I don't know how to explain everything. He remembers an explosion, a fire, but even that he's vague on. He's not asked me any questions about anything either. He sleeps most of the time, and when he's awake he's so quiet. How do I drop in that he survived a plane crash?' The absurdity of the event hits him again, the unlikeliness of it. 'Also, I don't know what he saw in there. I don't want to start dragging stuff up he's not ready to deal with.'

'But what do you think *he* thinks happened?'

Malachi shrugs. It's rare for him not to be able to read his little brother, but that's how he feels as he sits by the bedside day after day, watching Tristan lie awake, silently staring at the ceiling.

'When our mum passed away our nan never spoke about it. Even the day of the funeral, no tears, no words, just took us through the motions and never mentioned it again. I always hated that, that she wouldn't acknowledge anything.'

Harris sits down opposite him. 'I can imagine. It must have been difficult.'

'But it's all I know. I don't know how to talk about these things. Even to Tristan.'

He remembers when Nan first moved back into the flat after Mum died. How she continuously talked about the mess and dirt of the place, the mould around the edges of the bath, the smell of the unwashed bedding, the grease coating the hob. On and on she would go, about all these tiny things, but she never once raised the issue of why their mum was no longer with them.

A week after she arrived it was time to clear out Mum's room. Nan went to the market and came back with a bag of net curtains, pristinely white. She ordered Malachi to pull down the sheets that hung from the windows and replace them with the nets. As he hung them Tristan came in, confused, and said, 'But Mum doesn't like it when it's too bright.'

Nan's face wavered and Malachi, who up to that point prayed for her to give him some clues about how to feel or behave, suddenly was terrified by the idea of seeing his nan break down.

She took a breath and said, 'You can't live in the dark, not anymore.'

It was always like that: each time she noticed something not up to her standard, it felt like she was pointing out how Mum fell short of it.

'You both need to learn how to help,' she told them. 'Just because you're boys doesn't mean you can't pick up a cloth.'

Tristan loved having Nan in the flat; the order she brought in suited him and he responded to being kept busy after months of trying to play card games silently and avoiding Mum's dark moods. Also, Mum never trusted him to do anything right, so when Nan started giving him responsibility for things, like hoovering the carpets or standing on a stool at the kitchen worktop and peeling potatoes, he flourished. He'd never been recognized by an adult for doing the right thing before, so it didn't matter to him that Nan took away the photos of Mum or stood off to the side when they went to visit the grave.

But the silence didn't work for Malachi. He can't be like Nan. He knows he has to start talking.

'I don't know where to start, Harris.'

Harris leans across the table and puts one of his thin, tanned hands on Malachi's. 'It doesn't matter; you just need to talk to him. The worst thing that can happen now is that he hears it from someone else.'

CHAPTER THIRTY

Tristan

He pushes open the door of the day room with his arm and wheels himself in. After a week in the wheelchair he's definitely getting the hang of using it; the biggest problem is getting in and out of the damn thing, especially with his hand still in bandages and his ribs aching.

The room is empty and he wonders where the old biddies are. They usually sit in here after lunch to watch the soaps and bitch about their visitors. A man with a comical moustache stands on the other side of the glass with a squeegee in his hand. He gives Tristan a smile before going back to methodically wiping down the bubbles in straight lines. That's another thing Tristan enjoys about hospital: the reliable cleanliness of the place.

A youngish bloke – a biker, for sure – hobbles into the room and waves at the window cleaner, then he turns to Tristan. 'All right, mate? Good to see you getting about.'

Tristan looks down at his legs in the chair and shrugs.

'How you feeling? Is Olisa taking care of you?'

'Ha.' Tristan knows there's something wrong about fancying a woman in a nurse's uniform but he can't help it. 'She makes me not wanna get better. She's the world's hottest nurse.'

'Mate, I'd come off my bike a hundred times over if she'd give me a sponge bath.'

They laugh together and the man sits down in the chair next to Tristan's wheelchair.

'Look, I don't wanna pry or anything but I'll kick myself if I don't ask. It's you, ain't it?' He pushes a copy of *The Sun* under Tristan's nose. A photo of the retard smiling brightly in front of an ice-cream van at the seaside takes up quarter of a page.

'What?' But as Tristan says it he spots an image of himself, smaller, down the bottom, looking deceptively studious in his blazer and striped blue and yellow school tie. He's never even owned any of his school photos, only ever seen them with the word SAMPLE stamped across in bold red type.

'I knew it was you.' The biker smiles, as if he's just bumped into a celebrity.

'Yeah, it's me.' Tristan feels he has to say it out loud to confirm the headline: *Brave Elvis Saves Tower Teenager.*

'Crazy. I mean, what the hell was the plane doing flying so low?'

'Plane?' Tristan takes the paper and flicks through the pages, stopping on a photograph of the field in front of the estate. It's covered with debris, ambulances and crowds. Behind it Nightingale Point burns. It was true, a plane had crashed into Nightingale Point.

But it makes no sense.

In Tristan's head he had been trying to work it out. The fire and explosion, he knew it was because of something bigger than some guys attacking him for his trainers. He thought maybe a gas leak or something. But plane crash – well, he couldn't quite piece that together.

'I still can't believe this happened,' the biker says, then waits expectantly for some first-hand account of the sensational tragedy that, judging by the number of pages it occupies in the newspaper, has captured the public's interest.

A plane crashed into the estate. But Tristan can't remember this. This isn't why he's in hospital. It can't be. It's too far-fetched and ridiculous.

'It's an amazing story,' the biker says. 'I heard there were loads of you in here at first, from the crash, but think you're the last one now. You got it pretty bad, didn't you? But still, you're here, you're still going.' He slaps Tristan playfully on his upper back, in one of the rare spots that doesn't tend to hurt or smart.

'You finished with this paper?'

'Course, it's old. I only kept it to show you. Have it. Stick it on your bedroom wall.'

Tristan puts the paper on his lap and wheels himself out of the room into the hallway. It's been days since he woke up, days and days of not knowing, of lying in the bed trying to work out what happened. All those blurry memories he's been trying to make sense of, like the toilet bleach in the sink, Pamela crying on the other side of her security gate, the ear-splitting sound and chemical smell, and that retard looking scared in the stairwell. All of it. Tristan couldn't fit any of these things together and no one told him. He looks again at the date on the newspaper. So people knew about this, everyone in the whole fucking country knew about this, except him. They've been tiptoeing around, keeping secrets, everyone: Olisa, Dr G, the other patients. Even Mal kept this all a secret. Why? Why didn't Mal tell him? Why did he let Tristan believe that it was some random incident where he was the only one hurt? They didn't keep secrets from each other, this was always the deal.

Tristan rolls his chair further into a corner, away from passing footfall. He already feels like an idiot, sitting battered and broken in a wheelchair, crying; the last thing he wants is an audience.

Maybe Mal was trying to protect him, doing that stupid thing he always does of playing 'big brother'. But how could he? Tristan's almost sixteen; he could have dealt with knowing the truth straight away. It would have helped him feel less confused. And now, well, now he's got all the information in his hands. He works his way back to the front cover, putting a hand over the photograph of Nightingale Point, and begins reading the article. He's ready to know the truth.

Authorities are still searching for up to 250 bodies as a result of Saturday's plane crash, in which a Boeing 747 ploughed into a fourteen-storey London council block.

Reports from airline officials suggest that two of the aircraft's engines caught fire shortly after take-off, causing the cargo plane to plummet into the tower, killing all five on-board.

Police said anyone in the block near the point of impact is presumed dead, while more may have been killed in the inferno that followed. Nightingale Point, part of the Morpeth Housing Estate, has 56 occupied flats.

The block's caretaker, who has been a resident of the tower since it opened in 1969, described horrific scenes as he tried to help people to safety. Bob Ferris, who is in his last year before retirement, said, 'It's my home and I wasn't going to leave anyone behind. I could see they weren't all going to come out, but I had to try. I stayed helping till the fire brigade dragged me out.'

An emergency line has been set up for people concerned about relatives.

Tristan skim reads the rest, then goes back to the page the biker had the paper folded open on, the one with the photographs of himself and Elvis.

Elvis Watkins, a man with learning disabilities, has been hailed a hero after saving a teenager badly injured in Saturday's plane crash.

Watkins moved to the 'ill-fated block' several months ago as part of the borough's care-in-the-community initiative, which aims to prepare vulnerable adults to live independently.

Watkins was returning to his flat on the tenth floor, after a walk across the field, when the jet slammed into the side of the tower.

It was then that Watkins, who is currently the only known survivor from above the tenth floor, found the teenager semi-conscious and badly injured in a corridor. Watkins carried the boy down the stairs, before leaving him on the ground floor and going off to get help.

George Barker, Elvis's support worker, said, 'Elvis is kind and caring, so it doesn't surprise any of us here at the Waterside Centre that he put his own safety below saving another person's life. We are all so proud of his bravery and heroism.'

Watkins, who received ear damage and a minor head injury in the crash, is back in supported accommodation while recovering.

The teenager is said to have been able to talk to the paramedics, telling them his name and address before going into shock. He was rushed to the Queen Elizabeth Hospital, where he is still being treated for serious injuries, including extensive eye and leg injuries.

Elvis? Is that actually his name? Tristan remembers pushing him down the stairs, then seeing him again with Ben Munday. Tristan spat on Elvis, he called him a retard. And then Elvis saved him. His vision shakes and blurs, and he has to stop several times to look at something else, to wipe his streaming eyes.

So Elvis did more than simply help Tristan out of the block. He saved his life. Why? He should have left him to die. Why did he help? Tristan needs to find Elvis to check if he's okay. It said head injury. What does that mean? Tristan can remember it now, the blood pouring down Elvis's face. He needs to thank him, to try make it up to him somehow. But that's impossible, he can never apologise for what he did and he can never thank him enough.

He turns the page and looks at the list of the dead, their photos and stories wrapped up into a sentence.

The victims of the tragedy have so far been confirmed as: Annhagrid Davies, 67, retired teaching assistant. Billy Eastern, 24, father of three, plumber. Jane Fisher, 40, mother of three, retail assistant. Lina Baxter, 21, care assistant. David Tuazon, 58, musician. Pamela Prudence Harrogate, 17, student.

Pamela and David are both dead. Shit. He wonders if he was the last person to see them both alive. He feels like some kind of jinx. Wonders who else may have passed by him that day and ended up disintegrating into ashes or having their bodies crushed under the weight of the plane.

Why hasn't Malachi told him about David? Why hasn't he said anything about Pamela?

He feels sick. Images of people from the estate start to run through his head. What happened to the nutty old woman on the third floor with all the plastic plants? He doesn't even know her name. Or that little African kid from upstairs who always wanted to race him and talk about *Gladiators*. Tristan feels his scars weep, his bones ache.

There's a double spread photo of pastel flowers in front of the estate. All those people. All those dead. It's hard to believe it happened. Plane crashes weren't the kind of tragedies that ever happened to anyone you know. They happened to other people around the world. People you would never meet. No one ever knew anyone that was in a plane crash. Tristan wasn't meant to be *that* kind of victim. Getting hit by a bus while crossing the road with headphones on, maybe, or getting stabbed in a club for looking at someone else's girl, a strong possibility – but a plane crash?

Then a photo of a blue teddy propped among a sea of cards, flowers and football scarves. *The plane's youngest victim.* The pages flutter against the opposite wall as Tristan throws the newspaper across the corridor. He leans forward in his chair and rests his head in his hands. His face hurts, his leg hurts, his ear buzzes. But he's alive.

Though he's not sure he deserves to be.

He hears Olisa call him. 'What are you doing out here?' The melody drops out of her voice. 'Why are you reading this?' He listens as she gathers the pages. 'Well, when you're done feeling sorry for yourself, your brother's here to see you.'

*

'Hey.' Malachi empties a carrier bag of stuff on the bed: some sweets, a few GCSE textbooks, which are Harris's influence, and some imported American magazines. 'Some stuff to keep you going. Look.' He holds up a copy of *The Source* magazine. Lil Kim is on the cover wearing fishnet tights and a lacy bra, but Tristan isn't in the mood for it.

'You all right?'

'I'm always all right.' Tristan wishes he could lay back in his bed, close his eyes and not have to see Mal right now. But he's exhausted himself and doesn't have the energy to get out of the wheelchair without someone's support.

'Tris? Talk to me,' Malachi says.

'No, you talk to me,' he snaps.

How could Malachi keep so much stuff hidden? It goes against everything they've ever promised each other. Back when they were kids there were always adults whispering about them and passing looks, as if by keeping secrets they were protecting them from something. But they always knew when Mum's sadness was overwhelming her, people whispering about it just made it worse. So how can Mal do the same thing now?

'Why are you hiding so much stuff?' Tristan asks.

Malachi's face falls. He's not used to being the one in the wrong. 'What stuff?'

'You know what I'm talking about. Tell me what happened.'

'About what?'

'The fucking plane crash,' Tristan spits.

Malachi shakes his head, walks to the end of the bed and picks up the clipboard of doctor's notes, his back to Tristan. He flicks through a few pages, stops and raises a hand to his face. Finally, he slots it back and looks over, his eyes red, eyelashes wet. 'I don't know where to start. What do you want me to tell you?'

'Everything,' Tristan shouts. His voice attracts looks and Malachi draws the blue curtain around the bed. He pulls the plastic chair close and sits down.

'You don't talk to me properly anymore,' Tristan says. 'You can't even look at me half the time.' It hurts to say it, to acknowledge how messed up his face is that even his own brother sometimes flinches at the sight of the injuries.

'I'm not keeping stuff from you. They told me it would be better if you remembered everything in your own time. Gradually. I didn't want to hit you with the whole thing. Even Dr Gonsalkorale agreed.'

'And why did you listen? Since when do we listen to other

people? We don't keep stuff from each other. It's not what we do.'

Malachi rubs his face and stretches his legs out in front of him. His trousers are slightly too short, revealing his socks and a few inches of hairy legs.

'Where d'you want me to start?' he asks finally.

Tristan feels unsure of what he needs to know, where to direct his anger, if it's even worth asking anything. He starts with what seems like the most unlikely thing to hurt: Nightingale Point.

'Well, tell me what's left?'

'Of what?'

'The block, man. What's left?'

'The actual building?' Malachi looks up at him, confused by the question. 'Not much,' he answers quickly.

It's hard to picture Nightingale Point, the only home they had ever known, gone. For some reason it makes Tristan think of the hurricane years ago, how trees were brought down and the next day all the local kids went climbing over them. He still remembers the feeling of Malachi pushing him up onto the enormous trunk of one. The exhilaration of seeing something so great toppled.

'What about everything else? All our stuff?'

'It's gone. Everything's gone.'

He runs through a mental list of all the things he owns: his clothes, his music, magazines, a few action dolls and Spiderman comics he's long since too old for but has never wanted to get rid of. Surely something must have been saved? It can't all have gone.

'Everything?' he asks.

'There's literally nothing left.'

Tristan pictures himself opening the cupboard under the sink and untying Mum's scarf, the crust of limescale coming off in his hands.

'Do you think Nan has kept any photos of Mum?' He feels ashamed asking.

'I'll ask her for you.'

Tristan feels buoyed by the conversation and the strength he's pulling. It's time to ask about her.

'What happened to Pamela?'

Malachi flicks his eyes up to the ceiling, the same maze of white pipes and square panels Tristan has spent hours staring at. He crumples his mouth. 'She was in her flat. I don't know when she got back from Portishead because she never came down or called me or anything. She was so high up in the building,' he clears his throat, 'she probably died straight away.'

'But I was high up too. I don't get how people died but I'm still here.' He wells up.

'They think the stairwell protected you and Elvis when the plane hit the building. But Pamela was in her flat.'

That high up, Tristan and Elvis just managed to get out alive. But Pamela, in her locked flat, had no chance.

'And what about David? I saw his name in the paper. Is that why Mary won't come and visit me? Like, does she blame me or something?'

'Why would she blame you?'

''Cause I saw David last. Does she know that? Is that why won't she come and visit?'

'Tris, calm down. This was a bad idea. We don't need to

talk about everything in one go. You need to focus on getting better. So let's not talk about it anymore.'

'I can't believe after everything that you're still doing this.'

'What?'

'Trying to protect me. I can only see out of one eye, Mal. My foot is fucked – two operations later and I still can't stand on the thing,' he cries.

'Your Achilles was seriously damaged, Tris. You're lucky they didn't amputate. It's going to take time to heal.'

The fact they didn't need to amputate his foot has been the one thing Mal and Dr G have thrown around since he woke up, like he should be grateful that even though a piece of radiator pipe almost destroyed his foot, it's still connected.

'I was the last one in that fucking block and no one wants to tell me why. Why was I the last one to be saved? How comes I'm not dead when everyone else is.'

The curtain opens and Tristan hides his face in the crook of his arm from Olisa. She puts her hand on his wrist and turns to Malachi. 'This isn't helping, whatever you two are shouting about in here.'

'We're just talking.'

'That's not talking. You're stressing him out. Malachi, I think your brother needs to be alone for a bit. Come on, I'll walk you out.'

'No,' Tristan says. 'I need him to stay.' He lowers his voice. 'Please, Olisa.'

She looks at the two of them and steps back, leaving the curtain open slightly. They wait until she's walked away. Then Tristan starts again.

'You telling me you haven't broken down about this?

You've had weeks to deal with this, Mal. You've seen it unfold. Even now you get to go and look at it. All I've got is the newspaper and the images in my head. I can't even believe it happened.'

Malachi sinks his head into his hands. 'It's too hard, this is all too hard. I can't think about any of it, sometimes. It's like a big cloud or something.'

'How did you find out about Pam?' Tristan asks tentatively.

'I saw her dad at the relief centre after the crash. He told me . . . ' He trails off, looks away. 'Well, he told me she had been in the flat.'

Tristan feels cold as he remembers the black bars of the gate, her puffy red face behind it. Even if her flat wasn't crushed on impact she wouldn't have been able to escape anyway. He remembers the way she smiled when he promised to take the letter. The letter that now sits folded in a copy of *Men's Health* magazine in the bedside unit with his few possessions. The letter with Pamela's last message.

CHAPTER THIRTY-ONE

Malachi

He had hoped it would be Tristan's last week in hospital. The physiotherapy seemed to be going well, with Tristan already able to pull himself to standing using the parallel bars, as well as get in and out of the wheelchair. Dr Gonsalkorale said this kind of recovery was common in the young, but Tristan credited it to the hundred push ups he did each night before the accident.

Malachi wonders how his own body would have coped with all Tristan's has gone through. He'd probably be dead; he can't even trust his body to get him through winter without being brought down by a cold or virus. He's always been like that, sickly and prone to whatever bug's going around. And then there's Tristan, his foot almost blown off and already thinking about raving again. He seems better since they talked properly last week, though it doesn't feel quite the same between them, it's tense. Tristan's mood varies from one day to the next, sometimes hopeful, other times awkward and angry.

He smiles as Malachi approaches the bed; it's a good mood day.

'What were you talking to Dr Parma Violets about?' he asks. 'Out of all the women here she's the only one I can't get any banter going with.'

Malachi sits on the edge. 'Well, she has more important things to do than banter with a fifteen-year-old boy.'

'I'm practically sixteen.' Tristan smiles, pleased with himself.

His birthday felt so far away, but now it's looming and he's going to have to spend it in hospital. Malachi sighs, expecting this information will cause Tristan to kick off again.

'How old do you think Olisa is?'

Malachi shrugs.

'I know sixteen is too young for her but I want to keep the dream alive. Though I get the feeling she's swaying more in your direction. She wants your chocolate sauce, man.'

Why is everything still a joke to him? This is serious. There's so much at stake. They need to make plans and sort their lives out.

'Tristan?'

'What?'

'Dr Gonsalkorale isn't convinced you should leave this week. There's still a high risk of infection in your ankle so she's not going to discharge you yet.'

Tristan's face falls and he lays his head back on the pillow.

'Sorry. She only told me now. You knew this would be a possibility. What's another week?'

'Maybe I had plans.' Tristan reaches for a bag of sweets on the cabinet, but his bandaged fingers struggle with the packaging. 'For fuck's sake, man.'

Malachi takes the bag of sweets and unwraps one for each of them. 'I know it's not what you wanted to hear today. I'm sorry.'

'Whatever.'

'Where are you getting all these sweets from anyway?' Malachi asks, keen to change the subject.

'Annie Wilkes over there.' He points to a matronly looking nurse, who smiles back. 'She loves me. She'll be the one to mash up my other foot.' But there's little bravado in his joke. His mood is down.

'You feeling all right, Tris? Still up for meeting Elvis later?'

Tristan flinches as he chews. 'I can feel my stitches pulling.'

'I asked you a question.'

'I know,' he snaps. 'I'm thinking about it.' Tristan puts out his hand for another sweet, then says, 'Awkward. Pure awkward.' He turns to Malachi. 'Since we're on this whole telling each other everything, I need to tell you that I've met Elvis before.'

'Yeah? What, around the estate? I'd never seen him.'

'Well, actually, it was that day. He was, erm, following me about. It was weird.'

'What are you talking about?'

Tristan sighs. 'He caught me having a little smoke in the stairwell and threatened to report me to the police, so we had a bit of an altercation.'

'An altercation? Why are you only telling me this now?'

''Cause there's kind of been other stuff to cover,' he snaps. 'You know what I'm like, Mal, how I can lose the plot a bit easily, especially if I've been smoking.'

'What did you do?'

Tristan looks off and it's clear he's trying to get his excuses straight, to justify something to himself. 'I called him some names and I . . . '

It has to be more than that. Malachi almost doesn't want to hear it.

'I spat on him.'

Malachi stands. The curtain tears slightly from the hooks as he opens it and walks down the ward. The Annie Wilkes nurse approaches him.

'Everything okay?'

He manages to utter something but feels all his energy going towards not screaming or pushing Tristan off the bed. He steps outside the ward and seriously considers disappearing, just running off and never dealing with any of this again. But he can't, he knows he can't. Tristan is his responsibility.

As Malachi returns, even the way Tristan looks, so sheepish, small and bandaged, can't calm him down.

'Mal, think about it. Ever since I remembered this I've been questioning why he didn't just leave me to die in the stairwell. Like, if I was him—'

'Not only did he save you, but he also visited you every day you were out. Talking to you, checking that you were getting better. I did think it was weird that he kept putting off coming to see you once you woke up. But now it makes sense.'

'I don't know what to say.'

'Did you know he had a carer? A carer that died in the flat while making his lunch, 'cause Elvis can't even make his own lunch. That's how much support he needs.'

'I didn't think I could feel any worse about this, but I do now.'

'What were you thinking? Surely you could see he was a vulnerable person.'

'Yeah, course I could, but I also didn't give a shit. But that was *before*. I don't know why he helped me. I really don't. I can only say sorry and try and pay him back. But I don't even know how to do that. Mal, how do I pay him back?'

'You can't.'

*

Elvis is almost an hour late. The timing is terrible as it forces Malachi to spend time with Tristan when all he really wants to do is go back to Harris's and sleep off the morning. He's furious with Tristan and embarrassed.

George comes over and shakes Malachi's hand, and they make small talk while Elvis takes his time walking slowly up the ward, showing the potted plant in his hands to everyone polite enough to give him their time.

'Mr Popular,' George says. 'It's like this constantly at the moment.'

Elvis breaks into his wide childlike smile and encloses Malachi in one of the big, tight hugs he always gives, the plant bashing up against the side of Malachi's face.

'Hello,' Elvis says into Malachi's ear, too loudly, as he holds him.

'Hey, Elvis. How you doing?'

He nods, smiling, then covers his mouth with one of his large freckled hands. 'Is Tristan Roberts really awake?' he asks.

This is it, Malachi could stop the meeting from going

ahead. What right does Tristan have to talk to Elvis anyway? He can never make up for what he did that day.

'I bought a Solanum lycopersicum,' Elvis says, lifting the pot. 'That's the posh name for a tomato plant.'

'Really? I didn't know that. You brought one of these before, didn't you?'

Tristan was still unconscious when the plant had first arrived on the bedside cabinet, and Malachi was too out of it to care for another thing. But he does remember sitting by Tristan's bed, listening to the machines beep and watching the leaves turn yellow and fall off.

'Solanum lycopersicum can be a little bit tricky to look after at first and sometimes you can kill them by accident. But if you keep trying you will be able to keep them alive one day. Do you think Tristan Roberts will keep trying?'

Malachi shrugs. 'Maybe you should ask him yourself.'

Tristan is sitting up on the bed as they near, putting on the poker face he perfected on the estate to protect himself from being seen as soft.

'Hi,' he says. His bottom lip quivers and his eyes keep darting up to Malachi, as if asking for advice on what to do. Then he can't hold it in anymore, he starts to cry, a few tears that he wipes away quickly with his arm as Elvis leans across the bed to hug him.

It's almost too intimate to watch, and Malachi crosses his arms in front of his chest and turns to George. 'I'm going to get some teas or something.'

He takes the long way over to the café, stalling at the chiller and reading the labels on every drink, panini and pie.

He knows it's too late for him to have a reunion with

anyone saved from the tower, to have a second chance to start over and say sorry for messing up the last time. He knows, but still it's hard to accept.

It's quiet around the bed as he walks back over, carrying a tray of teas and chocolate bars. George has been keeping the small talk going, asking Tristan about his injuries, which is always the last thing he wants to talk about, while Elvis sits quietly until he spots the tray.

'Oh, KitKat's are my favourite.'

'Mine too,' Tristan says, and holds out his hands to catch one.

They all crowd around the bed drinking their teas and listening to the man in the next bed over snore. Elvis giggles.

'What you doing?' Tristan asks Elvis. 'You can't eat a KitKat like that. Look.' He demonstrates biting the edges off the ends of each stick of chocolate and sipping his tea through it. Elvis copies and George laughs, happy they've bonded, like this is enough.

It fills the time.

'Why didn't you leave me?' Tristan asks.

Elvis blushes, the butterflied scar on his forehead turning pink.

'Seriously, I need to know to why. Because I was such a dick to you.'

George bristles at the language. 'Tristan, Elvis sometimes finds it difficult to explain his actions.'

'No, he must know why. He had a reason. Why didn't you leave me?'

Elvis says, 'Because you cannot leave people behind.'

Tristan fingers the leaves of the Solanum lycopersicum and nods. 'I don't know how I can ever repay you, but I will.'

CHAPTER THIRTY-TWO

Elvis

Tristan Roberts was fifteen when the bad plane crash happened but now he is sixteen, as today is his birthday. Elvis has brought him a videotape of *Dr No* as a present, because even though Tristan Roberts says he likes Bond films he has not seen *Dr No*, which Elvis thinks is very strange as it is the best Bond film.

Elvis likes the Queen Elizabeth Hospital a lot more today than when he came before to have his forehead stitched up, and much more than the time when his arm was broken by the car and he bit the nurse. George, his care worker, is here too. He came in his car, which smells like Aztec the Labrador dog, but Elvis came all by himself on the 138 bus. The 138 bus stops right outside the Waterside Centre, where Elvis now lives again, but in a different room from where he lived before. But it is kind of the same as it has a small bathroom attached to the bedroom, paintings of lily ponds in the hallways and Tuesday night bingo with Bill.

Tristan Roberts has a little beige remote control in his

hand. When he presses it his bed sits up and then lies down again, which makes Elvis laugh.

A nurse comes over with a trolley of drinks. She is singing a Celine Dion song, which Elvis has heard on the radio and would like to join in with but cannot because he does not know all of the words.

'Hey, Sweet Sixteen,' the nurse says to Tristan Roberts as she pours him a cup of juice. But she does not say 'hey' to Elvis or George. She does not even offer them anything from her trolley of juice, which is a little bit rude.

Elvis enjoys visiting Tristan Roberts. He does not even mind when he has to wait outside the ward for visiting hours to begin. Elvis loves that the ward is called Xion, which sounds like the kind of planet a superhero would be born on. He also loves the green plastic chairs that make a clicking noise when you rock on them. But he especially loves the friendly doctors, who ask him how he is and remark on the scar across on his forehead by saying things like, 'Wow, quite a gash you got there'.

When Elvis visits Tristan Roberts, sometimes he sits up and together they look around the ward at other people. But most of the time Tristan Roberts sleeps, which Elvis does not mind. Yesterday was the first time he had seen Tristan Roberts' head without any bandages and Elvis was upset that the little zigzags he used to have shaved in his hair had all grown out and instead there was fluffy, furry hair, which Elvis really wanted to feel but knew it was rude to feel black people's hair. He had done it once before as he queued up in Tesco. He stroked a black lady's hair because it looked so nice and soft, and he did not think she would notice if he did

242

it inconspicuously, but she did notice and shouted at him, 'Do I look like an animal for you to stroke?'

Malachi Roberts is here too but is very busy chatting to a lady doctor, who has a very strange name and does not wear a white coat. Malachi Roberts is here every day. He always buys Elvis a cup of tea and a KitKat from the café, and Elvis practises the special tea-drinking trick Tristan Roberts taught him. But today there are no KitKats, today there are special Chelsea buns to celebrate Tristan Roberts' birthday.

Malachi Roberts comes over and gives out the buns, and everyone sits down and says 'Happy Birthday' and eats.

Elvis feels embarrassed that he eats his Chelsea bun the quickest and hopes the brothers will not think he is greedy and understand that he only eats nice things fast in case George tries to take them off him. Elvis is meant to be on a diet because his tummy is getting so huge. George says that Elvis is getting a big tummy because all the cooks feel sorry for him and keep giving him extra food and that when this happens he does not always need to take it. But Elvis feels sorry for himself sometimes so when the cooks offer him extra chips or a second ladle of custard with his Jamaican ginger cake, he thinks of the deep gash on his forehead and ugly Edward Scissorhand stitches, and of the sad message he had to write in the card with the cross for Lina's family, and he takes the food.

'You all right, Elvis?' Tristan Roberts asks.

Elvis knows he must have gone 'somewhere else'. This is what George calls it when Elvis stops paying attention to what is happening around him because he is too busy thinking about Nightingale Point and being sad.

He nods and tries to listen to the conversation that is about 'being sixteen'. Elvis would like to join in this conversation but he cannot because Tristan Roberts is getting out of bed and sliding into his wheelchair.

'Elvis, let's go. You push,' he says and begins to wheel himself away.

His brother stands up too. 'Tris, where you going?'

Elvis thinks Malachi does not like it when they are separated. Elvis understands this because if he had a brother he would never want to be separated from him either.

'Not as far as I'd like to. Come on.'

Elvis pushes the handles of the wheelchair and they leave the ward. 'Where are we going?' he asks Tristan Roberts.

'Anywhere you like.'

This makes Elvis happy as it is not often people allow him to choose where is best to go. They go around the main corridors, past the flower shop and out into the patient gardens, where Elvis points out some of his favourite plants.

'So, Elvis, do you have a garden at the . . . er . . . the place you live?'

'At the Waterside Centre, yes, we share one. I am going to grow some more Solanum lycopersicum, which is—'

'The posh name for tomatoes. See, I'm learning.' He smiles. 'But what's it like there? Do you enjoy it? Does it feel like home?'

Elvis has to think about this. 'Yes. It is my home. But it is not as perfect as Nightingale Point, which had all my perfect things, like my TV and my James Bond books and my Merlin Premier League sticker album and my jar of shells from Margate and my . . . ' Elvis stops talking as it is upsetting him to think about all these lovely things he no longer has.

'It's okay, man. I understand. Here.' Tristan Roberts pulls a packet of tissues from his pocket. 'Can't believe I've become the kind of person that carries tissues around with me. But it's tough, isn't it? There's always so much to deal with. It never ends. Getting out of the building should have been the hardest thing we had to do.' He shakes his head. 'But sometimes it feels like that was only the start.'

Elvis's nose runs and the tissue gets soggy so he takes another one.

'I know it's sad you lost your stuff, but it's just stuff. You're still here and that's the important thing. And anyway, when this is over and I'm a world-famous, half-blind rapper, I'll buy it all back for you.'

'You cannot buy shells. You have to collect them yourself.'

'Well, then, I guess we're going to Margate.' Elvis smiles. It will be fun to go to Margate with Tristan Roberts one day.

'Let's head back inside before Mal gets his knickers in a twist.'

Back on the ward there is a very boring and serious conversation happening about where the Roberts are going to live.

'Has the council rehoused you?' George asks.

'Not yet, but we're seeing some places soon,' Malachi Roberts answers. 'But for now we're going to stay with a friend.'

'Friend of a friend,' Tristan Roberts says as he gets back onto the bed.

'Good to hear the council are getting on with it,' George says. 'They're being slated in the papers over their handling of this. There are still hundreds of people scattered in hostels all over the city, far from their schools, families, jobs. Anyway, glad to hear you're on the mend Tristan, we better leave you to rest. Come on, Elvis, I'll give you a lift back.'

Elvis kneels down by the bed. 'I have to go now.'

Tristan Roberts winks his one good eye, which makes Elvis smile.

Elvis follows George into the dog-smelling car and sits quietly the whole way to his new home, which is really his old home at the Waterside Centre. Elvis is always happy when he returns to his new room there as it is so full of perfect things. Like his blue and white stripy bed sheets and his bookshelf of James Bond books and the sparkly silver frame with a photo of himself smiling in the newspaper after he saved Tristan Roberts from the bad explosion at Nightingale Point. But he does miss Nightingale Point. Just a little bit.

'Elvis?' George stands in the hallway. He does not come into Elvis's perfect room. 'There's a painting class in the activities room. Are you going?'

Elvis enjoys painting, especially when the class is run by Serena. Serena is from Trinidad and has a speaking voice that sounds like singing. It makes Elvis smile and want to sway at the same time. Usually on Tuesdays, after finishing his cottage pie, Elvis rushes straight away to painting class to get a seat right by Serena's side, but today he does not really feel like it. Today he does not really feel like anything. He often feels like this after he visits Tristan Roberts.

'No, thank you.'

'Okay. Maybe next time then,' George says.

'Goodbye,' Elvis says. 'I'm going for a little rest now.' He kicks off his shoes and lies on the bed with its lovely nautical stripes. He waits but does not hear George move and opens one eyelid to peek at him. George shakes his head and finally closes the bedroom door. Elvis bounces up. He lied, he does not really want to have a little rest. He gets out his new notepad and pencil case from under the bed and draws a huge lightning bolt across the first clean page with a red felt-tip pen. His scar. He likes drawing things from the plane crash and bad explosion that happened after. It helps him remember because sometimes he forgets bits and worries someone has put a magic spell on him and soon he will forget everything. At least if he draws it, he can remember. In his notepad he also has a drawing of the coffee-smelling doctor who stitched up his head. Underneath the drawing he has written *Dr Ross* for fun, even though his name was not really Dr Ross.

Elvis has to go to the hospital again next Tuesday. He needs to see a special ear doctor about why he can no longer hear anything in his right ear except for a buzzing, which sounds like the time bees swarmed near his old school and everyone panicked because they did not want to be stung, but Elvis ran outside to try and spot the queen. The ear doctor does not smell like coffee and does not look like anyone from *ER* or even anyone from *Casualty*. She is not that friendly either, and when he last went she poked him with a strange thing that she would not let him look at. Each time he tried to turn his head and see the strange thing she gave him an angry face, which made Elvis think of Lina.

Elvis misses Lina sometimes. He misses her pink fringe and the shiny pink polish on her toenails that reminded him of the inside of seashells from Margate. He did not go to her funeral but George helped him write a message in a card and send it to her family, who he said were very upset that she died in the bad explosion. The card had a white dove on it and a silver cross stuck on the front, which was not real silver but cardboard. Elvis liked it a lot because even when the card was in the envelope you could still feel that it was a cross.

Elvis takes a dark green felt-tip pen and draws the cross. Then he changes to the blue felt-tip pen and draws some zigzags around the cross. The zigzags are exactly the same as the ones Tristan Roberts had shaved in his hair. Elvis would like to have some zigzags shaved into his own hair. He had asked Alan, who comes every second Thursday to cut everyone's hair, but he said no because that would take too long and Elvis's hair was too thin and 'not afro enough' for it to look good.

Elvis does feel sad sometimes and also a little bit scared. Like when the alarm goes off at the Waterside Centre because someone is fighting with the people that work here. Each time this happens Elvis thinks maybe another plane has crashed and exploded. Once Elvis cried because he was on washing-up duty and his friend Archie was keeping him company but also telling him a sad story about pandas becoming extinct because Chinese people were eating them. Elvis stopped concentrating on the washing up and the water ran over the brim of the sink and all over the kitchen floor. He cried because he would get into trouble, but also because the way the water splashed as you walked in it was exactly like the wet floors of Nightingale Point that day. Elvis then had to go and see Sonia and her ugly puppets to talk about his feelings.

He closes his notepad and puts the lids on his felt-tip pens. George says that Elvis can leave the Waterside Centre whenever he feels ready, as London is full of perfect flats waiting to be filled with Elvis's perfect new things. But he does not want to move today, or next week, or even next month. He looks out of his window and up at the two planes that crisscross the sky. Maybe one day he will be ready to move out and try again.

ONE MONTH LATER

CHAPTER THIRTY-THREE

Mary

Instead of returning home with the food shopping Julia sent her out for, Mary walks towards Nightingale Point. It's a silly thing to do – the walk takes her almost an hour, the plastic handle of the bag cuts into her fingers and she knows her daughter will be panicking at home.

When she reaches the gloom of the field in front of the towers she sits on one of the benches that line the path. The shopping bag sags at her feet. The cold of a thawing chicken touches her foot and her fingers explore the slightly damp wood of the bench, pockmarked with cigarette burns. On the other side of the field police cordons are still in place and the council have erected hoardings that cut the space in two – the before and after, the living and dead. The destruction had smouldered for days and even now, a whole month on, it still occasionally lets out a puff of dust as the remaining parts of it are brought, slowly, to the ground. The breeze carries the smell of ash and rotting flowers.

What's the point of all those flowers and teddies and

football scarves sitting out here, being battered by the weather? All these messages of condolence made public for everyone to see. When will everything be removed? Who will take responsibility for such a task? Surely it's not rounded up with the normal rubbish. All those heartfelt messages scrunched into bin liners.

There are lights on in Barton Point, the sparse signs of life. Mary had read most of the residents don't want to move back there, and who could blame them?

With Sandford Road still closed to traffic, it's quiet and dark on the field. The only noise is distant; the only signs of life in those faraway windows. She takes in the still darkness, but swears she can see movement coming her way. She is not sure at first, has to squint as a man walks across the grass. There is something familiar in the slump of shoulders, the thin frame, something safe and earnest in the walk.

'Mary?'

It's Harris. She had called him as she stood outside the supermarket in tears, desperate to see him and tell him her decision.

'I knew I'd find you here. Please, let's not talk here.' He puts out a hand but she rises without its aid.

They walk to a pub, far from the estate. Inside it's empty except for a large group of cackling women on a night out, all in party hats and pink sashes. Mary listens to their laughter and wonders if she will ever feel like that again.

'Tristan will be leaving hospital soon,' Harris says.

The women explode into laughter again and Mary loses the thread of what she wanted to say. What is she doing here? In a pub surrounded by people enjoying life. She's acting like nothing ever happened. That's the problem with her and Harris. They don't take the real world into account; when she's with him she forgets about everything else. And it was fun back then, but look where it led them.

'Mary?'

There's a shade of tiredness across his face, but he seems brighter than usual today, his smile comes easily each time she looks at him. He tries to take her hand but she pulls it away and curls her fingers around the glass of Coke.

'Tristan's doing really well,' he says, 'though he seems to have fallen in love with one of the nurses. He thinks he has Stockholm syndrome.' Harris laughs. 'He's quite a character, isn't he? And inspiring too. The physiotherapy is gruelling, it really is, but he gets through it somehow. Every day he's there trying again. Makes me think back to when I was first diagnosed with my illness, I was an absolute wreck. Then I see this young boy facing up to challenge after challenge and it . . . ' He shakes his head, lost for words. 'Well, you know him much better than me. You know what a great kid he is.'

It almost makes Mary smile, to hear Tristan described in such an un-Tristan-like manner.

'But things are far from okay, Mary. He's got quite serious hearing loss, severe eye damage on one side and it will take him months before he's walking again unaided. And even then it's not guaranteed, they may still need to amputate his foot in years to come. Tristan won't even entertain that idea.'

'I know,' she says. 'They told me.'

Every few days Mary calls the hospital and speaks to Olisa, a young, discreet nurse who Mary helped to train a few years ago. Mary is still on long-term compassionate leave and can't quite bring herself to go into the hospital as a visitor, to face her colleagues and have their condolences pressed upon her. The cards they sent, through John and Julia, were bad enough, the odes to losing one's husband, one's soul mate.

'I worry more about Malachi,' Harris says. 'He seems to be drowning in this.'

'He'll be fine.' But this information scares her, for she knows how prone Malachi is to dark moods. How in the past he has blamed and punished himself for everything that has gone wrong. Just like his mum.

'He's far from *fine*, Mary. He's not eating well or sleeping much. Up all night. Sometimes I hear him leave the house, and he stays out for hours. I lie there worrying. Or he lays out in the garden all evening smoking. I don't know him like you. I don't know what's normal.'

'He likes to be by himself. I told you he's quiet.'

'His girlfriend was killed.'

'I know. I was there when he found out.' She had read about Pamela in the papers. It broke Mary's heart to see the little blonde head smiling in a photograph next to all the other victims. When Pamela had come for dinner that day at Mary's, she drank diluted juice from a plastic cup and picked all the green vegetables from her meal. She was a child. It's too cruel.

'Malachi is blaming himself,' Harris says. 'Thinks he could have saved her, somehow, yet he didn't even know she was in London at the time. He's tearing himself to pieces over this.'

He's too young to carry so much guilt around.

'I spoke to one of the counsellor's at my school; they said it sounds like post-traumatic stress. He needs help. I know he goes to the estate at night, and that he sits there looking at it, this big, empty space where his whole life once was. It's not healthy.'

She should never have left him. She was meant to be there for him.

'I do try with Malachi,' Harris says, 'and he talks to me sometimes, we get on well, but I don't know him. He needs you. Mary, please. Talk to me.'

'I told you I can't be there for him now, or Tristan. I need to look after my own children. They are grown-ups but they still need me.'

Harris nods.

The partying women continue to laugh and Mary finds it hard to deal with the fact people are having normal conversations. That life for others is ticking on like nothing ever happened.

'We have agreed that Tristan will stay at mine till the council rehouse them. It makes sense with the hospital so close and, of course, I have the space,' Harris says.

'You don't have to do this, Harris. You don't have to take them in and disrupt your whole life because you feel obligated.'

'I don't feel obligated. I actually like having Malachi with me. I like them both a lot. And I feel like I can help.' He raises his glass to his lips, then places it back down without taking a sip. 'Though Malachi keeps telling me how particular Tristan is about cleanliness. I've cleaned out my study for him, even got the duster out. What have the council said to you?'

Mary shrugs. She hasn't heard anything, but then she forgets she is homeless. It doesn't feel like she's truly lost anything. She still expects to walk back into her flat in Nightingale Point at any time, to find it intact, the spiral fly-catcher on the kitchen ceiling, a plate of prawn skewers in the fridge, and the folder with her passport and marriage certificates.

'Tristan's going to need a lot of support, a lot of care. That's another reason why I thought it would make sense if you moved in too.'

'I can't believe you're asking me this, that you're asking me this now.'

'We need to start rebuilding our lives, Mary.'

'No, it's my life, Harris. Nothing has changed for you.'

He straightens his back and looks across the table. 'Actually, everything has changed for me. Everything.'

'Do you realise what we've done?' she says finally. 'Do you realise that I sat in your car, thinking about divorcing my husband, while he was about to die?'

The hens stop and look over, but Mary doesn't care. 'Every time I'm with you I can only think about what we did wrong. And now all this has happened. Up shit creek without a boat.' She closes her eyes, places her left hand across her forehead. She needs to refocus on why she came here today, what she needs to ask him. 'Harris, no one else can know about us.'

'I don't understand.'

'Malachi knows, so that means Tristan does too. But no one else needs to.'

'Is that why you called me?' His face changes, that rare flare of anger that reddens his cheeks and makes him look like a stranger. 'You want me to silence the boys for you?'

She closes her eyes to his anger and nods.

'And your children?' he snaps at her. 'What about them? They must suspect?'

'No. I told them you're a friend from the hospital. They can't deal with this too. They have other things to think about.'

'So do the boys.'

A waitress approaches their table cautiously with two full plates. She looks of school-age. 'Did you order the burger and beer deal?' But as she speaks she realises her mistake. 'Oh, I'm sorry.'

Mary watches the girl scuttle off to the hen party's table, where she is met with smiles, normality, life.

'Mary?'

This time she allows Harris to take her hand and with the other she wipes her eyes.

'What about us?' he asks.

'It's over, Harris. It has to be.'

CHAPTER THIRTY-FOUR

Tristan

The boys hover around the bed in order of importance, headed, of course, by Ben Munday, who sits on the one plastic chair drinking the cup of orange juice that Olisa left for Tristan.

'Good to hear you're getting out soon,' Ben says. 'You're the last one in here.'

The stitches on the left side of Tristan's face pull as he smiles. 'Two more days. I can't wait. The food in this place is driving me crazy. How you been?'

'Okay. Still in the hostel, though.'

'Shit, man. I'm sorry.'

The other boys all drop their heads for Ben, who, like Tristan, lost his home in the crash and is now at the mercy of the council.

'Be good to have you back in school,' Sayeed, one of the younger boys, says. 'It's boring without you. No one is challenging these teachers.'

'Don't be stupid,' Ben interrupts. 'He can't go back to

school like this, all disabled and shit.' He indicates towards the mass of bandages covering Tristan's foot.

'You'd think so,' Tristan says, 'but I'll be back in September. My foot's fucked but my brain's fine. Actually, I'm looking forward to having something to do again, some normality.'

Ben laughs. 'Yeah, right. I give you a month before you're back to bunking off, sitting on the wall with us.' He strokes his beard and adds, 'If we had a wall.'

'Nah, things are going to change for me when I get out of here. Need to focus a little more.' Tristan has been giving this some thought, making plans for the future and setting himself a couple of life goals.

Ben sniggers. 'My brother says the same thing every time he gets out of prison.'

The boys laugh and Tristan does too, but he also feels he has to press his point, to share his newfound ambitions, hoping it rubs off on them. 'I'm done wasting time. First thing is quitting the weed.'

They all burst out laughing again and Ben leans forward to nudge Tristan's arm, which, while playful, actually hurts. 'The only time you go a day without smoking is when you can't find me.'

'Nah, I'm telling you, that stuff is killing my brain cells and I'm looking to get some GCSEs next year. I don't know why you're laughing, Sayeed, you know I'm top set for everything. Once I get focused, it's on.' Tristan claps for extra emphasis and watches as Sayeed, who is bottom set for everything, confirms the claim with a nod.

Ben clears his throat and asks, 'Is it true, what the papers said?'

'About what?'

'That the retard saved you? Carried you out? I know how the papers lie and stuff.'

'Elvis? Yeah, man. I should be dead. He picked me up and carried me out. Like a real-life hero.'

They snigger a bit and Tristan feels irritated by it. Why can't they see what he did?

'And you can't say that R word anymore, man, it's 1996. That's pure offensive.'

'Well,' Ben puts a hand on his chest, 'soon as I saw that explosion, I ran. Ran and didn't stop to look back or nothing. I was out of there.'

Ben is one of the most feared guys on the estate; it's hard to imagine him running from anything.

'But you were still outside on the wall,' Tristan says. 'If you'd been inside the block it was different. You had to help each other.'

'I don't have to do anything,' Ben snaps. 'I don't owe anybody my life.'

'Elvis could have left me in there. I could barely walk. Or see. Or hear. The pain was making me hallucinate and shit.'

The boys all exchange looks, confirmation that it's getting too deep, too heavy.

'Elvis stayed with me,' Tristan says, more adamant this time, as if they don't get it. 'Stuff was collapsing in there, it was dark, it was crazy. The smoke was choking us both. But he didn't run. He stayed with me and got me out.'

'After how you did him that day?' Ben says. 'Spitting on him'

Tristan nods.

'Man, if I was him I would have left you there. That's how I know that brer ain't right in the head.'

'He's fine in the head,' Tristan says. 'He just isn't a coward.'

*

Olisa's got on a reddish lip-gloss. It really suits her.

'So, Mr Man,' she says, 'today's your big day, huh?'

Tristan fusses with the plastic-covered remote to stop staring at her mouth.

'You all packed?'

'Yeah, took me all of two minutes,' he says.

She pulls her head back and looks at him with a raised eyebrow. 'Why are you sad? You've complained every day about being stuck here, and now it's time to leave you're sulking.'

'I'm not sulking.' He's embarrassed by how sulky he sounds.

Olisa leans next to him and he admires, for what he knows will be the last time, her impressive bosom. 'You'll be fine. Get out of here and get on with your life.' Her voice is soft but determined, and Tristan wonders how often she has to give this pep talk.

'I been in here so long now,' he explains.

'I know, it's like a jail sentence.' She laughs.

'This must be how people feel when they get out of the army.'

'Are you saying the hospital has institutionalized you?' She laughs again and her great chest jiggles in a way that cheers Tristan up.

Her tray is filled with lined-up cups of tap water and the tepid orange juice he has spent the last month drinking. He stretches from his bed to grab a cup.

'One for the road.'

There's that hollow kind of feeling again, the one that makes him feel like everything in his stomach has burnt out. He takes a sip, then pours the rest into the tomato plant Elvis brought.

'Don't worry, you're strong, and that brother of yours,' she shakes her head, as if searching for words, 'I'm sure he'll take care of you. And don't forget you've still got stuff here.' She nods down towards the bedside unit, where he's been dumping the revision guides Harris keeps dropping off.

'Olisa,' he whines, 'you know I can't reach down there.'

She bends over to get it out and slams the pile of books onto his bed.

'Nurse,' a voice calls from behind the curtain. 'Nurse, come quickly,' the disembodied pain in the arse calls.

'Olisa, let me whisk you away from all this.'

'There's my smart aleck.' She puts her soft hand on his shoulder and whispers, 'You're through the worst of it. Just keep going forward.' Then she moves on, humming 'In the Air Tonight'.

But how can he move forward if he can't remember the last bit of his old life? Also, Dr G keeps banging on about him still being an outpatient for the next year.

At the end of the ward he spots Malachi and Harris. They always seem to come in a pair at the moment. Harris pulls one of those tartan shopping trolleys every woman seems to acquire upon hitting sixty, for the sole purpose of smacking into everyone's legs on market day. Malachi has on another ugly brightly coloured sweatshirt, emblazoned: *Tigers Basketball Camp*. Who would buy such a thing? Tristan refused to wear any of the crap Malachi brought him from the relief centre. As if he would put his body in someone else's old garms.

'Right, this is it.' Malachi comes forward and slaps Tristan's palm. 'I just got to sort this paperwork first.' He beams as he holds the green hospital notes above his head, a fat booklet that details each of the four operations Tristan has gone through since arriving. Tristan had flicked through it once, but it was all jargon about lacerations and recovery and was way too impersonal to be interesting.

'May I?' Harris asks before he puts Tristan's collection of magazines in the shopping trolley. 'Enjoyable reading, were they?' he asks, indicating the revision guides.

'Yeah, riveting,' Tristan answers, but then spots the crusty yellow letter as it falls from within the pile. Harris picks it up. It's obvious that he clocks the name written on it and looks at Tristan for an answer. Tristan fractionally shakes his head and hopes it's enough to put Harris off. It's not his business, anyway. Slowly, Harris hands it to Tristan, who folds it back into a magazine.

Doctor Gonorrhoea comes over and talks with Malachi. Tristan is now the only one in the group without a full-watt smile on. It's all a bit too happy. He doesn't know how to feel. He shakes the doctor's hand, this woman who saved him. He wants to thank her but doesn't know where to start. He hopes he won't cry, but right now it's all he wants to do. It's overwhelming.

'You've done brilliantly,' she says. 'Really, well done. So I'll see you back here next Thursday. Your brother's got it all written down.' She turns to Malachi and they small talk for a bit. Tristan misses most of the conversation as the buzz in his left ear loudens. Finally the doctor shakes Malachi's hand, but holds it longer and stronger than she did with Tristan, and they leave.

He hasn't been outside the hospital gates since that day and everything seems too bright, too busy and too loud. He hopes Malachi and Harris don't look down at him as he wipes his eyes. Luckily they occupy themselves with chat about the logistics of their departure: who will run the wheelchair back and pay the parking ticket. Tristan is put out by how comfortable they are together, this relationship that has sprung up from nowhere and seems to have replaced all others. He looks around the car park and realises he doesn't even know what car they are looking for. The wheelchair bumps down a curb and his heart beats fast at the involuntary jerk, the clank of metal against brick. It brings to mind a memory he doesn't want to deal with, not now at this moment. They stop by a bronze Escort. Tristan wasn't sure what kind of car Harris would have, and he wouldn't have guessed it would be something so girlie.

Malachi opens the back door and helps him into the seat. It smells like Harris, like cigarettes, spicy food and the bars of pink soap you only find in school toilets. But his body is grateful for the way the caved-in padding holds him. Harris and Malachi fuss with the radio up front and Tristan begins to pull the seatbelt across himself, but then lets it reel back up. The odds of surviving a plane crash only to be killed in a car crash must be very low. Surely the odds of anything tragic happening to him ever again are minimal. It's a pleasing thought.

'Mind my plant, Mal.'

'Sorry, sorry.' He cranes his neck and flashes a big smile into the backseat. He always looks off when he smiles like that, like it's hurting his face. 'You all right, Tris?'

'I'm always all right.'

'You got enough room?' He inches his seat forward till his lanky legs are crushed in the front with the tomato plant on his lap, but the smile remains.

During the short drive, Tristan zones in and out of the conversations about traffic, dinner, and a morning meeting with the council. He looks out of the window but can't make up his mind about whether he wants to see it or not. He spots Barton Point and Seacole Point in the distance. Then the blackened stub of what must be Nightingale Point, burnt out and being taken apart by two large yellow cranes on either side, exactly like in the newspaper. He feels relieved as it disappears from view again and they carry on driving into a small close of single-storey houses, each one with a brightly painted door and no metal security gates. Harris drives as close to his green front door as possible and Malachi helps Tristan out and onto his crutches. He takes him straight through to a narrow, pastel-coloured bedroom.

'I know how you like stuff clean and Harris is pretty messy,' Malachi says, 'so I spent some time clearing it out yesterday. Probably not quite to your pristine standards,' he swipes a finger along a surface, 'but I tried.'

The room is bare, except for drawers, a wardrobe and a

single bed. The creases from where the sheet was folded in its packaging still show; they didn't even wash it first. Tristan lowers himself onto the bed and the sun hits his face, which causes Malachi to rush over to the window and pull at the slatted blinds. He stands there for a bit, a slight wheeze from his chest, before he pulls his pump from his pocket and shakes it.

'You all right, Mal?'

He nods and takes a few puffs. There had been a story in the papers about an upsurge in asthma and chest problems from people that breathed in the smoke that day. Does Malachi sound raspier than usual, or is it just noticeable because everything else is so quiet? No thump of children running wild in the flat upstairs or neighbours having a domestic, or televisions blaring or people whistling outside.

'Shit,' Tristan says, 'it's creepy silent round here. Reminds me of a horror film or something. Can't believe this is only a bus ride away from Nightingale.'

'Quiet is not a bad thing. It's a nice area.'

Tristan clocks a bowl of what looks like dried flowers on the drawers. 'I know what this place reminds me of . . . *The Burbs* – remember that one? We must of watched that a hundred times when we were kids.'

'You knew all the words; used to drive Mum crazy.'

'He's a stranger in an even stranger land,' Tristan says in his best American accent. The memory makes him smile as he leans his crutches against the bed. The pain in his left ankle is searing and it's a few hours before he's allowed another round of painkillers.

'You think Harris would be okay with Elvis coming over?'

'Course.'

'I think he's finding everything a bit overwhelming. Be good to keep an eye on him. Don't you think?'

Malachi nods and smiles.

'And Mal, I never said it before in the hospital, but I'm really sorry about Pamela. It's proper sad.'

He nods.

'Do they know if she . . . ' He's not sure how to say it, or if he even really wants an answer. 'Like, died straight away or if she suffered?'

Malachi sits on the bed and leans his elbows on his knees. 'I don't know.' He uses his hands to shield himself. 'Like I said to you, I didn't even know she was back in London. I wouldn't have believed she was in the block if I hadn't seen her dad. It was horrible. He was broken.'

'Who cares how he feels? He was the one that locked her in.'

Malachi snaps up, his forehead creasing, and he holds Tristan's gaze for too long. 'What are you talking about?'

'What?' Tristan can't think of a time he's ever lied to his brother and got away with it. He's not sure if it's because Malachi can always see straight through him, or if he's just a really bad liar.

'What makes you think he locked her in?'

'I don't know. I don't. Her dad was strict, right? It seems like the kind of thing he'd do.' Tristan opens his bag and takes out his pill bottles, then begins to line them up on the little set of drawers by the bed. 'But like you say, we didn't even know she was back in London.'

Malachi is still staring at him, so Tristan turns away and

lifts the bowl of rotten flowers and sniffs it. 'You think Harris would mind if I put this outside? It proper stinks. What is it?' Tristan feels as if he may blurt it out, what he knows. 'Y'know, I'm kind of tired. And I'm talking shit now.' The stitches around his eye hurt as he yawns.

'You want to be left?' Malachi asks.

'It's the pills, they turn me into a proper narcoleptic, man.'

Malachi gives him a sad smile and stands up. 'I'll let you get some sleep, then. I'm so happy to have you home, though.'

Tristan pulls off the one ugly trainer Dr G insists he wears while his foot heals and he practises to walk again. As Malachi closes the door behind him, Tristan mumbles, 'Yeah but this isn't home.'

CHAPTER THIRTY-FIVE

Mary

'Where have you been?' Julia's face is angry and overly made-up.

'I told you. I needed a walk, to clear my head.' Mary feels her daughter search her face, as if trying to work out if Mary's tears are part of mourning or guilt.

'Today of all days.' Julia snaps her make-up compact shut. 'You realise we're leaving at ten?'

'Yes, that's why I am dressed.' Mary knows what time they are leaving; the fact loomed over her all morning as she walked aimlessly through the Jewish graveyard in her black dress and tights. She keeps one hand in her pocket and rubs at the metal of her fob watch.

'You can't wear those.' Julia stares down at Mary's feet, horrified at sight of the stained plimsolls. 'I bought you proper shoes. I told you to chuck those.'

Mary knows she will not throw away these shoes, her only ones. She will hide them under the bed along with Harris's shirt and navy jogging bottoms and the newspapers she has been collecting with David's name in them. Mary likes her things, no matter how worn, useless or neglected, to surround her always. Especially now, as she has so few belongings.

She follows Julia into the living room, where the four grandbabies sit in a line across the sofa. They look like morbid bridesmaids in their black tulle dresses, each of their thick-haired heads adorned with a black sequined bow.

'I don't think I can do this, Julia.' But even as Mary says it she regrets laying it on her daughter.

'We don't have a choice,' Julia says in emulation of one of Mary's own lines. 'We need to say goodbye. So please, go and change your shoes.'

Mary pads upstairs and collects the clunky black shoes and ugly plastic handbag Julia laid out for her. Inside the bag she finds two packets of tissues and a roll of mints. She sits on the top step and waits for ten o'clock to come, for John's low voice to fill the hallway and for Julia to call for everyone to leave for the church.

Mary's life with David had been nothing but goodbyes: every few months another show, another goodbye. It had begun weeks after their wedding, a gig he could not turn down, the chance to sweat in closely fitting polyester trousers, singing 'Baby It's You' in hotel bars, while Mary laid alone in her marital bed wearing a lace nightdress. For the following fifty-three nights Mary told herself she was not mad at David. She knew the money would cover the costs of the recording studio he wanted to hire, for the breakthrough recording he had been dreaming of ever since he watched *A Hard Day's Night*. Singing was David's life but he also wanted to be a good husband, sometimes, so the day he returned, with a suitcase of clothes that smelt of tobacco and beer, he made the first, and only, completely selfless gesture towards Mary. He gave her the money. 'For your ticket to London. I know you are short. Go and I will follow next year.' So today, she feels she owes it to him to play the devastated wife.

*

The last time Mary was in a church with David's family would have been her own wedding at St Joseph's back in the Philippines. It was there, after eleven months of chaste looks, supervised lunches, and three sessions of quick, ecstatic sex at his house, that Mary and David were married. She had felt proud as she spoke the vows of 'forever', while glancing around at her smiling family and envious friends, many already married to men who were suffering premature balding and widening waistlines. Mary was the girl with the perfect catch and the glittering future abroad.

But now Mary is the woman with nothing: no home, no husband and children who feel like they don't know her at all.

Her feet smart within the stiffness of the new plastic shoes as she walks from the church. Men talk loudly as they walk, reminiscing about David, the talent, the jokes, the larger-than-life character. Mary stays silent. What can she add to this? That he was an absentee father? That he was a terrible husband?

Finally they reach the plot, a mound of freshly turned-over earth and a large hole beside it. She thinks of the thirty-eight other people who died that day, the thirty-eight other funerals. There is no body to bury for David. But they decided on a casket and only the closest family members know the make-up of its weight. She imagines the lightness of the David's possessions as they move about inside the bodiless box. His jewellery, his favourite cassette tapes – mostly his own recordings – and a series of headshots that, when lined up in order, chronicle how little he aged.

Despite the families wrangling about where to bury David, a will had been discovered, which spelt out his wish for British soil to be his final resting place. Julia and John are still angry about the will, the cold, legal document that said so little about them but contained lengthy details outlining David's wishes for his own funeral: white doves, a full choir, a painting of Mother Mary on the inside lid of the casket. But even the generous *abuloy*, raised by members of the Filipino Snooker Club, was not enough to fund such a production.

The casket is lowered. The guilt returns and Mary feels her knees wobble with it. She prays that she will not faint here in front of all these people. She does not want to make a spectacle of herself, even though that is probably what David would have wanted, that someone faint with grief at his funeral.

Julia raises a clump of sodden tissues, marked with black eye make-up, to her face and John puts an arm around her. He whispers something in her ear, which brings a thin smile to her lips. David's mother looks up at them from her chair; suspicion of her foreign and least favourite grandchildren floods her eyes, fuelled by an old-fashioned fear of twins.

David would taunt his mother with tales that the children could sense what the other was feeling when he would tickle one and get the other to laugh. Mary can suddenly no longer see all the hours David missed from their life but the minutes he spent bouncing a little Julia on his knee or swinging a pint-sized John upside down till he cried with laughter. Mary remembers the children's happiness each time David would return home and her own despair.

Mary looks away to search for a face not running with tears, and it's then she spots the tragic lone figure standing in an unoccupied clearing of grass. The floozy from the side of the stage.

Her hair is done up in an old-fashioned coiffed style, a whalebone hair clip in the side, a black skirt down past her knees. She is older than Mary imagined, nothing like the image of a young, laughing girl that has been etched in her mind for the last three decades. But of course, if this woman has been around since the start, then she would have aged, just as Mary has. This is her, the other woman. The real widow.

Mary tolerated the idea of David having a girl, several, even, but the idea that he had one other woman, one who loved him enough to cry this way and travel this distance to say goodbye, stings her. Mary wonders if this other woman has spent weeks sitting with red-rimmed eyes and dark bags, despite sleeping all day. She wonders if she too has been staring blankly at old photos. Or listening to records from The Mamas and the Papas and The Hollies, and remembering how disappointing the originals sounded after hearing David sing them first. The woman's face is obscured by a white handkerchief, which she stuffs in a sleeve before walking away from the church. Then, a few steps later, she takes another look behind her at the man she never truly had because of Mary. The man she had now lost because of Mary.

CHAPTER THIRTY-SIX

Malachi

He was always one of those children who wore the shirt and trousers of his school uniform to church. Suits were an extravagance. Even during that first year at university, when everyone, no matter how little was left of their student grant, had marched down to Hugo Boss and hired one for the summer ball, Malachi couldn't justify the cost. But for this, for today, he knew he needed one.

Harris had helped, forcing Malachi into a fitting room and passing him several pairs of black trousers, white shirts and jackets to try on. 'Don't worry about the cost,' he said. He was always saying that, but Malachi felt the debt mounting each time Harris did the food shop or topped up the electric. 'Pay me back when you're earning.' It seemed so far away, but then Harris pointed out that next summer Malachi would have graduated, be interviewing for internships and starting his career. It's difficult to think that far ahead. To imagine himself moving on. Surely it won't happen for him, this future he had envisioned. How would he ever be able to sit in an interview and talk about something as trivial as his professional goals, while wearing the same suit he wore as he watched his girlfriend being buried?

The bus goes over a speed bump too fast and he topples slightly onto a pile of shopping bags by an old man's legs. The man frowns and looks pointedly at each of the empty seats on the lower deck. But Malachi doesn't want to sit down, to crush the trousers and crease the shirt. He had attempted to iron them himself this morning, but Tristan had winced and given a running commentary on all the things Malachi was doing wrong before taking over.

The sky is mostly grey, but as he steps off the bus he realises it's warm, too warm for the jacket. Though he knows he won't take it off today.

The church grounds are unkempt and overgrown; there are crisp packets and newspapers caught in the bushes. Pamela hated litter. Along with the dirty air and lack of open space, she said it was one of the things she disliked most about living in London. Once, as they walked down Oxford Street together, she told off some tourists for throwing their empty coke cans on the ground. It had surprised Malachi because he'd never heard her speak up about anything before.

'Malachi Roberts?' A familiar voice – his old art teacher, Ms Biney. She looks different here today, with her bright colours muted. She steps forward and reaches up to put a hand on his shoulder. 'My goodness, you look so different. So grown. How are you?'

He manages a nod and hopes she'll remove her hand. Ms Biney was always like this with him, too kind and too intuitive. For the year she was his form tutor she was forever asking him if he was 'okay', if he needed 'to talk'.

'And how is Tristan? We do get updates. I heard he's out of hospital, but how is he *really* doing?'

'Great. He's doing great.'

They both step to the side, allowing a couple dressed in black to walk past. Malachi looks closely at the light-haired woman. Could this be Pamela's mum? Should he speak to her?

'Tristan's strong, isn't he?' Ms Biney says. 'You both are. So strong. What a tragedy, Malachi. I'm sorry this happened to you. Terrible. So terrible. And Pamela, poor girl. She was in my form, one of my Year Elevens.' Ms Biney puts her hand over her mouth, as if having overstepped something, then a few seconds later she shakes her head and continues. 'Sorry. Where is Tristan? I'd love to see him.' She takes a cursory look around.

'He's not here. He didn't know Pamela very well. Also, he's not very able right now.'

'No, no, of course not.'

He needs to get away from this, from the small talk that will ultimately lead to how he knew Pamela, why he's here today. It should be enough to say that they both lived in Nightingale Point, but Ms Biney's the type of person who always wants to know more.

'I'm going to take a few minutes before I go in.'

Again the hand comes up, and this time gently pats his arm. 'I understand. Take your time. I'll be inside if you need me.'

The crisp packets rustle under his feet as he walks over to

a bench and lets his head fall into his hands. The sun breaks through and spreads across the back of his black jacket. He doesn't want to be here, he doesn't want to have to do this. The last funeral he had been to was his mum's. But he doesn't remember feeling this kind of pain then, maybe because he had been waiting for it, for her death. It's difficult to remember much from that day; he kind of just went through the motions. Propped up by Nan, shaking hands with all those people from the past, Mum's past, Nan's past. People who hugged him hard and whispered prayers into his ears. People he rarely saw again.

Two girls, about Pamela's age, slow as they pass the bench and nod in his direction. Maybe they are from the school and recognize him from when he used to pick up Tristan, or perhaps they are friends of Pamela's, the small group of girls she spoke about, who occasionally chatted with her or tolerated her presence in class group work. One of them gives him a small smile, before walking on down to the church where a few people now gather outside.

Jay's there too, in a dark grey suit that is too big for him, his hair shaved closer than usual. He looks over at Malachi while talking to another man. There's no sign that Jay has softened, that his anger has been quelled. Even from here his shoulders appear too close to his ears, his face too contorted and red. The man turns to face Malachi, while still listening to Jay and nodding. He then begins to walks towards the bench.

'Can I help you?' he asks. It's not entirely unfriendly.

The sun obscures the man's face, so Malachi stands. 'I'm here for Pamela.'

The man sucks the air through his teeth. 'Sorry, but it's family only.'

Despite what happened at the relief centre, Malachi had never considered that he would not be able to sit silently, unnoticed, at the back of the church. He only wanted to see what photograph of Pamela they would display, to hear her name and know it was real, that she was gone.

'Look, I'm sorry, mate. I don't know the story, don't need to, but—'

'Jay doesn't want me to come in?'

The man looks over his shoulder, back at the church, but Jay is no longer there.

'I'm here to say goodbye to her. That's all I want. I have a right to do that.'

'Look, my brother's just lost his little girl and, for whatever reason,' the man rubs the back of his head, 'he doesn't want you here.'

'I have a right to be here,' Malachi repeats, his voice trembling.

'Come on, it's a funeral. Don't make a scene.'

Malachi can see it now, the way the man looks a little bit like Jay, a little bit like Pamela. She had never spoken about an uncle before. But then they tended to stay away from talking about family. It suited him at the time, but now it makes him feel like he didn't know her.

'He's really going to stop me from saying goodbye to her?'

The man drops his head fractionally, as if embarrassed by what he's been tasked to carry out. 'The family don't want you here. You should leave.'

CHAPTER THIRTY-SEVEN

Elvis

Tristan Roberts has a wheelchair now, which Elvis likes very much as wheelchairs always make him think of Professor X and Elvis loves Professor X. But Tristan Roberts does not like Professor X, as he thinks all the X-Men are 'inadequate' and he does not like the wheelchair.

Instead, he is trying to get much better at walking using only two sticks, even though it hurts him very much and he has to wear special trainers, which he says are 'ugly' and 'uncool'.

Elvis sits in the garden on a fancy white chair and watches as Tristan Roberts walks up and down the grass doing his exercises, sometimes stopping to lean on the fences. A big, bushy ginger cat walks along the top of the fence and stops to stare. Tristan Roberts looks up at it and barks like a dog.

'I feel like this cat is mocking me,' he says, 'prowling about with ease in my face.' He bangs on the fence and the cat jumps away. Finally he makes his way back over and slowly steps up onto the decking. 'Right, I'm tired. You wanna go play cards or something?'

Elvis nods, excited because this is what he loves about coming to visit Tristan Roberts: firstly that there are always snacks and no one to tell Elvis 'that's enough now', and secondly that there are always so many games to play.

They go inside the kitchen, where Harris is sitting at the table with lots of reading books. Elvis does not know how anyone can read so many books at a time, but Harris is a super clever teacher, so he can because his brain is huge.

'I'm making lunch. Do you want some?' Harris asks.

Elvis is hungry but the last time Harris gave him something to eat it did not taste nice and Elvis did not want to be rude by not eating it so he went to the bathroom and hid until dinnertime was over.

'It's a kind of bean stew,' Harris says.

Tristan Roberts sticks out his tongue and makes a funny face, which makes Elvis laugh.

'No, thanks, we'll wait for Mal to get back and run down the chip shop.'

They leave Harris to his bean stew and lots of books and walk very slowly over to the sofas. Elvis likes the sofas here because they are covered in squashy cushions that have pictures of elephants sewn onto them.

'Elvis, I almost forgot, I got you something.' Tristan Roberts hands Elvis a little blue-wrapped parcel. A present – this is exciting. Elvis has not received a present since Christmas, which was already so many months ago.

'Can I open it?' he asks to be polite.

'Course, go for it.'

Elvis rips the paper and inside is a very fancy notepad with drawings of small tomatoes all over the cover.

'I've wanted to get you something for ages, but I don't have much money. In fact, I have no money. But when I saw this I thought of you. Solanum lycopersicum. You can start to keep notes on things again, like you used to. Just don't go drawing me this time.' He smiles and shrugs.

Elvis knows when you get a present you should always say thank you, even if the present is something rubbish that you do not want. But Elvis does want this present and likes it very much, so it is strange that he cannot say thank you straight away. Elvis feels a little bit sad but also happy.

'There's so much I regret about that day, Elvis.' Tristan Roberts looks sad too. 'I'm so sorry about what I did to you, what I said. I was an idiot. Sometimes I don't even feel like I deserve to be here. But there must be a reason, right? For you to have found me behind the door? To have had the strength to get me out of there. I think about it a lot. My flat was destroyed completely by the plane.'

Now Elvis does feel really sad, because he does not like to hear about the plane and everything it destroyed. He does not want to remember that horrible day and the way Tristan spat blood, and the vomit that came out of his mouth and went all over Elvis's shorts.

'I only left to go and see Pamela, Mal's old girlfriend, the one who used to run around the field all the time.'

'The running girl who died?' Elvis saw her photograph in the paper and was very upset as she was so pretty and so fast.

'Yeah, that's the one. As much as I didn't like her, thought she was a bit dull and that, I knew Mal was really into her. So I went up to her flat to get some love letter for him, then *boom*.'

Elvis is interested in the idea of a love letter, especially from the blonde running girl. But love letters are private.

'I was only on the other side of the block because she called me up. First she saved my life, then *you* did.'

Elvis knows he saved a life, that is why he was in the newspapers, why the nurses were all very kind to him and why he got a free dessert at the café George took him to last week. Everybody loves heroes.

'Do you like the book?'

Elvis allows the pages to flick over from the first to the last. So many pages to fill with important information. He nods.

'Elvis, you saved my life. We're like brothers now.'

Elvis smiles as he thinks being Tristan Roberts' brother is a good idea, a very good idea.

THREE MONTHS LATER

CHAPTER THIRTY-EIGHT

Malachi

Harris turns up the car radio and slaps the steering wheel as the newscaster announces Labour gains ahead of next year's election. Malachi smiles at him, then catches Tristan's look in the rear view mirror.

'You all right? Comfortable?'

'Yep,' Tristan says.

He's been in a mood all morning after he found Malachi's letter from the university, expressing regret that he's 'chosen not to progress with his studies'. Malachi should be the one in a mood. Why should he have to explain his life choices to his little brother? Giving up university to sell flat-pack furniture and sovereign rings on the high street was hardly an easy decision for him, but it was one he had to make.

Malachi has come to the realisation that easing Tristan's physical pain is the easiest part of his new role. He bought him a watch to beep reminders to take his painkillers, he helps to clean the hard-to-reach weeping wounds, and he makes sure Tristan rests, despite a stream of visits from Elvis, as well as a girl from the youth club, nicknamed Red Weave. But the psychological pain, mood swings and attitude are things he can't help with. He hoped the course of therapy they had both been directed to through the survivors' network would take care of this, but Tristan went just once, returning home furious that the therapist, who he described as 'an old guy with tattoos and a ponytail', asked him to say what he liked best about the way he looked.

'Besides,' Tristan said, 'I don't need to see some fruity therapist. This is the clearest I've felt in ages.'

The clearness was probably because after smoking weed every day, Tristan declared himself 'reformed' and said that his former favourite pastime now only served to make him nauseous. Weed was now Malachi's thing, his only break from reality, a slow spliff while sat on the wrought-iron chair in Harris's garden, despite how much Tristan bitched about it. Always the opposite of Tristan, weed and therapy was what got Malachi through one day and onto the next. Malachi loves how he feels so light after each session of therapy, exhausted yet purged of all the things that eat away at him day after day. Therapy is a chance to talk, to ask all those questions out loud. Will he ever be able to be with anyone again? Or will every woman have to compare to the girl he lost at twenty-one? The girl he wants to stop thinking about. When she enters his mind, he pushes her away. It hurts too much. Though he enjoys when she appears in his dreams, sitting in their booth at the café, picking at a plate of a chips, gossiping about the arguments her insane neighbours have with each other.

'I think this is it?' Harris says as he pulls in by four small blocks of flats.

The letter from the council confirms it. 'Yeah, it's that one on the left.'

It's almost half three on the dashboard clock – it has taken them fifty minutes from Harris's place, without traffic. Malachi calculates this in his head: that's a two-hour round journey to the hospital for every appointment. He hopes Tristan hasn't noticed. Between the fortnightly check-ups with the consultant, weekly physiotherapy, and random scattered appointments with the ear consultant, his recovery was already a full-time job without adding in a commute.

Malachi jumps to open the back door and put his arm out for Tristan, who, despite obviously struggling to rise, pushes the helping hand away. Why can't he be grateful for the help? It's Malachi's role as big brother to be there.

'I'll wait here,' Harris says as he takes out his box of cigarettes.

It's a bit chilly and Malachi pulls a grey fleece jacket on over his red work shirt. He catches Tristan glance over. 'What?'

'What is this look you've got going on today?'

'I'm on shift at two. I'm not going to go back just to get changed, am I?'

'I know, man, but *Argos*.' Tristan shakes his head and grabs the paper from Malachi's hands.

Something about this housing estate doesn't look quite right. Each block is three floors high and white pole bars run alongside ramps up to the front entrances.

'An old people's home?' Tristan says. 'Three months waiting and this is what they offer? Are they serious?'

'I don't know, Tris. Let's look properly.' Malachi can feel

his brightness fade, his shoulders slump. He's too tired for disappointment.

'This place is adding insult to injury, ain't it? Literally.' Tristan leans his weight on the roof of the car, then takes hold of his crutches.

They move slowly towards the glass entrance doors and both sets of eyes go to a hand-drawn poster. *Do you want to learn cross-stitch in a friendly environment?*

'Yeah, this is not going to work,' Tristan sulks. 'Let's go down the council now. Let's kick up a fuss.' His voice echoes around the silent close. 'They can't palm us off with this. It's been months. They need to house us.'

'They need to house a lot of people.'

One of the wall boys had told them the council had dispersed families across bedsits all over the city, sharing kitchens with battered wives and ex-junkies, while the housing office struggled to find permanent homes. It was a scandal. Worse still, one of the tabloids had run a story last week about residents being 'picky'.

'But we get priority, Mal.'

'A priority case', those were the exact words Tina from the council had used when their application was made.

Tristan begins to read the letter: 'We are delighted to have found you somewhere that fits with your brother's physical needs. Flat Seven, Bridge House.' He huffs. 'We need our own place again, man. We need it to be like the old days. Can't stay homeless.'

'We're not homeless. We have somewhere to stay. What? Why you shaking your head?'

'We can't stay there forever. We don't even know him. I

mean, why's he being so nice? What's in it for him?' Tristan looks over at Harris, a cigarette between his lips.

'Harris has been amazing to us.'

Tristan wobbles slightly and Malachi's immediate reaction is to reach out and grab his arm.

'Get off.' Tristan pushes away and stumbles over to rest against a low wall. 'We need to get our own place,' he says in frustration. 'Our own lives. And you too – this is not just about me. I know you're still hurting about Pamela, but you need to start looking forward. I mean, how long you gonna work there?' He nods towards the red shirt.

Malachi doesn't want to deal with this. He heads back towards the car.

'What about university?' Tristan calls. 'Mal? Don't walk off. Say something.'

Malachi turns and heads back to the wall, keen to shut down this conversation. 'I've only just started working. Why are you stressing me about this now? Can't you see how hard I'm trying?'

'Yeah, I can. But I don't understand why. You keep acting like you're all right to give up everything you worked for, 'cause things have gotten off-track.'

'Off-track? You call what happened to us going off-track? Are you fucking kidding me?'

Tristan flinches at the outburst and Malachi feels embarrassed at the sound of his own raised voice, unfamiliar and uncontrollable. A net curtain twitches on the first floor of the old people's block; the outline of a face appears and vanishes just as quickly.

'I want you to be your old self and get back to the original plan: university, internship, career.' Tristan uses a finger to mark out each stage. 'I don't get why you're giving up.'

'I'm not giving up.' Again, the anger escapes into his voice. He feels his heart race and pats his pocket for his inhaler. 'I'm working.'

'What, this shitty job? You could've left school at sixteen for this job.'

'So you expect me to go back to studying full-time, spending every evening at the library, trying to write a dissertation, while all this is going on? Does that sound like something I could do right now?'

'Yeah. Why not? You've done it before; you can do it again.' Tristan now raises his voice too.

'Because you need me more than I need to graduate.'

'Me?' Tristan asks, incredulous. 'I don't need you.'

'You do need me.'

'I'm fine, Mal. Get on with your—'

'You do need me,' Malachi cries.

'No. I don't need you.' Tristan throws his crutches to the ground as he leans his full weight against the wall.

They each take a few breaths to calm down.

Malachi walks over to where the crutches have rolled along the pavement.

'Not everyone needs you all the time, Mal,' Tristan says gently. 'I mean, listen to yourself, man, you're like one of those controlling boyfriends or something.'

Malachi breaks into a laugh, then feels guilty for allowing himself to laugh when everything is in such a state.

'Gimme those.' Tristan takes back the crutches and threads his arms through, though he continues to rest against the wall.

He's meant to be taking it easy, yet still insists on using the crutches rather than the wheelchair the doctor recommended.

'Please try to understand. We won't stay with Harris forever. I'm not going to work in the stockroom forever either. But, till we are strong enough, this is how it's got to be. I'm not ready to take on everything myself again. Bills, cooking, cleaning, studying, begging my tutors for hardship loans and deadline extensions. I did it for years when Mum was sick and I can't do it again. I'm tired. I'm really tired, Tris.'

'But this ain't like when Mum passed. I'm sixteen now. I'm not some little kid you need to protect from everything. Besides, I can survive anything.'

'It doesn't work like that. You're not on the other side yet. We've spoken about the possibility of you needing more surgery. If that happens things are going to get hard again, really hard.' Malachi thinks of the very real possibility of Tristan's left foot needing to be amputated in the coming year, of how this will throw everything off course for both of them again.

'Whatever, Mal. You can't protect me from everything, so stop trying.'

Malachi nods. He knows it's the truth. 'Come on, let's go back to the car.' He notices Tristan wince as he uses the wall to push himself to standing, but this time Malachi doesn't jump to help.

*

Despite his initial demands of descending on the council, Tristan sleeps for the rest of the afternoon, and even when

Malachi comes off shift, keen to talk through what they can do next, he finds Tristan still in bed, exhausted from the day.

Malachi heads to the garden and rolls up. He's never been a huge weed smoker, always saw it as one of those things capable of distracting him from what he needed to be doing. But there's nothing he needs more in life right now than a distraction, to be taken away, and for life to be made a little fuzzy. Even the concentration it takes to roll the thing is enjoyable.

He lays on the decking and closes his eyes to the thick grey sky and the planes that cross it. This silence, this peace, has become the only snatch of his day where he feels anything close to contentment. Lying here alone, replaying all those conversations he had with Pamela, laughing at the way her accent would come out when she said words like 'something' and 'bothered'. He misses her. He misses watching the swing of her ponytail as she ran around the field. He misses making fun of her shameless nosiness and the way she always eavesdropped on others' conversations while they sat in the café together. He misses her. That's what the pain is. He missed her before, during those twenty-nine days when he thought she was in Portishead, but this time it's different because he knows she's never coming back.

It gets dark and the lights come on inside the bungalow. Malachi wonders how much longer they can stay here. Tristan's right, they don't even know Harris and they've gatecrashed his life.

He walks into the house, his back stiff from lying on the wood.

'Hey,' he greets Harris, who's at the table marking a pile of his students' books.

'Evening. How long have you been out there?' Harris grabs Malachi's hands as he walks past. 'You're freezing.'

He pulls away to open a cupboard door, then realises he's shivering.

'Malachi?' Harris says. 'What's wrong? What's happened?'

Malachi leans his elbows on the counter and puts his head in his hands.

'I don't know how to stop thinking about Pamela. How can I get on with things knowing that it was my fault she died that way?'

'It wasn't your fault.'

'It was.'

He walks over to the sink and splashes water on his face. Outside a fox winds its scrawny body across the rear of the garden. It visits often, on the hunt for the peelings Harris piles into one of his green tubs to compost. Its fur is sparse and wet, making it look more thin and desperate than it probably is.

'I never really thought it was over for us. The way things ended were weird, her dad got involved, made her doubt if I was serious about her. I *was* serious about her. I loved her. But I never told her that, so when her dad said I didn't care about her she believed it. Then she moved away. I was hoping she'd come back and we could work it out. That I could somehow prove to her dad that I wasn't the guy he decided I was.'

'Which was who?'

'Just another black guy on the estate, I guess.' Malachi shakes his head. 'It was never said, but I don't know, as much as Pam talked about our future, she always skipped over the part where I would meet her dad. Obviously, with me being older than her, I thought it best that we wait, at least until she started college. But when I finally met him it felt like there was something else. Something he would never be able to get over.'

'Don't add his prejudices to your worries.'

'But it all ties in, Harris.' Malachi sniffs, a shiver running up his back. He can't afford to get sick now, to take time off from his new job. He closes the window, making the fox jump and scamper. 'If I didn't get involved with her she wouldn't have been at home in the first place—'

'And if the plane didn't have a technical failure none of this would have happened, but it did and it's no one's fault.'

Harris isn't listening; he doesn't understand what Malachi is trying to tell him. 'Her dad was so strict, so furious when he found out that she had been seeing me. He used to threaten that he would lock her in. Maybe he did—'

'This thing,' Harris interrupts, 'this terrible thing that happened to you all at Nightingale Point was random, unpredictable. It was just bad luck.'

Malachi straightens up. 'It's life. The way things go. Especially for me.'

'No, it's not. This is not how life should be. Tragedy after tragedy.'

It's the first time he's ever witnessed Harris raise his voice.

'I should leave, Harris. Tris and I, we shouldn't even be here.'

'You're not leaving, I won't let you, not in this state. I promised Mary I would look out for you both and that's what I'm doing. But you need to look after yourself as well. I know you're grieving but you do need to get out of this hole you're in. I was with my wife for thirty years when I lost her, so trust me, Malachi, it will never stop hurting. But you can move on.'

Malachi sits down at the table and watches as Harris takes the bottle of whiskey from the cupboard and pours them each a drink.

'Mary's so fond of you boys, I felt I knew you both before I ever met you.' He takes a swig of the drink and tops up his glass. 'She talks about you more than her own children. I understand why you feel so guilty in all this. Mary told me what happened with your mum, how you've always blamed yourself for it.'

How could Mary betray his confidence and tell Harris about this?

'I know you don't want to talk about it and it's not my place to try and make you, but again, you were unlucky. And it wasn't your fault.'

But Harris doesn't know that Malachi was the one in charge of booking her hospital appointments and making sure she had her pills each morning. It was up to him to make sure her mood didn't darken enough to the point where she would no longer be able to look after herself, or them. So, when she died, it was partly his fault because he didn't see it coming.

'I knew Mum was going to take her own life.'

'You were a child, Malachi.'

'So? I should have helped her more. She relied on me.'

'Stop punishing yourself. You need to let go of this because you can't change what's happened. And maybe your mum did rely on you, and maybe Pamela was in her flat because her dad grounded her, but it still doesn't mean these things are your fault.'

'They are, Harris. I keep letting people down. People I'm meant to be taking care of. Mum, Pamela, Tristan.'

'Your mum was sick. There was nothing you could have done. And Pamela lost her life in that tragic accident, like everyone else that day. It was no one's fault.'

'But Tristan, he's my responsibility.'

'Yes, and you've given up your whole life to look after him. What more? What more do you need to sacrifice of yourself?'

'I don't know.'

'You can't be everyone's hero all the time.'

Malachi knew all this, said it to himself every day, but this is the first time anyone else has ever told him.

CHAPTER THIRTY-NINE

Tristan

Malachi takes his keys from his pocket and slides them over the Sellotaped flaps of the box.

'It's a cheap one but it should do the job,' he says with a kind of pathetic pride.

The plastic wrap falls to the floor. Back in the day Tristan would have dived straight down to clean it up. But now the move from his position – propped up on the bed in Harris's spare room – down to the floor would be too much effort. It almost makes him jealous to see the amount of ease Malachi uses to kneel and plug in the television–VCR combo.

'What do you think?'

'It's old school, man,' Tristan says.

'Better than nothing.' He fiddles with the aerial and attempts to tune in the channels. Each one fuzzes for ages before a picture slowly emerges. Terry Wogan fills the screen and it's like seeing an old friend. 'There we go.' Malachi chucks the remote down on the bed. 'I give you entertainment.'

'Hmm, guess I can watch half a show now.'

Malachi rolls the plastic wrap around his arm and huffs. 'Why you staring at me like that?'

'You're looking skinny, man. I think it's Harris's food. It doesn't make you want seconds, does it? I could well go for some of Mary's fried pork right now.'

The name hangs awkwardly; she's a sore subject in the bungalow. Tristan usually tries to catch himself before he talks about her. It hurts too much. How could she leave them like this? Tristan had called Julia's place a few times, but Mary wouldn't come to the phone.

'She won't get out of bed,' Julia told him. 'Stays there all day. Hardly eats, hardly talks. We're worried.'

Tristan couldn't imagine Mary immobilized like that. He'd hardly seen her sit still his whole life. She used to drink her tea standing, eat her dinner perched on the edge of the sofa and watch the *Eastenders* omnibus at the same time as ironing. She must be feeling bad, really bad.

Malachi wipes his face with his hands and holds them there. 'I'm so tired.' The bed gives way a little as he sits on it and leans his head against the wall. They used to lie like this as kids, Malachi reading Tolkien until they fell asleep in the same bunk.

'I need something from you, Mal, and I don't want you to make a big thing about it.'

Malachi keeps his eyes closed. 'Does it require me moving from this spot?'

'Well, I know it's hard to believe, judging by Harris's poor choice of hairstyle, but I did notice he's got some clippers in the bathroom. I've got a proper 'fro going on.'

'You want me to cut your hair? Now?'

'Yeah. Why not?'

Malachi's eyes flick open. 'Don't we need to wait for the scars to heal up a little more?'

'No. It's been long enough. Come, help me out.'

Malachi sets up a chair in the bathroom and comes back to help Tristan through. Neither of them mention how much harder it's getting for Tristan to walk, how he can only stand for a few minutes at a time unaided.

Malachi stands behind the chair, sorts the blades out and rests the small round mirror in the sink bowl.

'Nah, Mal. Put it on one.'

'Why?'

''Cause I always have it on one.' Tristan rubs at his thick hair. 'Can't wait to see it off.'

'Tris, if I shave on one, it's going to look patchy.'

'I know. But I always have it on one. So put it on one.'

Malachi tuts as he changes the blade back and starts to cut. Back home they would always play music while doing this, but the CDs went with everything else and the one thing Harris can't share is his radio. Besides, it's kind of calming listening to the buzz of the blade. It nears an area of scar tissue, still tender, and Tristan flinches.

Malachi pulls away. 'Knew this was a bad idea.'

'It's okay, carry on.'

Malachi straightens up Tristan's head before continuing. 'It's a bit flaky. I'm going to rub some coconut oil on it.'

'Argh!' Tristan jumps forward. 'What's wrong with you? You're like Mum, always with the cold hands. Can't you warm them up first?'

'Stop complaining. Be grateful I didn't cut you.'

'Wouldn't make a difference anyway.' Tristan holds the pot of coconut oil to his face, then wiggles his fingers. 'Mirror, please.'

Malachi huffs. 'Really?'

Tristan kisses his teeth and keeps his hand raised until he's passed it. He sees the scars on his body every day, the wide graze across the left side of his face and the deep line that curls around his ankle and shoots halfway up his calf. These no longer have the power to shock him. But this tiny maze of cuts is jarring. How can the back of his head be so damaged?

'You're right, it's pure flaky,' he says glumly.

'Yeah, but it's healing. Right?'

Tristan moves his head about to reassess his reflection. 'Yeah, it's healing.'

*

Tristan's glad he took the leap and cut his hair. He should have done it ages ago. It's almost like he's his old self again. He takes his crutches and fills the kettle, looking about for Malachi, who disappeared straight after cleaning the bathroom. The evenings are the worst here, it's too quiet. Everyone seems to stick to their individual rooms. Harris listens to the radio and marks his books, while Malachi sleeps for hours, and Tristan sits bored out of his head alone. Maybe that's what the TV is for. To keep him occupied. It never used to be like this back in the flat, even when Malachi had exams on or was out with Blondie, there was always time together to watch pirate videos and listen to music.

There's a faint smell of weed in the air. Tristan opens the kitchen window and spots the long outline of Malachi as he lies across the wooden decking, staring up at the sky.

'Oh, you're out here. You want a tea?'

'If you're making one.'

'Yup.' He goes to the cupboards and sniffs the teabags to check they're proper tea and not the weird herbal kind Harris is always boiling up. He puts the mugs on the window ledge and knocks for Mal to get them while he makes his way out of the back door.

'Here.' Tristan takes a Mars bar from his pocket and throws it down before checking on the progress of his tomato plant, which now has three greenish bulbs hanging from the hairy vines. The only sound is of Harris's smoker's cough over his radio. It always creeps Tristan out that he can hardly hear the neighbours. 'So quiet out here, eh, Mal?' Tristan's mug clanks as he puts it down on the iron table.

'Hmm.' Malachi's eyes are now closed, his hood up.

Tristan taps a beat from an old track, he's not heard in ages, on the table with his fingers. He thinks he hears a baby cry and listens for a few more minutes, turning his head to the right, where his hearing is strongest. No, nothing. The tea is too hot and he has to slurp it.

'Could you be any louder?' Malachi says.

Tristan laughs. 'Dunno how you can lie on that mouldy old wood down there, Mal. You're gonna get bugs crawling up your arse. I can smell those compost tubs from here. Why can't Harris use the normal bin like everyone else? He's so extra. And what's with the dressing gown? When he wears that little gold and green ensemble I feel embarrassed for him.'

Tristan slurps his tea again. 'I like sitting up here on this chair. It makes me feel like I'm at a garden party or something. So ornate.'

Malachi pulls himself up to sitting. 'I thought you came out here to chill, not talk my ear off.' He sips his tea and flinches. 'And when are you going to learn the difference between a tablespoon and teaspoon?'

'Whatever, Mal. I'm only sitting out here with you till *Eastenders* comes on. Got to kill time somehow.'

'Can't believe you're still watching that.' He lies back down. 'As if real life doesn't have enough drama.'

Finally, it feels like they're back to their old ways, how they used to be with each other in the flat. It makes Tristan feel good. He doesn't want to rock the boat, yet can't help but think now would be the perfect time to talk, to open up, then they can start to properly move past this.

'You all right, Mal?'

'You know me. I'm always all right.'

They had first started the mantra after their mum died as an easy way to shut down conversations with prying adults, to get out of talking about how much they were hurting. When had they started using it on each other?

'You miss Blondie, don't you?' Tristan can hear the nerves in own his voice.

'Course I miss her.'

'I never really got it, Mal. Were you two serious? Like, did you wanna do it properly?'

'Do what?'

'I dunno, get a dog, buy a sofa together.'

Malachi sighs.

'I mean, would you have gotten back together eventually? Did you want to start a family with her?'

'Tris,' he says, 'stop going on.'

'You're meant to talk about stuff, Mal. Isn't that what your fruity therapist says? Don't bottle this shit up.'

'I'm not.' He shoots up to sitting again, pulls his hood down and stares. 'I just about have enough energy for each day. There's no point in me talking about stuff that doesn't exist anymore.'

Tristan feels the heat rise behind his ears. 'But I'm not talking about *stuff*, am I? I'm talking about her – Pamela.'

'Yeah, but what about her?'

'Well, was it real between you two? Were you getting back together?'

'I don't understand why you're asking me all this?'

''Cause I saw her.' Tristan's been holding it in for so long that it almost explodes out of him. 'I saw her right before it happened. I knew she was back home.'

The door to the house opens and Harris comes out, looking ridiculous in his dressing gown. 'Boys? Everything okay out here?'

Malachi ignores him and holds Tristan's gaze. 'Did she come to the flat?' he asks.

'No, I went up. She called. She wanted me to give something to you.' Tristan should have kept his mouth shut. He doesn't know what to say next, what to keep a secret. As Malachi comes closer Tristan sees an unfamiliar desperation in his face.

'What did she want to give you?' he asks.

'Just some book, that's all.'

Malachi's eyes zone in on him. 'What book?'

'I dunno.'

'What book? What did it look like?'

'I dunno. Just some uni book you must have left in her rucksack.'

'You kept this from me? All this time? All that shit you said to me in the hospital about never keeping secrets and you had seen her and didn't tell me?'

Harris tries to put his arm around Malachi. 'Come inside.'

Malachi shoves him away and slams his fist on the table. 'We're not meant to keep stuff from each other.' The tea splashes everywhere; it runs through the twists of iron and onto Tristan's legs. 'It's not what we do.'

'I'm sorry, Mal. I didn't mean—'

'I can't believe you kept this from me. I can't believe you saw her. Right before it happened. You saw her last. You realise that? You had her last words. Her last smile. Her last . . . ' He throws his arms up and lets his hands come to rest on his face.

'I'm sorry, Mal. I was too confused at first and then I didn't know what good it would do for you to know. It wasn't a big deal.'

'So why tell me now? Why wait till I'm just getting okay, then tell me?' He drops his hands and shakes his head at Tristan. 'I can't be around you.'

Harris follows Malachi back into the house. The muffled sound of their voices briefly fills the air, then the front door slams. Malachi's probably gone back to the estate, to stand on the field and torture himself by looking at it. Tristan wishes he could chase him, stop him and apologise, put things right again. But none of this seems within his power. His head feels heavy; he lays it in his palms. He can't let things get worse than this, he knows that for sure.

All sounds quiet in the house and he heads back in.

Harris looks down at Tristan's wet trousers. 'Are you okay?'

'Course, just a little fallout. He'll be all right?' Tristan doesn't mean it as a question but that's exactly how it comes out.

'I've not wanted to get involved with this,' Harris says. He stops and pinches the bridge of his nose. 'But if you're hiding something from Malachi about Pamela—'

'I'm not hiding anything.' He feels defensive again.

'Tristan, I know there's a letter. I saw it at the hospital.'

'I know Mal and I can't give him that letter. It would kill him, the stuff in it.'

'Well, then, that's your decision. But whatever you decide you need to stick with it for the rest of your life. So think about it. Think about if it's really a secret worth keeping.'

Tristan doesn't need to think about it, he already knows what to do. He goes to his bedroom and from under the bed he pulls out the plastic tub that contains his school books and hospital records. Under this is a pile of magazines, well-thumbed and read cover to cover during his hospital stay. He finds the issue of *Men's Health*. Pamela's letter falls out. Flat thirty-three had been destroyed the minute the plane exploded. He would have been dead if Pamela hadn't called him up to get this letter. He was meant to have it. It rips slightly as he pulls it from the envelope and unfolds the three pages of Pamela's big, swirly writing.

He sighs as he skim reads. It feels different to how it did before when he read it in the stairwell. He remembers laughing then, thinking Pamela was just some ridiculous girl quoting Aaliyah songs at his brother. But now, reading this is upsetting and kind of emotional. He stops on the third page, he knows what's coming, and feels the urge to destroy the letter. But no, he needs to be one hundred percent sure that he's doing the right thing here, so he takes his time and tries to imagine what each of Pamela's last sentences would do to Malachi.

I know this wasn't part of our plan, Mal, but it's happening. I'm pregnant. I can't believe we did this and now here's the consequence. Obviously I've not been to a doctor yet but I think it's still really early days (I only realised once I arrived back in Portishead and started feeling sick). We need to talk about this. We need to make the decision together and quickly. There's so much we both want to achieve and I realise how this will make things harder for us both, but I'm prepared for it, if you are. But of course if you're not then let's talk about that too. I'm so confused. Don't know what I want, except for us to be together again.

Please, please let's talk. Dad is still furious, locking me in and even talking about walking me to and from school! But he can't stay mad forever. He's working long hours, so please phone me and we can talk properly, like we used to.

I love you. I miss you.
Pam

There's no way Mal can know about this, no way it will help. Tristan begins to rip the paper up into the tiniest pieces his fingers can manage. Then, despite his exhaustion and the pain in his left leg, he walks back outside to the end of Harris's garden. There, he puts Pamela's last words into one of the big green compost bins.

SIX MONTHS LATER

CHAPTER FORTY

Malachi

They sit outside the town hall in the little bronze car. Malachi's knees bend awkwardly as his seat is pushed forward to make space for Tristan in the back. He feels so big for everything these days, like he can no longer fit into his old life.

''Arry, this lack of heating is becoming an issue,' Tristan says.

Harris turns the engine back on, filling the car with air that's too warm and close.

Malachi was the last one to get up this morning. He didn't want to face this day, this six-month marker, but they had made him, insisting he came along to the town hall to walk with all the other survivors in solidarity. His head thumps; the headaches are coming more often these days.

'Mal, there's Bob Ferris.' Tristan taps on the window as he spots the caretaker from the estate. 'Don't think I've ever seen him outside of the blocks before. In fact, I've never seen most of these people anywhere other than on the estate. Weird, innit?'

Malachi vaguely recognizes some faces as they pass. No one in the car needs to say it but it's obvious the only person they all really want to see here today is Mary.

Little crowds form, coming together in hugs and tears. Some have brought signs and placards painted with demands for answers. Others hold flowers and unlit candles. On the other side of the road stand a huddle of photographers talking among themselves. One breaks away from the pack to take pictures of the three men in navy uniforms: representatives from the airline.

What's the point of gathering here today, asking for answers about what happened, going over what could have been? None of that will change anything.

'It's quite a crowd now,' Harris says. 'Well, they said from midday, so we should go. Are you both ready to join?' He switches off the heat.

The cameras flash in the corner of Malachi's eye and when he looks over he spots Pamela's dad, Jay, sloping in behind the crowd. His isolation makes him stand out. Had he always looked so dirty? So poor? Malachi hadn't thought about him in months, but now he wonders about this man, where he was when Pamela was dying in the flat.

'Tris, I need you to tell me the truth about something.'

The car falls silent.

Malachi watches Tristan's face in the rear view mirror. 'This book you got from Pam. You told me you went up to get it. Why would you do that?'

The backseat squeaks as Tristan shifts in it. 'I already told you what I remember: she had a book to give you. You two were always swapping books and stuff.'

'Yeah, but why did you have to go up?' Malachi turns around now, needing to see his brother's reaction when he asks the question he should have all those months ago. 'Why didn't she come down and post it through the letterbox?'

'Is this really the right time to do this?' Harris asks.

'Why didn't she post it?' Malachi asks again.

'I dunno. Maybe she was still funny about seeing you after whatever happened—'

It's obvious now, the story doesn't make sense, and he can see it in the desperate way Tristan keeps looking out of the window, fussing with the blanket over his legs.

'You're lying to me.'

'Mal, why would I lie to you about something like this?'

'Because you know she was locked in, wasn't she? Her dad locked the gate. He always used to threaten her with it, ever since she lost the key. He did, didn't he?'

Harris intervenes. 'Malachi, what is the point of this? Stop.'

'Why?' It's the only thing he can think of now, *why why why*. He's filled with questions, they take over and push him out of the car and through the crowds towards Pamela's dad. Malachi doesn't even know what he's going to say or do, all he knows is that he needs to be standing in front of him right now.

The man flinches as Malachi approaches. 'What do you want?'

'You locked her in?' He can feel it now that Jay killed her, locked her in that flat, and made sure she couldn't save her own life. 'Say it out loud. You locked her in.'

Jay stands, blank-faced.

The silence builds and Malachi moves closer, the rage mounting as he imagines what Pamela's final moments must have been like, alone and scared, waiting for the smoke or flames to take her. It makes him crazy to picture it; it hurts.

He grabs at Jay's jacket. 'I want to hear you say it. You killed her.' Their faces are so close now and it makes Malachi sick to notice, in this moment, a reflection of Pamela in the colour of Jay's eyes.

'What does it matter?' he finally says. 'She's gone. I locked the gate to keep her safe from you. And I would do it again if I had to. You wanna blame me for it?' Jay spits. 'You wanna put it all on me?'

'Of course it's on you. You killed her.'

'Why d'you think I had to lock the gate? You think I liked doing it? You're the one who gave me the reason.'

Other people surround them now. Malachi can feel them looking, questioning what's going on.

'You're the reason I locked her in that day,' Jay shouts. 'You're to blame.'

When Malachi hits him, it's not only from anger about Pamela, it's a build-up of rage from everything that's ever happened to him: of losing his mum, of watching Tristan in pain, of every time he said he was all right when inside he felt like he was one step away from giving up.

Malachi's not to blame. He would never have hurt Pamela.

He hits Jay again and again, until he stumbles backwards and Malachi feels his hand go limp and tingly from the impact. An unwashed smell rises from Jay as he falls to the ground, not even putting up a fight. Malachi pulls him up by the jacket and stares at the white and red clusters of skin gathered on his cheeks and forehead.

He's vaguely aware of Tristan's voice calling him, someone screaming, but he can't stop now. Something takes over, causing him to wrap his fingers around Jay's neck, which feels easier and much more satisfying than the punches. But then he's being pulled up, his fingers peeled away from the stubbly skin of Jay's neck, and it doesn't matter that he didn't finish what he started, because for the first time in months, he feels like he's let it out.

CHAPTER FORTY-ONE

Mary

It's another normal day in Julia's house. Mary gets dressed, she eats breakfast, she marinates the beef and grates the papaya for the empanadas – the only traditional food her grandbabies will tolerate. She complains about her daughter's kitchen, the electric hob that burns everything, the ordeal of removing tea stains from the white worktops. Julia asks several times, 'Mum, you sure you're okay today?' and each time Mary replies, 'I'm fine. Go out.'

But then Julia leaves, and without her distraction, Mary feels herself shrink. She sits on the sofa and watches TV for hours. She absentmindedly scratches at her left elbow till the skin breaks and bleeds. She doesn't feel like she is okay today after all.

The headline on the newspaper bothers her. *Mourning Dad Battered by Local Thug.* And next to it a photo of Malachi, looking as he always has, fed up and miserable, but in this context he also looks malicious. Maybe this is who he's become, another violent stranger angry at the world.

It would be impossible to go through what he has without being changed by it.

'Nanny Tuazon!' Ruby, the oldest of Mary's grandchildren, shouts as she runs through the house. 'The washing's getting wet.' She stops in front of Mary. 'Nanny?'

Mary folds the paper and throws it under the coffee table. Then the other two children bound into the living room. They're draining to watch, the speed of their movements, the life that radiates from their small flushed faces and the smell they carry, of grass and rain, tinged with something sweet like Coca-Cola.

'No, stop it,' the youngest child squeals as she grabs Mary's skirt. Her big sister pokes and tickles through the material.

'Get out,' Mary tries. The children run away. As they leave, one of them knocks against the small wooden table, on which stands a gold-framed photo of David and two burnt-out tea lights. Mary walks over and lifts the frame. It's an old photograph, David at his peak. Years ago she had told him how disappointed people must be when he shows up to bookings with his middle-aged face, but really she could not deny how little he aged over the years. This will forever be the case now: she will age and wither, and he will always look like this, beautiful and wrinkle-free, preserved.

The children play on the stairs now, a game Julia shouted about when she caught them playing, a game she slapped her oldest child for making up.

'Fire! Fire!' Ruby's call makes Mary recoil. She needs to stop them, but can't face the march out to the hall, the energy it will take to discipline them.

The children share tales of their imagined heroism and

bravery should a plane ever crash into their home, how they would run fast, save one another and put out fires, throw mattresses from the top floor and jump down to safety.

'Fire! Fire!' The imaginary plane has crashed.

Mary walks to the conservatory, to silence, to watch the slow soaking of the bed sheets and school uniforms on the line outside. She wants to relive that day too, the day the plane came. She wants to bump into David as he gets off the bus on the other side of the field and tell him there and then that she wants a divorce, that she plans to marry someone else, someone she loves. Then she wants to watch him rage about a wasted journey, his wide face reddening with anger, before turning on his heel and dragging his suitcase away, out of her life and into that other woman's.

Ruby comes in and presses her nose against the glass by Mary's leg. 'Nanny, the clothes are getting wet. Mum will be cross.'

They watch as a plane draws a soft wisp of white in the distance.

'Nanny, why didn't the people on the plane parachute out?'

'Stop it,' Mary says.

'Do you think Grandpa Tuazon was really a spy and the baddies were trying to get him?'

'Ruby, stop.'

'I think it was done on purpose. Maybe someone wanted to have a war with England.'

'Leave me alone,' Mary shouts.

Ruby looks up, her face a replica of her mother's at that age, and Mary feels guilty for snapping. The child's bottom lip trembles before she runs away.

Mary presses her face against the glass and slides down it. She closes her eyes to the clothes, the rain, the many different scenarios that could have produced a different outcome that day. She isn't even aware of Julia's car in the drive, or the front door as it opens.

'Mum?' She sounds angry. 'Why are you out here? The kids are running riot.'

Mary turns to face her daughter. The powder on Julia's face is splattered from the rain, her hair slightly frizzed.

'You look exhausted. I shouldn't have left you.'

'We were never happy,' Mary says now, because she realises there is no better time. 'We were never enough for each other.'

Julia throws her keys into her bag. 'I think you need to go upstairs and lie down.' She uses the same tone she uses on her children, on her husband, even – patronising and forever exasperated.

'I'm trying to tell you something.'

'Yes, but I'm not sure I want to hear it,' Julia snaps. Yet she sits down on one of the wicker chairs and drops her bag on the floor. Mary can feel her daughter's anger; it seeps off her in fierce waves, the same way her grief at losing her dad does.

'Julia, you are not a child anymore. I need to be able to talk to you like an adult.'

'I don't want to do this, Mum,' she says quietly. 'I don't need to know about your marriage.'

Mary realises that her daughter knows about the affair. 'So you want me to pretend? To act like we were Brady Bunch happy? We were strangers in the end, you must understand.'

'Oh, so it's okay that he died then? Because you weren't in love anymore?'

'No. Of course that's not what I am saying, but—'

'I don't need to know!' Julia screams.

Mary is taken aback by her daughter's fury. It makes her weep.

Ruby pokes her small head in. 'Mummy?'

'Ruby, go upstairs,' Julia shouts, without turning to face the girl. 'I understand that you and Dad didn't always get on. But for John and me, we've lost a parent. And we're struggling. We need time.'

'But I don't have time anymore. I've waited my whole life. It's all I've ever done. Wait for tours to end, for kids to grow up, for him to return home. You have no idea how much I wanted to do in my life, but missed because I was waiting. I cannot wait anymore. I cannot wait for it to be all right with you and John. I am sorry.' Mary feels herself truly exhale for the first time in months, for mixed within the sea of grief and guilt, she feels the first flutters of relief.

Julia stands up and shrugs her shoulders. 'Do what you want, Mum. I don't need to know about it.'

CHAPTER FORTY-TWO

Elvis

Tristan Roberts loves pizza. The last time Elvis went to see him they had three huge pizzas delivered to the bungalow and everyone shared, except Harris because he is a vegetarian, which means he does not eat anything that once had a face. Elvis hopes this evening they will order pizzas again. Especially the Hawaiian flavour as it has pineapple on it, which is strange but also very tasty. Though, even if there is no pizza Elvis knows he will have an excellent time at the bungalow as it has become one of his favourite places.

'Right, Elvis, I'll drop you here.' George hands Elvis the lemon drizzle cake they picked up at the Co-op. It is to share with Tristan Roberts as he loves cake. 'Get Malachi to call you a cab when you're ready to go home, all right?'

Elvis steps out of George's car, very carefully holding the cake.

There are a lot of big trees in Vanbrugh Close and there are also a lot of crunchy leaves on the ground, which he likes to kick through as he walks. Archie, his friend from the Waterside Centre, once said that if you kick through leaves your shoe could get covered in dog poop or, worse, you could break your toe on a hidden rock. Archie thinks too much about all the bad things that could happen and most of them never do.

A girl with amazing red hair comes out of the bungalow. She stops and kisses Tristan Roberts on the mouth and Elvis looks away, as he is not a pervert.

'Laters,' Tristan Roberts calls to the girl as he leans on his special walking sticks, which Elvis tried once but they made his arms very tired.

When Tristan Roberts sees Elvis, he laughs. 'Ah man, that girl is trouble.'

Elvis would not be smiling if someone with red hair was giving him trouble, but he knows sometimes Tristan Roberts says things that do not always make sense.

'Come in. Thought you were coming at six?' he asks.

'George had to walk Aztec.'

'Damn social worker,' Tristan Roberts says as he hobbles over to a dial on the wall and fiddles with it. 'Drafty, ain't it? I'll put the heating up.' He winks at Elvis. 'Don't tell Harris.'

They put on a film called *The Usual Suspects*. It has some shooting in it, which Elvis does not like, and it is a little bit confusing, especially as Tristan Roberts talks all the way through the start, so Elvis misses some parts that are important.

The front door opens and Malachi comes in. Elvis always feels pleased to see Malachi, but Malachi does not look pleased to Elvis. He does not look pleased about anything. He picks up the remote control and turns the volume down.

'I can hear this from outside,' Malachi shouts. 'Put the subtitles on.'

'Elvis can't read that fast.'

'How many times you seen this anyway? You already know the ending.'

'Shush, Elvis don't know.'

Malachi then goes to the dial on the wall and shouts again. 'It's not even cold outside. You're ridiculous.'

'Oh, stop bitching, Mal. Sorry, Elvis.' Tristan Roberts knows that Elvis does not like bad language. He has promised to stop using it so much when they are together but sometimes he forgets.

Malachi takes a slice of the lemon drizzle cake and eats it standing over the sink. Tristan Roberts does this too and Elvis does not understand why both of the brothers do not like to use plates.

They continue to watch but now Tristan Roberts looks grumpy. He even stops telling Elvis about the film, which is great because it means Elvis can do very good concentrating. When he looks up again, Tristan Roberts has fallen asleep. He does this a lot when they watch films together.

Elvis does not want to sit by himself, so he goes outside to find Malachi, who is smoking his funny cigarettes, which are very bad but allowed when you are at home.

'Hello,' Elvis says as he sits down on the wooden decking, which is a little bit wet and mouldy.

'How you doing, Elvis?' Malachi stares down to the end of the garden at the big rubber tubs of compost.

Last week Harris showed Elvis inside the tubs. He took a stick and poked at the compost, which was crawling with thousands of worms. It was amazing but Tristan Roberts made lots of gagging noises, but he was not really sick, he was pretending, or being what Harris called 'theatrical'.

'You look sad,' Elvis says.

Malachi raises his eyebrows. 'That's because I am sad.'

'Tristan said you loved the blonde girl from the eleventh floor. She could run very fast. But I know she is dead now. Is that why you are sad?'

He stubs the smelly cigarette out on the decking. 'Yep. That's exactly why I'm sad.'

'How long will you be sad?'

Malachi laughs, but it is not a funny question, it is a serious question. He does not answer.

It is getting a bit cold now and there are some fireworks in the sky, which look pretty but also make Elvis jump a little when they go 'bang'.

'Are you still sad, Elvis?'

Elvis nods. He is still very sad. Sad about losing his perfect flat and all his perfect things, sad about Lina dying and her family crying, sad about Tristan's operation next year, where the doctor might have to cut his foot off, and sad about his own ear, which still is a little bit broken even though the angry ear doctor has looked at it lots of times. Elvis thinks maybe she is not a real doctor after all.

'Yes, I am sad. But also quite happy.'

'Really? Why?'

'Because I have a brother now who will take care of me forever. Tristan Roberts said he is my brother.' Elvis is suddenly excited by a thought, which has not been discussed yet, but Elvis thinks it is a great idea. 'Do you want to be my brother too?'

Malachi looks at him and smiles. This is a good thing, a very good thing, because he does not usually smile very much.

'If we are all brothers then we can all take care of each other. Then none of us will get hurt again.'

'That's a nice idea, Elvis. But remember that one day Tristan might not be stuck at home so much, he might be off at school or hopefully college, and when that happens he won't be around to hang out with you as much as he does now.' Malachi is no longer smiling but making a very serious face at Elvis. 'Does that make sense? You can't stop spending time with all your other friends just to hang out with Tris.'

'I only have one friend. His name is Archie.'

'And when was the last time you hung out with Archie? You always seem to be here at the moment. Don't you think it would be fun to hang out with Archie some time too?'

Elvis is not sure. Archie is his friend but now he has a brother, he likes to hang out with him more.

'Elvis, what happens when Tristan's not around to watch films and eat pizza with you anymore?'

'Then I will watch films and eat pizza with Archie again.'

Malachi sighs loudly, like he is getting very fed up. 'Yeah, but will Archie still want to be your friend then?'

Elvis crosses his hands in his laps and thinks about this very complicated question.

'If Archie does not want to be my friend anymore Tristan

Roberts will help get us back together again like he did with you and running girl. That is what brothers do.'

Malachi relights his smelly cigarette. 'Forget it.' He starts to smoke and the smell is not very nice, but Elvis cannot tell him off because it is a garden and people are allowed to smoke in their own gardens.

'Anyway,' Malachi says, 'what makes you think Tristan helped with me and Pamela, the running girl?'

'He told me.'

'Told you what?'

'He told me that he did not like her very much because she only liked practising running fast and was boring. But he said you liked her very much and that you should have been able to be her boyfriend again.' The word boyfriend makes Elvis laugh, especially when he thinks that maybe Malachi and the blonde girl kissed each other on the lips. 'That is why he helped.'

'Helped with what?'

'He tried to help get you back to being boyfriend and girlfriend again. But then the bad explosion happened and the letter got lost.'

'What letter?'

'The love letter from the running girl. She asked Tristan Roberts to give it to you.'

Malachi stares for a very long time, then throws his hood up over his head, even though it is not raining. 'Oh, you mean the book?'

'No. It was a love letter. He told me. But I did not read it because it is private.'

'You're confused, Elvis. It was just a book. Tristan can't even remember which one, anyway.'

Malachi lies down on the decking and closes his eyes, even though there are pretty fireworks in the sky and the conversation about brotherhood, friendship and the love letter is not finished.

CHAPTER FORTY-THREE

Tristan

He watches Harris come up the gravel path. He's got on his smart camel-coloured jacket – Humanities Teacher jacket, Tristan calls it. All that's missing are the patches on the elbow and some ballpoint pens poking out the breast pocket. A cold rush of air sweeps the room as Harris comes in, a bundle of yellow exercise books under each arm.

''Arry,' Tristan shouts from his spot perched on the window ledge.

'I can't believe they still haven't swept the street. The leaves are wet now, it's dangerous.' Harris drops the books and ugly jacket on the sofa. 'Just where is my council tax going?'

'I like it, man. Looks atmospheric and shit,' Tristan says. He turns back to the window and watches as two teenagers cycle about the close. One of them attempts a wheelie. 'Pussy,' Tristan says under his breath as the boy's wheel slams back down on the pavement a few seconds later. Back at Nightingale Point, Tristan was the king of wheelies; he could do it all the way up Sandford Road without even breaking a sweat.

The boy peddles faster this time and Tristan thinks about the book of prosthetic feet Dr G showed him the last time he went in to see her. Still, it might never happen. Maybe never getting to ride a bike again will be another one of the *life-changing consequences* of the accident. Like never being able to step into a bath, or hear that low whine on a Snoop Dogg track, or have patterns shaved into the side of his hair.

'Who are you spying on?' Harris asks. Dark pouches hang below his eyes, and his skin, though still unexplainably tanned, has a greyish sheen to it.

'I'm waiting on Red Weave. Wanna make sure I see her coming. Can't have her sneaking up on me.'

Harris stifles a laugh. 'And will she be joining us for dinner?'

Tristan grins with relief as Harris pulls a pile of takeaway menus from under the coffee table.

'Nope. She's not the kinda girl you need to feed.' He'd asked her to come over earlier in the day, while everyone would still be at work, but her timekeeping was poor. He never thought twice about having girls over when it was just him and Mal in the flat, but there's something embarrassing about doing a girl while Harris is home. He had tried it once and even with a girl as hot as Red Weave, he was distracted by the sound of the kitchen radio as it drifted through the bungalow.

'Tristan, are you actually going to look at these books, or is this some kind of display you're creating here?' Harris indicates the spread of GCSE revision guides, which have sat on the table, untouched, since this morning.

'Pah.' He waves his hand. 'I got ages for that. Besides, the mock tests were a piece of piss.'

Tristan mistakenly thought that after doing so well in his mock tests, despite missing such a big chunk of school, Harris and Malachi would back off constantly trying to get him to study. But the opposite happened and now they are both wetting themselves about the prospect he could get enough A to C grades to do A levels.

Tristan had made plenty of big plans while lying in that hospital bed, mostly lofty ideas around music. But once out and hobbling around in the real world, he realised he needed some sort of plan B in case he didn't make his fortune from rapping. He's always been good at maths, but those suit-wearing number jobs like accountancy, engineering and finance simply didn't float his boat, even though the money was appealing. After what he'd been through, Tristan felt he needed to focus on something a bit more wholesome. He just didn't know what and felt too stupid saying it out loud.

'I was always appalling at science,' Harris says as he flicks though a book, frowning. 'Tristan, you haven't highlighted a single thing. Come on. Put in some effort.'

'Gimme a break. You want me to spend my life learning from books? I got the real biology report right here. People should be studying me,' he says as he taps his chest. '*Ay yo, they said I'd never walk again, but boy I knew I would, and then the lady with the lamp came and fixed me a new foot. Connect the tibula and fibula, the tendons and the tendrils, mix it with some gin and juice, and boy you know it's been real.* Eh, Mal,' he shouts through the hallway. 'Come hear me spit this verse.'

Malachi emerges into the room and shakes his head. 'I can't believe you're rapping about tendrils.' He rubs his temples and Tristan suspects that he was in the bedroom rolling a spliff to have out in the garden later. The thought of smoking weed still turns Tristan's stomach. Even the smell of it on Malachi's clothes in the evening is enough to put Tristan right back in the stairwell. It's one of the few things that makes him feel down. But most days, Tristan wakes up feeling like a light has been cracked open inside him and he can take on any old shit that comes next. Nan says it's the light of God, but it's probably more to do with not being able to remember everything.

Last month the Civil Aviation Unit contacted him to ask if he wanted to see the surviving parts of the plane. Harris angrily called the invite 'macabre' and Tristan later asked his physiotherapist, a Scottish man who wore trainers and had an impressive knowledge of old school hip-hop, what the word meant. Tristan's since decided he doesn't need to see the wreck of the plane. It's just another one of those things people suggest, like therapy, thinking it will be helpful, when really there's been nothing in the last few months that's made Tristan feel worse than when he sat in that dingy grey office being asked about his appearance and how it made him feel. The whole time he kept looking at the wall of shelves, home to hundreds of ring binders containing everyone's problems, all stacked up like a wall of misery. Besides, Tristan's demons aren't with the plane or even with his injuries, they're with his lack of memory. The feeling that his life has been altered and he missed it happening.

It's all clear up until a point: the heat in the flat, the splash

335

of melted blue ice pole on his white T-shirt, David arriving for the keys, and Pamela, red-eyed and tearful, passing him that letter through the black bars of the security gate. Then it all stops with a bang. After that he can only recall the sound of a sharp ringing bell, the smell of sulphur, and Elvis, encouraging him, reassuring him, and saving him.

That damn letter. It's not even worth thinking about what it would have done to Malachi if he found out about it.

The room brightens.

'Why are you two sitting in the dark?' Malachi asks. He looks thin, his shirt hanging off him. Tristan makes a mental note to order a tub of ice cream with dinner.

Malachi's only just started talking to Tristan again. It isn't quite the same as before, but at least there is some conversation between them. Still, it hurts to think that their relationship is damaged. It hurts more than anything else Tristan has endured over the last six months.

'I don't have the energy to move,' Harris says.

'I didn't even notice it get dark.' Until Harris came in, Tristan thought it was still about one o'clock. The days seem to fly when he's at home doing nothing other than 'studying'.

He treads slowly over to the sofa and lowers himself down next to Harris, who stretches out his legs.

'So, let's talk film choices.' Tristan pulls a bag of videotapes between them. 'I got *Se7en*, I got *Casino* – I know you love yourself a bit of Sharon Stone – *Ace Ventura*, which is obviously one for Elvis. These are all pirates, but all right copies.'

Harris observes one of the photocopied covers closely before he bends over to pull off each of his socks. 'They all look terrible.'

'Come on, this stuff ain't even out in the cinema yet. Give it a chance. You liked *Johnny Mnemonic*.'

'I tolerated it,' he laughs.

Tristan knows Harris still needs to pretend that he regrets allowing them to move the television–VCR combo into the living room, but really he loves an action film as much as anyone.

'Mal, you wanna watch something with me and 'Arry tonight?' He asks hopefully, like a real beg-a-friend.

Malachi shrugs, non-committal as always. Probably the best Tristan is going to get from him tonight.

'Come on, 'Arry, what we eating?' He throws his arm around Harris. 'I well fancy some curry goat. You up for driving me down the takeaway?'

'Tristan, I'm exhausted. Order something to be delivered.'

'I'll go and collect it,' Malachi says with huff. 'Hurry up and decide.'

'You want me to hobble on down with you?' He never misses a chance to be alone with Malachi. 'Be good to stretch my legs,' Tristan tries again, but Malachi is staring out of the window at something in the close.

'Mal, what's up?'

'Mary's outside.'

Tristan pushes himself up and goes over to his brother's side. The street lights always come on too early in the close and everything looks brighter than it should be. One of the kids has fallen from his bike and now stands with one trouser leg rolled up while his friend inspects for damage. A car slowly reverses into the drive across the way. One of the neighbours pulls her wheelie bin up the path. And then, on the other side of the close, is Mary, her feet hidden by the build-up of brown leaves, her face lit brightly by the orange lamp above her head and what's left of the fading sun.

No one speaks. No one knows what to say. Tristan hears his watch beep in acknowledgement of the hour – a reminder to take another line of painkillers. Harris sits on the sofa, blank-faced like he's not bothered, like he's not been waiting for her to return all this time. Missing Mary was the one thing they all had in common, the thing that helped them to bond. But Harris never spoke about her and the only sign she had ever been with him at all was a photo of them both cuddling outside some church. Sometimes, Tristan found himself slipping into doing an impression of her, mimicking one of her sayings in the hybrid Manila-come-London accent of hers he had perfected over the years, and everyone would recognise it and laugh, but afterwards there was a weird, sad silence. The bottom line was Mary left them all, and it was kind of painful.

''Arry, what you going to do?'

The fan of takeaway menus falls to the carpet as Harris sprouts up and heads out. The temperature of the room drops as the November chill enters. Tristan and Malachi edge closer to the window and watch as Harris's bare feet take the leaf-covered path, flanked by cut-back rose bushes and wilting pink flowers, before stopping.

'What's he doing now?' Tristan asks in frustration. 'Why's he just standing there?'

Malachi leans his elbows on the ledge like a keen bird watcher. 'I dunno, Tris. Give him a chance.'

CHAPTER FORTY-FOUR

Mary

She finds herself grateful for the cold, the way her eyes water in the stinging, frosty breeze, the sensation of her toes going numb within her plimsolls, the feeling of being woken up sharply. As she enters Vanbrugh Close, her stomach churns with emptiness. If only she had eaten something before she left Julia's home, then she would not feel so weak and light, so insubstantial. The streetlights come on, signalling the failure of the weak autumn sun, its inability to see the day out. Everything is now too bright and too real. She needs more time, even a few more minutes in the dusk to gather her thoughts and strength. Two schoolchildren on bikes skid to avoid her. Their unbuttoned blazers flap open to reveal the thin lemon shirts of the school Harris teaches in. They're untouched by the cold as they show off for one another, tipping their bikes up onto the back wheels like the kids on Morpeth Estate used to.

Mary should have waited until morning before coming here.

The front garden is a little sparse, in line with the season, and the path is covered with leaves. Inside a light blinks on and she imagines Harris at the switch, illuminating the room, like a shop window for all the neighbours to see the mess and clutter of his home. There is a figure at the glass, familiar, but not Harris.

Mary grips the handle of her bag tightly. It contains all she owns in the world: Harris's work shirt, navy jogging bottoms, her broken fob watch, some newspapers and a few items of clothing bought by Julia.

'Stupid old woman,' she mumbles. 'Cross the street, cross the street.'

The front door opens and Harris appears. He stands in the doorway, motionless, his expression unreadable. Then quickly he walks down the path, until he is on the other side of the street, facing her. The teenagers, now back on their bikes, whizz between Mary and Harris. He waits till they have passed before he crosses and takes her in his arms. The smell of his embrace is so familiar: heavily spiced stews and cigarettes on a cold patio. A shiver passes between them and she doesn't know if it's her body or his that has succumbed to the cold. His back convulses with sobs and she's embarrassed for him, for herself, for anyone happening to walk or drive by and see the scene: two old lovers crying in the middle of the pavement. But she can't stop herself.

She pulls away slightly and looks down at him, at his astonishingly tanned bare feet on the wet ground. 'You've got no shoes on.'

'So what?' He takes her hand and they walk together up the path.

Malachi emerges. He stops at the threshold and leans on the doorframe. He wears a thin-looking red shirt and pulls his shoulders up towards his ears with a shiver before giving Mary one of his brief hugs. She's shocked by the size of him. Has he always been this tall and lanky?

On the stripy woven mat by the door sit the brown sandals Harris wears in all weathers, alongside two large pairs of white trainers.

'Tristan?' She hears the shock in her own voice at finally seeing the damage. Even after all these months, she pictured, at the most, a cursory bandage, a bruised face, some quick-healing scabs that would not alter his young face too much. But his left eye is slanted, the colour replaced with grey, and his face is littered with small scars.

Still, she awaits the toothy smile she's missed, the crush of one of his bear hugs, and when it doesn't come she goes to him.

'Hello, sunshine.' He feels rigid in her arms.

She takes a few steps into the middle of the room, the middle of them all, and feels so small. All the words she practised on the way over vanish and she can think of nothing to say.

Harris's sniffing breaks the silence. He takes a napkin from his pocket and says, 'I wasn't sure you would ever come back.'

'I'm sorry.' Again, she's shocked by how Tristan looks, how much the child she always saw in him has gone.

'I'm going to make some tea,' Harris says and goes into the kitchen.

She sits on the sofa and puts her bag by her feet.

'It's good to see you,' Malachi says.

She smiles, grateful for his kindness. She wants to tell him she's sorry about Pamela, about running off and leaving them, about them losing their home and having to stay here, but she can't speak. The bungalow seems so different with the boys, oddly not crowded, but their influence is clear: a television, a stack of pirate videotapes, crisp packets and magazines on the coffee table.

Harris places a mug of tea in front of each of them, leaving one for Tristan on the side, along with a tablespoon inside a jar of sugar. Mary laughs.

'What?' Harris asks.

'I never thought about what it looked like here, with you three living together. It's very strange.'

'It made sense,' Harris says, embarrassed by his own generosity. He sits on the arm of Malachi's chair and they sip their tea silently. 'Won't you join us?' he asks Tristan.

There are empty spaces either side of Mary, but Tristan shakes his head, wobbling slightly as he leans on the window frame.

Finally, Mary puts down her cup. 'My husband . . . ' She falters. 'My husband David and I were married for over thirty years. We were not together for most of that time, but still.' She looks up at Harris, prepared to see hurt in his eyes, but also some kind of understanding. 'He was my husband and I cheated on him. I started something I shouldn't have. I kept so many secrets. From everyone. I knew David had died, I felt it in my stomach that day.' She turns to Tristan. 'And at first I thought you were gone too, and I blamed myself because I knew something was going to happen but I didn't know what to do about it. So I did nothing.' Her voice breaks. 'I did nothing except come here.'

'You can't blame yourself, Mary.' Harris comes besides her and takes her hand.

'But I did. I don't anymore. I've grieved for my husband. Now I want to start rebuilding my life.'

Tristan huffs.

'Tristan, please say something to me.'

'What do you want to hear?'

'Anything. I am trying.'

'So what if you're trying? You should have tried when I was lying in the hospital bed. When I couldn't remember shit. When Mal got turned away from his girlfriend's funeral.'

'Stop it,' Malachi cautions.

'Why should I? She's rolling back in here like it's a day later and nothing's changed, but she needs to know what it's been like.'

She's seen Tristan kick off many times over the years, especially at his mum and Malachi, but never has it been directed at her. It hurts. She thought she was prepared to hear it today, to feel his neglect and accept how much she hurt him, but it stings more than she predicted.

'You couldn't even be bothered to call me back. I called the house so many times. Every week at one point, and Julia couldn't get you to the phone.'

Those days, an awful blur where Mary wore the same clothes and ate what little food her daughter pushed in front of her. Unthinking, only feeling all she had lost. It was like coming out of a tunnel, when the haze of grief finally began to subside, when she realised that although she lost David she still had her family, her children and grandbabies, her boys and Harris. She needed to get them all back.

Harris puts his arms around her as she starts to cry.

'It's been half a year,' Tristan shouts. 'Half a year. So how can she expect to walk back into open arms from everyone?'

She jumps as Malachi slams his cup down on the table. 'We're all trying to forgive someone something here, Tris. Every one of us. Remember that.'

The look that passes between them has weight to it, another thing Mary has missed. But she no longer has the right to intervene in their arguments.

'I knew you weren't alone. I knew you had each other. Even my children, they shared a womb and they're not as close as you two; they don't look out for each other like you two do. So I knew I could stay away and you would look after each other. You would be okay.'

'But it wasn't okay. We weren't okay.' Tristan is shouting again. 'Why the fuck does everyone keep leaving us to get on with it? I can't believe that you, of all people, walked off. I don't get it.'

'Tris.' Malachi takes hold of his brother's shoulders as he tries to calm him down, but Tristan shrugs and looks directly at Mary. 'You're like all those teachers we had, those social workers. But no, actually, you're worse than them because you pretend to be different. You pretend we're part of your family. But we're not. We're no one to you.'

'Don't say that.'

'It's the truth. You've proven it's the truth. I can't deal with this.' He walks off, away into a bedroom.

Malachi rubs his face with both hands and sighs.

'Tell me the right thing to say to him,' she pleads.

He keeps his face covered and shrugs.

'Malachi?'

'Mary, I don't know anymore.'

She follows Tristan down the corridor. The television goes on inside the end room and she hesitates, wondering if maybe he needs time to calm down. But time is the problem here; she's already wasted too much of it. She opens the door to what must be the tidiest part of the bungalow, void of the knick-knacks, photos and bowls of potpourri Harris scatters about the place. The television gets louder and Tristan focuses on a wildlife programme, the kind he's always loved watching, shouting encouragement at the screen as if his words can save the wildebeests from getting devoured by lions. Mary sits beside him and reaches out to touch his face, like she used to do so freely. She was always pinching the cheeks he never quite lost the chub from, or patting the fluff that gathered on his chin. 'Bum fluff', she called it, much to his annoyance.

'Stop.' He pulls away. 'I don't get why you've bothered to come back at all.' His voice is littler now and he seems almost tearful.

'To say sorry.'

'Well, you said it now, so . . . ' He stalls and in this moment Mary takes the remote from his hand and turns off the television. He doesn't protest, but continues to ignore her, focused on the now blank screen.

'I made a mistake. Too many mistakes. I wasn't well; I had to stay away. But I'm better now, stronger than I was. Before I was acting like a stupid old woman. Worry, worry, so much worry. About you and Malachi. My children. My grandbabies. The hospital. David. Harris. Everything I was worrying about all the time. For what?' What else can she say? How can she explain to him how much she's missed him? How terrified she now is that he will reject her? 'I'm sorry I missed your birthday.' It's probably the wrong thing to say, but it's been hanging over her, the fact that she missed this marker. He had told her of his ambitious plans for his sixteenth: the VIP area he and his boys would dominate in a club, the gold velvet suit he had seen some rapper wear in a magazine and wanted to copy.

'Surprisingly, you didn't miss much.' He pulls a pillow towards himself and leans back.

'I will make it up to you.'

'It'll take a bit more than a cake to make up for this.'

'I can try, if you'll give me a chance to put this right.'

'You been gone six months. That's long. What did you expect?'

'The talk show reunion,' she admits.

Tristan snorts. They both always used to comment on how strange it was that no one ever screamed and shouted during these TV reunions, why the abandoned daughter never swore at her dad, or why the adopted son never lashed out at his birth parents who wanted him twenty years too late.

'I wanted everyone running to me, hugging, crying, saying: "Oh Mary, we missed you, we missed you".'

He stifles the smallest of smiles and she uses this as an in to take his hand, but it remains limp in hers and eventually she lets it drop.

'I saw David,' he says suddenly. 'Right before it happened. He knocked at the flat, looking for the keys, looking for you.'

In all these months she never considered that David would have crossed paths with anyone other than death that day. So it's odd to hear he spent his final moments with Tristan.

'How did he seem? What did he say?'

'I'm not sure. My memory of everything is kind of muggy. I can only remember bits and pieces.'

'Oh. Of course. It must be difficult to think about it.' But she wishes he could tell her something about David that day, his last.

'He literally collected the keys and left. I'm sorry, there's not much else to say. He looked the same as he always did, I guess tired from the long journey.' Tristan finally looks at her and smiles. 'Smooth, he looked proper smooth.' He laughs and she wipes her eyes. 'I missed you, Mary. Why didn't you call?'

'I was scared. At the start I had to get away. And then a few days became a week. Then it was already months. Then it got longer and longer and I lost myself.'

'And what happens now?'

'I don't know. It's up to you and Malachi.'

They come out of the room, Mary first, and she notices how Harris and Malachi look past her to Tristan, to gauge his reaction.

Malachi steps forward and hands Tristan his stick. 'You want to get out for a bit?'

Tristan nods and allows Mary to squeeze his hand. She watches the boys leave, noticing how sloped Tristan is when he walks, how slow. He's right, there's so much she's missed.

'I'm sorry it went so badly,' Harris says as he joins her by the window. 'Tristan has missed you so much; I'm surprised by his reaction.'

But Mary isn't. With every day she stayed away, every call from him she didn't take, she knew it would hurt him more and more.

'What did Malachi mean about everyone needing to forgive something?'

Harris pulls the curtains shut and then sits on the armchair. 'They've both been through a lot; those first few months after the crash were quite intense.'

It's clear Harris is not yet ready to tell her the details and nor does she deserve them. She takes the tea in her hand and it feels so silly, how they are pretending to be normal.

'And you? Do you think you can forgive me?' she asks.

'Of course I forgive you, but . . . ' He sighs. 'Things can't go back to how they were before. What's happened has changed everything and I want different things now. Having the boys here, it's been challenging but it's made me want more than I had before. I don't want you to be a woman I see once in a while. I want more than that.'

But again, the vows, she took them, all those years ago in the local church, with the baskets of sun-bleached plastic flowers. They are set in stone.

'Mary, I don't need an answer now, but I do want you to be clear on what it is I want.'

Finally, Mary thinks of the engagement ring studded with rubies as pink as the hibiscuses back home, and then she gives Harris her answer.

FIVE YEARS LATER

CHAPTER FORTY-FIVE

Jay

After so long alone, Jay finds he enjoys the company of sound: the coughs and grunts, the snoring and clearing of throats, the breathing and movements of others. A door is dragged shut against the uneven carpet in the corridor, the lock turns and the handle is pulled to double-check the security of the valuables inside. Jay waits for the sound of footsteps, fingerprint unique, and by the fourth step he is able to identify which of the nameless occupiers of forty-nine Cassland Road has just left. He listens to them constantly, these footsteps up and down, some heavy and deliberate, others quick and skittish, and this particular one, careless and clumsy.

It's 10.55 a.m. The new kettle is taking too long to boil. Jay flips the lid. The steam wets his face and inside small pieces of polystyrene bob violently in the water. The instructions read: *Rinse before first use*, but he chose not to follow them. The tortellini looks unappetizing as it falls into the plastic sieve in one solid lump. He'd found the sieve in the sparsely stocked cupboards. 'All your essentials,' his caseworker said, to which Jay smirked about how indulged a man would have to be to think a sieve essential. The boiled water cooks his meal and he sits on his bed to consume the soft, wet globules, filled with something vaguely cheese-like. It's always the same crap they press on him at the food bank. The kind of stuff people are always clearing their cupboards of: sweet corn and baby potatoes in tins, red lentils, muesli, cup-a-soups.

11.04 a.m. He will leave soon. He has to.

A patch of dried red skin on his elbow flakes. Is he pouring the washing powder too generously? Pamela always used to say that was the cause of his psoriasis.

There's a lopsided mirror on the back of the door. Despite a grey face and lined skin, the reflection looks like a man much younger than Jay feels. The longer he looks, the more he recognizes the man as a ghost, still in the same camouflage trousers and yellow T-shirt he wore that day, five years ago, as he stood and watched the building burn.

Pamela, at five years old, comes to mind: her refusal of haircuts and brown bread, the snorting noise she made when giggling too enthusiastically, the *Rainbow Brite* pyjamas she ordered him to buy her. Jay wishes his memories could make him smile.

11.30 a.m. He needs to leave now or risk being late. Or risk changing his mind about going at all. He grabs his oxblood boots. The original ones were pulled from his feet years ago as he slept under a carriageway. His feet smart as he pulls at the laces. Last Christmas at the shelter there was a podiatrist, who was too young and too kind. She bathed his feet in a bucket of warm, soapy water before chipping away, and Jay wondered what kind of father would let his daughter spend Christmas Day at a homeless shelter with men like that? Men like him. If Jay had his daughter back he wouldn't let her out of his sight ever again.

He locks the door to his room tightly, and wonders if anyone is listening to his footsteps as he descends the staircase. What would his slow and careful walk say about him?

The walls are lined with posters, which spell out the price of violating house rules. Strongly worded threats of eviction, decorated with clip art images of sad faces and the charity's sunny logo. They sit alongside posters for AA meetings, the Samaritans, the local needle exchange and methadone clinic. The back of the front door hosts a new sign: *Please respect our neighbours when coming and going.* As Jay steps out of the house, he clocks a woman, one of the neighbours, her eyes full of disdain. She glances at him and quickens her step. No one wants a house on their street to be filled with men like Jay, the dregs of society. The smell of destitution probably emanates from number forty-nine; he can imagine it flowing between the plane trees and Volvos as it pollutes the air.

On the tube he closes his eyes and hopes for the heat and motion to put him to sleep. But he can't drift off, so instead he reads every advert and studies the spider of coloured lines on the map. The carriage fills and he looks into the faces of others. They all have secrets, dark pasts and regrets. No one has ever asked his story, not on the streets and not in Cassland Road. Sometimes other men talk about their histories, to share or brag, even to confess, he is never sure. Tales of wife-beating, affairs, loss and unemployment, gambling, drugs, drink. They all have a similar tale, but no one has been through what Jay has, no one has suffered such a great loss.

As he waits for the bus, he becomes aware of the quiver in his legs. The journey is going too smoothly, too quickly. He will soon be there, and will have to face it.

The bus passes by the William Hill. It's shocking to see the unchanged exterior and how it pulls him back to the moment he has replayed in his head many times over the years. Perched on one of the high stools at the bookies, his hands clutched together as he urged the horse on under his breath. It was hot that day, the air was close, and sweat ran down the back of his T-shirt. His luck was about to change. Then, over the sound of a fast-talking commentator and slap of the horses' hooves, there was a sharp bang followed by a boom. Everyone looked at each other. Jay slid off the seat and saw that the man beside him was wearing plastic beach shoes; his pale, naked toes blended in freakishly with the paper betting slips that littered the carpet. People began to move outside, to stand on the street and look up at the smoke and flames in the sky, so close to where they stood. Too close. The memory hurts; physically he feels it.

The two fourteen-storey towers that make up what remains of the Morpeth Estate come into view, and he gets off the bus on the other side of the field. Everything looks so different; the estate has been remodelled around its famous missing piece. There are new trees and flowers to be neglected, a swing park to be ruined by local street rats, a sandpit for dogs to shit in. Bile starts to rise in his throat. The key is in his hand again, the gate locked, his mind at rest knowing Pamela is safely out of harm's way.

He stalls on the green and lets a bench take his weight; he can't go any further.

'Has it really been five years?' A woman in a black felt hat beside him asks. Between them sits a bunch of roses, in romantic shades of pink and red. 'Feels like yesterday.' She tips her head to one side as she waits for him to agree. 'Don't it?'

But she's wrong; it feels so distant, a lifetime ago, almost as if it happened to a different person. Sometimes it's like Pamela never existed at all.

The woman's flowers are plastic.

'I lost my photos in there,' she says. 'Ten years' worth of photos from the Chelsea Flower Show. Used to go every year. Even had photos of Her Majesty.' She tuts several times, as if seducing a bird Jay can't see. 'All gone; the fire took them. But it didn't take me.'

Pamela's school had given Jay the photo they had of her on file, smiling brightly in her uniform, her ponytail high on her head, her tie slightly wonky.

He feels the light hand of the woman as she pats his shoulder. It's embarrassing, he doesn't want to sit and cry on a bench like this in front of this stranger.

'You never get over something like this, do you?' the woman says.

She removes her hand and uses it to push herself up slowly from the bench. Quickly she switches her handbag from one arm to another, before collecting up her bunch of plastic roses and crossing Sandford Road to join the crowds.

Every year on this day he comes here, and every year he can't bring himself to get any closer than this. Grief is meant to be private, but these people make such a scene. He hates the way they dress up for it, the way they let the cameras in, the way they think some stupid memorial stone will make any difference to how much it still hurts.

Five years. It's a long time. Long enough for him to get closer today, to see the place where he lost her. Slowly, he crosses the road, taking care not to make eye contact with any of the others; he's not part of their group because he's not blameless.

It doesn't take long before Jay spots him, standing out in the crowd, taller than Jay remembers and looking older, because of course he got to grow up while Pamela is stuck as a sixteen-year-old. Malachi turns and they lock eyes, the first time since the six-month anniversary. Jay often reimagines that fight happening in private, where Malachi would have been free to let all his aggression out, to keep hold of Jay's neck so he wouldn't have to deal with any of this anymore.

Malachi's face momentarily hardens and he looks away, off to the pointless block of stone everyone is here to see. Somewhere on it is Pamela's name, but he won't be able to look at it, not yet, not today. Perhaps Malachi feels the same way, wandering around the edges of the crowd, his head bowed. He stops and turns to face Jay once again. So much happened back then, so many things that can't be unsaid or changed. But today isn't about that, it's not about Jay or Malachi, it's about acknowledging Pamela, the sixteen-year-old girl who loved laughing and milkshakes and running till she could no longer feel her legs. The girl they both loved. They share a look, which Jay feels is not filled with violence or regret, but with understanding of what they've both lost.

CHAPTER FORTY-SIX

Mary

The memorial has been placed in the middle of the field rather than in the actual space where Nightingale Point once stood. It is bordered tastefully with flowerbeds and in her head Mary hears Harris listing the merits of each plant. How they would have been chosen for their beauty or hardiness across the seasons. She is glad he is here to support her today, yet knows that when she comes face to face with David's name cut into the memorial stone for the first time, she should be alone. The memorial itself is not what she expected: three thick concrete discs stacked one on top of the other. A loop of text is chiselled into each ring: one bears the date of the crash, the other the names of the victims, and the final holds a sentiment of how we must never forget. Mary looks at the thirty-nine names etched around the rings, like declarations of love on a wedding band. Then she sees it: *David Tuazon*. She places her flower on the top, a single white lily like the ones David's mother used to grow in her garden back home.

Mary has waited for this. This place to sit quietly and

remember the man she had, as a nineteen-year-old trainee nurse, fallen in love with. In a few months, on David's birthday, she will make his favourite food – oxtail stew – and bring it here, along with her Discman. She will listen to sixties pop music while overlooking the Morpeth Estate, the place they were meant to start their lives abroad together.

Nothing ever works out how you planned it.

She thinks back to that strange time when she was reunited with Harris, Malachi and Tristan. How odd it was to find them all cooped up together in the bungalow and how warm it felt when she moved in there too. They spent that winter squeezed in, eating soup and arguing over what films to watch. Tristan's anger towards her slowly thawed, but even now she occasionally catches him looking at her curiously, like he's trying to work out who she really is.

Then the boys were finally rehoused, and for the first time, it was just Harris and Mary. And it was wonderful.

The Virgin Mary's arms on the old broken fob watch, which she keeps in her pocket, show half past twelve. Mary rubs the face. She decided years ago there was a kind of beauty in its cheapness, the way the saint's arms have to reach awkwardly to indicate the numerals, the greening of the silver that has become more prominent over the years, the way it smells both metallic and perfumed. Soon, someone will ring a bell and everyone will stand in silence to think of all they lost on that day.

'Is that it?' A woman stands next to her and huffs. 'Some poxy bit of concrete?'

But no, it's beautiful. Even next week, when the flowers wilt and brown, and next month, when the polish dulls, and in the coming years, out here in the wind and rain, isolated in the middle of the grass, with the cold sinking into it, it will still be beautiful. This memorial will have a whole life out here. A piece of David will always be here.

Harris is talking with Julia and John, the awkwardness of their relationship more evident today than any other. He catches Mary's eyes and they smile at each other through the small crowd.

'Goodbye, David,' she says, then walks over to her husband, her son and daughter, and her grandbabies.

CHAPTER FORTY-SEVEN

Malachi

'Malachi Roberts?'

He turns towards the familiar voice, grateful for a distraction after seeing Jay.

'It's so good to see you.'

He struggles to place the face of the woman in front of him, but allows her to hug him; her hair smells like fried food. As they part, Malachi checks his bunch of blue and white flowers haven't been squashed by her embrace.

'You look well,' she says. 'Oh, I'm so pleased to see you.'

He nods. It's hard to remember everyone from back then and he is yet to attend one of the Nightingale Point Survivor Meetings, the invitations for which still arrive at Harris's address twice a year. The very idea of being a 'survivor' makes him feel like a fake.

'So, how have you been?' she asks. There's a softness in her face, which takes him back to those afternoons with Pamela in the Turkish café. It's then he realises she's the waitress, one of the few people who played audience to his short relationship with Pamela. It sends him back five years, to big white plates of greasy chips and thick splodges of unmixed milkshake powder.

'I'm okay. And you?'

'Well, you know what it's like, busy as always.' She laughs. The blue evil eye pendant stares at him from her cleavage. 'You don't live around here anymore, do you? Most people moved away after. It must make it easier.' She looks to the ground, embarrassed, as if she's spoken out of turn.

'Yeah, but my brother's still in London, though not around here.'

'How is your brother? I'll never forget reading his story.' She closes her eyes and puts a hand on her chest. 'Poor kid.'

'He's fine. He's around here somewhere. Do you know him?'

'Oh no, love. I only read about him. I don't think he ever came into the café with you. And what do you do now? Did you get those big dreams you were chasing? Always with your head in a book. It was architecture, wasn't it?'

He feels embarrassed for his younger self, the ambitious twenty-one-year-old, focused on getting qualified and making a success of himself. That's all most people knew him as from back then: Tristan's older brother, the one who was always studying.

'Well, I'm still an assistant. I'm two years off my original plan because of,' he nods up towards the blocks, 'because of what happened.' He is never quite sure how to refer to 'it'. He's uncomfortable with the words 'tragedy' or 'accident', nor can he bring himself to use the simple drama of 'the plane crash'. It sounds so sensational, too cinematic.

'And I know you're still young – ' she blushes – 'but I'm curious, did you meet anyone? I always think how close you and Pamela were. How hard it must have been to go through losing a girlfriend like that. Sorry, I'm prying,' she says. 'Ignore me.'

'No, it's fine. Actually, I did meet someone.' He smiles at the ground, but it feels wrong to talk about his happiness today.

'That's great.'

What are they expected to talk about next? Malachi wishes Tristan, the king of small talk, was by his side.

'It doesn't feel like five years,' he says, to get off the subject and because it's what he thinks he's meant to say, to feel. It's what people have been saying all day. 'Or does it?'

'Sometimes it feels like yesterday and other times it feels like it never happened at all.' She looks up at the space left by Nightingale Point, then turns back quickly, a small smile on her lips. 'It's good to see you again. Take care.' She pulls him in for another hug, squeezing his arms as they part.

Everyone has moved on. Most of the time Malachi feels like he has too, until he returns to this area and spots the two surviving towers in the air, the marker of the event that threw his life into chaos. No matter how much they remodel the estate, he will only ever see the flames on the balconies and the field filled with crowds and ambulances. He swears he can still smell the smoke and gas that wound his chest so tightly. The memory has the power to shorten his breath. Discreetly he takes a few puffs of his inhaler.

'That's nasty.' Tristan shakes his head with mock disapproval as he walks over. 'How can you be flirting with women on a day like this?'

'What are you talking about?'

'I just seen you, squeezing up on some woman.'

'That was someone from back in day.'

'Aren't they all, Mal? Aren't they all?' Tristan throws an arm around Malachi's shoulder. 'What?'

'Why are you wearing such a bright top to a memorial?'

Tristan tuts. ''Cause yellow is my colour. What did you want me to wear? A black veil?'

'No, but maybe something a bit more sombre.'

'I been sombre for too long. Now come on, you wanna go do your . . . ' He trails off and indicates down to the bunch of flowers.

'Yeah,' Malachi says sullenly. 'Let's do this.'

Together they walk over to the memorial and add the flowers to the pile. Carved into the stone are the names of people he knew, like David Tuazon, and people he only ever passed in the stairwell or shared a lift space with. But now, after so many years of court hearings and newspaper write-ups, he can put a face and story to each one. The worst, of course, is Pamela Prudence Harrogate. It hurts so much to see it here, so permanent. He had become used to the endless reproduction of her smiling school photograph, the photograph in which she never changed, always sixteen, almost seventeen, in her uniform. It helps to imagine that Pamela simply never came back from Portishead. That she stayed on there, rebuilt her relationship with her mum, set up her own running club, and even met someone else.

Suddenly he feels overcome, sickly and tearful. He can't believe he's back here, in this place where he lost his mum, then Pamela, then his home, and where he almost lost his brother. He had always been able to hold everything together until this *thing* happened and caused him to finally unravel. He rubs his eyes with the back of his wrist, and while he is grateful Tristan doesn't draw attention to the tears, he doesn't mind that they're falling here so publicly. Tristan leans in and hugs him, one of the quick bursts of affection they allow themselves every so often before they fall into another argument. Malachi can't remember how his little brother used to look or walk before the crash, or if he always spoke so loudly. He doesn't care, he's just glad the name Tristan Roberts doesn't appear on the stone today.

'I half expect to see my name on here,' Tristan says on cue. 'That would be some Bruce Willis *Sixth Sense* shit. Like the last five years have all been a joke. Seriously, though,' Tristan throws his arm around Malachi's shoulders again, 'you good?'

'Yeah, I'm good.' Malachi nods. 'You all right?'

Tristan breaks into his wide Cheshire cat smile. 'You know me, I'm always all right.'

CHAPTER FORTY-EIGHT

Tristan

He steps back to allow Mal some peace as he lays the flowers for Pamela. It's taken years but Tristan has made peace with the fact that there will always be one secret he has to keep.

It's amazing to see how his brother has been able to move past what happened and stop blaming himself for everything. Though at first it did feel like Tristan was losing him. They had always lived within a few feet of each other, so it hurt when Mal picked up and moved to Surrey, of all places. But then Tristan can always call when he needs to discuss something important, like the new Eminem album or how to reference correctly in an essay. Plus he loves going through to the little suburban house Mal shares with Anna, a woman crazy enough to find a long-faced, badly dressed architect like Mal boyfriend material.

But next year, when the baby comes, everything will be different. Tristan never planned to become a dad at twenty-one, but he never planned to lose a foot and eye on a Saturday afternoon either. Shit just happens.

Girls were always his biggest weakness. The first year at university was the worst, getting into freshers week and realising how outnumbered he was by them. Sure, he expected a large number of females on a Performing Arts degree, but it wasn't his main reason for choosing the subject, despite what Harris says. Then, to top it off, they were all really keen on his survival story. He gave them the radio edit; no one really wanted to hear about the deaths or how his left eye gives no vision but waters constantly, and nothing kills conversation quicker than talking about night terrors. So while he hooked up with more than a few girls from the course, the one who finally broke him was Laura from the estate. She was the only girl that ever really got it, because she'd been there, on the third floor, looking after her little cousin while the building shuddered above her. They never spoke about the crash in the months that followed, preferring instead to use each other as a distraction. It seemed to be what they both needed and it worked. Looking back, Tristan's kind of embarrassed at how he used to treat her, even after she spent so many hours with him at Harris's place, when he was low and still looking mashed up from the crash. It's only since she moved into his flat share near campus, which originally was only out of necessity, that Tristan's been able to see her as more than a troublesome girl with a red weave.

Mal lost the plot when he found out about the bun in the oven. Still, that's Mal, overreacting to everything. How hard can it be to raise a kid, anyway? Most things are a piece of piss after what Tristan's gone through. What with the crash, then the recovery from that, then the months of pain, and finally, having to make the decision about the amputation. It was hard-going for a long time and the recovery was brutal, but Tristan doesn't regret a thing and his current foot allows him more freedom than he's had in years. He can even step into a bath without needing help. He's still not convinced on a hearing aid though, especially now he's got the lip-reading thing covered. Mal was the first he could 'read'; it was so easy, Tristan wondered if he had been able to do it all along. But it's hard with others, especially when there's a big group at the student bar.

Still, he's here, not dead yet. Got to be grateful for it.

He spots Ben Munday and some other boys from back in the day, wearing shirts and ties like they have court appearances. They all moved away in that first year, and Tristan didn't see much point in keeping in touch with them. They were never his real friends anyway, just people he felt the need to constantly impress.

'This is crazy,' he mumbles.

Looking about, some people are crying, but most are smiling, hugging others they haven't seen since the last time. Tristan doesn't cry about it anymore; each year this day just makes him feel lucky. Especially when he thinks about all those who didn't make it and how close he came to being one of them. He owes everything to Elvis. Where is he? They spoke last night on the phone and he promised he would be here today.

The memorial is a curved concrete wall with the names of all thirty-nine victims, as if there were only thirty-nine victims. It affected so many people; so much suffering came from that one event. The names of the airline crew are on there too, written in both English and Greek, but they feel so distant, like people from another tragedy.

Mary's over the other side of the chairs. He didn't see her arrive. She twiddles her elbows in that nervous way she always has and her shoulders jump gently. She's crying. He feels the urge to go and throw an arm around her, to make her laugh with some jibe about Mal's outfit or last night's *Eastenders*, but he knows not to. It still hurts when she shuts him out, but he gets it, it's her way of dealing with things, and it doesn't mean she loves him any less.

He wonders whether today is the right day to tell her he's going to be a dad. He definitely needs to break the news when Harris is around. That way he can jump in and stop her when she tries to kill him. He had told Nan last week and she put the phone down on him. He's still waiting on her calling back.

But him and Laura have it all planned out: Tristan will finish his degree next year and get some cushy paid internship role at one of the community theatre groups he's been helping out at. It might be rough for a few years, but the bigger picture is they will all be together and safe. And happy. They're both just so happy at the moment.

Tristan can't wait to be a dad. Ever since he found out, he's been trying to convince Mal to get Anna up the duff too. Surely it's only right that they both have a kid at the same time, then they can grow up together and have each other's backs.

Finally, he spots who he's looking for.

'Elvis.' The only person with worse hearing than Tristan. 'Elvis,' he calls again, attracting attention. Tristan hasn't seen him in nearly a year. His ginger hair is shaved so low his head looks like a fuzzy orange. 'Elvis?'

Finally he turns and runs straight over to crush Tristan in one of his too-tight hugs.

CHAPTER FORTY-NINE

Elvis

Elvis hates to leave his flat, as it is so full of perfect things. Like the squashy green armchair, the toaster that can toast four pieces of bread at the same time, and the fluffy orange giraffe on his TV, which he managed, after weeks of trying, to lift with the metal claw from the machine in the arcade. But today, Elvis has left his flat and got on the train to go all the way to London to visit the Morpeth Estate. He knows that today will be a sad day. There will be people looking sad, talking about sad things, and putting sad-looking flowers, like white lilies and carnations, near the place where Nightingale Point used to be. Elvis has not brought sad-looking flowers; he has brought a Schlumbergera, which is the posh name for a pink flowering cactus. Elvis is not sure if Lina liked cacti, but he knows that she definitely did not like fancy flowers. Once a boyfriend bought her a big bunch of red roses and she said, 'Waste, man, I'd rather he gave me the cash.' Elvis chose the Schlumbergera as it was pretty but spikey, like Lina.

He stands on the field in front of where his home used to

be, which kind of looks the same as five years ago but also looks very different too. As he walks towards the group of people in the middle of the field, he passes a man in army trousers, who is not a real soldier, crying on a bench. Elvis has some tissues in his pocket but does not stop to offer them to the crying man because sometimes men who cry on benches have been taking drugs and are very dangerous.

Elvis walks past the swing park, which is new and shiny and looks much more fun than it used to look back when Elvis lived here, but not as fun as Dreamland, which is next to Elvis's new perfect flat. At Dreamland there are hot, sugary doughnuts and a ghost train and a big wheel, which is so tall you can see France when you get to the top of it. There is also a stand where you can buy pink candyfloss from a blonde girl in a blue sweatshirt, who says things like, 'All right, captain, what can I get ya?' This always makes Elvis smile because blonde women are his favourite kind of women, and he is not a captain but would like to be.

'Elvis!' someone shouts.

He gets excited as he recognises the voice straight away. It is his good friend and brother Tristan Roberts. He wears a T-shirt in Elvis's favourite colour too: macaroni yellow. Elvis gives him one of his very special big hugs.

'How you been? How's life on the old promenade?'

'Promenade? I live in Margate,' Elvis tells him.

'Yeah, I know. Bet you're loving it? Sun, sea, fish and chips?'

Elvis nods. He really does like living in Margate a lot. Though there are some drug addicts there that shout things at him like, 'Oi, fatty, get a clue', and in the winter when Dreamland is empty it can get a bit boring.

'You look good, Elvis.' Tristan reaches out and flicks the collar of the new grey and red checked shirt Elvis bought to look good for this very special, but very sad, day.

'Thank you.' Elvis had looked in the toilet mirrors at King's Cross station and Tristan Roberts was right, he *did* look good today.

'So, have you seen the memorial yet?'

'No.' He has only just arrived and has not yet had time to look at the memorial, which everyone here must look at because it is what makes the day so special.

'You want me to come with you?'

Elvis nods and together they walk over to the big grey stone with lots of small, neat writing on it.

'It looks like a wedding cake,' Elvis says.

Tristan Roberts laughs loudly and slaps Elvis on the back. 'Ah, you crack me up.' He leans in and whispers, 'It ain't what I was expecting neither, to be honest.'

'But it looks nice,' Elvis lies, as he knows that someone must have spent a lot of time carving all those tiny names into the stone. Also, he does not think it is so bad that it looks like a wedding cake, because wedding cakes can sometimes be fantastic, especially when they have tiny plastic models of the husband and wife sitting on the top.

He looks for Lina's name, but there are so many names, so many other dead people to remember. This makes Elvis sad and he does not want to be sad, so he tries to think of something happy, like the orange giraffe he won from the claw machine, the blonde candyfloss girl in the blue sweatshirt, and the inside of the seashells, which are shiny pink, like the colour of Lina's nails.

'Do you feel sad?' he asks Tristan Roberts, who looks at the concrete cake with a sad face.

'Yeah, course. It's sad for everyone.' He reaches out and puts his hand over the names. 'But the important thing is, we're still here. Right? Can't get caught up in feeling sad. Sadness will drown you.'

Elvis is not sure how anyone could drown in sadness, but he nods anyway to agree with Tristan Roberts, and decides to think about this properly, a bit later when he has more time.

'There.' Tristan Roberts points to a name: *Lina Baxter*. Elvis runs his own fingers along it; it feels sharp and scratchy and a little bit powdery. He takes the sheet of newspaper off from around the pink painted terracotta pot with the Schlumbergera inside, and stands the plant up between bunches of white lilies and carnations, which, while sad-looking, are also a little bit pretty too.

Elvis touches the scar on his forehead, which is kind of like the slots in the arcade machines where you put in your 2p. Elvis loves those machines because when your 2ps run out, more 2ps fall out of the machine, and you can play all over again.

His scar is a light silver colour now, not like Tristan Roberts' scars, which are light brown. When people ask Elvis what happened, he tells them the truth: that he was hurt by broken glass. He does not tell them the whole long story, as people might not believe him and call him a liar. Or people might ask him too many questions, which would make him confused, as he does not remember everything that happened that day. But he does remember how he was brave and how he grabbed Tristan Roberts and made him escape the building. This makes Elvis so happy because if he had not saved Tristan Roberts then he would be another name carved in tiny neat writing on the big concrete wedding cake.

'Will you come to Margate?' Elvis asks. 'The train is twelve pound fifty return from London King's Cross.'

Tristan puts his arm around Elvis. 'Margate? Yeah, I'd like that.'

A sign at the bottom of the memorial says: *In memory of the thirty-nine who lost their lives here on Saturday, 4 May 1996. May we never forget.*

Elvis knows that he forgets many things, such as what time *Countdown* is on, how long to boil a steak and kidney pie for, and why double-glazing salespeople are not his friends. But he will never forget the day the plane came.

AUTHOR'S NOTE

On 4 October 1992 a cargo plane crashed into two high-rise blocks of flats in the Bijlmer, Amsterdam, killing up to forty-seven people. The survivors of the destroyed blocks lost everything: loved ones, homes, belongings and community.

Then came the aftermath. The media wanted to talk to them, the authorities questioned who the victims were, and challenged their right to be rehoused. They suffered health problems, both mental and physical. They had questions about the accident, the rescue operation, the advice they were receiving. They were angry.

When Grenfell Tower happened, despite it being a different decade and country, a similar narrative played out. Yet again, people felt they were not being listened to.

While the characters in *Nightingale Point* are fictional, the spirit that drives each one is based on those from the Bijlmer, who rebuilt their lives after losing everything. It is also a tribute to those from Grenfell Tower, who continue their fight.

Luan Goldie, 2018

ACKNOWLEDGEMENTS

Thanks to my agent, Eve White, who championed this novel ever since the first phone call. Your enthusiasm, belief and support kept me going through every setback.

Thank you to everyone at HQ for welcoming me so warmly, and a huge thanks to my editor Manpreet Grewal for helping me shape my original manuscript into the novel it is today. I do hope your talent and precision rub off on me.

Back in 2014 I read my short story, called *The Day the Plane Came,* at one of Elise Valmorbida's writing classes, to which she said, 'I don't think this is a short story'. It wasn't. So thank you, Elise.

I am eternally grateful to my first readers: Kevin Linnett and Holly Rizzuto Palker. From critiquing in the backrooms of Selfridges to cross-Atlantic Skype calls, you have both been there all the way. What can I say, except the drinks will always be on me.

To everyone who has attended The Salon over the years, each week you've inspired me with your talent, intelligence and thoughtful feedback. Special thanks to Gill Haigh and Paul McMichael.

A huge thanks to my early inspiration to write and former mentor, Courttia Newland.

Finally to Annabelle: I did try to write this during your nap times, but as we know, girls grow quicker than books, so sorry for all the CBeebies you watched while I typed.

READING GROUP QUESTIONS FOR
Nightingale Point

1. Which character in *Nightingale Point* did you most identify with and why? Did your view of the characters shift as the story progressed?

2. Tristan decides to keep something a secret from his brother Malachi. Did you agree with his decision? Would you have acted differently if you were in the same situation?

3. Did you feel sympathy for Jay? Discuss if you think there should have been greater consequences for his actions.

4. Mary seems to have a much closer bond with Tristan and Malachi than her own grown-up children. What did you make of their relationship?

5. Elvis and Tristan form an unlikely friendship as the story progresses. What do you think each of them ended up learning from the other?

6. Out of all the characters, Tristan undergoes the most dramatic journey, emotionally and physically, over the course of the novel. The last time we see him he's on the cusp of another momentous life event. How do you think he'll cope with this event?

7. *Nightingale Point* is not an overtly political novel, but issues of race, class and the duty of care we owe to those in our community underpin the story. Discuss which political issues in the novel have changed since 1996 and which are ones we are still grappling with today.

8. Mary is a strong, independent woman who moved from the Philippines to London as a young woman for a very different kind of life. But Mary stayed married to David for all those years despite his behaviour. Why do you think Mary was so intent on trying to make her marriage work?

9. Discuss the representation of disability and mental health in the novel.

Other Reading

If you loved *Nightingale Point*, then we think you'll also love these books:

The Bricks that Built the Houses by Kate Tempest
My Name Is Leon by Kit De Waal
White Teeth by Zadie Smith
Brick Lane by Monica Ali
In Our Mad and Furious City by Guy Gunaratne

Keep reading for an exclusive extract
from *Homecoming*, the upcoming book
by Luan Goldie – coming soon!

CHAPTER ONE

COFFEE SHOP

September 2020

The coffee shop is one of a chain but this particular branch seems to have lost its way. The tables are filthy; the pleather seats are burst in places, and two men sit closest to the counter openly making their way through a six pack of supermarket croissants.

Yvonne finds an empty table, next to the toilets. The armrest is spotted with dried milk; it's the kind of dirt which signals neglect, it unnerves her. The walls are lined with photographs of generic Italy, wicker baskets of tomatoes, mopeds, skinny women in large sunglasses drinking espressos at pavement cafés. The door opens and a homeless man emerges, bulging carrier bags at his side, smelling of urine.

She doesn't want to be here.

Deep down she hoped he would cancel, was almost waiting for it. But when he texted her in the morning it was to confirm this address and time.

He's late.

Maybe he won't come at all.

Then she sees him on the other side of the glass door, taller than she imagined, far from the gangly eight-year-old he was when she last saw him. His hair is long and sits in a curly mass on the top of his head. He's wearing a pale pink sweatshirt with the sleeves rolled up, his arms marked with random tattoos. He's a man now, completely unfamiliar. But as he spots her and squints, she sees it's him, it's Kiama.

Her hand goes up but she feels too stunned to smile as he makes his way over.

'Hi,' he hovers near the table.

She stands up, 'Hello, Kiama.' It's awkward but she feels grateful the furniture blocks the hug the situation requires.

He scratches at his hair, 'Wow, this is crazy.'

'Yes,' she laughs. Nervous.

'So weird to see you again.'

They stand like this, locked in the act of looking each other over, before he snaps out of it. 'I'm getting a coffee.'

'Okay.'

He begins to back away then pauses, 'Sorry, do you want anything?'

Yvonne gestures to her cup before sinking back into the chair, relieved to be able to return to poking her Earl Grey teabag with a wooden stirrer.

Kiama joins the small line at the counter, he dives for his phone, not content to wait and waste the moment. Yvonne knows she's in the minority of people without such a habit, without the need for continuous entertainment.

As he reaches the front of the line there is talk between him and the pretty barista, definitely more words than it takes to order a coffee. The stud in his nose catches the light and his face breaks into that smile, his dad's smile, it's uncanny. The barista beams too and lowers her reddening face as Kiama walks back to the table.

His knees knock Yvonne's as he slides into the seat opposite her. He was always a lanky child, all elbows and knees; they used to call him a baby giraffe.

'What?' he asks.

'Nothing.' Yvonne looks down at the smudged table and flicks away the crumbs of previous customers. This is harder than she thought it would be.

Steam floats from his take-away cup. Why take-away? Is what he has to say to her so short? He catches her eyeing it, 'I get fed up of spelling out my name.'

She's confused, but then notices the scrawl of *Kev* on the side. It sad that's he's not proud of his name. But it was simple for her, growing up with a name like *Yvonne*, something everyone could spell and pronounce without a second thought.

'Kev?' Yvonne says.

'It's an easier name.'

'But Kiama's a beautiful name. You know it means—'

''Course I know, *Light of life*. But most name meanings sound poetic when you look them up. Here,' he takes his phone back out of his pocket and types something in. 'See, Yvonne means Archer. I don't know what that is.' He furrows his thick eyebrows and reads on, 'Ah, listen, *people with this name are dynamic, visionary and versatile*. Any truth in that?'

Then despite the pink, the tattoos, the hair, the nose piercing, Yvonne says, 'My God, you're so much like your Dad.'

'Lucky me.' Kiama puts his phone on the table and sits forward in his chair, his eyes seem a darker brown than they were when he was a kid, but he's still never quite grown into them. 'Dad asked me if I'd found any photos of you online.'

'Photos? Why?'

He shrugs, 'I don't know. Maybe he wanted to see what you looked like after all these years. You do look quite different. Especially your hair.'

Her hair? She had it cut last week, but has worn it in this bobbed style for as long as she can remember.

'Funny,' he says, 'I can't remember it being so ginger.'

It breaks the tension and makes her laugh, but not him. 'Sorry, is that rude? I didn't mean it.'

She rubs the back of her neck. 'I know I'm a redhead.'

He holds his palms up, 'I just remember it being lighter, that's all.'

'It was. But I don't dye my hair anymore.'

Kiama stares at her hair as he takes the lid off his drink. 'I like it,' he says, 'the red; it suits you more than blonde.'

The way he looks at her, surveying and watching, it's too intense.

Her tea is stone cold, unappetising; she raises the cup then puts it straight down. 'Your arms,' she says, 'you really are covered, aren't you?'

He stretches them out across the table, and under a tangle of festival wristbands and beads, they're a mess of tattoos: feathers and roses, playing cards and Kanagawa waves.

'My best mate is training, so I'm sort of like his guinea pig. He's done all these in the last six months. A few of the crappier ones I had done when I was sixteen.'

'That's surely not legal?'

''Course not. But it's free.'

'What did your Nana say when she saw them?'

'She cried. I stopped showing them to her after a while. When I find a good portrait artist, I want one of her face right here,' he slaps the left side of his chest.

'How is she?'

'She um,' he looks away and Yvonne knows what's coming. 'She passed away last year.'

'I'm so sorry, Kiama. I didn't know.'

'Nah nah. You wouldn't have.' He rolls his sleeves back down and adds four packets of sugar to his coffee. Noticing her watching he explains, 'I used to be bang into the energy drinks, but they were giving me heart palpitations, so I gave up. But you got to replace it with something.'

'Sounds logical.'

He smiles back at her, then his face changes. 'I'm glad you were up for meeting me.'

She takes a breath; she's not yet ready to hear the reasons he got in touch with her, why he wanted to meet in person and talk. 'How is your dad? Does he,' she pauses, searches for how to frame the question, 'I don't even know what he does for work these days.'

'I don't want to talk about Dad.' Kiama leans forward again, he's staring at her and she can feel his energy, his nervousness. This was a mistake. She should never have come. Should never have responded to his original message, but she couldn't ignore him. It would have been so wrong.

'Obviously, I asked you here for a reason. I need to talk to you about something.'

'Okay.'

He moves his coffee to the side of the table and fidgets with his bracelets, rolling them up and down. 'I'm going back to Kenya.'

It's not what she expected to hear from him. Though, what did she expect? 'Why?'

He wraps an empty sugar packet around his thumb and purses his lips. 'I don't know,' he says quickly.

'You don't know?'

'No, I *do* know.' He puts a hand over his face, as if embarrassed. 'But I don't know how to say it.'

She waits for him, to compose himself, to explain, but he just stays hidden. 'Kiama?'

'I'm not okay.' He removes his hand and looks straight at her. 'I need to go back so I can deal with things properly. I can't keep carrying this.'

'Carrying what?'

'What happened there,' he says, 'don't you ever think about it?'

There's no response that will do.

'Don't you ever think it would help to go back?'

'I'm not sure what you're—' she stops. She looks away, at the men polishing off their croissants, the barista who glances hopefully at Kiama, the glass door she wants to escape through.

'Yvonne, I have so many incomplete memories about what happened. I can't even tell the difference between what I saw and what I heard from others. What I've read in the papers.'

'Why would you read the papers?'

'Because I wanted to know,' he says quietly, almost

embarrassed. 'I was only eight. It's hard to trust my own memories. And I think that's why I'm stuck, like not able to move forwards. No one ever talks to me about Kenya. About what happened there. We came back to the UK and everyone just got on with things.'

'Got on with things?' she almost laughs, it's a ridiculous way to describe those months which followed their return from Kenya, the months in which Yvonne 'got on' with nothing.

'I can't talk to Dad about this,' he says. 'I used to talk to my Nana but—' his face falls.

Yvonne lifts her hand to put it on his arm but pulls back. She hasn't seen him in a decade, she can't suddenly step in and start comforting him. It's not her place.

'I don't want to do this alone.' His voice cracks slightly. 'I can't. I can't do this alone.'

She knows what he's about to ask.

CHAPTER TWO

SNAKEBITE

May 2001

The middle step is prone to squeaking, so Yvonne carefully avoids it as she heads downstairs. She tiptoes past the
downstairs bedroom. Though she doubts a little noise will
be enough to stop Emma and her latest fling doing whatever
it is they're doing.

Emma squeals from behind the sky coloured bed sheet
stapled in the doorframe. The door fell off weeks ago. The
hinges, like everything else in their dump of a student house,
rotted, and one night Emma drunkenly slammed it too hard
and it swung from the frame with a crack.

It was Yvonne's idea to put up the sheet.

There's a growling noise from behind it now, followed
by laughter, delight. It's too intimate, Yvonne shouldn't be
listening to her housemate having sex, but it's that car crash
thing. How can she not?

The bed creaks and someone groans, guttural, she's not
sure if it's Emma or *him*. Him being SWEETBOY76, his screen

name on MSN Messenger. Over the last month, Yvonne has wasted so much time in the library, helping Emma to become her sexiest, smartest self, which mostly consisted of correcting the spellings of words like *risqué* and *licentious*.

The groans die down to light laughter followed by whispering, and in a way, it's more intimate. They really need to get the door fixed.

The kitchen looks worse than usual this morning, past messy and dirty, now firmly in the realms of filthy. Fairy lights twinkle around the whiteboard, Christmas every day, the board itself covered with doodles of lecturers doing inexplicable things to each other and Box Room Bethany's complaints about people using all her tampons.

If someone would have asked Yvonne years ago, back when she was living in the cramped flat of her childhood with her three older brothers, what she imagined it would be like to live with three girls, she would probably have used the word *clean*. But here, in this house, there is only grime. A saucepan of congealed pasta rests on the hob, surrounded by dried white froth from where it was allowed to boil over. And there, on the counter, amongst the crumbs, empty CD cases and dirty dishes sits an open take-away box from *California Chicken*, a few brown thigh bones and a smear of ketchup left in it. So, Sweetboy's not a vegetarian then. That would be Yvonne's deal breaker. She could never bring herself to share saliva with someone who had dead animal on his breath. She lifts the gaudy box; its slogan proclaims to be '*Hot and Tasty. Just the way you like it*'. The smell disgusts her, but the bin is full, close to overflowing. She should take it out really, like she always does. But instead she drops the box back on the counter and grabs a whiteboard pen, scrawls a note on the board.

Clean your shit up! I'm not your slave. Y.

Yvonne dumps her notepad in her rucksack, checks for a working pen and refills a Poland Spring bottle with tap water while rereading her whiteboard message. It's a bit strong. She drops her rucksack to wipe it off with a sleeve and rewrites.

Please can whoever cooked last night clean it up. Thanks. Y.

The male voice in Emma's room says, 'Not now.'

He doesn't sound how she expected. But then, what did she expect? That he would 'sound black'? Her mum always says you can tell on the phone, but Yvonne doesn't think so, or at least, she would never admit it.

Are they coming out of the bedroom? This will be awkward. She doesn't want to meet him. Quickly, in the hallway, she kicks off her slippers and grabs a battered pair of pink Dunlops from a pile by the front door. They smell. Emma's been wearing them without socks again.

'Dude?' Emma whispers as she comes into the hall, a short towel wrapped around her like a toga. She grabs Yvonne's wrist and pulls her into the kitchen. 'Did you hear us?' She drops open her bottom jaw and fakes a silent laugh.

'I think I would have heard you if I was in John o'Groats.'

Emma slaps Yvonne's arm and laughs.

'You're ridiculous. No one likes sex that much.'

Emma shushes her. 'He'll hear you.'

'Don't shush me. You're the one with no volume control. And I'm fed up with this,' she points to the sheet. 'Call the landlord and tell him you need a proper door. No, tell him you need sound proofing.'

Emma laughs, then mouths over enthusiastically, 'I've not slept all night.' Her chest is red, her mascara smudged making her green eyes look liquidly cold and pale. 'Seriously, like, seriously.' She says with the international school twang she's never quite managed to shake. 'I love a guy so open to trying new things.'

Yvonne fake gags. 'Please, stop talking.'

'Wait till you meet him.'

'I don't want to meet him. It's bad enough I'm talking to you post-sex.'

Emma covers her mouth to stifle a laugh. 'Why are you going out so early anyway?'

'I've got my final tutorial at eleven. Surely, yours is today as well?'

'Urgh, for what? So, they can tell me how unreadable my last essay was. I know that. Stay home today?'

Yvonne thinks about the cost of truancy, all that student debt she's racking up to sit on the sofa and watch *Diagnosis Murder*. 'Nope. I'm going in.'

Emma frowns. 'Well, he's going to work so I should like drag myself in as well. Wait for me.'

'No. You'll make me late.'

'I'll be quick. Talk me up to him,' she whispers.

'No. I'm leaving.'

But Emma's already halfway up the stairs pulling off her towel. 'You know me, three minutes and I'm done.'

Three minutes to shower followed by an hour pottering about the house. Yvonne steps outside and closes the front door. There's a car parked on their usually empty drive, a Volvo Estate, not the kind of car a young guy would drive. A crucifix on a purple beaded chain hangs from the rear-view mirror, surely it's his parents' car, she thinks as she walks towards the bus stop at the end of the road. But then, stops, she's left her rucksack on the kitchen counter. She runs back to the house and looks in the hall, but it's not there. A tap is running in the kitchen, and as she goes in she sees him there by the sink, bare back and a pair of black jeans.

She averts her eyes and grabs the bag from the floor.

'Morning,' he says brightly.

'Morning.'

'I know you,' he says.

She looks up; he leans against the kitchen counter and narrows his eyes at her.

It can't be.

'No way,' he says loudly.

It can't be. There are over eight million people in London. How is it *him*? The odds are impossible; they have to be.

'There's no way.' He smiles widely, the smile that got her the first time around. 'I can't believe it's you.' He drops his head forwards and laughs, then stops to look up and confirm it. 'This is messed up. Emma's going to freak out.'

He can't be serious. He can't tell her.

The water from the shower runs loudly through the pipes. Emma will be downstairs any minute, ready to deliver her patter about quick showers and water efficiency.

Again, the narrowing of his eyes, he pulls back and leans against the counter. 'What are the odds?'

Yvonne is aware of all she hasn't said, but right now, she doesn't know where to start. 'Emma doesn't need to know we know each other. I mean, we don't really know each other, do we?'

He clocks his head to one side and smiles. 'Actually, we kind of *do* know each other.'

The water thumps off. The time ticks.

'Please, don't say anything,' she rubs her head.

'Calm down, Evelyn.'

'It's Yvonne.'

He puts his hands up in mock defence, 'Don't get like that. It was months ago. You probably don't remember my name either.'

But, of course she does. She remembers everything about him. How he smelled, how he danced, how he wrote down her number on the back of a travel card the next morning. How he never called. Emma can't know about any of this. 'Please, don't say anything to her.'

'I only just started seeing this girl and you're asking me to keep a secret.'

'Yes. Well, no. Not a secret, it's not worth mentioning, is it?'

He nods. 'Sure. I can keep a secret if you can?'

The bathroom door opens upstairs.

'I need to go.'

When Yvonne gets home later that evening she's greeted by the sound of the television coming from the living room. She puts her head around the corner but no one's in there. She walks towards Emma's room and pulls back the bed sheet from the doorway, 'Em?' The sheets are still ruffled and she wishes she'd never seen it.

'Hey,' Box Room Bethany shuffles past holding a plate of potato smiley faces, a fleece blanket thrown over her shoulders.

'Oh, you're in. Where's Emma?'

'I don't know where that little cow is,' Bethany says as she walks through to the living room. 'What was she playing at last night?'

Yvonne follows her through and checks the time, it's late. This is a bad sign. A sign that Sweetboy's maybe not kept his mouth shut.

Bethany forks a piece of potato into her mouth. 'I don't want to hear all that moaning and shit. And to be honest, it sounded like she was faking it. Was it the guy she met in a chat room?'

Yvonne nods.

'So, basically, he's a complete random? Some stranger she met on the internet, the home of the world's paedophiles and weirdoes.'

'He's not a stranger. She was talking to him for weeks.' But really, it was Yvonne talking to him, typing all those witty, flirtatious lines while sharing a chair with Emma in the library.

'So? People aren't who they say they are on the internet. He could have been anyone. Can't believe she let him in our house. Oh,' Bethany suddenly shouts, jabbing her fork in the direction of the TV, 'I bloody hate this guy. He needs to get evicted.'

'How can you keep losing so many hours of your life to this?'

'I know, I know. It's trash.' She whoops as some of the TV contestants start dirty dancing with each other.

The front door opens, Emma's home. This is it. Yvonne goes out into the hallway but Emma has already run upstairs to the loo. Yvonne waits in the hallway for a minute, before returning to the living room, where Bethany explains in depth which contestant is her favourite, which one is a slag and so on.

Emma takes ages. Then finally, when she comes into the living room she sits in the armchair, rather than next to Yvonne as she usually does.

He's told her. Shit.

'Well, look what the cat dragged in?' Bethany shouts.

But Emma's expression is far from the proud smirk she usually sports after subjecting everyone to one of her noisy sessions. 'I've had the worst evening.' She glances at the TV. 'Oh no, not this. Why is everyone watching this?'

'Because it's amazing,' Bethany says licking ketchup from her fingers.

'Emma? You okay?'

'No. One of the boyfriends turned up at the shelter.'

'Can this story wait till the ad break?' Bethany asks.

Yvonne sinks further into the sofa, relieved that something upsetting happened at the women's shelter where Emma volunteers. 'I didn't realise you went in today. Thought maybe you decided to stay home. In bed.' She hopes Emma will take the bait and start talking about Sweetboy. But she doesn't.

'This guy turned up and started screaming about wanting access to his kids. It was awful. The kids could see him from the window and well I actually don't want to talk about it. I can't.'

She doesn't know about Sweetboy then, and there's no way Yvonne is going to tell her. He's just some guy after all.

He doesn't matter. He didn't call Yvonne after sleeping with her and he probably won't call Emma either. It makes sense to forget about the whole thing.

'Do you want a cup of tea?' Yvonne asks.

'A cup of vodka? Yes, please.'

'I'll make you a tea. Beth, do you want one?'

Emma lifts her head. 'I need a cigarette.'

Yvonne goes to the kitchen to make the tea, and clean up the huge mess Bethany managed to create while oven cooking a few potato products. The security light in the garden flicks on as Emma walks across the overgrown grass and sits in a cloud of moths and cigarette smoke.

Yvonne takes the tea out and sits next to the paddling pool bought last month during the heat wave. Both of them could just about fit in it, their knees bent, the water flowing over the side each time one of them moved.

Yvonne offers Emma the packet of Chocolate Digestives stolen from Box Room Bethany's cupboard. 'When are you due back at the shelter?'

'Not till the weekend now.' Emma takes two and shoves them into her mouth in one go.

'You're so classy,' Yvonne laughs as she kicks at the mushrooms dotted around the edge of the paddling pool.

A phone tones from within the overgrown grass.

'Urgh, dude,' Emma says through a mouth full of biscuit, 'I dropped my phone somewhere.'

Yvonne finds the small square of light next to a pile of burnt out disposable barbecues and hands it over, trying her best not to look at who the message is from. But it's clear from Emma's smile that it's him.

'Can you believe Sweetboy is trying to invite himself over again?' she says.

'He's coming over? Now?' Yvonne panics.

''Course not. I'll get cystitis if I have another night like last night. Such bad luck to meet someone right before I go away for the summer.'

'So you like him then?'

'Yeah. He's so fit.'

'I know he's fit. You've said. Several times actually. But do you *like* him?'

Emma looks up and smiles, 'Yeah. But I'm not sure how much he likes me. He sort of runs hot and cold. But this,' she holds up her phone, 'the fact he got what he wanted and is still messaging me is a good sign. Right?'

Yvonne attempts to formulate a response, a confession of sorts, but all she can do is nod.

The phone tones again. 'Ah,' Emma says, 'he's being quite persistent.'

Then, despite herself, Yvonne says, 'Maybe it will cheer you up to go out tonight, take your mind off what happened at the shelter.'

'He can wait,' Emma hops up. 'You fancy dinner at The Plough? It's two for one?'

'You're choosing me over Sweetboy?'

Emma pulls Yvonne to standing. 'Always. Are you okay though? You seem distracted?'

Yvonne wants to stay in this moment and tell Emma the truth, for them to have a laugh about the coincidence and their scarily similar taste in men. But it's embarrassing, so embarrassing that she slept with him after a few drinks, that he never called her and that this morning he struggled to remember her name. Besides, Emma's relationships always fizzle out to nothing. What would be the point in telling?

The student bar is holding its final Pound-a-Pint night, the monthly promotion Yvonne and Emma have attended religiously ever since they met at one during Freshers Week almost three years ago. It's hard to believe that this will be their last. That they soon will no longer be students. That this bar, which is always the same, a dense wall of smoke and heat, backed by pop music and the smack of snooker balls, will no longer be their space. Yvonne looks about the booth, lined in tacky pink velvet, at her group of friends and suddenly feels nostalgic for something she still has.

Sweetboy has been invited along tonight to meet Yvonne, for what Emma thinks will be the first time. Hopefully he will cancel. He's already cancelled several times before, and the one time he did show up, Yvonne made sure she was on a train back to her parents' house in South London for a fabricated family birthday.

Emma jumps as her phone vibrates in her lap, she squints at the screen then her face breaks into a smile. She starts finger combing her hair roughly and wipes at the corners of her mouth in that self-conscious way she sometimes does.

He's on his way then. There's no getting out of it.

Of course, Yvonne should have come clean that night in The Plough as they sat drinking shitty house ale and reminiscing about all their past flings. She should have light-heartedly said, 'Here's a funny coincidence', but she didn't. She kept silent each time Sweetboy was mentioned and prayed nothing would come of it.

Box Room Bethany is talking about the topic they can't seem to escape at the moment, their post-university lives. The group go round and round with it, bragging about the securing of internships and further education until Emma declares loudly, 'I'd rather fucking die than endure a Masters Degree.' She's tipsy. They've all been down here since lectures finished three hours ago and it doesn't take much with her.

When Sweetboy arrives, it's almost like the crowd parts for him as he swaggers over to their table. Yvonne doesn't think she's ever seen a man look more pleased with himself.

Emma bounces up from her seat to kiss him. 'Dude, where have you been?' He pulls off his jacket and gives Yvonne the briefest moment of eye contact.

'Everyone,' Emma says, 'this is Lewis.'

He slumps into the booth and slings his arm around Emma. His property. Yvonne hates that. Hates him.

Punjabi MC comes on over the speakers and everyone in the bar cheers, except Box Room Bethany who mouths, 'How many times?' and mimics hanging herself.

A tacky big faced watch glints on Lewis's wrist; he looks like one of those ridiculous American rappers. It's exactly what Yvonne needs to see. 'Love this track,' he says while bopping his head.

'Finally,' Emma shouts as the barman puts down a paper boat of chips in the middle of the table, 'I ordered these fries hours ago. Shit, this is a big portion. Guys help me out, save me the hassle of puking it all up later.'

Stools are pulled from other tables as more people join and

it quickly becomes one of those group conversations where bits and pieces get lost in sound, where you catch some of one topic, none of another. Lewis stifles a yawn and coils Emma's hair around his fingers till she turns to him.

'So Lewis,' Box Room Bethany says. 'Are you studying?'

'No. Studying wasn't really my thing.' He explains how he could never have afforded it and didn't need it to set up his men's fashion label anyway. The label. Of course. Yvonne's heard some of this spiel before: 'Street fashion for the modern man', 'limited run T-shirts with a message'. They'd been standing outside The Troika bar that night surrounded by ravenous drunks demolishing kebabs, and he had stunned her with his ambitions.

'I'm all about doing something for real, you know,' he explains. 'I'm not one of those people who sits around talking about how to change things; I'm more about making it happen.' Everyone nods along, even Box Room Bethany, whose sole purpose in life *is* to sit around complaining about not being able to change things.

'T-shirts are hardly going to revolutionise the world.' Yvonne says. She's only had one drink. What possessed her to speak directly to him? Now, he's looks straight at her. 'Yeah, well, no, 'course not. But it's a start. My label's like a stepping stone to other things I want to do. Music. Art. Marketing. I like to have my fingers in a lot of different pies.' He holds her gaze steady; he's challenging her and she can't rise to it.

'Well,' Emma shouts, 'Yvonne and I are also going to change the world.'

Yvonne cringes, she doesn't want Emma telling him about

their plans, the things they discuss when it's the two of them, their bright-eyed ideas to save the world. She tries to get Emma's attention from across the table.

'Oh no, is this your Crayons for Kenyans company idea again?' scoffs Bethany. 'As if anything is ever going to offset that your parents drill oil from the ocean.'

'Whatever,' Emma laughs, but it's a sore point, the fact that, despite her self-righteousness, she can never win an argument on ethics because her parents work for an oil company.

Lewis smiles. 'So, tell me about this idea then?'

'Backpacks for Africa,' Emma drops her jaw as if to say, 'wow'. 'Yvonne and I have been trying to work it out ever since we met.'

He pulls himself up straight and smiles across at Yvonne. 'Really? Keep talking.'

'So,' Emma starts, 'remember how at the start of a new school year your mum would take you to Woolworths to buy you a pencil case and stationary, ready to start fresh? Remember how great it was? How it made you excited for school? Well, the kids where I grew up—'

'You mean the kids of your maids,' interrupts Bethany.

'Fuck you, Beth. Everyone has help in Kenya, okay. It provides jobs. It's nothing to be embarrassed about.'

'Everyone? Were you seriously that cocooned in your privileged little expat bubble to think that's true?'

'Look my parents aren't rich; they're not these oil tycoons or whatever you think. My dad's a normal hardworking man, he just happens to work in—'

'A former British colony,' Bethany laughs.

Lewis steps in. 'Let's talk about something else. This is a bit heavy.'

Emma looks relieved. 'Yeah, you're right. Proper vibe killer. Back to fashion talk.' But since when did she care about fashion? Her wardrobe mostly consists of things she's borrowed from Yvonne and never returned; even the suggestion of going shopping causes her to start quoting passages from *No Logo*. It's as if with him Emma's a completely different person. There's nervousness in her voice, an exaggeration in her laugh, and the way she keeps packaging up whatever he says and giving it back to the group with an excess of enthusiasm is pathetic. She must really like him. A lot.

His phone rings several times and cuts out. 'The reception is terrible down here.'

Yvonne wonders if her name and number ever made it into his phone. If he ever intended to call her.

He stands and makes his way out of the bar. She considers following him, but for what? Her stomach lurches at the thought of being alone with him, away from the eyes of everyone.

'So?' Emma slides in next to Yvonne and wriggles her eyebrows comically, like a children's TV presenter. 'What do you think?'

'I think that you need to stop drinking.'

'I'm talking about Sweetboy.'

'Yeah. He seems nice.'

'Nice? You can do better than that.'

'What do you want me to say? He's not what I expected.'

'How comes?' Emma's eyes fall down to the now crushed

paper boat, smeared with grease, she pushes it back and forth with a finger. 'You knew he was black.'

'I didn't mean that. But, I am surprised by how all over him you are. Do you even know his last name?'

'Dude, I've only just found out his first name. We're taking things slowly. I think it was all that chat room stuff, it really built the tension. I like the way he's so focused too, not like these uni boys.'

They both look up at Lewis as he makes his way back through the crowd.

Emma pinches Yvonne's thigh under the table. 'He's fit, isn't he? Look at that body. He told me he goes to the gym five times a week.'

'Yeah and he probably wears his T-shirts a size too small on purpose.'

'And for that, we thank him.'

'You're drunk.'

'No, I'm not. I've only had two pints. Small ones,' Emma holds up a thumb and forefinger.

'A pint comes in one size.'

'Urgh, you're in such a mood at the moment.'

'No, I'm not.'

'Yes, you are. I'm trying to cheer you up. Maybe have a drink and loosen up a little.'

Yvonne sighs, careful not to invite Emma to probe her moodiness further. A few drinks may be the answer; it was all it took that night with him.

The stickiness of spilt drinks pulls at Yvonne's thin rubber soles as she makes her way over to the bar and crowd waiting to be served. 'Can I have a snakebite and black please?' She drops the hot pound coin from her pocket into the bartender's hand. 'And a tap water.'

Lewis brushes against her arm. 'Are you buying me a drink?'

Why is he here? She briefly glances at him. 'I've already ordered.'

'I don't remember you being so cold.'

'This is all a joke to you, isn't it?'

'Sorry, but you've got to admit, this is kind of a funny situation.' He waves over the bartender. 'Can I get a Pepsi please?' He pulls a note from a money clip.

A money clip? He's ridiculous.

'Your girlfriend wants another pint.' It comes out childish, snarky. She's embarrassing herself.

'I think she's had enough.'

Yvonne is pushed closer to Lewis as a few drunken girls jostle her to get closer to the bar. She feels her face flush as she steps back, away from him.

The drinks are set in front of them. The cold runs down the side of the plastic pint glass.

'You look pissed off, Evelyn.'

This thing with her name, he's doing it on purpose. As if she doesn't already get it, that she was a mediocre shag, forgettable as a human being. Good job she doesn't have to stay and listen to it.

'Don't storm off to the table with your face like that. Stay.'

He's right. She places the drinks back down on the bar, puts her purse away, and takes a breath. How can this work? This secret.

'Emma says you want to go into advertising when you graduate?'

'Why are you discussing me with Emma?' It makes her nervous, anxious, the thought that her name has passed between them.

'You guys are best friends, right? She talks about you a lot. She talks about *everything* a lot.'

Is there some scorn in his voice? Some hint of boredom?

'I'm really interested in advertising too. Marketing. Branding.'

'Hmm, good for you.'

He laughs. 'It's competitive, though. Emma knows she doesn't stand a chance working in that kind of field. But then, she's going on about training to be a teacher. As if. The kids would eat her alive.'

'And you'd know, would you? Emma's quite tough actually.'

'Look, my mum's a secondary English teacher,' he says. 'It takes a lot more than liking books to be good at it.'

'Whatever.' She swallows quickly and reminds herself not to get drunk tonight.

'My mum had me reading Wordsworth in primary school. Can you believe that? I used to perform poetry at family barbecues.' There's a dimple on the right side of his cheek, it gives him a warmth she couldn't see before, almost boyish.

'Why are you telling me all this? I'm not interested.' But she can see him, as a child, up on a stool in front of his whole family.

'*She was a phantom of delight, when first she gleamed upon my sight. A lovely apparition sent.* Why are you laughing?'

Her mouth needs to do something other than encourage him, so she takes several mouthfuls of her drink. 'I don't want to insult your mum so I can only assume you were a horrible student.'

He straightens up, 'I can't be good at everything, can I?'

'You're unbelievable.'

'You said it. So, what you drinking?' he nods to her cup.

'Snakebite,' she answers shortly, wondering how much longer she needs to keep up the farce of talking to him before she can go back to the table, back home even.

'What? You're drinking something called a snakebite? Can I try it? It's always good to be reminded of why I don't drink beer.' He takes the cup from her hand and slowly raises it to his lips, watching her sceptically as he has a sip. His face snaps into a wince.

'Not to your taste?'

'No,' he chases it with his own drink, 'not quite.'

'How much longer do I need to pretend I'm enjoying talking to you?'

'Well, that all depends, doesn't it?'

'On what?'

He sidles closer, his arm hot against hers, 'How much longer will it take me to get back into your good books?'

ONE PLACE. MANY STORIES

Bold, innovative and empowering publishing.

FOLLOW US ON:

@HQStories